Left, but Not Alone

Left, but Not Alone

FINDING TRUE LOVE WITHIN

DE'MONICA N. COOPER

iUniverse, Inc.
Bloomington

Left, but Not Alone
Finding True Love Within

This is a work of fiction. All of the characters, names, incidents, organizations, and dialogue in this novel are either the products of the author's imagination or are used fictitiously.

iUniverse books may be ordered through booksellers or by contacting:

iUniverse
1663 Liberty Drive
Bloomington, IN 47403
www.iuniverse.com
1-800-Authors (1-800-288-4677)

ISBN: 978-1-4620-4409-2 (sc)
ISBN: 978-1-4620-4411-5 (hc)
ISBN: 978-1-4620-4410-8 (ebk)

Printed in the United States of America

iUniverse rev. date: 09/08/2011

Chapter one

1990 . . . Growing up in "the ward" had its privileges and setbacks. The way I see it either you learned to love it or you learned how to survive in it. The "ward", was filled with people that had big dreams and visions but not many ever saw them come to reality. We heard about their dreams whenever we would pass by the local corner store.

"I should be on the road touring . . . uuhmm hmmm . . . but I am here in this hell hole baby, that 'cane got me stuck and now I live in a rut . . . ohhh yeahh," the local wino mellowed out his blues tune for the world to know.

It was pretty funny to me because I couldn't see him on anybody's stage or tour bus even though he swore up and down he sang with stars like Natalie Cole, Luther Vandross and Aretha Franklin. I believed his dreams had always been just that . . . dreams. Everybody dreamed in the ward. That was the only way to believe we would someday get out. Since there were so many wards in Houston and where we lived was named the Fifth Ward, the local residents shortened the phrase and simply called it "the ward." Most of the neighborhood was related in some sort of way. Either a brother married the neighbor's sister and had babies or the hoeing grandfather got the church usher from across the street pregnant more than once. There were lots of secrets that were only spoken through "pillow talk," so it seemed everyone knew everybody's business except for the Rideaux's. We were the family that people loved to hate because we had it going on. No one could run out and say they knew anything about us unless we told them. And that was highly unlikely.

Our house, like most in the ward, stood on bricks on all four sides and was built by my grandfather in the early 1950s. It was rickety and every time the wind blew hard we prayed that it would remain standing. The house originally only had two bedrooms but before my Papa died he built an extra room on the back and turned the garage into a bedroom, too. That was the thing to do in the ward I guess, because everybody had extra people living with them. Our bedrooms were small and only a twin size bed could fit with one chifferobe. The kitchen probably was the sturdiest place in the whole house. That is where we mostly hung out anyway because someone was always cooking. That was another way the neighborhood knew us, from Big Mama's good cooking. You could smell her fried chicken and cornbread from around the corner and mouths would begin to water. Big Mama was a quiet, dark-skinned lady with long gray hair. Her skin was smooth and her body was toned like she'd been lifting weights. People knew when she was coming because she always walked fast and her steps were real hard. She stood about five feet ten, but by the way she talked you would swear she was a giant. That is where she got the name "Big Mama." Papa told us a story of Big Mama fighting some boys in New Orleans because they were trying to jump her little brother. After the fight, the two boys looked like they had been beat with a bag of bricks due to the fast hands of one little lady. Papa and Big Mama met when they both lived in New Orleans, Louisiana, right after Big Mama graduated from high school. Papa said he always knew Big Mama, but was scared to talk to her because her daddy was crazy. Papa was a tall, slim man who always dressed the part and smelled very good. Whether it was his deodorant, Brut, or soap and water, when it reached his body the smell stayed with you long after he was gone. He wore his height very well too, with broad shoulders and a smile that made you melt. That is what Papa said caught Big Mama's attention, along with his light green puppy dog eyes. It seemed that back then the ladies loved light-skinned men with light eyes, Papa once mentioned.

"I've loved your grandmother since the first time I saw her in the French Quarters with her sisters," Papa explained one night before we went to bed. His stories were always lengthy and seemed to do the trick of putting us straight to sleep.

"She was the talk of New Orleans and I knew that she would be my wife, but her daddy was crazy and was known for protecting his girls."

Papa's face turned upside down when he mentioned Big Mama's daddy. I could tell there was unspoken anger because the conversation ended at that point.

I was surprised that our house was still standing after thirty-odd years, but it was and that's where you would find our whole clan every Sunday. When Papa and Big Mama moved to Houston, Papa knew he wanted to leave something for the family that the white man couldn't take away, so he built our house with his bare hands. It wasn't a mansion, but it was ours.

Rideaux, our last name, was French and came from Papa side of the family. He was Creole, but looked like a white man, so when most people saw us in the ward they thought we were mixed with black and white because we all were very light skinned with hazel or green eyes. It was sometimes hard living in the ward because people thought that since you were pretty you couldn't fight. So whenever there was a fight at the local park or in the street we knew that there was a good chance one of the Rideaux clan was probably defending himself again.

My family loved living in the ward, but sometimes the mundane of the day got old and seeing people shot, drunk or just crazy was not how Mama Betty wanted to raise her kids. Mama Betty was the oldest girl out of four kids and had a heart of gold. She stood about five feet three and had long coarse hair that was always braided up and put in a bun. Her deep chocolate eyes were so mesmerizing that when she looked at you, it felt like she looked deep into your soul. Her light brown skin was smooth and always glowing as if she tanned each morning. Mama Betty was the name she told everyone to call her and it was used by not only her family but the entire community. Her voice and presence demanded our attention, so when Mama Betty spoke, we listened. She, her brother and sisters were all born and raised in the ward. They had seen the good and they saw the bad, people robbed and killed, but yet they stayed. I often wondered if they were like the winos who had a dream to get out of the ward but would never see it come to reality. She often dreamt of us moving to a nicer house when she got a little more money saved up and all the family knew she would do just that! Since I was the baby, Mama Betty would come and talk to me. She figured I had no one to tell and I was too young to understand most of what she was talking about anyway. But the truth is I knew everything and forgot nothing. Big Mama and Mama Betty had a really special relationship because of my dad, Tommy Boy. He was Big Mama and Papa's baby son and was a major hustler from the time of birth. Slim, tall and quiet were his greatest attributes and when anyone mentioned his name on the streets it demanded respect; he was the "Don."

Mama Betty claims she didn't want to talk to him when they met, but it was Tommy Boy's charm that swept her off her feet. He had the same infectious smile his father had, with those big green eyes that obviously made Mama Betty melt. Most of the women in the ward became jealous of Mama Betty because they couldn't understand why Tommy Boy chose her over all of them. Mama Betty said it was because she was a good Christian girl with values and morals. Most of the women that Tommy Boy dealt with before her were what she called "skanches."

Since the streets knew Tommy Boy was the man, some were jealous and wanted to take him out, but he was too smart and kind-hearted for that. You could always catch him helping someone in some way or feeding the homeless. That was the kind of heart that was passed on to his kids and even to Mama Betty. So when the laws raided our house that early Sunday morning,

Mama Betty already knew what to do. She grabbed us all and told us to go out the side door to Mrs. Lorraine's house and she would meet us in a minute. Tommy Boy got a call from a "lookout" that warned him the Feds were coming. He had already prepared Mama Betty on what to do in case anything like that ever went down and she followed his plan precisely.

"Mama, where we going? I'm sleepy!"

"Hush up Pearl and go in there and hurry up and put your shoes on and get your backpack that's hanging on the door in the closet. Get Brooklyn out of her bed and carry her with you."

Mama Betty told me she had prepared Mike because he was the oldest and had to take the role if anything happened to Tommy Boy as the head of the house, so he was the first one out and knocking on Mrs. Lorraine door. Mrs. Lorraine was the most trusting neighbor around. Tommy Boy knew he could trust her, so he paid her early to take care of us if anything jumped off.

"Betty, remember I told you where everything is and who to talk to. Do not talk to anyone else except the ones I told you to, okay? I love you, take care of business and hold your head up. I will be back. The house is ready for y'all to move in to. Do not procrastinate about leaving; the Scott boys will be here to move all of our things out tonight at 10," I remembered her telling me. She said Tommy Boy kissed her for what seemed like an eternity and motioned her out the back door. Mama Betty was a very strong lady and did just as Tommy Boy asked her and she didn't even shed a tear like he had told her not to do. From then on, Mama Betty never looked back and never talked about Tommy Boy again.

The house was Mama Betty's pride and joy; it was everything that Mama Betty and Tommy Boy talked about when we were still in the ward. He made sure that there were enough bedrooms, a big kitchen and backyard for family outings and when the

Rideaux clan would come over. Big Mama loved the kitchen because she could cook up a storm and still have enough space to pop her peas right in the same room.

"Y'all see God has blessed us with a new house and I be damn if anyone of y'all gone run my house down. God will only bless us with more when he sees that we can take care of what we have."

Those were Mama Betty's favorite words that echoed throughout the house every Sunday morning right before we had prayer and got ready to leave for church if ever something wasn't cleaned or put back right.

Early Friday morning one hot summer day, everyone ran to the door to see who was coming in with Mama Betty. I stayed back on the couch with Madear because *The Price is Right* was on and I didn't want to miss the Plinko game. My brother and sister ran to the door as if they were expecting someone. But I didn't hear anything about a visitor coming over, so I stayed on the couch.

I usually knew everything that happened in our house before it happened; everything *had* to come through me. As Mama Betty walked in the door carrying a pink bundle and a diaper bag on her shoulder, I couldn't help it, I became curious.

"Is someone having a baby?" I thought.

I knew Mama Betty wasn't having a baby and no one in our house had better be having one either. When they walked through the door everyone went straight into the kitchen. I stayed on the couch because now the "showdown" was coming up next and a black lady was in the running. You know when blacks get on a game show we have to root for them whether we know them or not.

I heard a baby's cry coming from the kitchen and then I heard Mama Betty tell someone to get a bottle out of the diaper bag. "WHAT?" That was all I could say. I wasn't talking to anyone in particular; I was just shocked at what I was hearing.

"Brooklyn, who do you think you are saying what to?" Mama Betty yelled from the kitchen.

You see in my house saying the word "what" could've easily got your teeth knocked out of your mouth.

"No one," I yelled back, but tried to yell gently. By this time I am tripping because no one told *me* I was getting a new baby doll and no one told *me* that we were having company. I jumped off the couch and headed toward the kitchen. Madear looked at me like "oh no there she goes." I wanted to ask her what was that look all about, but I was too curious and almost upset because I did not know what was going on 20 feet around the other side of that wall.

Madear was Mama Betty's mother and she had always lived with her since she moved out at age eighteen. Short, petite, and full of life was the best way to describe Madear. She wore her caramel skin well and always kept her gray hair rolled in rollers for days at a time. Madear was the jokester of the house. If you said the wrong thing you would get cursed out, and if you looked the wrong way in her opinion, you would get cursed out. She had those same big deep brown eyes that Mama Betty had and it was almost scary to look at her because she made faces that reminded me of the man from the movie *Candyman*.

When I got around the corner all I saw were smiles and people standing around something on a big pink blanket that was stretched out on the floor.

"Is that a baby?" I wondered.

I just knew that she did not go and get another baby. For what? I'm the baby! Is she trying to replace me? Thoughts of neglect and rejection began to run a marathon in my head as I looked at the little baby on the blanket. She was a little chubby with Chinese eyes and very light skin that resembled my Papa. Actually she was cute.

"What is her name?" I asked looking toward Mama Betty.

"This is Chrissy. She's going to stay with us for a while."

I went over to touch her and she smiled at me. I smiled back but quickly regained my composure because I was not going to like this little girl. I couldn't understand why she was at my house *or* why she had to live with us. Where was her mama and daddy?

I needed answers so I went to my big sister, Pearl, to see who this baby was and why was she at my house. Pearl had gone into Madear's room to watch TV but I knew *she* could tell what was going on.

"Pearl, who is that baby for Mama Betty just brought in the house and why did Mama bring another baby home?"

Pearl was the no-nonsense one of the family. She didn't know how to sugarcoat anything and she always spoke her mind. Most times she and Mama Betty were at each other throats because they both were hot-headed. Even with a no-nonsense attitude, Pearl was still very popular in our neighborhood and her school. She was very athletic and most everyone knew her because of the records she held in track and basketball. Pearl and I had the same daddy so that Rideaux blood ran through her as well.

There was a tremble in my voice and it made Pearl look up at me.

"Girl that is our new baby. Her mama didn't know how to take care of her because she is sick, so our mama decided she could help her mama out. The baby will live here with us for a while like Mama said."

I almost choked when I heard those words. Now I knew it was true. She is staying and Mama Betty wanted to replace me with this other baby! Was I not a good kid? I make straight As in school, I don't get in trouble and I sing in the choir at church. What else does she want from me? I ran back into the living room and noticed it was all of a sudden quiet. Mike was holding the baby. NO . . . . not him, too! I went over and stood next to my brother and looked up at him. I gave him the biggest smile I could.

"Hey big brother you wanna go play gymnastics?"

We always played gymnastics. He would pick me up and throw me in the air and then catch me and throw me up again. We also played wrestling and would sometimes accidently pull up the carpet from running and sliding so much. That would make Mama Betty furious but Mike was like the man of the house since Tommy Boy was in prison. Mike would look after us and he also helped Big Mama with the bills, so she didn't get too upset.

Mike was a giant, too! So throwing me up in the air and catching me was no problem. His big brown muscles reminded me of the wrestling men we watched on Friday nights. I almost thought he wanted to be like them because he would practice the same moves they did on TV on me! That was okay because it was fun and it was "our" time together. Mike was six years older than me, so I almost looked at him like my dad. Whenever he got his checks from McDonald's he would buy me something. Once he got me the newest Adidas for school and once he got my hair fixed. He even took me to the movies with him and paid for everything. Even though Tommy Boy was not his dad, he still respected and looked to him for advice. That was my brother, Mike. He had all the girls after him too because he was so nice and smart, just like Tommy Boy. All the uppity white folks knew him as well because he was on his way to Harvard and he was the valedictorian of his school.

"Naw Brook, not right now. I am trying to put the baby to sleep."

Uggghhh! She has him too! Her cooing and goo-gooing has sucked everybody in and has left me out. This is not fair. I need somebody to talk to and play with, but they all have their hands full with this new baby. I walked to the front door and stopped. Usually before I could even walk out the door my mama yells, "Brook where are you going?"

I stood at the door for what seemed like an eternity waiting for her or someone to ask me where I was going, but no one said a word. The baby had started crying and mama was trying to help Mike calm her down. I stood there a little longer and this time opened the door so the alarm would make that beeping noise. I knew that would get somebody's attention. But nothing! Fine, nobody loves me anymore so I will just go on about my business. I walked out the door and decided to slam it. I knew in just a few seconds my mama was coming behind with a belt because she told me the next time I slammed a door my behind was grass.

I walked down the driveway slowly looking back for my mama. No show! Okay, fine! Maybe she really didn't hear me and in any minute she will be coming out here with a belt. I walked around the perimeter of our yard for what seemed like an eternity and still no show. This is crazy! What is she doing? Why hasn't she come out here to whip me yet? I decided to take matters into my own hands. I went back in the house with a major attitude. I didn't speak to anyone when I walked in, which, by the way would get you sent right back outside in my house. I went to the den . . . no mama. I looked in the kitchen . . . no mama. I looked in the living room . . . no mama. Where did everyone go? I walked to the back towards her bedroom and then I heard them.

"Oh my goodness she is so beautiful! Look at those big brown eyes! She looks like a little doll!"

I wanted to scream "don't forget about me" but I was sure no one would listen, so I kept quiet aftering hearing all the good things they had to say about her. I swallowed a big knot in my throat, trying real hard to keep my tears from falling. I stood there in the doorway and nobody looked up, not even once. I slowly turned around headed straight to the room that my sister and I shared, thinking to myself maybe they really don't love me anymore!

Later that night I overheard Mama Betty's phone call from her sister in Chicago.

"Hey sis, listen I need you to get the boys because I can't take it anymore. They are ruining my business and my relationships. So I have bought them tickets to come out there this Saturday," Renee said in a matter-of-fact tone.

"Wait one minute, I already have a house full and you think you can just drop those kids off on me? You told Sheila that you would take care of her boys and now you going back on your word?"

"Like I said Betty, they are ruining my business. Every time I look up, something is missing out of the store or their hoodlum friends are hanging in front like it's a club or something. My customers are scared to come in and I am losing money!"

Renee owned several convenience stores on the South Side of Chicago and was a widow. Her husband was killed in a car accident while driving home from work one night. They had no kids, so since his death she spent all her time in their businesses.

"No one told you to make that promise to Sheila like you were Mother Teresa. She trusted you to take care of her boys while she was locked up and I tried to help in the beginning, but you wanted to save the world. I can't afford any more kids right now so you're going to have to wait."

Mama Betty and her sisters never really had a good relationship, but she was always bailing them out if she could. *The woman with the heart of gold but little willpower to say no.*

"I am sorry Betty, but I already told them they were coming to stay with you for a while and I have their airline tickets already reserved. I really appreciate this, thanks."

Just as Mama Betty was about to speak, Renee hung up the phone.

"Mama Betty, can I spend the night at Staci's house?"

I came in the room right as she was hanging up the phone. I would usually knock, but I wanted to make sure I got to her before dark.

"Brooklyn, I need you to go in there and sit your tail down somewhere. I need to clear my head and talk to God right now."

God seemed to be another person that lived in our house because she was always talking to Him. He must not have said much because she was still pissed at the world after they finished talking.

Tears began to roll down her face and she got up off her bed and walked into the bathroom. Seeing my mother cry was the hardest thing in the world an eight-year-old could watch. I wanted to make things better, but I had no clue of what to do, so I walked in behind her and gave her a hug.

"Sometimes Brook, people will try to run over you and take advantage of you just because you are a nice person, but don't let them. Stand up for yourself and let your yes be yes and your no be no."

I didn't really understand what she meant, but I knew she was trying to teach me a lesson.

∽

The following week the doorbell rang early in the morning and I could hear voices outside my window. I knew I was not about to get up so I rolled over and pulled the covers over my head.

Ding Dong, Ding Dong, Ding Dong. The doorbell rang over and over and the voices outside grew louder and louder. I looked over at Pearl to see if she was moving, but she was knocked out.

Ding Dong, Ding Dong, Ding Dong.

"Pearl, somebody at the door," I yelled so she would wake up.

"Go see who it is then and leave me alone!" She rolled on her side and pulled the covers up to her ears.

I knew I would be the one getting up to answer the door. No one ever came to our house this early except Jehovah Witnesses and I really hoped it wasn't them.

"Who is it?"

As I made my way to the door I saw Madear peeking around the corner.

"Who is that coming over here so early? You better tell your friends we don't have guests this early in the morning."

"Madear, this ain't nobody for me!" I wanted to tell her to go back to bed but I forgot she was the night watchman and her shift didn't end until 7 a.m.

"Who is it?" I said again hoping someone would say something but they didn't. I opened the door reluctantly without removing the chain and asked again, "Who is it?"

Three boys with two bags each in their hands were standing at the door with frowns like they had just woken up. The cab driver blew the horn and waved as he drove off. I didn't know what to do, so I closed the door and headed back to my bed. The boys did not look familiar to me so I figured they had the wrong house.

"Brooklyn, who was that at the door?" Mama Betty asked as she tied up her robe.

"I don't know, some boys with suitcases, but I think they have the wrong house Mama!"

"Girl, those are your cousins! Go back and let them in!"

Mama Betty had the biggest smile on her face I had ever seen. She seemed happy to have "these cousins" at our house.

"I don't know where they gone sleep," I murmured while walking slowly to the door.

Ding Dong, Ding Dong, Ding Dong . . .

"Dang, here I come," I yelled as I approached the door.

"Why you close the door on us girl? Where is your mama?" The tallest one spoke with a baritone voice that almost scared me.

"Mama . . ." I yelled as I rolled my eyes and walked away leaving the door open.

"Pete, come here boy. You've gotten so tall! Ooh, and you look just like your daddy! Look at John Boy and Anthony . . . y'all growing up to be some handsome young men!"

"Hey Mama Betty! We missed you!"

These boys talked like they had known my mama forever.

"Y'all come on in here and meet your cousins and see your grandmother."

Pearl finally walked out of the room with dried slob on the side of her face, squinting her eyes and yawning. Mike came out of the restroom and smiled at Pete while giving him some sort of funny looking handshake. He patted the other two boys on the head like they were his little brothers.

"Dang man, y'all getting tall! In a minute y'all gone be taller than me."

"Hey y'all," Pearl said. "What's been going on?"

Okay, was I the only one who didn't know these guys from Adam?

"Look over there, that's your grandmother! Don't she and your mother look just alike?"

Madear came out from around the corner and smiled. She headed straight to her favorite spot on the couch that had begun to sink in and cut the television on.

"This is your cousin Brooklyn, I know Anthony you don't remember her because y'all both were babies when you all moved to Chicago and John Boy you might remember her but you were small too! Come on in here and put your things in Mike bedroom. He has a bunk bed so two of you can sleep in the bunk and the other one will have to make a pallet on the floor. I got plenty of sheets and pillows so you will still be comfortable."

Mama Betty was too excited but I was pissed. My introduction was very short and almost irrelevant. I'm supposed to be okay with a new baby coming to live with us and now three more mouths to feed! Ugghhh . . . . left again!

Chapter two

T he summertime in our new neighborhood was always fun. Our neighborhood had a pool that was open throughout the summer and it had a diving board. I didn't know how to swim but my new cousins did, so I trusted they wouldn't let me drown. One Friday afternoon we decided to go to the pool while Mama Betty, Mike and Pearl played with the baby.

"HELP . . . !" I knew somebody heard me screaming for my life, but no one came to my aid. I felt myself sinking and my throat swallowing the water.

"GHELPPP!!"

Was anyone coming to my rescue? Finally I felt a slinky arm pull me up and out of the pool to the side. I knew I was dead but I tasted the gel from my hair in my mouth and it brought me back to reality.

"Brooklyn, Brooklyn are you okay?"

Jared's eyes were staring at mine and all I could focus on were his humongous teeth. Jared was our neighbor from across the street who was always being nosey and in our business. He lived with his older brother and mother, who worked all the time, so we often stayed outside being nosey. He was a nerd to me, so I never really had much communication with him, but he always seemed to know everybody else's business.

"Yeah, I'm fine! Where are my new cousins? They were supposed to be watching me!"

I knew if I went home and told Mama Betty that those boys let me drown she would kill them. To my surprise I looked around and they were still jumping off the diving board and having a grand ole time!

"Hey, didn't y'all see me drowning? What's wrong with y'all?"

I was pissed and Jared knew it, so he slowly walked away. My new cousins jumped into 10 feet and then swam to three feet where I sat on the side in a daze. As they got out of the pool all I could see were their yellow teeth and fingers pointing while laughing. How could these jerks laugh at me when I almost lost my life?

"Dang, girl I thought you knew how to swim. Your mama said you would be okay," Anthony said.

Anthony was close to me in age but he seemed a little slow. Whenever I tried to talk to him he just stared at me like I had something on my face. I knew he was the baby of the three boys, so I figured they always talked for him . . . until today.

"She told *y'all* to watch me . . . I do know how to swim but just in three feet."

I was not about to let them clown me in this pool so I managed to pick my feeble body up and walk toward the lockers.

"Girl, where you think you going now?" asked Johnathan.

"I'm going home . . . y'all gone get it!"

"You better not go home and tell your mama nothing. I will beat your ass if you do!"

Dang, why was he talking like a grown man? If Mama Betty heard him talk like that she would beat his tail.

"Now go home and tell her I said that and watch what happens," Johnathan said with a growl.

For the first time ever I felt I had no control.

As I walked out of the pool area and down the street alone I pondered the threat and death wish placed on my life. I really didn't know these new cousins and I wasn't sure if they were all talk or if they would follow through with their promise. I circled the cul-de-sac a block away from my house to weigh out every option.

"Dang, it's hard being a kid. So many decisions," I said out loud.

I must've felt like Mama Betty did every time she broke out her Kool Filter Kings. She told me she began smoking right after I was born and before she hated the smell of cigarettes. She was only 25 years old at the time but her nerves she said were getting worse by the day. As time went on she began smoking up to three full packs a day. I figured if one pack of 16 cigarettes couldn't take the pressure away, then she needed to kick that habit.

Now with three kids, a live-in mother, an adopted baby and three new cousins all under one roof and all her responsibility she moved up to four packs a day.

"Mama Betty, can you get cancer from just being around people that smoke?"

I knew that was a rhetorical question but I wanted her to know I knew she was trying to kill us . . . slowly.

"Girl, if you die before I do then tell the Father I'm right behind you . . ."

I didn't know if I should laugh or worry so I cracked a half smile every time I asked her that question which was often hoping she would get the hint.

The walk seemed soothing until I reached the corner and saw all the flashing lights at my house.

"Little girl we need you to move out of the way. Bring the smallest stretcher over here, Keith, I don't want to move her."

"What is going on?" I asked the man at the back of the ambulance.

"Little girl, go inside the house and talk to your parents but we need you to back away from this truck."

Oh my God, Mama Betty said I might go before her but she never prepared me just in case she went before me!

"Madear, why is there an ambulance outside?"

Madear looked at me and then went into the kitchen. I followed behind her because I needed to know what was going on. She began drinking her coffee without saying a word. I thought I saw a tear coming out of her eye, but she turned away quickly and walked out the back door.

"Mama Bettyyyyy!" I yelled but no one answered me.

"Pearl . . . . Mike . . . !" I yelled but there was still no answer. For some reason the house seemed quiet and still like someone was missing.

I walked down the hall and into Mama Betty's room. I saw the baby lying on the floor and Mama Betty standing next to a lady that was breathing in the baby's mouth and pushing her chest.

"Ma'am, why are you pumping so hard? She's only six months! You trying to kill my baby?"

"Mrs. Rideaux, please back up. We are doing everything we can."

Mike grabbed Mama Betty and pulled into her bathroom. Pearl was on the phone and I all I could see were black squiggly lines coming from her eyes and down her face.

"Big Mama, can you come over here? Something is wrong with the baby . . . she stopped breathing," Pearl asked while taking in a gulping breath after each phrase.

It was rare for anyone to get any emotion out of Pearl, so when I saw her face I knew things were serious.

"Yes ma'am, the ambulance is here and trying to resuscitate her now. Please hurry! Mama Betty is here with me and Mike but what about the other kids? We can't take them with us . . ."

Big Mama must've said okay since Pearl placed the cordless phone down on the counter. By now the medics were loading baby Chrissy on the stretcher and tubes were coming out of her mouth. For the first time I felt sorry for her and I wanted to cry seeing her like that. She looked so helpless and lifeless.

By the time Big Mama got to the house everyone was gone except Madear, me and my new cousins.

"Hey Big Mama," I said in a melancholy tone.

I felt drained . . . all the action at the pool and the drama with the baby had me tired.

"Hey baby girl . . . you doing alright?"

"I am tired and drained."

"Tired, you are too young to be tired. Go over there and bring me that quilt off the divan," Madear said in her matter-of-fact voice.

Big Mama looked at Madear and quickly turned her nose up and walked over to me. For some reason they never really got along and was always rude to one another.

"Well hello to you too! I know I didn't wake up with you this morning. It's just polite to speak when you walk in someone's house."

"Hi Madear, how are you?" Big Mama said sarcastically.

"I would be better if they would've warned me about you coming over here. I would've gone to my prayer closet. Everyone is gone except the kids, so how can I help you?"

"I was called and asked to come over until Mama Betty and the others come back from the hospital. So if you don't mind I am going to get some supper on before everyone gets home . . . is that all right?"

"So you are good for something!"

I was surprised Madear didn't give Big Mama more lip than that. She usually let's her have it as soon as she gets to the house.

The new cousins had come in from the pool and were dripping water all throughout our house and on the new carpet. I saw the look on Madear's face as they pranced around the living room and I knew she would be in their pants momentarily.

"Excuse the hell out of me, what are y'all doing? You need to make your way to that room and get out of those wet clothes. Since Mama Betty not here y'all think you can do whatever you like? You had better get out this living room quick and go change clothes."

The new cousins were stopped in their tracks and were in total shock.

"Listen, ole lady, you can't tell us what to do. It's not like you gone get up and whip us or something," Johnathan said to Madear with a hateful scowl on his face.

Obviously Madear was in total shock since she didn't say anything back and was totally silent.

"Excuse me little boys, you heard what Madear said! Now get in that room and get out of those wet clothes. And after you take a shower come back in here so we can have dinner. Do you understand?" Big Mama said as she walked out of the kitchen looking over her glasses.

"Yes ma'am," they all said in unison.

While waiting for dinner I wanted to relax and play solitaire but when I looked for my cards in the place I normally leave them they were gone.

"Anthony, have you seen my deck of cards? I left them sitting on the table and now they're gone."

"Go look on the table then, I've been sitting here watching TV since I got out of the shower."

"I left my cards on the table because I was coming back to play with them. Who's been in here besides you? Somebody moved my cards and I am gone tell Mama Betty when she gets home. So whoever moved them had better get them back on that table quick!"

I knew he was paying no attention to me as I sent out my wrath, but somebody had my cards and I didn't play when it came to my stuff. I walked through the house and into the boys' room looking, but to no avail. I sat on the couch next to Madear and began to question her.

"What's wrong with you li'l gul?"

Madear had a heavy southern accent and all her words sounded funny to me. I wanted to laugh but I was too upset about my missing cards.

"I left my cards on the table so I could play solitaire but now they are missing. I know where I leave my stuff and now all of a sudden they are gone!"

"Well, you know your new cousins have sticky fingers," she whispered in my ear while keeping her face toward the television, "so you might wanna go on in to their room and begin your search."

Those no good lazy new cousins of mine stole my cards and I was going to get to the bottom of it. I walked outside into the garage and sat on the ground. Where in the world would they hide my cards and why would they steal from me? I just met them; we don't even know each other like that!

"Say girl," Johnathan yelled, "I saw you coming out of our room. You had better keep out or you might get your butt kicked!"

I know he didn't! This ain't even his house; he just here temporary because my Mama Betty owns this house.

"Listen punk, I know one of ya'll got my cards and I want them back . . . RIGHT NOW!"

I felt strong, I stood up for myself and there was nothing that he could say or do so he walked away and slammed the garage door. Inside I was still mad because my cards were gone but I laughed inside because he had just been told off!

I went into the kitchen with Big Mama and watched her wash her greens in the sink.

"Big Mama, why you always wash greens in the sink with dishwashing liquid? Won't we get sick from the bubbles?"

Big Mama laughed like I had just told the funniest joke in the book, but I was serious. I was not about to eat them greens knowing I was going to get sick.

"No baby, I wash them off because they have dirt and debris from the ground and I don't want you to get sick from the dirt. Plus when I put my seasonings and my foot in them you won't even be thinking about dirt or dishwashing liquid."

I liked the way that sounded and she was telling no lie, they were the best greens I had ever tasted; the only greens I had ever tasted.

Mama Betty, Pearl and Mike were still at the hospital when dinner time came and I was beginning to worry. I paced the house wondering what time they would finally come back and hoped they would be back before I went to sleep. That really needed to be soon since I felt my eyes getting heavier and heavier.

The doorbell rang and I knew I was not supposed to answer the door but I was in charge since everyone else was gone.

"Hey ya'll, what took ya'll so long?"

"Chrissy is not doing too well. They say she had a stroke and they need to run more tests on her," Mike said.

"Yeah she is going to have to stay overnight. Dang, I feel so bad for her," Pearl said walking in behind Mike.

Mama Betty came in last with a very long face. I tried to think of something that would cheer her up but I didn't want to get cussed out in the process.

"Big Mama, thank you so much for watching the house and cooking. It smells real good in here. I am going to have to go in to the office tomorrow morning to make up for today so will you be coming by as usual?"

"Of course honey. I will be here bright and early. As a matter of fact if you want to go back to the hospital with Chrissy I will stay overnight with everyone. I know you are tired so I will make you a to-go plate that you can have once you get there, okay?"

"What would I do without you Big Mama? Thank you so much. Mike, Big Mama is going to stay here with yall until tomorrow. I want to make sure Chrissy is alright so I am going back up there. Madear, behave yourself while I'm gone."

"Whatever Betty. We don't need Godzilla here. I can take care of these kids."

Mama Betty gave Madear a "yeah right" look and walked into her bedroom.

"Pearl, make sure your sister takes her bath and cleans the tub when she is finished. And you go in there and help Big Mama with whatever she needs you to do. Pete, Anthony and Johnathan, I am leaving and I better not here anything about anything from yall when I get back," Mama Betty said as she gave out her orders.

"Here is your plate Betty. Drive safe and call to let us know how Chrissy is when you get there."

Mama Betty looked at all of us and broke a faint smile as she walked out of the front door, "see you all tomorrow . . . early."

It was Big Mama's routine to come to the house almost every Saturday morning and we loved when she came. She always came bearing gifts of some sort for me since I was her favorite. I loved the peanut brittle and hog head cheese that was always wrapped in wax paper to savor the flavor.

"Hey Big Mama, I know you are already here but did you remember to bring me something?" I asked when I woke up the next morning.

"Of course I did baby girl. You want some hog head cheese or peanut brittle? Oh and don't forget to save some for your cousins!"

Huhhh? Save some for them for what? I hope I was not about to have to share everything with them since they almost let me die and stole my cards.

"But Big Mama, I thought you brought this just for me," I wanted to yell at her but she was too sweet for anyone to yell at and I knew she wouldn't do anything anyways.

"Yes, Brook but now that our family is larger it's the Rideaux custom to share whatever we have."

I couldn't argue with that since I had seen Big Mama feed the entire old neighborhood.

The house smelled just like it did in the ward on Saturday mornings. Eggs, grits, biscuits and bacon were already on the table ready for us to tear into.

"Ooh, Big Mama your biscuits and bacon woke me up out of my sleep," Mike said giving Big Mama a kiss on the cheek.

"Me too," Pearl said as she came into the kitchen pushing up her glasses.

"Well, good! Yall come on in and eat before the food gets cold. Wait a minute, did yall brush your teeth and wash your face this morning?"

"I did," Mike said as he started scooping grits onto his plate.

"Ooops, I forgot! Don't nobody touch my food, Brooklyn. I will be right back."

"Brooklyn, did you wash your face and brush your teeth yet? Oh and go in there and wake up the Grouch and your cousins."

"I am already up Godzilla," Madear said creeping into the kitchen.

Everyone had come in and sat at the table ready to chow down. Pete, Anthony and Johnathan had no home training or respect for the Lord so they started eating before everyone else and before we said grace.

"Excuse me boys. I know you are hungry but around here we have to say our grace. So bow your heads and close your eyes . . . everyone please. Lord, thank you for blessing us with a nice meal and a place to eat it. Let this food nourish our bodies in your darling son Jesus name amen," Big Mama prayed.

"It does not take all that to thank the Lord for a meal. But I did forget we are dealing with Mary Magdalene," Madear said.

"Big Mama, has Mama Betty called yet?" Mike interrupted.

"Yes, they said Chrissy is doing so much better that she can come home today. Babies, I tell you there aint nothing like the power of prayer. I stayed up all night on my face praying to God for that baby. He is a healer, yall hear me."

Big Mama was about to start shouting in any minute and this would be a sight for my new cousins to see.

"Hallelujah! I praise you Father. Hallelujah!"

Mike and Pearl put their heads down and my new cousins almost choked on their food from laughing so hard at the uncontrollable shaking Big Mama did at the table.

"It does not take all of that," Madear blurted out.

"If you knew him like I know him then you would be careful about what you say," Big Mama suddenly stopped and corrected Madear.

We continued eating and Madear all of a sudden got real quiet. I gulped down my food and in a matter of minutes and so did everyone else. I jumped up from the table and headed to my room to change my clothes. I needed to go outside and play since summer was in full effect and I didn't want to waste a beautiful day. Pearl had gone into the kitchen to help Big Mama clean up and everyone else scattered throughout the house and out the door. Just as I was walking out of the door Mama Betty and Chrissy came walking in.

"Brooklyn, where do you think you are going?"

"Outside."

"Is your room clean?"

"It's Pearl's turn to clean it."

"Whatever, you just better be in hollering distance."

"Yes ma'am."

I wanted to ask how Chrissy was doing but if I showed any signs that I liked her Mama Betty would probably try to keep her. So I left without saying a word.

The door was cracked, so I figured Ms. Moore or Mama Betty had taken Madear out for a walk. Madear loved to be outside but she didn't need or want to be bothered while out there. I see firsthand where my independent nature came from. I sometimes thought it was just from Mama Betty, but I see Madear passed it on to her.

"Mrs. Mo? Madear? Where ya'll at?"

I knew they heard me call their names but no one answered. I looked all over the small three-bedroom house but no one was there. Mrs. Mo's car was outside and the door cracked open so I knew that someone was there. Bear, the family dog looked pitiful through the back screen door and then I saw Madear's walker.

"I was calling ya'll name," I said as I walked out the backdoor to talk to her. "Where is Mrs. Mo?"

Madear looked at me like I was wearing a fresh pile of dog mess.

"Madear, where is Mrs. Mo or Mama Betty?" I said it a little louder because I figured maybe she didn't hear me.

"Listen, little girl you do not have to scream, I may be old but I am not deaf. She should be in the house somewhere. Go get Bear some water . . . he look like he is about to roll over and die of thirst. Poor dog, they won't bathe you, feed you or even take you for a walk. Just pitiful!"

Madear was a character that no one could reckon with. She'd lived with our family ever since I could remember. Just recently she had gotten sick and had to have a home health nurse come in and assist her on a daily basis. That rocked her world because she liked things done her way or the highway.

"Mrs. Mo!" I began to search the kitchen and garage after I gave Bear his water. I searched all over the house but I still could not find her anywhere. I passed by Pearl and my room and there she was, caught red-handed.

"Mrs. Mo . . . what are you doing?"

When she saw me, she jumped like she had just seen a ghost and almost hit the floor. I laughed so hard that tears formed in my eyes and flowed down my plump cheeks. A 60-year-old plus-size lady jumping up off a bed in a hurry was the highlight of my day.

"Girl, don't come in here and scare me like that, I thought you were your grandmother trying to pull a fast one. You know she tried to call 9-1-1 on me today for giving her a bath!"

"Is that why you so tired and why she sitting outside with Bear? I knew something had happened when the front door was cracked and she was in the backyard with the dog . . . she don't even like dogs. Are you about to leave? Did you cook today?"

I was filled with questions since I knew Big Mama had left and Mama Betty and Chrissy were sleep in her bedroom with the door closed. I guess my cousins had made them some friends because they were all gone too.

"Yeah, your grandmother is a trip ya'll better be glad that I love and fear God because I could be like those nursing home workers beating her every day and ya'll never know anything about it."

"Oh yes we would! You see how she almost had you put in jail today for giving her a bath and you talking about beating her, I think she would be the one doing the beating."

We both laughed again and headed to the front room. I really liked Mrs. Mo because she was real. Some of those other nurses that the government sent over here were too stiff. They reminded me of the robot from *The Jetsons*, Daisy. I wanted to reprogram them with some soul and Jesus so they could understand our family like Mrs. Mo did. She was from the wards too, and wasn't afraid to see the down and dirty, roaches and Bear tied up with a steel chain. When we didn't have much food, Mrs. Mo made a way and we ended up with a whole meal. Mama Betty liked Mrs. Mo too because she not only took care of Madear but the whole house. There were many days when Mrs. Mo would use her own money to buy us food. Mrs. Mo was married to a shade tree mechanic, the kind that fixed everybody's cars in the neighborhood for half the price or for a case of beer, but we didn't hear about him or see him much. We just knew his name was Mr. Mo and that he worked on cars. Mrs. Mo had chocolate brown skin and a sad-looking face. You could tell that she had a rough life because her eyes were always puffy underneath and real low. I wondered for a while if she was on some sort of drugs but I never said anything. She was a lot like us, with a lot of people in her house too. I guess when you come from the wards and everybody had to live together you can't get that out of your system.

"Madear you ready to come back in? Because I will be leaving soon. I put your lunch that you threw at me earlier back on the stove and your milk in the icebox. Do you need anything else before I leave?"

"Yeah, for you to leave me the hell alone. I can get myself back in the house and I will tell Mama Betty that you tried to drown me today in the tub so you can go to jail." Madear didn't have any teeth so her lips smacked together so fast that nothing but spit flew out after every word. She was all of a buck o'five and about 5 feet tall but if you talked to her over the phone you would think she was a giant. I heard from Mama Betty that she used to be a major whipper snapper, whip butts and take names later. I can see her getting into it with those old ladies back in the ward. Mama Betty said one time Madear beat a lady so bad she had to stay in the hospital for several weeks. This lady thought Madear was going to let her walk away after cheating on a game of pitty-pat, but Madear caught her after finishing her beer. As soon as the lady stepped out the door, Madear got up from the card table, threw her empty beer bottle away and walked outside right behind her. Before anybody knew anything, Madear was back in the house and the lady was on the side of the house bleeding.

"Mama Betty, did she shoot her or something?"

I needed to know what kind of grandmother I had in my house.

"Naw chile, they didn't carry guns back then. She just beat the hell out of her and left her on the side of the house. Everybody thought she was beat by her old man because she was a prostitute with a pimp so nobody ever said anything."

"Did she live? I mean did Madear kill her?"

Tears began to well up in my eyes because I am now thinking my grandmother is a murderer.

"Girl naw, she was used to being beat so she got out the hospital and went on back to hoeing," Mama Betty explained.

From that story I knew that Madear could probably take Mrs. Mo even being old.

Mrs. Mo looked at Madear and shook her head. You can tell she wanted to say something, but Madear gave her a look like I wish you would. I almost think Mrs. Mo was scared of Madear and for very good reasons.

"Bye Brook, I will see you tomorrow and please help your grandmother back in the house because she can't lift her leg up over that step at the door," Mrs. Mo whispered because she knew if Madear heard her telling me to help her back in it would be drama all over again.

"Okay, I will see you tomorrow. Oh, Mrs. Mo did you cook anything?"

"Of course sweetie, there is a pot of your favorite chili beans on the stove and the rice is in the microwave."

"Did you make some cornbread to go with it?" We had to have cornbread with chili beans . . . shoot we had to have cornbread with everything. Jiffy cornbread was the best because it was already sweet and if you added a little more sugar and put more melted butter in the pan it tasted like pound cake. Just the smell of it in the oven made your mouth water.

"Yes sweetie, it's in the stove. I will see you tomorrow and make sure to lock the door when I leave." She sashayed out the front door and winked when she left. I blew her a kiss and she caught it and put it on her cheek! That was our thing, I knew she loved me even though she wasn't even family.

Mama Betty woke up and everyone was watching *Wheel of Fortune* in the living room. This was a rare occasion for all of us to be together at the same time. Pearl usually came home from summer track late and Mike was never really home.

"What ch'y'all doing? Whose turn is it to take out the trash because it is in here overflowing and I should not have to say that something is not done every time I walk in this kitchen!"

Here it comes. A bad day at work, stressing about the bills or just getting up on the wrong side of the bed brought wrath on us and hell to pay. This was the story of our lives with Mama Betty. She worked for Sons and Sons Insurance Agency as the secretary to the head guy. She complained daily about the job, but went back every day with a smile. I always wondered why she kept going back, but I figured that it was because of all the mouths she had to feed. Mama Betty was a real generous person and she had a heart of gold. If you told her you didn't have clothes, she would give you her shirt. If you said you didn't have food, she would give you her meal. That was just the kind of person she was, but along with her giving came hell and high water. Some of the things she requested and asked for was reasonable but sometimes things were just ridiculous.

"Brooklyn, give me that remote control over there."

Was she serious? She is sitting next to the television. I wanted to remind her of the proximity between her and the TV, but I would probably find myself picking up my teeth off the floor.

"Pearl, come in here and fix me a bowl of cereal. Don't put a lot of sugar in it this time, thank you."

Her sarcasm came across real rude and Pearl was not the one to take everything Mama Betty dished out but I guess this day she decided to keep the peace.

"All I do for y'all in this house and I can't even wake up to a clean place. I have been at the hospital with a sick child for 24 hours and I need to rest but oh no I have to come in here and be the maid and the drill sergeant. Get y'all tails up and clean my house! I am going to take a bath and eat my cereal. When I get back this living room better be clean, the trash better be taken out and those dishes better be washed. Pearl listen for Chrissy in case she gets up before I get out the tub. It's almost time for her medicine."

The house was not big at all so it wouldn't take long for those things she mentioned to get done. Mama Betty wanted things done in a certain way if it wasn't done her way we have to keep doing it until we got it right.

"Betty, leave them kids alone. We watching *Wheel of Fortune* and this our favorite part. They can clean up when it go off."

"Madear, mine your own business before I have you cleaning up something too! They should've had this done before I woke up and y'all could be watching whatever you want to but it wasn't. So like I said it better be clean by the time I get out the tub."

"I am surprised these kids ain't ran away from home yet . . . hard ass!"

Madear knew she could say whatever to Mama Betty and she would basically turn the other cheek because she didn't want to disrespect her mother. I could see it in her eyes that she was tired of Madear and her mess because she gave her a stare that could've burned a whole straight through her.

"Okay, I will wash the dishes; somebody can sweep and clean the stove and countertops."

"Brooklyn, you do not have to tell us what to do. Just do your part and we will do ours. Dang, you always think you running something."

"Pearl, shut up! I was just trying to help organize something so when Madusa aka Mama Betty come back out we will have this done."

Not only was Pearl argumentative with Mama Betty, but to anyone she could get at, she was the mouth of the house. Pretty caramel skin and long sandy brown hair with an hour-glass shape made her think she was God's gift to America and the Rideaux family. Her ravishing beauty and smooth moves made all the girls at her school jealous, but little did they know Pearl was not in the least bit interested in what they thought of her. Her mind stayed in her books and on trying to be the valedictorian of her class. She had everything it took except for her weakness to one boy, Brandon Daughtry.

He was her first real love and she would bend over backwards and forward again to make sure he was okay. I went into the kitchen and washed all the dishes and ended up sweeping and cleaning the counters too. Man, I felt just like Cinderella while my evil real sister watched and start talking on the phone.

"I don't know who gone clean the living room or take the trash out because I am done," I said with anger and force. Our two cousins Pete and Johnathan were looking dumbfounded at one another. Pete was the oldest and the laziest but Johnathan was the hot head. He volunteered to take the trash out while Pete went and laid on the couch. I wanted to call Big Mama so I went into the living room to call her but when I picked it up I heard Pearl's friend, Tonya, voice on the other end.

"Dang Pearl, how much work do you have? I thought we were going to the mall." Tonya was a no-nonsense friend who always shot straight. She and Pearl were a lot alike but they were very different as well. Tonya stood about 6-foot-2 and weighed about 250 pounds. She had lots of friends because she was fun to be around and she always dressed real good. Whenever new shoes came out, Tonya had it or if Girbeaux put out new jeans, she had that, too.

"Girl, I am almost finished. What do you need to go the mall for anyway? You know I don't have no money and you got everything as it is." Pearl obviously had an ulterior motive because she loved going to the mall.

"Well, the new Jordan's came out and I want to go see if they got my size? Listen just call me back when you get done and I will come and pick you up, okay?"

"Right, I will call you when I'm finished." For some reason Pearl didn't sound too happy when she hung up the phone, almost pissed off. I hung up the phone at the same time and marched into Madear's room where Pearl had gone to use the phone.

"You going somewhere Pearl? Tonya coming over here?"

"Why are you always in my business? She wants to get those new Jordan's but I really don't feel like going to the mall. Plus how did you know about that anyway?"

"None of your business. Where does Tonya get all of that money from anyway?"

"Why are you asking me? Why don't you ask her yourself when you see her again? Nosey tail!"

"You really get on my nerves Pearl. It's a simple question and you don't have to be so rude. UGHHH!"

Even though Pearl didn't tell me, I found out anyway from her diary that Tonya's dad was a major dope dealer and whatever she wanted he got it for her. They were from Colombia and I read that they came down here running from the feds. I guess Pearl knew to keep quiet about anything dealing with those Colombians.

"Pearl, telephone. I think it's your baby daddy!"

"Give me the phone dummy!" She jerked the phone out of my hand and I stood there listening.

"Hello . . . wait a minute, hold on! If you don't get your tail out of my face while I am on the phone its gone be on like Donkey Kong and you better hurry up before I tell Mama Betty you were talking to a little boy on the phone earlier."

She really knew what to say to get me out of her face. Just mention telling Mama Betty something about what I did would raise the hairs on the back of my neck. I walked out of our room giving her a look that said "I can't stand you" but little did she know I didn't go far.

"Yeah, I'm finished. Well me and Tonya suppose to go to the mall but I really don't feel like going. Hey, you wanna just come pick me up and we can go chill? You know what I mean, right?"

Oooh, she was making plans to go that boy house and "chill." I'm gone tell Mama Betty for real.

"How long will it take you? Okay, cool you can pick me up from Tonya house."

Pearl was not ordinarily a sneaky child but ever since Brandon, her new boyfriend, had come into the picture she had being done some real devious things. Brandon was the guy that everyone wanted to be with but *he* chose Pearl. Tall, dark and handsome was one way Tonya and Pearl described him. He reminded me of Morris Chestnut with Mekhi Phifer eyes. His arms were huge and he often wore those tight shirts to show off. He was the star quarterback for the high school and the best forward on the basketball team so everyone knew him. I could see why Pearl was in love with him because on the outside he was a beautiful specimen but on the inside . . .

"Mama Betty, I am about to go over Tonya house and I will be back in a few hours; we going to the mall."

For some reason Mama Betty had obviously forgotten about checking on the cleaning that we were all suppose to be doing because she was laid out across her bed and fallen asleep next to Chrissy. The annoying rattling sound from the ceiling fan was the only thing louder than her snoring. She had turned the TV up and let her bedroom window up to take in the fresh air and to cover up being sleep although none of that seemed to bother Chrissy. I guess her medicine had her really knocked out. Mama Betty never wanted anyone to know when she was sleep like she wanted to catch us doing or not doing something.

"Mama Betty, did you hear me?" Pearl knew she was sleep and she didn't go all the way into her room either to tell her that she was leaving. Another tactic of a sneaky person who was trying to do some dirt.

"Uughh hmm," Mama Betty said while still knocked out. Pearl grabbed her things and shot out the front door like she was late for something.

Should I tell Mama Betty what I heard her plotting with Brandon? Naw . . .

"Pearl, do you know what time it is? You better have a very good reason why you coming in this house way after dark!"

Uuhh oh, Mama Betty was pissed and I know Pearl was scared like a stray cat getting caught by the pound. Her light brown eyes widened with fear and sweat formed on her forehead.

"Please tell her the truth, Pearl, because she already knows," I thought as I sat on the couch pretending to be watching TV. I was hoping and praying Pearl could hear the thoughts in my head and know that Mama Betty had talked to Tonya's mom and found out she wasn't over there.

"Tonya and I were at the mall and I lost track of time, sorry."

"What mall did y'all go too? The one in Alaska? Because the malls here close at nine and it is a quarter to ten. And you say you were with Tonya, right?"

"Ye . . . ye . . . yes ma'am," Pearl had begun to stutter and that usually meant she was lying.

SLAPPPPPP! Mama Betty slapped the daylights out of Pearl. Mike ran out of the kitchen and into the living room where the two stood. He looked over at Mama Betty and she gave him a look like "You better get the hell back!"

Since Mike was the peacemaker and Mama Betty was a hell raiser he could usually calm her down with his presence or a calm look. But not today.

"Mama Betty what you do that for? I said I was sorry for coming home late, dang!"

"Pearl, you lying. You never went to the mall because I called Tonya's mother and Tonya was at home. For some reason you think I was born last night, but I can show you better than I can tell you. Give me that beeper. You won't need that for a while my sister. And no more track either."

"We have a meet tomorrow that I can't miss."

"Oh, well!"

Pearl reluctantly gave the beeper to Mama Betty and ran into our bedroom. She was mad and I knew that this was not the right time for me to go in and say anything to her. I heard her sobbing and I almost wanted to cry too. I knew Pearl was wrong but it was just something about when *she* cried I wanted to cry to because I felt her pain. I stood frozen in the hallway trying to figure out if I wanted to go to bed now or later and Mama Betty gave me that look.

"You got something you want to say?" I put my head down as if my master was reprimanding me. "I didn't think so! Gone in there and get in the bed."

That was the way it was . . . when one of us got in trouble everyone got in trouble. Was that closeness or insanity? We never figured it out.

"Pearl, you want some ice cream?"

I knew that she loved ice cream and hopefully this would cheer her up.

"Brooklyn, I want you to leave me alone, please."

That came out very sternly so I began to tiptoe around her trying to get on my side of the bed. She sat in the middle of the floor between the dresser and the bed, so I had to step over her several times.

"Excuse me . . . sorry . . . excuse me!"

"Brooklyn, hurry the hell up and get out of here!"

"Mama Betty told me to go to bed."

"I don't care what she said. I said get out."

Wait a minute, what does she mean get out? This was my room, too. Sharing a room as small as a matchbox with your older sister was difficult because the room was really hers. If I wanted to do something in the room I had to ask her. If I wanted to rearrange the furniture I had to get her permission. Community property was not upheld in that bedroom and therefore I felt like a tenant rather than a sister. We had to sleep in a king-sized bed that took up most of the room. The bed was an old Victorian-era Metal Poster Bed with leaf accents. It was a hand me down from Flo, Mama Betty's best friend in the ward, and was worn seriously inside and out. The mattress was so worn that we had to turn it over at least twice a month so we wouldn't sink into the box spring. Pearl actually liked sleeping on the side that sank in, so I gave her that side. I didn't care as long as I was comfortable.

"Pearl, what is this?"

I picked up a long cylinder package that read *EPT* on the side in big bold letters from the side of the bed. Now I know I was indeed younger than Pearl, but I was pretty bright for my age. I knew from seeing the commercials on Channel 11 that EPT stood for early pregnancy test and this better be somebody else's because Mama Betty would have a heart attack.

"Give it here, stupid!"

Pearl reached over and snatched the slim package out of my hand. She stuck it in her panty drawer, the one she knew no one would ever go into. My eyes followed her every move in slow motion. From opening the drawer forcefully, to throwing the pregnancy test in and slamming it shut. I was in disbelief . . . is she? No, Pearl knows better, could she really be . . . PREGNANT?

Chapter three

"**W**hat were you thinking? Better yet, why were you not thinking?" Mama Betty asked Pearl, "How could you be so dog gone selfish by going and getting pregnant? This is just another mouth that I have to feed and less money in this house. Pearl when did this happen?"

Pearl couldn't look Mama Betty in the face and her body language said she was ashamed and embarrassed. She kept pushing up her glasses and then Mama Betty helped her.

SLAAAPP, SLAAAPP! All we could hear coming from the back were slapping noises and what sounded like doors slamming. Were they fighting?

"Betty, leave that girl alone. She made a mistake just like you did when you were her age."

Madear was the one to take up for us when Mama Betty got on our cases. She was often mean, but she did not like to see her grandchildren get whippings.

"Betty, I said leave that chile alone!"

Madear raised herself up off the couch and headed towards Mama Betty's room. She was trying to walk fast but her walker would only move so much on the very thick carpet. Before Madear could reach the door, Mama Betty came out and looked at her like she had stole something.

"Madear, where in the world are you going? You need to mind your own business, this ain't got nothing to do with you. I am the one that will be taking care of that baby, not you!"

"Let me tell you something," Madear began while inching toward Mama Betty, "I am *your* mama and you better respect me! Do you understand?"

I had never seen Madear and my mama have such a serious conversation where Madear took the lead.

"You must remember not very long ago you were in her shoes with your first child. Do you remember what I said to you?"

I stood at the corner trying not be seen and the two had ended up in Mama Betty's bedroom and Madear stood next to the Chateau Frontenac bed that Mama Betty got as a surprise gift from Tommy Boy. Madear's voice rose as Mama Betty began cleaning her bed off and seemed to not be paying attention. As the two talked, Pearl slipped out of the room and into our bedroom.

"Madear, times are different and Pearl has been taught better. I work hard every day so that this family can have the best and not have to worry about anything. This is a slap in my face and yes I remember what you said . . . you will always be there for me no matter what."

Tears began to roll down Mama Betty's face as she talked to her mother now in a child-like tone. The hurt was very evident and Madear went over and held Mama Betty.

"So like I was there for you, be there for your first daughter. Betty, she needs you now more than ever so don't turn your back on her."

As Madear exited the room she blew a kiss to Mama Betty. Mama Betty caught it and put it on her cheek.

Pearl laid across the bed and fell asleep. By now the house was very quiet and everyone seemed to have settled down. I went outside to get some fresh air and to see if my best friend wanted to come out. If I was old enough I probably would have grabbed a cigarette because all that drama stressed me out.

"Staci, can you come outside?"

I made it to her house in a matter of minutes. The walk seemed like an eternity due to the block being so long. When she came to the door she had the biggest smile on her face and that was good to see. I needed somebody to be happy right now if it wasn't going to be me.

"Yeah, hold on let me tell my aunty where I am going."

She ran back inside the house and left the front door open. Looking through their dark house I could see her nosey cousin and the cute quiet cousin sitting in front of their big screen television. The nosey one started whispering something while looking at me but the other cousin simply ignored him. The nosey fat cousin reminded me of a girl and he always had something to say. He was shorter than the boys we all hung around and came just about to my five-foot shoulders. Dark as night with cold dark brown eyes I could tell that he either hated his life or hated me.

"Hey Brook! What do you want with Staci?"

The nosey cousin wobbled his way to the door and got in my face. Oh my gosh, I was not here for him and I really needed him to back it up because I was not in the mood. All the drama that was happening at my house and then to come over and have to deal with him, I don't think so. In the event that his fat behind said the wrong thing in the wrong way a butt-whipping was going to be issued and I was preparing myself.

"Could you please just tell Staci that I am about to walk down the driveway because you are bugging and I ain't got time for it, thank you!"

As soon as the last word left my lips a six-foot, athletic build statue came to the door and pushed fat boy out of the way. Before I could turn around and walk away I caught his smooth chocolate skin and caramel toned eyes that silently spoke "stay . . . baby, stay."

"Hey Derrick, what's up?"

I wanted to say more but four words were all I could muster.

"Hey Brook, you letting fat boy get you upset? Ignore this dude, he's whack."

As he spoke all I could do was visualize his LL Cool J lips meeting mine and us making sweet melodies together. The thought of us making out made me forget for a minute that I was standing outside waiting on Staci to come out.

"BROOK, BROOK girl what is wrong with you? Come on!"

Staci came out with her purse and a notebook like we were going on a tour of the neighborhood or something.

"See you later Derrick," I said blushing.

"Right baby girl, holla at me when you come back!"

I wanted to say definitely but Staci pulled me away too fast. She reminded me of a young businesswoman, so well organized and she learned to carry herself well too. Although she was a very humble person she was also a little self-conscious. There were times when she and I would cry together because we both were pushed to the side by our families in some kind of way. I remember Staci telling about all the times when she had to fight the crack heads in the ward. Her mama was on drugs and they would break in their house often even when Staci was home alone. Her aunty and uncle couldn't stand to see her in that environment so they moved her in with them. Staci stood about five-three with thick curly hair and light skin. Her little Chinese eyes made her look like she was mixed with something, but she was from the wards like me with some Creole in her too. That is why I confided in her so much because we understood each other when other people didn't.

"Girl where are you going with all that stuff? I just wanted to see if you wanted to go to the park. By the way, how long were you calling my name? Your cousin had me in another world, chile!"

We both laughed as we walked around the corner and Staci started digging in her purse for something. I guess lip gloss since it's like her American Express . . . she can't leave home without it. Taking red oil-based lip color; Staci smeared her lips with enough gloss to moisturize an ashy bum.

"Dang, girl you think you got enough on . . . you looking real shiny!"

"This is Avon baby and you can never have enough!"

I wanted to debate that fact but I needed to vent too badly so I dropped the issue.

"Guess what we just found out?"

I knew I wasn't supposed to tell anyone because what went on in the Rideaux house stayed in the Rideaux house! Staci and I were like sisters and I knew she wouldn't tell nobody so I spilled my beans.

"What . . . don't tell me your mama getting another kid?"

"Naw, not Mama Betty, but Pearl is!"

Staci dropped her lip gloss and compact to the ground and the mirror shattered.

"Oh Lord, what are ya'll gone do? I mean ya'll don't have that much space now since your mama took in those extra kids. Listen, if you get put out of your room and need somewhere to crash you can come to my house."

"Thanks for the invitation but I am not being put out of my bedroom because Pearl wouldn't keep her legs closed. They gone have to sleep in there with Madear or something because I ain't going nowhere."

Did they really expect me to give up my room? Shoot, this new baby thing is worse than I thought.

Whenever we were in the neighborhood or at school we hung tight and no one could tell us anything.

One thing I admired about Staci was her quick wit and nonchalant attitude. Most times you couldn't tell if she was for real or joking when we talked until she laughed or said she was joking. Her personality made her lots of friends and all the girls wanted to hang with her, but she was my best friend and I wanted things to stay that way.

We were "the girls" that everyone wanted to be around at school, but, it was "our" clique. We all ran track and played basketball, so most times when the boys were on a trip we were too. Amy was down with us, too. She was real tall and very slim. She didn't run but threw the discus because she was so long. She was good at it, too. Amy was the more subdued type that got along with everybody. It almost got on my nerves because people would try to run over her. I remember last year when Jennifer, the coach's daughter, embarrassed the hell out of Amy in the locker room.

She and Amy usually were cool until this day after practice when Amy wanted to use her hair dryer. We were all getting dressed as normal and then all hell broke loose.

"Hey Jen, can I borrow your dryer real quick?"

"Nope!"

Jennifer said that with a major attitude and everyone looked around to see what was going down.

"Girl, it won't take long I just need to blow my ponytail . . . let me see it."

As Amy reached for Jennifer's dryer, her hand was slapped down so hard I wanted to cry.

"Jennifer, I am sorry I just wanted to see the dryer . . . dang!"

"Well, I said no and that is what I meant!"

I couldn't believe my eyes as Amy walked away and back to her locker to get her things. Are you kidding me? I know this heifer did not slap my friend's hand and think she is going to get away with it. I walked over to Jennifer and gave her a look that said you had better watch your back. Now mind you this girl was about 200 pounds and I was a mere buck o' five and I knew she could whip my tail, but I could not let her know that. Amy got her bag and closed her locker.

"You ready?" she asked me in such a calm and pleasant voice.

"Ready? Yeah to whip this girl. You gone let her walk away unharmed while your arm is as red as that coke machine? Come on!"

Amy wasn't moved. I just knew that it was about to be a royal rumble in this locker room but she was ready to go to class.

"Amy, I know you hear me. This girl just pulled your card and you not gone do nothing? Fine, let me see her after school and I'm gone pull her card."

That was the last time I had to stand up for Amy. From then on she didn't have any more confrontations unlike me. Amy really wasn't bothered by much but I was about to get real mad, I was trying to help her out. Whatever . . . I had to let that ride because I would be the one suspended for three days while everybody else was chilling.

Staci and I stuck close together. She was like the sister I always wanted even though I had two others. I was a little afraid of Staci, too. She was a fighter and if anybody said or did something wrong, boy or girl, she would whip their butts. So I tried to stay on the peaceful side with her and we got along that way. She would come over and spend the weekend at my house sometimes, or I would go to her house. I believe she liked coming over because we always went to church. She never really had a chance to go to church at her house. They probably believed in God but didn't have a church home. My mama liked Staci, too. So my "loving" mother took her under her wings and catered to her like she was her child and once again I felt left alone.

"Girl, your mama cool as a fan. I don't see how you can get mad at her," Staci mentioned while walking from the park.

"Yeah she cool all right. To people that don't live with us. Try staying there for a while or maybe the rest of your life and see what you think then."

I was almost getting mad and slightly offended because people always made it seem as if it was my fault that my mama and I didn't have the best relationship. That was me though in middle school. Easily offended and always mad. Why? Who knows I guess just all the emotions of a pre-teen. And boy, were they out of control. If I wasn't crying I wanted to cry. No one really understood where I was coming from most of the time, so I acted out.

Staci changed the subject about Pearl. I guess I was starting to show that I was getting upset. The park was our sanctuary and our hideout. It was still close enough to my house where could get there if I saw the street lights coming on and close enough to Staci's house where she could hear her aunty calling her name.

"So are you ready for school?" I asked her.

"Of course, you know it's our year to run the school and to win every track meet and basketball game we go to."

"I know and I am so ready. I better hurry up and get home. I will see you later. Don't forget to be dressed to death on the first day of school. You already know I will."

Fall 1993 . . . When we walked in the building at Thomas Middle School you heard one of two things, "Look at them . . . man they look good," or "Who they think they are?" Most of the comments we heard made us laugh or either dared someone to jump stupid. But even in our tightness we still had much drama. Staci and I were the only ones that did not have a father figure in the house with us. The other three girls had their fathers living with them. That was intimidating and angering at times because rather we were playing basketball or running track their fathers were there. My mama had to work two jobs because of all the people that lived with us. Staci lived with her uncle and aunt and they always worked, too. We all lived in the same neighborhood except for Kim. Her dad worked for a company where they moved a lot. She lived in a neighborhood down the street from us and her mom was a "stay at home" mom. Mrs. T, is what we called her, always made us laugh. She was very stylish and she always had different fingernails or hairdos. I can remember her picking us up from practice and driving us home because Staci and I didn't have a ride. Her nails would be super long and I was afraid we all would get scratched up sooner or later. Mrs. T loved us all the same and when I started to feel lonely she made me feel good. I really didn't talk to Kim's dad much, though. He was there sometimes but for the most part he was working. He didn't like me anyway and he always looked at me upside my head. Whatever . . . he wasn't my daddy so it didn't matter.

"Okay, so I know you heard about Shae, right?" Staci asked after school.

That statement hit me hard and I had no idea that Staci knew this girl and I had beef. Shae was the new girl and she was from Third Ward. She was short, very skinny and quiet, so I just knew she was gone be cool. Her dark skin, short black hair and gold tooth made her come across as being very ghetto, but she was the opposite.

"What are you talking about?" I knew exactly what she was talking about but I didn't want to give way like I knew.

"You heard about Shae and Cory hanging out together *all* this week and now everybody saying you want to fight her because she was kicking it with your man."

"Girl please! First of all, you said it right, Cory is my man and ain't no hood rat from the third coming over here messing with my man. Plus Cory know what's up!"

My heart was in my stomach and I felt like I wanted to barf. Cory was the most popular guy at Thomas Middle and I had him. Taller than most eighth graders, Cory stood about 5-foot-6 and wore his height and build very well. Broad shoulders, beautiful white teeth, and those puppy dog eyes that made all the girls love to just stare at him, were his best attributes. His skin was the color of smooth caramel and his jet black wavy hair made him most desirable, plus he was the best dressed boy in the whole school.

Does this chick really think she can take my man away from me? What does she have that I don't? I immediately began to plot how I wanted to make sure this girl knew that Cory was mine and wasn't going anywhere.

"Hey do you wanna go to her house with me so I can let her know what's up?"

I knew Staci would say no. She had already been in trouble with her uncle for fighting her cousins at their family reunion this summer.

"Are you crazy Brook? You gone go to this girl house and do what? What if her people got guns or something? Naw, I am going home and you need to go home, too."

Staci looked at me with a look that meant she was serious and that I had better take my tail home. But I needed this girl to know who she was messing with . . . I mean Cory was with me first. After I got off the bus I ended up walking four blocks trying to talk myself out of going to her house but my pride said I had to prove to this third ward hood rat who ran Thomas. When I got on her street I really didn't know where she lived and I only saw one person outside watering their grass. The lady looked like a teenager so I dismissed the thought of her being anyone's mother. Just as I was politely passing her up and smiling, guess who walks out of her door? This was my opportunity to let her know that she needed to stay away from Cory or else.

"Brooklyn, what brings you down my street?"

Shae had a weird smile on her face like she worked for the city and could claim rights to streets in our neighborhood.

"Hey I need to talk to you," I said as I walked to the sidewalk in front of her house. Shae looked at her mom and then back at me. Her mother smiled at both of us and went into the house.

"Listen, I am not sure if you know, but Cory is my boyfriend and I heard you trying to talk to him. You need to step off and know that he is taken. If I hear anything else Shae about you trying to holla at him you gone wish you had stayed in Third Ward!"

My words came out frank and strong. I felt confident that this was all I needed to do to get her to back off of my man. As I stood there and nothing came out of her mouth I began to turn and walk away. Just then I felt something pulling my ponytail.

"Oh hell no, you better let my hair go!"

"Naw, Brooklyn, you think you bad so come here and let's see how bad you really are!"

Before I knew anything, the streets were filled with people and we were in the streets throwing blows like Foreman and Holyfield. I knew I could take this little girl because she was smaller than me and I talked a real good game that should have put some fear in her heart.

"Y'all stop it . . . stop it," Shae's mother came running out of the house screaming. She obviously knew that Shae could fight and must have done it a lot in Third Ward because some kind of way I ended up on the ground with her on top of me. I was not sure how I got down there except by someone obviously tripping me.

"Little girl, why did you come down here with that mess . . . take your tail home," her mother said as she pulled Shae off of me. I looked up and there she was celebrating in the streets like she had just finished a marathon.

I walked back home ashamed, embarrassed, and with a forehead full of knots.

"What happened? I was getting the best of her and then . . . ," I thought as I walked back, hoping no one saw me.

"Dangggggg . . . . what happened to you? You look like you've been fighting some bees." Johnathan always had jokes, but this time it was not funny. I tried to get in the house and to the restroom without anyone seeing me, but that was obviously not going to happen.

"Hey, Pearl, y'all come look at Brooklyn's head! Somebody whipped her ass! I mean tail! Do I need to go down there and put a Chicago-style beat down on somebody?" Johnathan made the entire house come and see what was going on with my head. There initially was sympathy but then that quickly turned into laughs and pointing. Mama Betty had still had her purse and keys in her hand but quickly dropped them on the couch. She told Pearl to go get an ice pack or a frozen piece of meat wrapped in foil. I didn't know what that was going to do, but I was okay with whatever it would take to get rid of the knots before school the next day. Madear came into the living room and began to examine my forehead.

"Brooklyn, you need to get yourself up and go back down there and whip that big girl ass. We don't walk away from fights like that no matter how big the person."

"Uhmm, Madear," said Anthony, "the girl was not bigger than Brooklyn. She was smaller!"

The laughs came pouring out even more and my head went down. No one could know that someone from Third Ward whipped a girl from Fifth Ward . . . that would be the end of my reputation. I kept quiet with the frozen meat on my forehead hoping the knots would quickly disappear and I got my pride back.

The only thing that I really knew about my father was that he was in jail from the time right after I was born and everyone called him Tommy Boy. I was not quite sure how I was conceived because Mama Betty said he stayed in the streets so much. Big Mama was adamant about making sure Pearl and I knew who our father was and that we knew he loved us. Mama Betty was so hurt and pissed at him leaving us that she never really talked about him unless we did something that reminded her of him.

One Saturday morning we took a trip to Rosharon where Tommy Boy was and the ride was the best part. Big Mama would stop and get crackers, hog head cheese, summer sausage, and root beer cream soda in the beer bottle for us. The bottles we pretended had real beer in them and so by the time we arrived in Rosharon we were all drunk! The ride took us about an hour from Fifth Ward where Big Mama still lived and since she drove slow what would ordinarily take thirty minutes seemed like forever. Actually getting into the place to see Tommy Boy wasn't easy either. Having to take off my shoes and jacket to let Barney Fife search me was the worst part.

"Dang . . . I am just a kid," I quickly reminded him.

"You would be surprised the number of kids we have to detain because their parents have them bringing drugs up here," the officer told Big Mama.

Big Mama nodded and pulled me closer to her. Pearl was already ahead of us since she had been there before and knew the routine. I wanted to run and catch up with her but I knew Big Mama would thump me on my ear if I started acting up.

When I saw him behind that big glass window I cried.

"Brooklyn, baby don't cry. Your daddy gone be home soon. You see when I get out of this hole we gone go to the carnival and eat candied apples and popcorn, okay?"

That was an awesome gesture, but where was he going to get the money from to take me anywhere?, I overheard Mama Betty and Big Mama talking about him being the big man in the ward and even while he was locked up. I remember different men coming to the house unannounced and dropping packages off to Mama Betty. She would refuse most of them but sometimes the men would leave them with her anyway.

"Daddy, when you coming home? I play basketball and run track and all my friends' daddies are at their games except for mine!"

I wanted him to know about me quickly so I was first to get my words out. I got the worst look from Pearl since I knew she needed to tell him that she was expecting a baby. All this time everything has been about her and now I was with someone that could listen to what was going with me.

"It won't be long now and remember when I do come we going to the carnival!"

Was that like a punch line for him or something? Because that is all he seemed to talk about. It sounded cool but I was in the eighth grade now and not really interested in carnivals like I was when I was five years old.

"Big Mama told me that you coming home before my birthday so I wanted to see if I could have a party at the skating rink."

Just when I said that I looked up and saw three huge men without their shirts on making their chests jump for Big Mama. I had never seen three gorilla-looking males put on a show like they were doing. Every time one muscle in their chest jumped the opposite one would soon follow like they were racing or something. Gross! Pearl looked at me and laughed. She was not as grossed out as me and obviously she had seen that mess before.

"Baby girl, do not look at them nasty fools. That is the reason they are in here, messing with little girls like you. Listen baby, you have to be wise as a dove and sharp as a serpent, okay?"

I did not really know what he meant but the being wise part sounded good to me and the being sharp part sounded better.

"Diiiinnngggg . . . . diiiinnngggg . . ." a loud sound came from out the ceiling that sounded like our bell at school. Pearl jumped up and headed to the door without saying a word. She had sat there the entire thirty minutes looking crazy. Tommy Boy looked over at Big Mama and then back at Pearl. His eyes began to water but he turned away.

"Come here Brook and give me a kiss 'cause I gotta go now."

I could tell that he wasn't ready to go since his eyes watered up again. It seemed like we barely had a chance to talk. Big Mama stood up and gave Tommy Boy a hug.

"Let's pray before y'all go . . . Father, I know these are your children but you trusted them to me. Please provide, protect and keep them safe for the rest of their lives. I will praise your name forever and ever."

The prayer was short and to the point. My hand was hurting after he let it go and Big Mama's face was wet with tears.

"Next week I will send you some money to put on your books, it may not be much because I have to get the car worked on too, okay. I love you baby and we will talk again soon." Big Mama hugged Tommy Boy tightly.

"Brook, Daddy loves you, do what your mama tell you and write me sometime . . ." was all jumbled in one sentence in about ten seconds. Tommy Boy walked out of the cold white box room and headed in the direction where the "nasty gorilla men" were standing. Big Mama and I grabbed our things and headed out the opposite direction. As I turned around to look at Tommy Boy and he blew me a kiss and wiped what looked like a tear from his face.

"I know he is not crying," I thought. I looked over at Big Mama as we walked down the long narrow hall and she wiped her eyes with every other step we took.

"Why are they crying like they not gone ever see each other again?" I questioned myself as we reached the outside of the prison walls.

"Stay far away from a place like this Brooklyn and from the things that put you in here, you hear me?"

Everyone was rushing to the malls to get the new Jordan's that had just come out. I knew we were not going to get them because Mama Betty had too many people to buy clothes for. I sat at the dining room table playing solitaire with my new deck of cards from Big Mama and that's when I saw my new cousins plotting something.

"Uhmm, Mama Betty, Johnathan, and me wanna know if you can buy us the new Jordan's?"

Anthony spoke up for the new cousins, which was rare. I guess Johnathan put him up to it and didn't give him any pointers on how to approach Mama Betty. Pete had not too long ago left for the army so maybe they thought that freed up some of Mama Betty's money.

"Baby, Mama Betty would love to buy you boys those whatever kind of shoes but I can't afford them right now."

"But Auntie told us that you would buy us whatever we wanted when we moved down here with you so why can't you get them? Everybody gone have new shoes except for us!"

Anthony must not know that Mama Betty didn't take that tone from anyone. So when she walked away and into her bedroom I knew it was on like Donkey Kong. I got up from the table and went into Madear's bedroom to be sure I heard all the action. Anthony walked behind Mama Betty slowly and slipped into the bathroom close to their room. Mama Betty went into her bedroom and came out with a leather strap that she had folded in half. Just as Anthony thought the coast was clear and headed out of the bathroom, he felt Mama Betty's wrath.

"AAAAHHHHH . . . hey what's that for?"

"Little boy come here, I am not finish with you."

"Mama Betty, I am sorry. I'm sorry! Johnathan told me to come ask you!"

"Johnathan . . . come here! You gone let this boy take a whipping for you That's sad! So you gone get it too!"

Anthony was real light skin so Mama Betty made sure she only hit him in certain spots. He jumped all over the hallway every time she swatted the belt. I am sure she missed him more than she hit him.

"Anthony, be still! As a matter of fact go in y'all room until I tell you to come out. Johnathan head to my room. You gone get it just like Anthony, lay over there across that bed and pull your pants down!"

Mama walked in behind him and closed the door. You really couldn't understand their muffled conversation but there had to be some pleading going on.

Mama Betty listened to Johnathan and didn't pop him as much. He didn't come out with dry eyes but he wasn't in there long either.

"Do you boys know why I whipped you," Mama Betty asked as she went into the boys' room?

"No ma'am . . . ," they all spoke in unison.

"First of all, don't put your little brother up to the dirty work. If y'all want to ask me something just come and ask and learn to stick together. Y'all are all you have. If no one else on this earth is there for you guys you have to be there for one another. I don't mind buying you all what you need but I have lots of mouths to feed now with one on the way so the name brand stuff may be out for a while. I will make sure you have what you need but don't try to make me buy you something. Do you understand?"

"Yes ma'am," they both spoke in unison once again.

Mike was already to go when his dad called. His bags were stuffed with sheets, towels, and lots of socks with his name at the bottom of them all. Mama's boss bought him a huge treasure chest trunk and he filled it with all his toiletries that he would need while in his dorm.

"Mike are you coming back?"

I needed to know that my best friend was not gone forever. Mike was the one I talked to about everything and he really took care of me since the new cousins moved in and we found out Pearl was having a baby.

"Naw, Brook. I'm just going to make a better life for myself and you. I want to be able to buy you whatever you want one day and I can only do that with an education. When I get a car I will come and get you, okay? So don't worry I won't be too far."

"I am going to miss you! Can I come live with you? It's too many people in this house!"

Mike was going to go to Harvard until Mama Betty got all those people in our house. She couldn't afford to send him out of state even with his scholarships so he decided to go to Texas A&M University in College Station.

Mike knew I was serious when my eyes began to fill with tears and my voice started squeaking. He leaned down and kissed me on my forehead.

"Brook, you know you my favorite girl so I am not really leaving you but you can't come stay with me. There will be more people in my house then there are here. I love you baby girl and I will keep in contact with you okay? Every day."

That was the last conversation that I had with Mike before he left. He was grown now and heading to begin his new life. His dad was supposed to pick him up at noon so he could check into his dorm by two o'clock.

"Ding dong, ding dong, ding dong!" Whoever was at the door was obviously wanting to be cussed out by Madear for ringing that doorbell so many times.

I ran to the door, "Who is it?"

"It's Stevie . . . tell Mike I said come on!"

I turned around and looked at the time on the VCR and it read 1:07 p.m. No he ain't trying to come over here and rush because he's late.

Mama Betty heard me talking at the door. She came and pushed me out of the way to open the door wide enough for Stevie to see her.

"Where do you get off coming an hour late and then trying to rush somebody? Brother you might want to take a chill pill and help Mike bring out his stuff."

"Good afternoon to you too, Betty! It's always a pleasure to see your beautiful face and hear your lovely voice."

"Don't try to patronize me! My son needs you to do one simple thing for him as his father and you are struggling with that task. Please . . . ."

Mama Betty looked Stevie up and down like he stole something and walked away. Mike began dragging his bags and treasure chest out of the room and into the living room looking for his dad to help him out.

"Hey son! Man you looking good! Just like me when I was preparing for my journey into college!"

"What journey, you never went to college? I hope you didn't fill Mike's head with that foolishness. You had a full scholarship to any college in Texas but you wanted to run the streets. Mike is taking after his mother and going to make something of himself."

Stevie looked at Mama Betty out the corner of his eyes. He stood a little taller than Mama Betty and wore his glasses at the tip of his nose. He reminded me of the librarian at the public library in the ward. His stomach hung over his pants; he was balding right in the front of his head and had several gold teeth in his mouth. I laughed when I saw Stevie because I could not believe that a beautiful women like Mama Betty would give this guy a chance. She once told me that when she dated him in high school he was the talk of Jeff Davis. He was an athlete, dressed nice, and charmed the ladies. They were not dating long before she ended up pregnant with Mike and had to drop out of school. That's when she met Tommy Boy and the rest was history.

"Whatever, Betty. Son are you ready to go? Here let me get that for you."

Stevie struggled to pick up one of Mike's duffle bags but Mike grabbed it with one hand and looked at Stevie with a huge smile on his face. He threw it out of the front door while we all stood and watched his strong arms pop. Mike was headed to college on a track scholarship and a football scholarship and his body was the epitome of a professional football player. Mama Betty pulled Mike over towards her near the garage door in the foyer.

"Honey, you know I love you and Mama is so proud you! You have done so much for this family and I hate to see you go. You have been my anchor and my best friend. It's now time for you to put all that you learned into practice and make a life for yourself. I know I'm not a man but I hope that I taught you a little bit of how to be one. You have grown into such a handsome person and I am so happy you learned something from Tommy Boy. You never let us down Mike and I am so thankful to have you as my son; my first born. Oh, please don't go down there and get wild, don't bring no babies home and please don't bring no diseases home either."

Mike and Mama Betty stood hugging each other for what seemed like an eternity. The floor was wet with their tears and I wanted to get in on the love. Before I knew it I was holding Mike by the waist and wetting his gym shorts with my tears. I was okay with him leaving since we had already had our little talk, but all the crying made me cry, too.

"Come on son, we're already late and we need to get on the road before your roomies get the better bed. Betty let him go so *we* can go, please,"

Mike went over and kissed Chrissy and Pearl on the cheek. He gave Anthony and Johnathan half hugs and waved bye to Madear.

A few months had passed and we ended up moving out of our "dream" house. Mama Betty got laid off from her second job, Mike was gone and now she couldn't afford the maintenance or taxes on the house. Mama Betty found us an apartment down the street. Even though she hated to leave her "dream" home she knew she had to do what she had to do. The apartment that Mama Betty could afford just on her salary was a two-bedroom apartment with two bathrooms. It was small and we had to turn the dining room into Madear's bedroom. By now Madear was getting older and sickly. She walked sometimes on her walker but mainly stayed in her bed and that was something that we were just not used to seeing. I felt bad for her lots of times until she began to cuss everyone out again.

"Madear, does your diaper need to be changed? I smell something and I know you didn't just sit there and go on yourself without letting someone know," Mama Betty would ask on many occasions.

"Betty, I am a grown woman . . . don't you think I know when I need to use the damn restroom?"

"I hope so, but recently you have waited to the last minute and these kids end up cleaning your mess."

Those were the conversations that were frequent in our two-bedroom apartment. Even with Mike gone it still seemed that our house was filled with too many people and I had a feeling that things were about to get worst and fast.

Chapter four

When Tommy Boy said he would be home soon I took it with a grain of salt since I was told those were always his parting words. I walked in the front door and Madear, Mrs. Mo and Mama Betty were all in the kitchen cooking, laughing and talking. I had to stop before I entered the kitchen and think about what day it was.

"Is it someone's birthday?" I wondered.

It really didn't matter because the aroma in the house made my mouth water and the laughs and giggling from the ladies made me laugh too.

"Hey everybody," I said with the biggest smile on my face, "what is all the laughing and cooking about?"

Mama Betty stopped and looked at me firmly.

"I thought I told you to say excuse me when you see adults are talking?"

"Yes ma'am, I am sorry . . . excuuse me but what is all the commotion about? Please tell me that we are not, ain't not, can't not, won't not be getting another child to come and live with us?"

I laughed as I said those words but I was serious as a heart attack. The smell of pinto beans and ham hocks made my mouth water all the more. I walked over to the stove to get a closer look at the contents in the four Teflon pots.

"Excuse me Missy." Mama Betty interrupted my journey to satisfaction, "please do not go over there putting your hands on that food or your nose in those pots. That is for tonight . . . we have a special guest coming over to dinner."

Her face lit up like an artificial Christmas tree and so did Mrs. Mo, who kept stirring some sort of batter in a large plastic white bowl. I moved away from the stove quickly before Mama Betty could get close and stood next to Mrs. Mo and the large white bowl.

"Little girl you sure are curious and I know exactly where you got that from," Madear said from her scooter that was next to the dinette table. She didn't like to stand long, so picking the snap peas was her favorite job.

"I just want to know what all this fuss is about and who is coming to dinner tonight and since when did we start eating dinner together? Will everybody be here? Where are they gone sit since we only have four chairs at the glass table."

All the questions I asked as I scooped batter from the big plastic bowl were ignored and unanswered. This was driving me crazy because I needed to know who was coming to *my* house. I really liked when we had company, probably because it was a rare occasion and especially for Mama Betty to be home from work early and cooking . . . that was all very rare.

I ran my two fingers that I used to lick the sweet batter from the big white bowl under the faucet. It was full of dishes but I ignored it and kept on rinsing.

"Sweetie, since you are over there can you go ahead and wash those dishes? Make sure you dry them off good and put 'em up too." Mama Betty was never short of things for us to do and I guess since I was the most curious one that came in the kitchen when I got home I made myself available.

"Mama Betty, it is not my day to clean the kitchen and plus I have homework. If I don't get this homework done by the time our special guest gets here then I won't have any other time to do it. Remember you always say education is first and I need to make sure I am making you proud."

I was a major hustler when it came to me getting out of things I was asked to do. I think it was innate from my daddy, because I usually won my cases.

"I do value education Brooklyn, but you not gone flunk behind a late assignment and if you do then that means you been flunking all year and I need to have a talk with your teachers."

Mama Betty was a major hustler who was quick with her words, too, and I think that was a learned behavior that she got from growing up in the ward.

"Well since you put it like that I will get right on it."

Everyone started laughing including me and I headed to the back room to change out of my school clothes and put away my backpack.

I wonder who is coming for dinner? Was it someone from the church? Maybe one of Mama Betty's coworkers, like her boss who would pop up every now and then and bring toys like he was Santa Claus. All this guessing was now starting to upset me and no one said anything about who was coming over tonight. After throwing my school clothes in the closet where no one could see them, I ran back into the kitchen to see if I could get some information before I washed the dishes.

"So, Madear tell me . . . who's coming over tonight?" I whispered. She sat at the table still popping peas and never turned around to face me when I asked her the question.

Mama Betty and Mrs. Mo were out on the patio getting more chairs to put in the dining room for tonight so I figured I could get some information from Madear.

"Tommy Boy," she said in a low voice, "and if you say I told you I will break your neck!"

Did I just hear her correctly? Oh my God . . . HE'S HOME! No wonder they cooking ham hocks and black eye peas. Big Mama told me those were his favorite foods when he was a boy. I kissed Madear on her forehead and went over to the sink to run soapy water for the dishes. All I could think of is me sitting on his lap and talking all night. We needed to catch up and I needed to tell him about my school and friends and everything. Why didn't Mama Betty want to say anything? Oh well it didn't matter because my daddy was coming home.

I had fallen asleep on the couch in the living room after cleaning and waiting for my daddy to come. I wanted to make sure I was pretty to him, so I combed my hair back and put it into a banana clip. I had little curly cues on each side of my ears like Shirley Temple would wear. I sat up on the couch and wondered why it was dark and quiet everywhere. The clock on the VCR read 8:33 p.m. and I hoped that my mama would not let me miss my daddy. I walked into the dining room and the lights were off, Madear was asleep and the chairs were stacked up against the wall.

"This is crazy; they didn't wake me up for my daddy!"

I felt a ball begin to form in my throat and tears swell up in my eyes. The aroma from the food in the kitchen had disappeared and no one was eating. The kitchen looked like it did when I finished cleaning the dishes.

"Did they eat, clean up and go to bed already?"

I now felt the tears falling but I had to get it together because I wasn't supposed to know that Tommy Boy was coming home. Just as I wiped my face Mama Betty walked into the kitchen in her bathrobe and began putting the pots and food in the refrigerator.

"Mama Betty, what happened to our guest who was supposed to come over tonight? Did they come while I was asleep and no one woke me up?"

She heard the shaking in my voice so I stopped talking because I did not want to give her Madear and my secret.

"No, Brook our guest couldn't make it tonight. Maybe next time." Her voice was low and melancholy as if she had lost her best friend. The disappointment on her face and in her voice moved me to give her a hug.

"It's okay, Mama! Thank you for leaving work and making the best dinner in the world. Even though I didn't eat any I know it was delicious. I love you, Mommy!" She took my skinny arms from around her waist and held them in her damp hands. She leaned over to my face and her deep brown eyes looked into mine.

"Brooklyn, no matter what happens around here, you will always be my baby girl and I love you too." She hugged me tight and quickly let go, she turned around without saying another word and finished cleaning up the kitchen.

Entering high school for the first time was a major accomplishment for anyone that came out of the ward. Most girls would either be pregnant, hoeing or trapped in an abusive relationship that they were scared to leave. Since we moved out of the ward our family now had hope. My same friends from Thomas would be moving on to John Maxwell High, so this was going to be the best year any freshman could have, and I was going to make sure of that. Being with my girls and meeting new people was on my to-do list for the first day of school. The teachers and class work could come later.

"Mama Betty, are we going school shopping? This year I have to be fresh to death since I will be a fresh-man . . . get it?"

I always cracked myself up, but Mama Betty didn't seem to think that I was real funny.

"Do you have a job? Can you go get a job? Money is tight right now and I am trying to do what I can to make sure y'all eat . . . so you may want to call Big Mama and see if she can help you."

Those words were like a two-edged sword that cut through my chest and sliced up my heart. This can't be happening to me now. School starts in three weeks and I do not have any new clothes for my new school. "Strategize Brook . . . how can you make some quick money?" I needed to come up with a way and quick. I could call my Big Mama, but she wouldn't get her Social Security check until the first of the month and by then I would have started school. I needed at least two hundred dollars and I needed it fast.

"Brooklyn, telephone," Mama Betty hollered from her bedroom. Normally she screened my calls like the FBI but I guess this one got through.

"I got it! Hello?"

"Wuz up Brook?"

"Who is this?"

"Oh you acting like you don't know my voice now. This is your man, Derrick. Staci cousin!"

The sound of his voice made me take a seat on the couch and close my legs real tight. I was not expecting him to call me and I know I didn't give him my number.

"Who gave you my number?"

"Does that matter? Whatcha doing? Can you come over here?"

This boy had obviously lost all of his marbles since the sun was already going down. Mama Betty didn't play that mess, you better be in before the sun went down not just when the streets lights came on. His questions came like I was on America's Most Wanted and being sought out by 5-0.

"No, I cannot come over there. What is it anyway? You never called me before and you see me all the time. So what's up with that?"

I wanted to ask him did he like me but I knew he was too old for me. Most all the high school girls in the old neighborhood liked him and I knew I couldn't compete with them. They were the girls that had the big booties and fresh clothes. Plus they were already having sex and I wasn't ready for that stage in life yet.

"Well, I was thinking that maybe we could get to know each other better since we obviously have a crush on each other."

Did this boy just say what I was thinking? Can he read minds?

"Plus Brooklyn, you know you the BOMB! These other girls around here are gold diggers and I ain't got time for any of that mess. I noticed you be about your business and that's fresh."

Derrick was about four years older than us and he was always at home. I wondered why he stayed home so much and didn't go to work like most people in the day time but Staci told me he worked at night.

"Well, I think you cool Derrick but you are too old for me and we both know what older guys want from younger girls."

"Listen here, I can get all the girls I want and they bring all the sex I want with them so it's not like I am trying to get at you for that so what's up?"

Who mentioned anything about sex? I see where his head was but for some reason I liked it.

"Okay, when I get up tomorrow I will call Staci and come over there."

I could tell that statement made his day because he started laughing and I could hear someone else in the background laughing too. That made me nervous. I didn't want anyone in my business like his nosey cousin.

"Cool baby girl, I will see you tomorrow!"

I decided to call Big Mama and ask her for the money so I could go school shopping. As I prepared my pitch to her I remembered that she bought Pearl clothes when she was entering high school a few years back and she was fly. My grandmother obviously knew how to dress and how to dress her grandkids. Okay, so the best time to catch her was after she had her morning coffee and her morning devotion time.

"Pearl, how did you get Big Mama to take you school shopping a few years ago? I need to use your same methods so I can get some fresh clothes like you had." I was full of excitement when I went into the bedroom, her sanctuary, to talk to Pearl.

"Girl, my grandmother does not have the money to take you shopping. You know she is on a fixed income and they just cut her Social Security down, so do not call her with that foolishness."

Pearl was always so helpful and kind when I went to her for advice. I knew the plan I had would work, so I ignored Pearl's warning signs and went into the kitchen to call Big Mama.

"Hello . . ." she answered in her sweet southern tone as if she knew all along that it was her favorite grandchild calling.

"Hey Big Mama, whatcha doing?"

"Hey Brook! I just finished praying and now I am sitting down with a hot cup of ole Louisiana coffee. What are you up to baby?"

I wanted to jump right into things but I knew I had to ease my way into the conversation.

"I was just talking to Pearl about going into high school and what that would be like for the first time. She gave me some good advice so now I am trying to prepare myself and soak it all up."

"Yeah baby, Pearl knows about high school and she knows a lot of people so you shouldn't have to worry about anything."

"But Big Mama I am worried about one thing."

"What's that honey?"

"I am not going to have any new school clothes to wear because Mama Betty say she don't have no money. So I decided that I would start working around the old neighborhood to earn a little bit of money to at least buy some panties and bras."

"Oh no ma'am! You will not be working around that neighborhood! Tell Mama Betty I am coming over to pick you up tomorrow and we are going shopping. I will not have my grand baby working just for some clothes. The devil is a liar! Okay, baby let me go before I get upset. I will see you later okay, bye."

"Thanks Big Mama, bye-bye." Mission accomplished!

"Hello . . . may I speak to Derrick?" I really hoped Staci did not answer the phone because I knew if she found out that Derrick and I were seeing each other she would have a hissy fit.

"This me . . . what's up baby girl?"

He called me his baby! A smile as wide as the Rio Grande River came across my face and I knew he liked me now.

"Hey, what are you doing?"

"Nothing. Is everybody gone? I ain't got time to play Brooklyn. I told you I ain't coming over there unless everyone is gone."

"Boy, I know that! Yeah everybody gone but my grandmother coming to pick me up in an hour so if you coming you better hurry up."

It was a very rare occasion for everyone to be gone at the same time. Madear would still home but she was in Mama Betty's room watching TV and I knew I could sneak Derrick into the other room without her knowing.

"Dang baby girl you serious about me coming over there huh? So what we gone do when I get there?"

"Come over and find out."

I knew I had no clue what I wanted to do when he got there but I was certain what I wasn't going to do. I mean I am just fourteen and I knew I wasn't going to lose my virginity to the neighborhood thug. I just wanted him to kiss and touch me in places I've never been touched before.

"Ding dong! Ding-ding!"

That fool rang the doorbell like he was 5-0 looking for one of my new cousins or something. I hurried and ran to the door before Madear had a chance to get up. I knew if she made it out of Mama Betty's room before I got him to the other room I was in big trouble.

"Dang boy, why you ringing that bell like you 5-0? Come on before Madear gets up," I said as I approached opened the door. The look on my face said I was agitated and didn't want to hear his foolish talk, so he complied.

"Brooklyn, who is that?"

"Nobody Madear, the FedEx man dropped off a package. Come on in here before she gets up!" I pushed Derrick down the hall in the direction of the other room. His face looked rough as if he hadn't shaved in a few days but I liked that. The shoes he wore looked like the ones he cut the grass in, with no strings and a little run over. He wasn't the freshest dude in the old neighborhood but he liked me and that's all that mattered.

"Come in here but don't close the door all the way . . . I need to be able to hear if someone is coming."

He walked slowly behind me and began rubbing my back.

"What are you doing?"

"I am rubbing your back! Don't you like the way that feels?"

"Uhmm, yeah. I guess it feels good."

Just then Derrick grabbed my back and pulled me close to him. My legs began to shake and I knew that I was about to become a woman. He kissed my neck as he undid my bra clasp and all I could think of was this man being my husband and all the kids we could have together. I was in love and I knew he loved me, too. My shirt came over my head and he then caressed my fourteen-year-old breasts and I melted. Picking me up and laying me across the bed, I could slowly feel his hand moving up between my legs and the sweat beads popping up on my forehead. I couldn't help thinking someone would catch us, so I became very tense.

"What's wrong baby? Why you so scared?"

"I don't know . . . I just feel like somebody gone catch us."

"Come here, hold me and close your eyes," Derrick gently whispered in my ear. "I love you but I understand if you not ready. I will stop if you want me too."

I wanted to say okay stop, but something inside me said let him go all the way. He did love me and that is all I wanted to know from him anyway.

"You don't have to stop . . . ," I barely said as he pulled my shorts and panties down in one simple grip.

"Have you done this before, Derrick? I mean I am your first too, right?"

"Uhmm, yeah baby! Now come here and let me make you feel good!"

"Wait, where is the condom?"

"Come on sweetie, I'm clean! Just come on and I promise I will pull out!"

At that very moment I could see Pearl's face and the pain she caused Mama Betty getting pregnant. I was not about to let that happen to me.

"Hell naw! I mean I love you and all but I ain't stupid! If you want me you better put a condom on now!"

"Damn, Brook that is exactly why I like you! You gone give it to me straight and not let me do whatever I want to do! You not like most hoochies . . . you different!"

Just then a smile filled with confidence came across my face like none other and I knew for real that this man was for me. I quickly forgot about Cory and all those middle school dudes! I needed an older man to handle me.

At the blink of an eye my innocence was gone and I was now A WOMAN.

Chapter five

For some reason I woke up before the alarm clock went off feeling nauseated. Derrick and I used protection so there was no way I could be pregnant, but why was I feeling sick? I got up anyway and took a shower. I started preparing for my first day of high school with a load of excitement and anticipation. I totally dismissed the idea of me being pregnant, took some of Madear's Pepto Bismol and went on with preparing for my new day. By the time I finished dressing Anthony was already hogging the only bathroom we had permission to use.

"Open the door stupid, I need to brush my teeth before the bus comes!"

"If you were popular like me you would not be riding the bus on the first day of school. See baby I can take my time because somebody coming to pick me and Johnathan up. So come on in here because we do not want you to miss your first day of high school."

Oohh, that boy makes me sick! How did they get a ride to school and I didn't get asked?

"Whatever, let me in here so I can hurry up and get out!"

I was looking fresh to def! Mama Betty gave me some money to get my hair done and for a few new outfits from Weiner's. Big Mama also gave me some money and I bought two new pair of sneakers and one pair of penny loafers with it. Of course they would not let me go shopping without buying new panties, bras, and socks. Those were a must have and I had better not be caught dead with anything with holes in them.

"Girl, you better always have on clean underwear and nothing better have holes in them. You never know when you gone get in an accident and they have to cut all your clothes off. Remember you represent the Rideaux family and we always look good."

Those were Big Mama's famous words to me every time I went to spend the night at her house. As I brushed my teeth and cleaned my face (including behind my ears) I couldn't help but think about Derrick. It had been a few days since I let him hit it. I wondered if he was thinking about me and if he would come and see me after school today. I began to feel moistness in my panties again as I thought about him and my heart began to beat rapidly.

"Brooklyn, you better hurry up because I hear the bus coming from down the street!"

Dang, I needed to put some powder in my panties but I knew I didn't have time. I grabbed my bag and purse and ran out of the door. Just as I exited out of the gate and reached the corner, the bus driver closed her door and took off.

"Hey," I yelled. "What's wrong with you? I need to get to school!"

The kids on the bus looked out the window and shook their heads. I guess they knew this bus driver was a fool because they looked as if they felt sorry for me.

Just as I began walking back into the gate of the apartments I heard a horn blowing.

"Hey li'l mama you missed your bus? You wanna ride?"

A 1990 candy apple red Cadillac Deville with shiny chrome Momo rims pulled up behind me. The passenger window was down and all I could see was a beautiful specimen with light brown eyes and a bright wide smile.

"Brook, you wanna ride to school baby girl? I know you don't want to miss your first day and plus you look to fly to miss today."

Derrick came out of nowhere and when I saw him my heart was filled with happiness. Not only would I make it to school but I was being dropped off by the tightest dude in the neighborhood plus he didn't forget about his baby, either!. Man, I know people gone be jocking now.

"Yeah, I want a ride! Where you get this fly car from? I thought you had a truck?"

"I do have a truck and don't worry about where this car came from, you keep acting right and I might teach you how to drive it."

Those words were music to my ears and now it was confirmed, he does love me! I opened the door and put my backpack with all my supplies in the back seat.

"Brooklyn, I'm going to tell your mama! You bet not leave with that man ... you don't know him!"

Anthony came out the front door to see whose music was beating so hard.

"Derrick, turn that down for a minute so I can tell this boy something."

Anthony came toward the car and I was almost nervous for him. I'm not sure if he knew Derrick but I knew Derrick didn't play. Living in the ward and running up on somebody car would get you killed but no matter where you are now days running up would still get you killed.

"Say girl, get out of that man car. You don't know him like that and you don't know what he's about either. You can ride with us since you missed the bus."

"I know him better than you think and I'm good. I will see you at school!"

Derrick rolled up the window and turned his music back up. I felt good and special. Anthony shook his head and went back into the house.

"What are you about to smoke?" I yelled.

"It's a joint li'l mama, you want to hit it?"

"Hell naw! I am about to go to school and I can't go in there smelling like weed. You trying to get me kicked out on my first day?"

"Just take one puff, it ain't gone kill you and I will let the windows down so you can air out."

"No thanks, I'm good."

"Okay, listen. Do you think I want to hurt you? I care about you. I just want you to feel good like I feel right now. I love you Brooklyn Rideaux."

Damn, those words made time stop for me and my head spin. I grabbed the joint out of his hand and took a heavy puff.

"UCHGHH, Uchghh . . . damn what is in this stuff?"

"You need to slow your roll, you hit it too hard! Here puff slow and hold it in your mouth for a second then let the smoke come out of your nose."

I took another puff, this time slowly and held it for a while. I felt funny and I saw Derrick laughing, so I guess I looked funny. After a few puffs and holding I began to feel sleepy and everything started moving slowly around me. I put my head back on the seat and before I knew it I was out.

"Brook, get up! You got to get home before the school bus come by your apartments," Derrick was pulling his shirt over his head and zipping his jeans up as he walked out of the room.

I looked down at my body and my clothes were gone. I looked around to see where I was and for a minute I could not figure things out. I sat up and looked around again for my clothes.

"Where am I? What time is it? Why am I here?"

I began to cry and couldn't believe that I had obviously missed my first day of school and that I was in this unknown place naked. Derrick walked back into the room and saw that I had been crying.

"Baby, don't worry about anything, I got you! I told you I would take care of you if you stick with me. You don't need school because I got you. Whatever you want I will get it for you."

That kind of made me feel safe but I wasn't sure about this dude. I had given him my virginity and I did want to be his girl forever so I guess it was okay. I found my panties at the bottom of the bed and quickly slipped them on while Derrick wasn't looking. I saw my Baby Phat jeans and Polo shirt on the chair next to the door so I jumped out of the bed to get them. When I jumped up I stumbled so I had to slow down and sit on the floor while my head spun around for a minute. I wasn't sure why I was still feeling like I was high but I prayed silently that what I smoked didn't have any extra stuff in it that would make me go crazy.

"Brook, you ready? Come on lil mama, I need to get you home. I don't want your cousin trying to jump stupid again and I have to hurt him."

"Derrick, did that stuff we smoked have something extra in it because my head is still spinning?"

"Naw, you just ain't never had it before so it feels funny to you. Just slow down and everything will be okay. But, if you want to hurry up and get home you better come on!"

He gave me a smile that was comforting and so I did what he said. Derrick's smile was wide and his teeth straight. I wanted to jump up and hug him tight, but my head was still spinning so I just finished putting on my clothes and left.

As we drove home I thought about expressing my love to Derrick and letting him know that I was down for whatever, but something kept my mouth shut. Even though I had missed the first day of school this was the best day of my life . . . . so I thought.

"Here you go baby girl! Hurry up and get inside before that bus come! I will call you later, okay?"

"Thank you . . . you took care of me today and I appreciate that even though I don't remember half the day. Don't forget to call me!"

I jumped out of the freshly washed Cadillac and ran in the house. Madear was sitting on the porch near the steps and I almost tripped on her wheelchair.

"Madear, what are you doing out here?"

"Minding my own business, thank you! Who was that man in that Cadillac that brought you home? Why didn't you ride the bus like the rest of the students?"

"Uhmm, his name is Joe! He brought me home because I missed the bus trying to get all my stuff. I gotta go use it Madear. I'll be back."

I hurried in the house in hopes of avoiding the rest of Madear's interrogation and as I opened the door Mama Betty was coming out.

"Girl, where you running to? You know I don't allow running in this house! And where are your cousins? Ya'll all left here this morning but only you coming home this evening?"

"Uhmm, I missed the bus because I was trying to get all my stuff," I said while doing the restroom dance, "so I got a friend to drop me off. The bus should be coming in a minute."

Just as I said that the big yellow school bus pulled up and began unloading. Johnathan and Anthony got off the bus last. As they approached the apartment Anthony looked at me and shook his head in disgust. I rolled my eyes and went inside the house. Mama Betty followed us all asking how our first day of school went especially being at the new school. My heart dropped. I went into the restroom and tried to stay as long as I could.

"Brook, how was your first day?"

"Yeah, Brook . . . how was your first day," Anthony asked sarcastically?

"Oh, Mama Betty it was good! Busy . . . but good!"

"Come out of that restroom . . . no one wants to talk to someone in the bathroom!"

I wanted to jump in the shower because I felt sticky and dirty, but I knew I had better go and see what was going on in the living room. As I got ready to walk out of the restroom I overheard Anthony laughing with Johnathan.

"Man, Brook is about to get her butt beat! If her Mama finds out she didn't come to school today and was with a grown man who is a drug dealer . . . oooh, I can't wait to see what happens!"

"Brooklyn," Mama Betty yelled from the living room again, come out here now!"

"Mama, I had to go real bad and plus I am on my cycle so I needed to take care of that. What's wrong?"

"The boys say they didn't see you at school today."

"Maybe because I have AP classes and they are in basic classes. I don't even have a locker on the freshman hall. My locker is where most of the juniors and seniors are and I have lunch with them, too."

I had just lied through my teeth but I couldn't go out like that. I didn't want to tarnish the view my mother had of me, especially with me skipping school.

"Well, who was that little boy that took you to school this morning? From now on you better get your tail on that bus with your cousins, do you understand?"

"Yes ma'am, and his name is Derrick. He's just a homeboy. He was behind the bus and saw that the stupid driver wouldn't open the door so he gave me a ride. I was running trying to get outside on time but my new cousins were hogging the bathroom. I asked if I could ride with them and their friends but they told me NO!"

Mama Betty was in the kitchen now seasoning her famous pork chops. I could taste them in my mouth already but for some reason I still felt queasy.

"I know what I need to do," Mama Betty said, "I need to be here when y'all get ready to go in the morning so no foolishness will happen. I'm going to talk to Mr. Spartan and see if he will let me come in later. I would hate for something to happen to you or your cousins because no one was here."

She sounded very serious and that was cool with me because I wasn't going to skip school and get high like that ever again.

∽

"Hey girl, whatcha doing?"

"Nothing, just watching TV. You know someone moved in y'all old house right? Some Chinese people but anyway where you were today?"

"Listen, what I am about to tell you is top secret and better not be heard again, you understand?"

"Dang, like that! What's up?"

I took the cordless phone and headed outside the front door. Madear had come back in so I knew I could have a little privacy.

"Girl, your cousin was behind my bus when the driver shut the door in my face. He asked me if I wanted a ride to school so I said yeah. Well, he was smoking something and asked me if I wanted some. I said no of course at first."

"What do you mean at first?"

"You know I am in love with your cousin, so I wanted him to know I was down for whatever so I took a few puffs!"

"Stupid, don't you know that stuff they be smoking is dipped in the stuff that they use on dead people. Oh my God, I can't believe you stooped so low for that thug!"

So that's why my head won't stop spinning and my fingers still feel numb. I wanted to tell Staci the truth but I knew she would get worried and want to tell my mama.

"I didn't know that . . . anyway I obviously passed out because when I got up I was naked at y'all house in his bed."

"Brook, did he rape you?"

"Naw, we been there before so I am sure I just gave him some. I love your cousin and he told me he loves me too."

"If you believe that line you crazy. Do you know how many girls he tells he loves on a daily basis? I can't even keep up with all the chicken head girls that come over here for Derrick. Please do not get involved with him. He does not LOVE YOU!"

Her words hit me like a Mac 10 truck. This man told me whatever I wanted he would get it and that I was different. I know I'm different from the rest of those girls because he came after me. I am not running behind him. The long pause on the phone made Staci a little worried.

"Brook, you okay? I am your best friend and I know my cousin. He will say whatever to get in between your legs and most girls are dumb enough to believe him."

"So what you saying, I'm dumb? I know you not calling me dumb, I got a lot of class and common sense."

"Then use it! He is not worth it! Listen, I got to go I have a lot of homework to do. Oh yeah, we have a lot of the same classes so just thought you should know you got a lot of work to make up. Bye!"

Staci hung up the phone in a hurry before I could get my rebuttal in. I wanted to tell her that Derrick and I were different. I wanted her to know that he really did care about me.

"Hey, I thought you were going to call me?"

"Oh hey Brook, listen li'l mama . . . I got real busy. You okay though right?"

Derrick seemed concerned but it also seemed as if he was rushing me off the phone.

"Yeah, I'm good. I just wanted to know why it's ten at night and I hadn't heard from you? You miss me right?"

"Yeah, I miss you but I can't just sit around and talk on the phone. I am a businessman and I have to take care of business so don't worry about calling me . . . I will call you."

"Derrick, do you have another girlfriend? Staci told me that you tell other girls you love them but you just told me that you loved me!"

"Listen, don't start questioning me about who I talk to and who I am with, okay? If I told you that I love you then that means I love you. Don't listen to Staci and the mess she talking. I am a grown man and I don't answer questions from little high school girls."

I was embarrassed and ashamed. I gave this man a part of me that no one had ever had because I thought he really loved me and now he trippin! I wanted to cuss him out and hang up the phone but I didn't.

"Beep, beep, beep" the sounds of a beeper were going off in the background and Derrick didn't try to hide it.

"Listen, I gotta go, business is calling. Remember, don't call me I will call you, okay Brook?"

I didn't know what to say because I loved this man, but he was telling me not to call him.

I began to feel the tears run slowly down my face but I didn't let him know it. Who does he think he is talking too? I am Brooklyn Rideaux.

"Pull it together Brook. You don't need that buster and you don't have to deal with him anymore," I convinced myself.

"Really? Okay," I said as I hung up the phone.

Since I was in honor classes and on the basketball team I didn't have to worry about homework much. The conversation with Derrick was so draining I wanted to get in a hot bath and relax my nerves. The house was in full effect as usual. Everyone was either eating or in the living room watching TV. The coast was clear for me to take an uninterrupted bubble bath before I went to bed. I grabbed the small bottle of Palmolive dishwashing liquid from under the sink and squeezed a generous amount into the steamy running water. I eased in and just as the bubbling water began to soothe my body and mind I started dozing off. Just as I made it to la-la land I heard a lot of commotion coming from the other side of the door.

"MAMA . . . MAMA, come here quick!!!"

"What is it Pearl, are you okay?"

"I think my water broke and my stomach is cramping really bad!"

"Okay, its time . . . Johnathan call Big Mama and tell her Pearl is going into labor! Brooklyn! Brooklyn, where in the hell is Brooklyn? John Boy, I am going to need you to stay here with Chrissy and Madear okay."

As soon as I heard my name I jumped out of the tub and began to dry off. Anthony came and started beating on the door.

"Brook, your mama want you. Pearl is having the baby. Hurry up!"

I threw on my basketball warm-ups and opened the door. Pearl and Mama Betty were already headed out of the front and Johnathan was still on the phone with Big Mama.

"Mama, wait here I come!"

I wasn't going to miss this for the world. I really wanted to be there for Pearl and give her my support. I made it just in time to the car with one shoe on and one in my hand. Mama Betty drove about 80 mph the entire way and Pearl screamed. I sat right behind Pearl, rubbing her hair and Anthony sat behind Mama Betty looking out for cops.

"Anthony, you better tell me if you see the po-pos somewhere you hear me? If I go to jail for failing to stop you getting put out!"

Even though Mama Betty probably wouldn't put him out she would make him pay for her ticket or work off the cost to get her out of jail.

"UUUHHHH, hurry Mama. This baby is coming fast."

"Okay, Pearl, we here. Anthony go in and tell them you need a wheelchair. Tell them that your cousin is out in the car going into labor. Brooklyn, come over here and get these bags. Stay with Pearl until I park the car."

All at once three nurses and a doctor ran out of the emergency room doors with the wheelchair. Anthony looked like he had seen a ghost but his job was done.

"Ma'am, what is your name?"

"UUUUHHHH, please get this baby out of me!"

"Her name is Pearl Rideaux," I interrupted.

"Okay, do you know her doctor's name?" the nurse asked frantically.

"TTTTHHHOOMAS, Dr. TTTHHHOOMAS," Pearl yelled.

"Okay, guys let's get her to labor and delivery fast," the male doctor finally gave some direction as he motioned for me and Anthony to stay out of the way.

"Sir, I have to stay with her until my mother parks the car," I urged.

"Okay, only one of you . . . hurry let's go."

I ran on the side of the wheelchair and tried to grab Pearl's hand. She moved them both so fast I couldn't catch them so I grabbed her forearm and held on tight.

"Young lady, here is where the family stays until after delivery. She'll be okay, don't worry."

The doctor and nurses took Pearl behind two swinging doors and I stared through the lined windows. I never ever wanted to feel what makes a woman scream like Pearl screamed. I thought she was dying and there was nothing I could do to help.

"Lord, please let Pearl and her baby be okay, please!" I whispered prayed while standing at the door. Mama Betty and Anthony came off the elevator looking around for Pearl.

"Mama! Anthony!"

"Where is Pearl? Did she make it?"

"Yes ma'am, they took her behind those doors and told me to wait out here."

Me, knowing Mama Betty, she was not going to stay out there with me and Anthony. She handed me her purse and keys and barged through the double doors.

"That's my daughter. I need to be with her!"

That must've worked because she didn't come out for another two hours. Anthony and I had fallen asleep on the couch in the waiting room while watching *In the Heat of the Night* on television. I didn't know what time it was but I knew it had to be late since the waiting room was now empty.

"Brook wake up! You and Anthony come over to the window so you can see the baby!"

For it to be so late Mama Betty was too excited. When I heard her I jumped up and ran over to the window. Anthony stayed on the couch and rolled over. I looked through the lined window and saw the nurse holding up a bundle wrapped in white blankets. I really couldn't see much except a black face with lots of curly black hair.

"Look, Brook! That's your little niece . . . Jasmine Monique Lewis. Doesn't she look just like Pearl?"

I didn't know what to say. She didn't look like anything to me. I thought maybe they were holding up the wrong baby.

"Mama Betty, where is Pearl? Can I go see her?"

"She is sleep baby girl. It was hard to keep her awake long enough to push the baby out. The medicine they gave her made her very drowsy. You can see her tomorrow but we need to go so y'all can get ready for school."

I was worried about Pearl, but Mama Betty let me know that she was in good hands there at the Women's Hospital.

"School . . . we still have to go to school?"

Chapter six

"**M**ama Betty, there is a party this weekend at the community center in our old neighborhood. Is it okay if I go?"

I wanted so bad to go to this party because I knew Derrick would be there. I had not spoken to him since he told me not to call him and he had not called me yet. I was miserable; I needed to see him and I would do so by any means necessary.

"No, you need to spend time at home and with your new niece. Plus I may have to work and someone needs to watch Chrissy."

"But, I am always here. I go to school, practice and back home. I don't have a life and I am always cleaning up around here after everybody else. So why can't I go to the party just this once?"

I knew I had crossed the line but I was pissed. Everything I do around here and she wants to keep me from hanging out with my friends. I knew the party would have all my friends from school there and some cute guys from other schools but that was not my main focus; Derrick was.

"Brooklyn, I am not about to get into it with you. I said no party and that is it . . . no party."

"Ugghhh, I hate this house. Ever since you brought Chrissy here and the new cousins I can't do nothing!"

"If you don't like it Brooklyn you can leave. No one is making you stay here. You starting to smell yourself and I am about to put my fist in your mouth!"

"Whatever . . . ," I mumbled under my breath.

This was madness. I walked out of the extra small living room and went into the back room. Pearl was there watching television with Jasmine in her lap sucking a bottle. She looked at me with a smug look like get out of here but I ignored her since I was too mad to talk.

"Brooklyn, come here," Mama Betty yelled from the kitchen.

I didn't move. I sat in front of the dresser and folded my arms and legs. If she wanted me she was going to have to come to me. I was tired of being everyone's pushover.

"Brooklyn Michelle Rideaux, I know you hear me calling you. Bring your tail here now!"

I still didn't move. Before long I heard Mama Betty tell Madear she was about to beat my ass so I jumped up and headed her direction.

"Little girl, you seem to think that I am your friend or someone you can play with but the next time I call you and you don't come, you will be picking your teeth up off the ground. Do you understand?"

"No, no I don't understand. I don't understand why I am treated like the evil step child and everyone else around here gets treated like royalty. I ask one little simple thing and I get told no."

SLLAAAPPP...

"Oh no she didn't!" I thought. Tears began to roll down my face and Mama Betty stood at attention like a trained soldier.

"Why did you slap me? I thought I was your baby. I could be out there getting into trouble or pregnant like Pearl but I am trying to please you and you're still not satisfied!"

"Get out of my face right now," she muffled with turned up lips. I walked back to the room with Pearl and Jasmine.

"You gone learn Brook," Pearl said while burping Jasmine, "you gone learn."

Derrick said he was going to call me and I couldn't understand why I hadn't heard from him yet. I went into Mama Betty's bathroom and dialed his number.

"Hello, may I speak to Derrick?"

"Who is this?" a female voice asked.

"His girlfriend," I answered.

"Excuse me, his girlfriend? This is his girlfriend that you are speaking to now, and his baby's mother."

I almost vomited as soon as those words made it through the phone.

"Give me that phone, girl. Who is that you talking to anyway? I told you to stop answering my phone."

Derrick grabbed the phone from the girl on the other end and told her to get out of the room.

"Hello, who is this?"

"Derrick, it's me, Brook. Why haven't you called me? I've waited for days and you still didn't pick up the phone to check on me or nothing. I thought you loved me."

This was really hard for me especially since Staci told me about the other girls that Derrick tells he loves just to get in their pants. Plus my mama and I were at odds and so there was no one for me to talk to and tell what this man was doing to me.

"Girl, I told you not to call me. Look, I gotta bounce. I have a baby on the way and I got to handle that, okay?"

"No, it's not okay. You said you loved me! What am I supposed to do now?"

"Leave me alone . . . I got what I wanted from you and I'm good. You too young for me anyway."

The conversation we were having seemed like a bad dream and I needed to wake up in a hurry. Why was this happening to me? I am a good person but no one seems to understand me.

"Derrick, don't do this! I love you. I need you in my life, please!"

"Brooklyn, you begging? That is very unattractive and you are starting to sound like these hoochies around here in the neighborhood. Listen, I gotta go. Peace out."

Derrick hung up the phone and there went my self-esteem right with that call. I felt tears rolling down my face so I got up and locked the door.

"How could he treat me like this? I thought he loved me. Was I not good enough for him?" All these questions flooded my mind but with no answers. I didn't want to be around anymore if

I couldn't have Derrick in my life. I was ready to check out of this place and no one could stop me.

"Brooklyn, hurry up in there I need to use the restroom," Pearl came to the door with urgency. I wiped my face with the towel hanging over the tub and opened the door.

"What were you doing in here so long anyway?"

"Thinking," I replied walking out with my head down. I wished I could tell her what happened, but I knew she had her own issues to deal with and I didn't want to stress her out.

I didn't know what it was going to take to release myself from all the hurt and pain from the fight with Mama Betty and the break-up with Derrick. I went into the other bedroom and grabbed my diary from my sock drawer.

"I can't do this, I can't even write! I am so stupid for letting that jerk into my life," I thought.

It was getting late and I began to feel sleepy. School was in a few hours and if I was going to do anything, now was the time. I got up and went into the dining room where all of Madear's medicine was located. I grabbed all five of her medicine bottles and emptied them into my hands. I swallowed three pills at a time without water. Once all the pills were gone I walked into the living room while stepping over Johnathan. Anthony was on the couch so I sat on the small sofa and waited. And waited . . .

Everything happened so fast that Anthony had to tell me the whole story.

"Mama Betty, come here. Something is wrong with Brooklyn," Anthony said he found me passed out on the sofa when he tried to wake me up for school, but I never responded.

"Brooklyn, wake up . . . wake up! What happened to her? Did she drink something? Wake up? Pearl call 911 and get an ambulance over here."

They said Pearl ran as fast as she could into the kitchen and dialed 911. "Yes, please send an ambulance. My sister won't wake up and we don't know what's wrong. Please hurry, please!"

He said Mama Betty lifted me off the sofa and held me in her arms. Madear got out of her bed and came into the living room.

"Betty look, all my medicine bottles are empty. I think she took all my pills, there's nothing left."

"Lord, help me! Help my baby, please help my baby," Mama Betty screamed and cried.

The ambulance drivers knocked on the door about five minutes later and rushed in to the small matchbox apartment.

"Ma'am, please move back and let us help you. Please we need to take her and give her CPR!"

Anthony said Mama Betty would not let me go until she was forced. The paramedics performed CPR and brought me back to consciousness. They strapped me to the stretcher and put me in the back of the truck. Mama Betty grabbed her purse and followed behind the ambulance closely. Pearl and Anthony jumped in the car with her just in case she couldn't keep her composure.

"Mama Betty, you need to slow down before you run into the back of the truck," Pearl commanded. Anthony said he put on his seatbelt and locked his door in the backseat.

"Sir, is she still breathing?" Mama Betty asked while jumping out of the car once they all made it to the hospital.

"Yes ma'am, but you can't park there. You have to move your car around to the emergency parking lot." The paramedic wasn't very sympathetic, so Mama Betty ignored him and handed her keys to Pearl.

"What do we have here guys" asked the receptionist?

"Suicide attempt we believe. She was unresponsive when we arrived so we performed CPR. Her vitals are here and this is her mother."

"Ma'am, do you know what she took or drank?"

"My mother brought her empty medicine bottles to me so I am assuming that she took several pills of all kinds."

Anthony said Mama Betty seemed reluctant to tell the receptionist about the pills. He believed she wanted to remain as dignified as she could without ruining the family name.

"Looks like we are going to have to put her in a room with supervision and pump her stomach," the nurse who read my chart commented.

"What is her name?"

"Brooklyn Rideaux," Mama Betty answered.

"Brooklyn, open your eyes honey. Do you know where you are," the nurse asked? Anthony said it took a few minutes but I finally opened my eyes and looked up and saw the nurse standing next to Mama Betty, who was still crying.

"What is she crying for," I thought, "just earlier she couldn't stand me and wanted to beat me now she crying?"

"Okay, she is responsive so we can take her from here, thank you gentleman."

The nurse began to push the bed toward the elevator and I became very dizzy. I leaned over toward the floor and vomited everywhere.

"Oh no, ma'am please do not step in that . . . we can't pump her stomach now. She is going to have to drink liquid coal to kill the toxins. Excuse me for a minute," the nurse said as she walked over to a phone on the wall, "can I get a clean up near room B12? Thank you. Okay, let's get her in the room and out of those clothes."

As the nurse and Mama Betty changed my clothes I could see Pearl and Anthony looking at me with the saddest faces. I really didn't mean to hurt any of them, just Mama Betty and Derrick. I wondered if someone would tell Staci and then she could tell him. He probably wouldn't come see me anyway.

"Okay, sweetie lay here for a second and I will be right back. Ma'am, make sure she stays lying flat because I don't want anything else to come up."

The nurse walked out the door and Mama Betty began to cry again. I turned my head because seeing her cry would make me cry as well.

"Brooklyn, why did you do this to yourself? You got too much good going in your life for this mess. If anyone needs to try to check out it's me, hell. I have 8 mouths to feed daily with a minimum wage job. So, baby girl why did you do this?"

I turned and looked at Mama Betty but didn't speak. I really wish she could have read my mind. All the answers to her questions were waiting to come out.

"Mama, she was in the bathroom earlier today for a long time. When I asked her what she was doing she said thinking, but I could tell she had been crying."

"Pearl, why didn't you tell me that earlier? This could have been prevented."

"I thought she was okay since she went in the other room and started writing in her dairy."

"Well, here we go," the nurse interrupted, "she needs to drink this entire cup of liquid coal and she can't have any water after she finishes. The coal will kill the toxins from all the pills that she swallowed. I will be back in a little while to check on you guys."

The nurse walked out and Mama Betty went to grab her purse. Pearl and Anthony looked at her to get their cue. She motioned them towards the door and walked over to me.

"Make sure you drink all of this Brooklyn. We got to go and check on the kids and Madear. I will call you in the morning . . . I love you, okay?"

I looked at her and gave a half smile. I turned my back to them and began drinking the liquid coal. Every drink I took tasted like mud and I just knew I was going to puke. I managed to drink the entire cup and soon laid back in the bed and fell asleep.

"Excuse me, I am here to check your vitals," another nurse in all white with short sandy blonde hair whispered.

"What time is it?"

"Oh, it's about 2:30 a.m., are you feeling okay?"

"My stomach hurts from that coal they made me drink."

"I see you're here because you tried to take your life. Listen, you are such a beautiful girl and don't you know the Father loves you? He has a real special plan for your life! So don't ever try to hurt yourself again, okay?"

Her words were so comforting and warm. I smiled for the first time in 24 hours as she gave me a hug and rubbed my forehead.

"What is your name?" I asked.

"Nurse Karen, I will be back soon to check on you."

I rolled over and went back to sleep without a fear or worry. I woke up a few hours later and I realized my new friend didn't come back to check on me. I figured maybe her shift changed and I would see her again before I was discharged.

"Knock, knock, knock," came the loud banging from the other side of the door.

"Come in," I mumbled.

"Hi Miss Rideaux, I am Nurse Lisa and I will be seeing after you today. Is there anything you need right now?"

"Yes ma'am, could you send Nurse Karen in for me? I need to ask her a question."

"I'm sorry sweetie, but we don't have a Nurse Karen here."

"Maybe she was on the last shift, but she came in my room at 2:30 this morning to take my vitals."

Nurse Lisa looked in her chart and a puzzled look came over her face.

"I am so sorry dear but no one came in to do your vitals this morning. We've been short staffed but I will ask the doctor to come in and check on you."

"Uhmm, that's okay. I must've been dreaming."

"Okay, well call if you need anything."

She walked out of the door with the same puzzled look as before. I didn't want her to think I was crazy but I knew Nurse Karen came in and talked to me. I felt something that I never felt before when she spoke to me. For once I didn't feel alone.

Chapter seven

"**B**rooklyn, why are you always wearing my stuff without asking me first? If I catch you in my new shoes again I am going to whip your tail," blared out from Pearl's lips like fiery darts as she stood in the hallway.

"I asked you if I could wear your shoes and you said yeah so what are you talking about?"

I knew I had asked her when she was asleep and also about another pair of shoes but if I made her seem crazy then she probably would be okay with it.

"Girl, don't play with me you know I was talking about those Adidas and not my new Jordan's."

Just then I felt a slap across my face. "Oh, no she didn't just slap me!" I thought. So, me being me, and knowing I couldn't whip her, I had to let her know she was not about to push me around, so I slapped her back and headed for the door. Her eyes looked like the devils when she realized that I slapped her back. As I was walking out the door I felt her grab my shirt.

"Come here you heifer. Who you think you slapping? If you put your hands on me again I am going to knock the fire out of you!"

At that moment I knew it was really about to be on and I wasn't going to back down. Yeah she was older than me but I was tired of being bullied by her and everybody else. Shoot, I was in high school now and those baby days were over.

"Pearl," I yelled, "get your hands off me!"

Before I knew it we were outside the front door. I saw the stairs to our neighbor's apartment out of the corner of my eye and tried hard to stay back so I wouldn't shed blood. I hit her back knocking her glasses off her face and onto the ground. She grabbed my neck and began choking me. All I could think of was "Lord here I come!" I knew she was about to kill me. Some kind of way we ended up rolling in the grass in front of the whole complex. I needed at least one of them to have some sympathy and come over and help, but no ever did. I tasted grass in my mouth as I lifted my head off the ground and that made matters worse. Not only was I being beat to a pulp everybody that lived in our building was watching now! This is not only embarrassing but it also made our family look divided. Man, when mama hears about this I am going to be beat again.

"Heyyyyyy . . . y'all stop all that fighting. You two are sisters," I heard screaming from one of our neighbors. Since we lived in the corner apartment on a main street, everybody knew of us, rather for good or bad. Pearl and I was so taken by his comments that we stopped fighting and hugged and made up, right there on the spot. YEAH RIGHT, in another life. We kept fighting and cussing at each other until we got tired. Finally our neighbor from upstairs came down and pulled us apart. Dang, what took him so long? I was bleeding from somewhere because it was on my clothes but I couldn't feel anything.

"You girls know better to be causing all this commotion especially when your mother isn't home. Pearl, you should be ashamed of yourself. You are the oldest . . . you should be trying to lead by example." Mr. Johnson was one of the oldest yet wisest men in our complex. When he talked we listened. He too came from the street of hard knocks and he had the war wounds to prove it.

"I am sorry Mr. Johnson, but I cannot keep letting Pearl and everyone else in this house push me around no more," I made sure he felt my words and saw my tears because I really meant business. "That girl told me I could wear her shoes and now she tripping so she got what she deserved."

I looked over at Pearl and she was trying to fix her glasses and turning up her lips at what I said.

"You make me sick Brooklyn, every time I get something you always got to mess with it!"

Pearl couldn't seem to fix her glasses and I saw a tear coming out of her eye. Did I make her cry? I began to feel bad for causing all the drama. I looked back at Mr. Johnson and he had already walked back into his apartment. I then looked at Pearl and saw that both of our shirts were torn and our hair was all over our head. I felt really bad because mama had just bought her those glasses and I broke them. I knew she was going to be in trouble so I started crying.

"What are you crying for? Shut up." Pearl looked at me with so much hatred and I could hear it in her voice.

"I am sorry Pearl for breaking your glasses," I wanted to say more but nothing else would come out. Just then Mama Betty pulled into the gate and waved. The feelings of worthlessness filled my heart and I ran to the back of our building where no one could see me and cried. I wanted Pearl to give me the attention she gave to everybody else. I loved her and in many ways wanted to be like her but she couldn't see it. Tears covered my face now and the longer I sat there alone the quicker it began to get dark outside. I needed to talk to somebody that would understand my feelings. I felt so alone. Left . . .

"Madear, can I turn the television to something else?" I really wanted to watch wrestling but I knew she wasn't having that.

"Hold on for a minute Brook, these kids over here by us were in a bad car accident and some of them died. I want to see what happened."

The area we now lived was crowded with Asians and Latinos with high profile cars. I was almost positive that some of those kids were playing and got into a wreck and this time it was fatal. I walked out of the living room where the television was into the bathroom to run my bath water.

"Brooklyn, telephone. Somebody name Derrick is on the phone for you," Johnathan yelled from the kitchen.

Oh my goodness, Derrick! For a moment it seemed as if time paused . . . should I take his call or pretend that I wasn't interested in talking to him? I still loved this boy but my pride wouldn't let me go down like a sucker. I had just come out of the hospital because of him and if Mama Betty found out who was on the phone she would have a horse.

"Tell him I will call him back . . . I am about to take a bath."

That took guts but a wide smile came over my face. I did it and it felt good. I knew he would not ever call me again and I was okay with it.

I lay in the tub for what seemed an eternity and thought about the fight with Pearl. Mama Betty never said anything to me so I guess she figured it was handled . . . just sibling rivalry. Even though it was over I still wanted to talk to Pearl and let her know I was truly sorry, that I needed her.

"Girl, did you hear about the accident last night?"

Keke, my play cousin knew everything and everybody's business. I arrived to school during second period and she was the first person I saw when I walked through the door.

"What accident are you talking about Keke?"

"Have you talked to any of your friends since yesterday?"

"No, why? You asking me too many questions. I need to get to my English honor class before it ends."

"Well, go to class. I will catch up with you later."

Keke walked away and headed into the front office. I still didn't find out about the accident she was talking about so I headed to my class not worried about it.

"Brook, come here sweetie! I am so sorry! Are you okay? Have you been with his mom? Is that why you are late?"

My girlfriend Kelly ran up to me in the hallway and began to hug and hold me real tight.

"Hold up, what is going on? No one is telling me anything! What's up?"

"You haven't heard about Stephon? They all were in a car accident last night and he is in the hospital right now. We are about to leave here and go up there to see if he is okay."

"WHAT? No one told me anything. Why didn't you call me last night? Oh my God . . ."

I hit the floor and put my head to the ground. Stephon was my best guy friend since I got to the new school. He took me under his wing and introduced to me to his clique. I was like his little sister and no one told me that he was hurt. I didn't know what to do. Immediately our conversations about God and church began to run through my mind. I didn't know if I should stay on the floor or get up and go. I was at a lost.

"Brook, come on girl. Get up! We are headed over to the hospital and you can pray for him over there!"

I jumped off the floor and grabbed my bag. I knew I was about to miss another day of school but this was my friend. I needed to be there for him . . . at least to pray for him.

On the ride over to the hospital I could do nothing but pray silently and cry.

"Lord, please don't take my friend from me, please!"

Kelly drove her mother's Jeep Cherokee to the hospital and it seemed that most of Stephon's friends rode over with us. I wanted so bad to know the details, but no one spoke a word during the ride. When we arrived at the hospital the waiting room was full of Maxwell High students and some of Stephon's family. I looked around the room for his mom and a girl that I didn't know told me she was in the room with him.

"Brooklyn, his mom wants you to come in the room with them. She told me to tell you she needs you when you got here," another girl from the school said as I walked in.

I was scared at what I would see but I knew I had to be strong for her. I walked to the nurses' station and asked for Stephon Jones' room.

"I am so sorry but only two family members are allowed in the room at a time and his parents are already there."

"I was told Miss that his mother wants me to come in and see him. So can you please let me in," I said in a matter-of-fact tone?

"It's okay, ma'am, she can come in with me," Stephon's mom said as she walked out of the room. I turned around when I heard her voice and she grabbed my face.

"I need you to be strong for everyone out here. My baby needs you to be strong, too."

"Yes ma'am," was all I could say as I wiped my face with the bottom of my t-shirt.

We walked down a hall with very little light and into a large room with several doctors and nurses standing near the monitors talking. I really wanted to know how all this happened but I wasn't about to ask any questions. Stephon's father was sitting on a stool next to his bed holding his hand.

"Honey, Brooklyn is here. I'm going to step out because only two of us can be here at a time," his mom said.

"No, I will leave so you two can talk to him. If you need me I'm right outside the door." Mr. Jones was a well-respected man in the community. He was almost like a civil rights activist because he was always helping the less fortunate and fighting at city hall for their rights.

"Hi Mr. Jones, are you okay?"

"I'm good Brooklyn, thank you for coming in to see him. He needs you more than ever right now. Talk to him like you always do, honey. Tell him what's on your heart." Mr. Jones wiped a tear from his eyes and put his shades on as he walked away.

I sat down next to Stephon on the stool and grabbed his hand. I could barely recognize him with the tubes and bandages around his head. His head was swollen and his eyes were closed tight. I was unsure if he could hear anything going on around him. Immediately, I began to cry as I started talking.

"Hey Stephon, it's me Brook! I love you my friend and you are so strong. I know you will pull through. There are so many people here praying for you. Everyone loves you and wants you to come out of here with that famous smile that warms everyone's heart. You're my friend and I need you. Please don't leave me!"

Just then his mom rubbed my back and motioned for me to come outside.

"The kids have gone over to the chapel to pray. Do you wanna go over and pray with them? Remember Brook, it's in God's hands now."

"Are you okay? Are you coming over too?"

I didn't want to leave her alone but as soon as I looked up Mr. Jones was coming back towards the room.

"Go ahead Brooklyn, we'll be all right," Mrs. Jones said.

I gave her a hug and walked out the door. I really didn't know what else to say to God. I wanted to ask him to make all this go away, but I remember Big Mama telling me sometimes God's plans are not man's plans. When I walked into the chapel people were standing around crying, consoling one another or sitting alone. I walked over to the altar and bent down.

"Lord, if you are up there please save my friend's life. Give him another chance, please. I am not sure if he talked to you but I am talking for him now. Please save his life . . ."

I heard a loud scream from behind and then more moans and groans all at the same time.

"Brooklyn, he's gone! He's gone!" someone whispered in my ear. My heart and head dropped to the floor.

"Lord, why? Why did you take my friend . . . what am I going to do?" Left . . .

∞

Stephon's family was Catholic so the funeral was very solemn and quiet. I was use to going to funerals in the ward where family members tried to jump in caskets so this was all new to me.

"Hey Brook, honey. Do you want to come sit with us in the front," Mrs. Jones asked?

The church was crowded with all of Stephon's friends, teachers and a lot of people I didn't know from the school. As I walked to the front with Mrs. Jones I saw our principal, Mr. Taylor, sitting next to a couple of teachers. I smiled at them as I passed by on my way to the front. I wanted to see Stephon one more time but his casket was closed and covered with flowers.

"We love you Stephon!" Someone from the back of the church yelled as the priest approached the podium.

"Yes we do," the very proper looking priest said. I looked over at Mrs. Jones who silently wept while grasping Mr. Jones' hand tightly.

"Today we lay to rest a young man full of zeal and a passion for life. Everyone he came in contact with he inspired them or encouraged them in some sort of way. His smile was infectious and his humor cheered everyone up. Mr. and Mrs. Jones have asked that one special friend would come and speak on behalf of all those that loved Stephon. Ms. Brooklyn Rideaux will you please come at this time."

My heart pounded and my hands began to shake uncontrollably.

"Brooklyn, it's okay. Stephon is here today with us and wants to hear from you," Mrs. Jones whispered as she squeezed my shaking hand.

The walk to the podium was hard and it felt like I was lifting cement blocks every time I took a step.

"Good morning. I didn't know Stephon long but the day we met he hugged me so tight. I thought he was a long lost cousin or something. He then showed me around the school and introduced me to all his friends as his little sister. Like the priest said his smile was infectious and his personality made everyone want to be around him. I remember one day it was real cold in the building so he took my knitted sweater and wore it around the school."

Several laughs in the audience broke out and smiles filled the room.

"It was so funny because I'm only 5'1 and he was 6'1 so the sweater was extra small on him. But he didn't care what other people thought he just wanted to make people laugh. That's why we loved him so much. Stephon, I know you're listening to us so from all of us I want to say thank you. Your purpose on this earth was to bring joy to hurting people and you did just that. My grandmother told me that once your mission or purpose on earth has been fulfilled the Father will bring you back home with Him. So Stephon I will see you when I'm done down here."

As I exited the podium applause rang out as people rose to their feet. Mrs. Jones came from her seat and hugged me right next to Stephon's casket.

"Thank you Brooklyn, thank you."

Chapter eight

"**B**rooklyn, are you okay honey? You've been moping around here all week long, not really talking to anyone. Do I need to send you to the doctor?"

Mama Betty was concerned and wanted to help but I had to grieve by myself.

"No, ma'am. I am okay. I just need some time to be alone."

"Well, your brother's college choir is coming down here for a musical and we are going to see him at the church. Do you think you'll feel like going later?"

"WHAT, Mike is coming to Houston? Of course I want to go! Of course! What time?"

"I thought that would cheer you up! We have to be there by 7 so I will be ready to leave at 6:30. Can you help Pearl with Jasmine? I will see if Anthony can help get Madear dressed and I will take care of Chrissy? Brook, you gone be okay, right?"

As I sat there and listened to her and all her plans, my heart began to leap. I was going to see my brother who I hadn't seen in forever. He told me he was singing in this college choir but I guessed he wanted to surprise me so he didn't tell me he was coming out here.

"Yeah, Mama! I'm fine . . . dang!"

"Okay, okay . . . I won't bother you anymore."

I went into the kitchen hoping to get me a sandwich before I started working on my homework. I opened the refrigerator and there was lunch meat but no bread. So I settled for cereal but there was no milk. So I settled again for Ramen noodles. I opened the pantry and of course no more noodles.

"Dang . . . is there ever going to be food around here?" I yelled.

"Brooklyn, who in the hell do you think you are talking to?"

Mama Betty asked walking towards the kitchen. Like Dr. Jekyll and Mr. Hyde out came the other Mama Betty.

"I am sick and tired of coming in here and never having nothing to eat. All these doggone people in this house that eat us out of house and home yet nobody is replacing anything!"

"Little girl you have lost your mind. I am the only one around here working and putting food in that refrigerator. I work long and hard at both jobs without complaining and all you have to do is wake up and go to school. So if somebody should be mad it should be me. I can't get a thank you, Mama you are great or anything. So until you get a job and start putting some food in this house then you need to keep that trap of yours closed."

Did she just go off on me? I am almost sixteen years old. Who does she think she is talking too?

"Whatever, Mama. Maybe if you get some of these people out of this two-bedroom matchbox then we can live like a family again. You always trying to save everybody and you losing those closest to you."

Before I knew it Mama Betty was in the kitchen in my face and I wasn't backing down. She grabbed my shirt and tried to push me into the bedroom for a whipping. I held my ground and I could tell she was tired. I braced myself up against the stove and dropped my head. All of a sudden I felt her fist going to work.

"You better stop hitting me in my head," I yelled!

Without thinking twice, I pushed my mama off me and into the table. The look on her face showed she was afraid but her actions couldn't show it. I ran over to Mama Betty and held her down on the table fearing what would happen if I let her up. She struggled to get loose from my grip but it wasn't happening. All the anger and frustration that I felt from Stephon leaving me and my mom replacing me, I wanted her to feel. Tears flooded my face and soaked my shirt. I let go.

"Brooklyn," Mama Betty said in a low voice over her tears, "I never thought it would be you. I thought you would always be my baby. You have just stepped over the line into womanhood and you need to get out of my house. Like you said this is a matchbox and it is not big enough for that many grown women. You have one hour to get your things and leave."

Pearl, Anthony, and Johnathan were standing in the dining room next to Madear watching nervously. The tension was so thick in that house that everyone watching was frozen with fear.

"Mama, where is she going to go," Pearl asked?

"I really don't care. When you've gotten too grown for me to tell you anything then you definitely need to be on your own or at least away from here."

"I HATE YOU," I yelled as I walked out of the kitchen into the bedroom to pack my things.

"I know, Brooklyn. I know."

Mama Betty walked out the front door. Pearl followed me into the bedroom trying to talk.

"Pearl, leave me alone. I can't take it anymore. I have done everything I know to be all that she wants me to be and it's not enough. I am tired of trying to please her. She loves you and Chrissy more than me anyway. If she didn't then she would not have tried to replace me with Chrissy. It's okay I will just leave and y'all can be happy."

"Girl, you talking stupid. You know Mama loves you just as much as she loves the rest of us. Just like you going through things emotionally she is going through some things as well. Y'all need to slow down and talk to each other. Think about everything she is going through right now. Taking on our cousins, me having a baby and Mike going off to college. That's a lot Brooklyn for one person to do on her own. Tommy Boy ain't here to help Mama out so she doing the best she can."

I had never had a conversation like that with Pearl and it actually felt good. I wanted that sisterly bond with her that I felt she gave to our cousins and Chrissy. I needed to know that she at least loved me and cared for me. Now I had to figure out where was I going to go? I let my mouth get me in trouble again and I didn't know how to handle it.

"Thanks Pearl but Mama and I ain't gone make it. I need to be on my own and learn my way. I mean I have tried and nothing seems to work with her. I am going to call Big Mama and see if I can at least stay with her until the summer. Maybe then I will have worked things out with Mama and some of these people will be gone."

I really wanted to run outside and hold my mama and beg her forgiveness but pride kept me still. I grabbed the phone off the receiver and dialed Big Mama's number.

"Hey Big Mama, are you busy?"

"Naw baby girl. You know I'm never too busy to talk to you. What's going on?"

"Can I come to your house? Me and Mama Betty just had a fight and she put me out. She loves all these people over here more than she loves me and I am tired of being pushed away. I need somewhere to stay until the summer."

I really didn't want to go to Big Mama house since it was so far away. How was I going to get back and forth to school every day? Big Mama did have an extra car but I wasn't sure if she would let me drive since I didn't have a license. She was my only solution unless I called Derrick. Lord knows I didn't want to open that can again but I gotta do what I gotta do.

"Well baby girl, you know I don't mind you coming over here but you need to make things right with your mama. I am not all right with y'all being at each other's neck and fighting. If Tommy Boy was home he wouldn't have it either. So yes you can come over here for a few days but you need to talk to your mama."

"Okay, I will! Can you come pick me up from the bus stop in front of our apartments? I don't want her to know where I'm going. Hello? Big Mama, did you hear me?"

I wasn't sure if she hung up the phone or was just being quiet. Lots of times we would be talking to Big Mama and she would burst out into a prayer and I just knew it was coming.

"Father, in the name of Jesus . . . I command those demons that are trying to interfere with my family to flee! Satan, you have no power and I cast you back into the pits of hell from where you came from. RIGHT NOW! RIGHT NOW! Father send peace, send your comforter and let your presence rest, rule and abide in that house. Hallelujah!! Hallelujah!! Thank you Lord. It's done baby girl. You go in there and talk to your mother and let her know your pain and ask for her forgiveness then you call me back."

Pearl held Jazmine while sitting on the edge of the bed watching me sympathetically. Tears covered the receiver of the phone as I hung up. I was tired of crying. I wanted this madness to be over and things to be better. I wanted my mommy back and my family back. Being teenager came with too much drama . . . who thinks I am strong enough to handle all of this? I am too young!

"Mama, can we talk?"

I stood next to the stairs where she sat smoking a cigarette. I really didn't know what to say but I knew I had to say something. I walked in front of her and bent down on my knees. The smoke from her cigarette covered my face as I held my breath.

"Mama, I am going through so much in my head right now. School, boys, my best friend dying and you picking everybody over me."

"What do you mean me picking everybody over you? Brooklyn, I never picked anybody over you."

"Why did you go and get Chrissy? I was the baby! Was I not good enough? Then you went and got my new cousins and brought them here. I need to talk to you sometimes but you are too busy either at work or at the hospital with Chrissy or taking care of somebody else. Where is my mama? When is it my time to be your baby? You let them come in and take that away from me. Pearl has Jazmine, Chrissy has you and the cousins have each other. Who do I have?"

Tears covered Mama Betty's face as if she had just received the worst news ever. Her cigarette had gathered an inch long in ashes that were about to drop at any minute. She smashed the cigarette on the step with one hand while wiping her face with the other.

"Brooklyn, I didn't know that is how you felt. I am so sorry that you feel pushed away. Your cousins were about to be sent to foster care by your dumb aunt and I couldn't let that happen. Chrissy needed someone to care for her because her mama wasn't able too. I was not about to watch a baby die because she didn't receive the care she needed. This is the hand the Lord dealt me so I am doing the best I can with what I have. Trust me, if I had a choice I would have chosen a different path for my family. I love each of you and I want the best for all of you. I have Madear and now Jazmine to add to that list. So please understand the stress that I am dealing with every day. But let me tell you one thing, I am your mother no matter how old you get. You are about to turn sixteen and now you starting to smell yourself. Just like I brought you here you better believe I don't have a problem making sure you have a real nice funeral. Don't ever in your life put your hands on me or push me to a place where I am willing to let you find out how grown you think you are!"

I understood everything my mother was trying to tell me. She broke it down for a sixteen-year-old mind to understand and I finally got it. I took my hand and wiped the tears from her smooth face and pulled her close to me. We hugged on the steps until tears and smiles came out and the love was apparent.

"Does this mean I can stay now?"

Grinning, "Yeah you can stay for now but you are on punishment from my car, the phone, and any outside activities until I tell you to come off punishment."

"Okay, I understand! I promise, too Mama, I will never put my hands on you again."

"Oh trust, I know you won't because if you try it you gone be missing a hand, finger and arm or something."

I knew she was serious and it was nothing but God that kept her from killing me this time. I went back into the house and everyone was in the living room waiting for the verdict.

"Dang, what y'all sitting in here waiting for?"

"Brook, stop playing. Do you still have to leave," Anthony asked?

Mama Betty walked through the door looking as puzzled as I was.

"She staying this time but guarantee if any one of you in here tries to jump stupid like Brook tried today you may not ever see daylight again. Do y'all understand?"

In unison we all cried, "Yes ma'am . . ."

Chapter nine

"Hello . . . ," a deep voice came through phone. I was hoping it wasn't Derrick. Maybe he moved away or fell off the face of the earth.

"May I speak to Staci?"

"Who is this?"

I tried to disguise my voice in hopes that no one would know it was me on the other end. I couldn't really catch who answered the phone so I kept my act going.

"Is she home? This is her friend from school. We run track together." I prayed that I didn't give myself away with too much information.

"Hold on . . . Staci . . . telephone. Some girl you run track with at school wants you."

"Hello?"

"Hey girl! Who was that who answered the phone? I didn't recognize the voice."

"Chile, that was my Uncle Jeff from Detroit. He came down here to see my grandmother so he staying over here for a little while. What's up? What are you doing?"

"Getting ready to go see my brother sing. His college choir is coming to a church in Fifth Ward and we are about to head over there now. I was just hollering at you because I never told you what happened between me and my mama."

"Oh yeah, you almost started crying and then we had to go. Are y'all okay? I mean you don't get emotional like that for nothing, well not lately."

"Whatever, we had a big fist fight and she was about to make me leave. I was so mad Staci and no one said anything to me except Pearl and I couldn't believe she said something."

"Wait, you need to start from the beginning and tell me what happened!"

"We were in the kitchen and we exchanged words. Next thing I knew she was throwing blows at my head. Before I knew it I was on top of her holding her down on the table. It was like I had lost my mind I was trying to kill this lady. Man, I looked up and everybody was looking at us but they were frozen stiff. I was like a beast after this lady. She told me to pack my bags and get out. I headed for the room to get my stuff feeling pathetic."

"Where in the hell were you going? You don't have no family that lives out here that you can stay with except your Big Mama!"

"I know, so I called my grandmother and asked her if I could come and stay with her."

"That's so far Brooklyn. How were you going to get to school with no car? Anyway, what did she say?"

"She prayed . . ."

"Prayed," Staci said in a confused voice? She and her family didn't really go to church except for holidays so when I told her my grandmother prayed instead of going off that threw her for a loop.

"Yeah, she prayed and after she finished I immediately felt different. I mean at first I was all macho and stuff like I could take on the world. I mean you know I had to really be out of my mind to hit my Mama Betty but that prayer did something to me. I went outside where she was and knelt down in front of her and begged for her forgiveness. We cried and hugged and I told her why I felt like I went off and she told me why she went off. It was like we both were going through similar stuff, but we never said anything to one another."

"So did y'all make up? Did she forgive you? Because if you were my child I would have buried you under the apartment and forgot about you!"

"Whatever! Yes that's what I am telling you. That prayer that my grandmother prayed did something to me that changed my whole attitude toward my mama. I was like putty in her hands. But listen, we are about to go and I need to help Pearl get the baby things together. If I don't call you when I get back I will talk to you tomorrow."

"Okay, tell your fine brother I said hey and I hope he still waiting on me! Hahh! Bye!"

"Bye crazy girl!"

As I walked into the bedroom where Pearl and the baby were I saw what I always envisioned a mother and her new-born baby looking like. Pearl held Jazmine while feeding her and singing her a lullaby. I never really knew Pearl could sing but I guess it sounded okay for the baby so it was all good for me.

"Pearl, let me take Jaz so you can get ready. Mama Betty say she wanna leave by 6:30 so we can get there and get a good seat."

Pearl knew Jaz would be asleep in a minute so she handed her to me gently as I sat back on the bed. I had on my nicest black dress with red stripes across the back shoulder. My brother loved that dress and I wanted to make sure I was beautiful for him since I am his favorite girl! I held Jazmine in my left arm and rocked her to sleep while she sucked her bottle. She was so little with beautiful ebony colored skin. Her hair was silky and curly and her face reminded me of my only black baby doll when I was little.

"Y'all ready? Its time to go," Mama Betty yelled from the dining room with Madear.

"Yes ma'am," I replied. "We are ready." Pearl stepped out of the bathroom and gave me a look upside my head.

"Please don't try to suck up to Mama Betty. She knows when you're being fake or when you're for real. Give me Jazmine and grab her baby bag. Look in there and make sure I put all her bottles and diapers in there please."

Suck up, whatever! I felt good about our new beginning and I wasn't going to let anybody ruin it for us.

CO

When we arrived at the church Big Mama was already there waiting for us. I knew it was her by the bright red suit and matching hat tilted to the side. Her suits, shoes, and hats always coordinated whenever we went to church and she was definitely stylin. The church parking lot was small and adjacent to the church so we had to walk across the street in hopes of not getting hit by any passing cars. Madear was in her wheelchair so Anthony helped her get across pretty fast. Pearl got Jazmine out and Mama Betty got Chrissy out as we all rushed to get inside. I saw Big Mama so I hurried over to give her a hug.

"Hey Big Mama! Man you look phat! You know pretty, hot and tempting!" I wanted her to know that I was not calling her fat or it would've been on in my world. I also had to hurry and let her know me and Mama Betty were good. I gave her a wink and she gave me one back. Our code system that only we understood.

"Hey everybody! Come on let's go on in before more people get here. The church is not that big either so we gone have to get some seats quick."

As soon as we got in the church I felt like I was going to suffocate. There were only about 10 short pews and a choir stand that had about five short pews. The pulpit was the size of a small closet and it looked as if only two preachers could sit in it at a time. I walked in right behind Big Mama and sat next to her on the second pew. Mama Betty took Madear out of her wheelchair and sat her on the third pew behind Big Mama.

"Hey, where is Johnathan? Didn't he want to come hear Mike and his choir sing?" Big Mama asked.

"Johnathan had a basketball tournament today. He is staying with his coach after the game until we get back," Mama Betty replied while straightening Madear's dress in the seat.

"Has Mike made it here yet Mama?" I was still on a high from knowing that I would see my brother real soon.

"I didn't see their school van outside unless they parked behind the church. They may be in the back. Here watch Chrissy while I go see if they are here yet."

I had begun to accept the fact that Chrissy was in my life for good. I decided that I shouldn't be mad and hate her since she was just a baby when Mama Betty got her. She deserved to have a mama that loved her too.

"So, did you talk to your mother, Brooklyn?" Big Mama whispered in my ear.

"Yes, after that prayer you prayed for me I felt sorry for what I did and I begged her forgiveness. I told her exactly how I felt about her pushing me to the side for everybody else. She told me it wasn't like that and in many of those situations she had no other choice but to take them."

"So do you better understand now?"

"Yes ma'am. I do. But I still think if you hadn't prayed for me and I heard your prayers then things would probably be the same."

"Okay, y'all they are here and the pastor is about to come out. I saw him and another preacher talking in the back." Mama Betty grabbed Chrissy out of my lap and sat down next to Madear. Pearl, Anthony and Jazmine were on the row with me and Big Mama waiting for Mike and his choir to do their thang.

"Mike!" I jumped up and yelled.

Mike came out of the back door. He looked around for someone until he heard my voice.

"Hey everybody! Y'all made it here early, that's good because it is supposed to be packed! Hey Pearl, Oh my God is that the baby? She is beautiful . . . she look like she could be my child with her skin tone and all! Hey Madear and Big Mama! Look at Li'l Anthony . . . man you been working out!"

"Well, yeah a little bit," Anthony said grinning from ear to ear.

Mike walked over to Madear and gave her a hug and kissed Mama Betty. You could tell he was rushing as he picked up Chrissy and spun her around.

"Okay, I have to get back with the choir but I will see you all after church." Mike walked away swiftly leaving without speaking to me. Did I do something to him? Did Mama Betty tell him about our fight when she went to the back? Did I yell too loud in the church and he was embarrassed? I am his favorite girl and he didn't even speak to me.

As the music began to play the pastor asked everyone to rise. The church sang the congregational song we sing every Sunday at our church, *This Little Light of Mine*. I knew the song so I sang it loud in hopes Mike would hear me.

"Thank you; now turn in your Bibles with me to Psalm 100. This is a familiar passage of scripture so let's recite it together. Amen. Make a joyful noise until to the Lord . . ."

As the church recited the scripture I kept my eyes on Mike in the choir. I was hoping he would look up and I could give him one of my beautiful smiles that he always loves to see. But he never looked up.

"Amen, amen you may be seated. It is a blessing to be in the house of the Lord one more time. Amen."

If the short bald man said "amen" one more time I was going to get up and go to the restroom. The pastor almost looked like Mike's dad with the bald head and fat stomach that hung over his pants. I looked very carefully but it wasn't him. He didn't have the glasses sitting on tip of his nose.

"Now we are going to get started with musical selections from our host college choir all the way from College Station. Give the president a hand as he comes."

I had my head down fixing my stockings that had turned around when I heard Mike's voice.

"Good evening. We are so honored to come down tonight and share with you in praise and worship. The members of this choir have practiced long and hard and we hope you get into the spirit with us tonight, Amen . . . amen."

Most of the choir was filled with women but there were some men. Everyone had on some form of red and black just like me. I didn't know those were Mike's school colors or at least his choir colors.

A lady with long fingernails and blonde hair approached the microphone and began to bellow out a song. She sounded really good and Big Mama started rocking back and forth.

"Father, I just want to thank you . . . ." she sang as the choir joined in behind her.

The night was going great and we even saw a few people shout.

"The Lord is showing his presence in here tonight! Amen," the other preacher stood and said after they had sang three songs.

Time quickly passed and it was getting late. Mama Betty tapped Pearl on the shoulder for her to let us know to get ready to go. The choir had sung about eight songs by now and it was extremely hot in the church. More people had crowded in and as we prepared to leave Mike stood up and headed towards the microphone.

"Wait a minute y'all," Mama Betty whispered, "Mike is about to sing and then we leaving."

Our eyes opened wide with expectation. Mike had been singing since he was little I was told and he always tore the church up. The music played softly for what seemed like a while and then there it was.

"Lord, thank you for saving me. All the wrong I did you washed me clean. I am sorry for the mistakes, sorry for taking your love for granted . . ." Mike sang out!

Had someone told him what was going on with me? Did he write this song just for me? Tears flowed out of my eyes uncontrollably.

"As the brother continues to sing, is there one here tonight? You know you've messed up somewhere and you really need to repent. You need to turn it all over to God and let him clean you. He loves you no matter what has happened. If that's you come tonight," one of the ministers stood at the pulpit and said.

Somebody has told these people what was going on in my life and it ain't even funny. I was so sorry and I needed God to forgive me so I could be on the right track with him and Mama Betty.

I stood up with tears covering my face and slowly walked to the altar with my head down.

"Praise the Lord; hold up your head baby this is your new day," The preacher said!

I stood in front of the church as others slowly began to come to the altar. The preacher kept talking and I knelt down on the floor.

"Lord, please forgive me! I hurt my mama and my family. I am so sorry. I need you to come into my life and heal me. Please!! I love you and I need you. Take all this hatred that's in my heart for my family away. I was mad at you for taking Stephan but I know your will had to be done. Please save me . . ."

I felt a hand on my shoulder and it was Mama Betty.

"Come on Brook, it's okay God loves you! Come on baby girl."

I sat up and wiped my nose and face with the back of my hand. Church was over and some people had begun to leave but I was still there at the altar. Mike and Big Mama were sitting in the pew nearest me praying and Pearl had gathered everyone else to the back of the church.

"Mama, I am so sorry," I said with eyes still full of tears.

"I know Brook, I know. It's over now . . . God has you now!"

Chapter ten

I thought things would immediately change when I accepted Jesus into my life that night but nothing did. I still found myself thinking about Derrick and wanting to call him. I knew he was no good for me but for some reason it was hard to let go.

"Why didn't he want me? I am different from them other heifers," I thought while sitting in the bedroom before I got ready for school.

"Brook you up?" Mama Betty asked. Lately, I had been sleeping in her room on the floor next to her bed.

"Yes ma'am."

"Okay, if you want me to take you to school for practice you better get up and begin getting ready."

I really didn't feel like going to school but I knew we had a game coming up that would determine if we went to the state championship or not. I had to go to practice to let the coach know I was ready to play again.

"Brooklyn, you have missed several afterschool workouts and several morning practices so I don't think you will be playing in the next few games."

Her words tap danced in my head and I didn't want to let her or my team down anymore.

"Mama, is Mrs. Mo coming for Madear today?"

"Brooklyn, why you asking me such a dumb question? If she don't come then who will stay here with her?"

"Dang, my bad. Let me get my tail up and go get ready to go," I said to myself.

"Brooklyn, not today. Not today!"

I got to school early that morning for basketball practice but things just didn't seem the same. When my mama dropped me off I wanted to say bye but before I could close the door good on the car she sped away.

"Well, goodbye and I love you too!"

Right there I knew this was going to be a crazy day. That was rare for her to leave without saying anything unless we were arguing or something but this morning was cool, I thought. Whatever, I tightened up my black and white converse and pulled the hood of my sweatshirt over my head. I almost felt the need to run a lap or two to warm up my muscles before going in to the gym but that motivation quickly faded. The parking lot was empty and dark except for one old black Ford pickup truck and it belonged to the boys' basketball coach, Mr. Pye. He obviously didn't have a life because he was at the school more than any other teacher or coach. I know he was there sometimes longer than the principal. He looked like he had a hard life and was ready to give it all up, like me.

"Yo Coach, what's the dillio," I said in my fun-loving and chipper morning voice?

"Why in the Sam Hill are you here so early? Every time I look around you have your tail up here probably chasing after some little boy. Gone over there and cut the lights on and get the balls out of the supply closet. Do not go into the small gym because it's locked."

Dang, what in the Sam Hill was wrong with him? He acted like I was the one that pissed him off before he left home this morning. Whatever. I am not going to entertain that fool this morning. I put my bag and sweatshirt against the wall and grabbed the rack of balls out of the supply closet. As I walked out I flipped the switch for the lights and all at once the room was lit. I guess I wasn't ready for all 1,000 volts of electricity to come on at one time because it made me lower my head and cover my eyes. I grabbed the first ball and started doing layups. This was my best shot, I guess because it was the easiest. After about 10 shots

I heard the back door to the small gym open and my homegirl Meithy walked in.

"Hey girl! Wassup?"

I guess she didn't hear me because she kept walking and headed straight into the girls locker room. The gym seemed a lot colder this morning for some strange reason and almost eerie like something bad was about to happen. I gave no attention to that feeling and I was not about to let a "feeling" get me off today. I have had too many of those these last few weeks and I was tired of it. I grabbed my ball again and went to start bouncing it but the air was leaking and the ball stayed on the gym floor. What happened to the air in this ball from thirty seconds ago? I picked up another ball and by this time the other girls had arrived to the gym. Coach Miller, the varsity girls' coach had also arrived with rollers in her hair and what I thought looked like shaving solution above her lip.

"Good morning ladies. I want you all to get into pairs and practice your free throws because most of you are under 60 percent and that sucks! I am not putting you all into pairs because I trust that you can pick your partner and get the job done."

That was music to my ears, I needed to practice, but who would be my partner? I didn't feel like hearing no mess so I asked the white girl, Sara, to be my partner. She agreed and we headed to the gym floor with a new ball.

"So where have you been," Sara asked very nonchalantly?

"What do you mean? I been here."

"No ma'am, you have not been here. You've missed practices and even a game. We need you Brooklyn and you seem to have kicked us to the curb. You know scouts are here watching at all the games and this could be your big break."

"Yeah, I know but I been going through some stuff at my house. Family issues."

"Well we all have family issues but this is like my refuge. When I come here and get on this court it's just me and the ball and the goal."

119

I wanted to tell her that my problems are probably different from her problems. I wasn't about to tell her that I had been in the hospital for trying to take my life. Or that I had a bad fight with my mama and almost got put out of my house.

"Yeah, you're right," I said, "but that's why I am here now and will be here from now on. So I see you've been practicing. You've made all of your shots. You have a goal at your house or something that you've practiced on lately?"

Most white girls at Maxwell lived in a very nice house with all the amenities. She looked like she had been working out with somebody, her form and everything looked good.

"Naw, I come up here on Saturdays and I play with the guys in my apartment complex."

"Apartment complex? What? Sara lives in some apartments," I screamed inside my head?

I guess you really can't judge a book by its color.

"Ladies, it's almost time for you to go in and get ready to go but before you go I want everyone to do 50 suicides and then you can go."

I hope coach wasn't doing this to punish me and therefore punishing the whole team. Damn . . . 50 suicides! I haven't run laps in a minute let alone some stupid suicides. I had every mind to walk off the gym floor and go into the locker room but I saw Sara looking at me to see what I was going to do. I headed to the line . . .

"Brooklyn, Mama Betty taking you to the dealership today when she get off work?" Anthony asked after we got home from school.

I had saved up about $500 from Big Mama giving me money and from past birthdays so I was ready to get my first car. Mama Betty said she would match whatever I saved so I hope she could hold up her end of the bargain.

"Yeah, why you wanna go?"

"I was going to ride just to see what you were thinking about getting. Do you know where y'all going to look?"

"Yes and what is this Jeopardy? Either you going or you not."

I wanted to jump all over him for irritating the heck out of me but I knew he was super sensitive at times so I let up. We sat outside on the steps waiting for the house to air out from Madear's accident.

"Brook, Mama Betty say you ready? She will be here in about ten minutes for y'all to go to the dealership," Pearl asked while holding the phone on one shoulder and Jaz on the opposite hip.

"Tell her yes I'll be ready when she gets here."

I was so excited to be getting my first car; the only problem was I didn't have a license. I figured Mama Betty was tired of having to get up extra early to take me to practice every day. She said she would get the car in her name and let me drive it to school but I had to get a license soon. I had seen several cars in the newspaper and I knew that we had enough money for either one of them if Mama Betty held up her end of the deal. I was kind of unsure about asking her especially the way she dropped me off at school this morning. Just think, I no longer have to ride the stupid bus with the dumbest bus driver in the world. I can take myself to basketball practice in the mornings and even stay after school for extra practice. I can go to parties and hang out with my friends without Pearl or Mama Betty having to come pick me up. This was the best day of my life.

"HONKKKK, HONKKKK!"

A horn blew outside and I jumped off the steps and ran back into the house. I quickly grabbed my purse and ran back out the door with Anthony right behind me on my heels.

"HONKKKKK, HONKKKKKK . . . . y'all better come on if you wanna go today," Mama Betty yelled as we approached the car.

"Hey mama, you look very pretty today," I said in an oh-so-sweet voice.

"Whatever Brooklyn, come on and get in this car so we can go before it gets too late. I am already tired and I don't feel like doing a lot of driving so I hope you know where this place is located."

Man, this is what I had to look forward to when getting my first car? I was really hoping the pleasant Betty would take me to look for a car but this is what I have to work with today.

"Yes ma'am, its right off 45 and Gulf Bank. As soon as you exit it is to the right."

We drove in silence the entire way there. I wanted to ask about the other $500 but was too afraid of talking and getting the wrong Betty again. Anthony had fallen asleep in the backseat like we were on a road trip and Mama Betty punched his leg to wake him up.

"We here, come on let's get in there and see what they got."

As soon as we walked up I saw the car that was in the paper. Black with chrome wheels, a sunroof and leather seats. A cute 1992 Honda Civic with only 52,000 miles. I knew this was the car for me. I would be the envy of school when I pulled up in this baby and all the boys would try to get at me then.

"Mama, this is the one right here!"

She walked over to the car and looked at the sticker on the window . . . it read $1,500 down and $200 a month.

"Brooklyn, we can't afford that car. Keep looking and let's find something cheaper."

"But Mama, I can get a part-time job and pay the note every month. Can we please talk to the man about it before we look at something else?"

"Hell no, if you don't find a job who will have to pay the note? I am not about to put myself in a predicament like that where I have to get a third job to pay for something you want."

Tears began to well in my eyes but they quickly went away when I saw the look on Mama Betty's face. Her Chrysler Dynasty was in tip-top shape and Pearl drove a nice hatchback as well. I wanted to make sure I looked good and drove something dependable too, but she wasn't having it.

"Good evening ma'am," a tall heavy-set gentleman in a cowboy hat and boots said while holding a cigar in his hand, "is there something I can help you with or something you would like to test drive?"

The man's nose was red as fire and his lips were as dry as the desert. I didn't want to keep looking at him because he almost looked scary.

"Hi! I am here looking for my daughter a car. She needs something dependable and inexpensive."

"Yes ma'am, I understand you there. What type of budget are we looking at for this car?"

"Well we have about a $1,000 to put down and I really don't want to pay any more than $150 a month."

"Okay," the cowboy said with a twisted face like that wasn't enough, "so let's come over here and take a look at these cars."

Was this the poe-people section? I mean these cars looked like they had been through hell and high water and left on the side of the road for the tow truck. I really hope my mama would want me to have something better than this to ride in.

"Okay, great! If these are DEPENDABLE and in our price range let's take a look. Brook, look over there. There's a nice one that you may like and he said it's dependable."

She pointed me in the direction of a small yellow car with tinted windows. The hood was dented in and the passenger side door looked like it wouldn't open because it was pushed all the way in.

"Mama, are you serious? You didn't do Pearl like this when you got her car."

"Pearl had more money saved than you do and she had a license," she spoke in my ear with tight lips.

"Well, what about this one? We just got it here about a week ago and it is a pretty nice car."

He took us to look at a light blue Hyundai Excel Hatchback. It looked pretty decent from the outside and the inside was a little worn but not too bad for me. The only problem was it was a stick shift. Oh well, I thought let's move on to something else.

"Brooklyn, this car is nice. Its small enough for you and it has low mileage. It looks to be dependable too."

"Yeah, but it's a stick shift and you know Mike didn't teach me how to drive his car, just your car."

"Well, ma'am this here is a really nice car and I think I can get you around what you are looking to pay for it and I will even give your daughter a few lessons on how to drive a standard before you leave today."

"Well if she is going to get this car she has to learn how to drive it today because I don't know how to drive a stick."

I couldn't believe my ears. The car was nice but how was I going to learn to drive a stick in a matter of minutes? I looked inside the car and before I knew it, Mama Betty and the cowboy had walked inside the building to work out a deal. I was frustrated and scared that she would leave me there and I would have to pray the whole way home. Anthony walked around looking at other cars as if he was in the market to buy one so I let him keep looking.

"Brooklyn, everything is set! You have a new car! I am so happy and your notes are what we were looking for too! You need to tell this man thank you since he is willing to show you how to drive this baby home."

Mama Betty had obviously fell and bumped her head. Was she serious?

"Sir, thank you so much but I am not sure that I can learn how to drive a stick shift in a matter of minutes and I normally ask a lot of questions."

I wanted him to say he didn't have time and tell Mama Betty never mind.

"Well, young lady your mother is such a sweet lady and I like her spirit. So I will take as long as you need," Mr. Cowboy said smiling from ear to ear.

"Brook, Anthony and I are going to go now. Don't forget to give him your half of the down payment and we will see you when you get home in your new car."

"What about gas," I yelled as she walked away?

"With every new car you get a free full tank honey so you are in good hands," Mr. Cowboy grinned.

Mama and Anthony drove off and I was left with the cowboy. I was nervous since I wasn't sure of his background, if he had ever been in prison, his credit score, or if he believed in Jesus. I wanted to make a phone call to Big Mama and ask her to come get me but Mama Betty would have a cow.

"Okay, sweetheart! You ready? I am going to drive us out of the parking lot over to that larger parking space next door. There you can practice using the clutch and shifting gears. Then we will get on the feeder and let you get in traffic. You think you will be okay on the freeway?"

Was this man losing his ever loving mind? The freeway? I don't know if I will be okay in that parking lot let alone the freeway.

"Father, if you hear me please help me learn fast and get home even faster," I said quickly as we got in the car.

"Okay, this here car has five gears. This is first, second, third, fourth and here is fifth. Anytime you want to change gears you have to stay on the clutch. If you come off the clutch while the car is in gear the car will cut off."

By the way he was talking I wasn't going to get home till tomorrow after school. I paid close attention and tried not to ask any questions. It was my turn to drive it and I was extremely nervous but to my surprise it was easy.

"Wow, young lady you are doing a hell of a job. It took me days to learn and you've picked this thang up on your first try! Keep going and let's go ahead and try to get on the freeway."

Did he say freeway? I once again tried to keep my cool since I was now behind the wheel and I didn't want to forget everything he had just taught me. Okay, Brook you can do this . . . just get on the freeway and get off.

"Man, this was easier than I thought. You are already a pro," cowboy said as we pulled back into the dealership, "now do you think you can get back home by yourself or do I need to follow you?"

Oh no he didn't! Follow me home, I don't think so. I do not know where this cowboy is from and if he comes to that house and Madear doesn't know him trust and believe he will get the tongue lashing of his life.

"Naw, I will be okay. I got the hang of it now. Thank you so much," as I held my hand out to shake his, "I really appreciate your help."

"Ahh, come here," he said while pulling me towards him, "you are a special young lady and I am honored to have helped you out! But uhhmm young lady, I need the other half of your down payment before I can let this here car leave the lot."

I quickly pulled away from this could-be pedophile and handed him five $100 bills. I then jumped in the car and locked the doors before he could say anything else. I was glad he helped but he was a little too friendly and I did not want the Rideaux's on COPS for knocking this dude off.

"Bye," I said waving as I drove off the lot.

The ride home was calm and relaxing to say the least. I was smooth with changing the gears and thank God the road was pretty clear.

"OH NO, he forgot to tell me how to reverse," I screamed as I made it to our apartment complex. The gate was closing on me and I needed to back up or the car would be hit.

"Okay, think Brook. REVERSE . . . ," I screamed hoping the car would supernaturally move backwards.

BOOM . . . BOOOM . . .

"Oh no, Lord help me please. This gate is janky and it has hit my new car. AAAAAHHHHH . . . Lord . . . Mama Betty is going to have a fit!"

I pulled the car into a parking space after the gate bounced off my front bumper and remained opened. I jumped out of the car to observe the damage. NONE . . . what? That gate is brutal on cars.

"Hallelujah!! Thank you Jesus," I screamed while dancing around the car. I grabbed my purse and keys and made sure the windows were rolled up. I slammed my driver's side door closed but then I heard a loud noise, like something hit the ground.

"What in the hell I mean heck was that," I said as I walked to the front of the car. My entire bumper had fallen completely off and was lying there on the ground.

"UUUUGGGGHHHHHH . . . . what kind of mess is this?"

Chapter eleven

Having a car was cool but having a car with no bumper was embarrassing. Since I was still a little shaky on how to reverse, I parked in a space at school that allowed me to simply drive forward.

"Girl, what in the world happened to your bumper," Staci asked when I pulled up to her house?

"Duhhh, it fell off. I don't know how but I pulled into my apartment complex and closed the door. Then out of nowhere the stupid bumper hit the ground. And you know that was after our janky gate hit it first."

I was getting more and more upset just talking about the car so I abruptly changed the subject.

"Hey, do you want to ride to the store with me? I need to get some gas and I'm hungry."

"Uhmm, naw I will chill. Call me later when you get home."

Was she acting saditty? I know my car wasn't a Mercedes Benz but at least I had a car.

"That's cool," I said throwing my hands up, "you gone want to ride one day."

I pulled up to the gas pump at the convenience store around the corner from my old neighborhood and a group of guys in a Mustang GT pulled in right in front of me.

"Oh my God, they can see my bumper is gone. Lord, please let this gas come out faster so I can get out of here!"

The guys looked familiar but one guy in particular I knew went to school with me. I had seen him in the cafeteria on several occasions and I think he played baseball too. I turned my back to them as I heard giggling and sneering. The tallest guy who drove the car wore a red shirt and white shorts. In his back pocket was a red bandana which made me believe they were in a gang.

As I put the pump back on the holder and closed my tank the guy that I recognized from Maxwell began to walk over to my car. I knew he probably had a joke about my car and I wasn't in the mood to hear it.

"Hey! Don't you play basketball for Maxwell?" He stood in front of my car with a wide grin and his grill shining.

"Yeah, I play basketball. Don't you play baseball for Maxwell," I asked in my I-really-don't-care attitude? His light brown eyes stared at my black tights and flip flops. I wondered if he was cross-eyed because he never looked up while we talked.

"Yeah, I play baseball. I remember you from the hospital with Stephon and his parents. Was that your boyfriend?"

"No, he was my best friend. We spent a lot of time together and I know his parents really well too. So how did you know him? Were y'all good friends too?"

"We were cool, we had a couple of classes together. I stay in the same neighborhood he stayed in and we played ball together sometimes. So how are you doing? I heard you took it really hard."

Was this guy trying to be sympathetic and compassionate? What does he want? He doesn't even know me and he asking me too many questions any way.

"Yeah, I'm good. Like I said he was my best friend so it's like losing a brother. By the way, what is your name?"

A wider smile came over his face as he headed closer to the driver's side of the car where I stood. I moved back and gave him a look that wasn't too friendly.

"I'm sorry li'l mama . . . my name is James. And may I ask what your name is?"

His grammar was horrible but I told him anyway.

"I'm Brooklyn."

"Well, Ms. Brooklyn do you have a boyfriend?"

I thought about Derrick and how I hadn't really talked to anyone for real since I was with him. I had been with David, Lamarcus, Xavier and some other guys that I don't remember but none that I will actually call my boyfriend.

"No, I don't have a boyfriend. Do you have a girlfriend?"

By now his friends had pulled over to the side and sat in the car with the music blasting. I wanted to ask him were they all in a gang but I didn't want to become a part of a homicide for being nosey.

"No, I don't. Do you think I can get your number and call you sometime? I don't mean to rush but those guys are being stupid and are ready to go."

"That's cool . . . I will give you my beeper number. I need to get in the store and pay for this gas before that Arab come out here tripping."

I grabbed my backpack and snatched a sheet of paper out of my binder. I took the pencil lodged in my ponytail out and wrote my number down.

"Listen, I will take care of your gas and I will beep you tonight . . . is that cool?"

"Yeah, that's cool. Oh and thank you for taking care of the gas. I'll talk to you later!"

I jumped into my car and closed the door. Lord, that boy looks good and I really hope he beeps me tonight, I sat in the car until he and his friends drove off. I knew they were already cracking jokes about my bumper and I didn't want to give them another reason.

I made it home after stopping off at McDonald's and going inside instead of using the drive-through. The last time I went through the drive-through my car became the comedy show for the evening. The cashier purposely messed up my order so I could stay in the line longer for her coworkers to come out and see my bumper. Never again.

As soon as I walked in the door my beeper went off and I didn't recognize the number. I put all my stuff down and headed into the kitchen.

"Excuse the hell out of me but I know you didn't walk in this house and not speak. What's wrong with you?"

I forgot about speaking and I went straight into the kitchen to grab the house phone. James was in my head and his beautiful smile and tall physique really turned me on.

"My bad, Madear, how are you?"

"I was good until Johnathan brought his black tail in this house. I really can't stand his ugly self," Madear said while looking at Johnathan and shooting the dozens at him.

Madear for some reason loved Anthony and Pete but had it out for Johnathan. Every night Mama Betty would come in from work and ask either Anthony or Johnathan to help Madear get in her bed. She often times cursed Johnathan out and showed Anthony so much love.

One day while Mama Betty was at work Madear laid into Johnathan, but what she failed to realize is John Boy had a tape recorder. He recorded everything she said and every name that she called him.

"Mama Betty I want you to hear something," Johnathan said when Mama Betty walked in one evening.

"John Boy this better be good because I am ready to shower and go to bed."

"Oh, I think you will like this tonight. Remember I told you every time you leave Madear cusses me out and shoots me the dozen? Well I have her on tape."

"What, you have her on tape? I can't believe that . . . let me see it."

Mama Betty pushed play and you would swear her ears began to bleed.

"Listen here you little mother f . . . . , you better leave me the hell alone. Kiss my black a . . . , suck my big toe and go to hell. You black ba . . . . son of a b . . . . !"

"Madear, I can't believe what I am hearing. You know this is the Lord's house and you can not use language like that in here."

"Betty, that ain't me! That punk is lying. That is Brooklyn or Pearl but that ain't me!"

Madear knew she had been cussing John Boy out on a daily basis while Mama Betty was at work or at church. She didn't want Mama Betty to look at her any differently and I didn't blame her.

"Madear, you ought to be ashamed of yourself for this mess. I am so hurt that you are talking to your grandchildren like that and then try to act all holy when I get here."

"Ahh, hell Betty! You ain't no saint. Those kids get cussed out every Sunday morning right before church and you get to church and try to act holier than thou. So get over it and throw that foolishness in the trash."

Madear had just given Mama Betty a piece of her mind and there was nothing she could really say back, so Mama Betty walked away. She threw the recorder on Madear's bed and John Boy ran quickly and grabbed it.

"See you bet not mess with me anymore . . . I got you on tape!"

"You better get your black ass out of my face before I poke your eyeballs out."

"Hello, did someone page Brooklyn from this number?"

"Yeah, hey you! This is James, what are you doing?"

"Oh, hey! Nothing much, just walked in the house about to shower and do some homework. What's going on with you?"

"Nothing much here either. I just wanted to call you and let you know I enjoyed talking to you for that brief moment. I also wanted to see if you were busy this weekend. My homeboy is having a party at his house; you think you would be able to join me?"

I don't even know this boy and he already asking me to go out with him. I mean yeah I can go but I think I need to get to know him before I hang out with him. He is trippin' . . .

"No, I don't have any plans this weekend. Does your friend go to Maxwell?"

"Man, please. Do you know how many times I get laughed at and talked about for going to Maxwell? My homies think Maxwell is a bougie school and especially since I play baseball. My homie goes to a school on the south side but his parents live out here on the north."

"Talked about for going to Maxwell? Maxwell ain't all that and don't they know baseball is the highest playing professional sport?"

I wanted to kind of impress him with my sports knowledge. Everyone in my family played some kind of sport and Big Mama told me that Tommy Boy was the star basketball player at his school so it was natural for me to be heavily into sports and love guys that were athletic too.

"Of course not, those dudes not worried about their futures. They just like to gang bang and go after girls. My dad ain't trying to hear that from me but they still my friends. And I see you know your sports . . . how long you been playing ball?"

"Since I can remember. Everybody in my family played something at some point in their lives so it came natural for me. My brother Mike went to college a few years ago on a football scholarship and before my sister Pearl had her baby she ran track at Maxwell."

"Wait a minute, Big Mike is your brother? Man, that dude was the best high school player I ever seen. He killed them on the field and he was smart too right?"

Was he jocking my brother? This was starting to be a major turn off and I needed to get some work done before I went to bed.

"Yep, that's him. Say, it's cool for us to hang out this weekend. Do you have a friend for my home girl? Maybe we can double date. My car may be too small for your long legs though so you may have to drive."

"I know you don't want your home girl hooking up with a gangster so I will call one of my teammates and see if they want to hang out. And by the way, I don't have a car."

No car? I can't talk to someone who doesn't have a car. What are we gone do? Shoot just like today I guess he will be putting gas in my car and getting it washed on a regular basis.

"That's cool. I will come and pick you up. Make sure before Friday you let me know where you live. I will talk to you later okay; I gotta go do some work."

"Hey, you wanna grab something to eat tonight before you go to bed?"

I know he didn't. Did he know what time it was and he didn't have a car so how were we getting to the restaurant?

"Where are you trying to go? My curfew on weekdays is 10 and my mama don't play. So we have to make this thing quick."

"That's cool! I will get my dad's car and meet you at Burger King off the highway . . . say in ten minutes?"

"That's cool . . . bye!"

Dang, I just walked in the house. I need to freshen up and make myself look and smell good before I walk back out the door. Should I keep these tights on or change into some jeans? He was looking at my legs at the gas station and my freshly pedicured feet. I ran in the bathroom and brushed my teeth, shook my hair out and put it back in a ponytail. I sprayed my body down with some of Pearl's real perfume. I was a little nervous because this could be it for me. I could finally have that relationship that I truly desired and I didn't have to worry about looking anymore.

"Madear, I am about to run over to Staci's house so she can help me with my homework. Tell Mama Betty if she gets home before I get back, okay?"

I said where I was going loud enough for Pearl and Johnathan to hear me in the back room. I knew they would act like I never came home if Mama Betty asked them so I made sure Madear knew too.

"Okay, you better be back here before it gets late. You know how your mama is and I am not trying to hear that foolishness tonight!"

Was Madear trying to check me? That's cool at least she responded and knew where I was going. I walked out the door and took a deep breath as I headed to my car.

"Lord, please let this be it so I won't have to go through drama with boys anymore. Let him fall in love with me and take care of me," I whispered as I got in the car.

I pulled into Burger King I heard a loud horn that scared me and my foot came off the clutch. The car shut off and began to roll back. I quickly hit the brake and clutch to restart the car and put it in first gear. I pulled into a space where I could drive forward and get out easily.

"Am I really that nervous . . . Lord help me please. This guy can't know that I am nervous, I'm a basketball player," I silently prayed.

"Hey Brooklyn, I see you looking good! Can I have a hug?"

"You are moving kind of fast, huh? Are you like this with every girl you meet? And plus, this is the same thing I had on when I met you!"

James got out of his dad's black Mercedes C class and all I noticed was his beautiful eyes and wavy low cut. He stood about 6 feet tall and hovered over me. That was cool because I needed to make sure he could hold me up when it was time.

"No, I just feel like I already know you. That's why I say you looking good because it is the same thing from earlier . . . I like that, baby girl! Are you this cool and laid back all the time?"

"Pretty much . . . I like to just chill so things don't get to me easily."

I was lying through my teeth but I had to get him to see something different in me . . . something that I hadn't seen. Did he call me baby girl?

"Well, can I have my hug before we go inside?"

I leaned in towards James and I came just above his waist. His cologne smelled like something Mike used to wear and

I immediately liked it. His strong arms held me tightly as he slightly lifted me off my feet. I wanted to stop and ask him did God send him to me. He was everything I prayed for in a guy; but back to reality I really hoped he wasn't expecting me to pay; all my money had gone toward my car but I had to play it off like I had some money.

"Are you real hungry," I asked him as we approached the counter?

"Yeah baby girl, I haven't eaten since practice. What about you? Are you hungry?"

Did he call me baby girl again? Where did he come from? I think I'm falling in love.

"No, I stopped when I left the gas station and got something to eat. I think I will just get a milkshake."

"Okay. Excuse me; can I get two whoppers with cheese, large fries, large coke and a small milkshake," James asked the cashier, who was paying more attention to her hairnet than to him?

I need to speak to the CEO and ask them if I can teach customer service skills to these people up here. I gotta keep my cool so he won't figure out that I will go off on somebody around here. Our order almost came out too fast for me and I was happy I didn't get anything. We sat in a booth near the door and just looking at him I felt ready to profess my love.

"Tell me about yourself Brooklyn. I know you play ball already but what else is there about Ms. Brooklyn?"

As I began to talk I noticed how fast James ate. I wondered if he was just hungry or greedy. I was almost embarrassed as we sat there and other people began hearing him smack and slurp his straw. So I decided to help him and talk a little louder.

"I am the baby of my family, technically, but I have an adopted little sister. My daddy is in prison, my grandmother lives with me and so do my new three cousins."

"Dang, y'all got a house full! That's cool because I am an only child and there is only me and my parents in our house. I would love to have a little brother or sister but they not trying to hear that."

Our conversation was continuous and we even laughed together. I didn't have that with Derrick and it seemed too natural. I was done with my milkshake and James had finished his meal so we decided to ride to the lake at the apartments behind Burger King.

"Come ride with me, we can leave your car here. We not gone be over there long."

The inside of his dad's Mercedes was clean and smelled like baby powder. I didn't want to ask him if he was rich but I kind of go that from the six-disc changer and navigation in the car.

"Have you ever been over here to this lake before? I come over here after practice sometimes and just sit and think."

"No, I've never been over here before but it is beautiful."

I was lying again. I realized that I had left my purse in his car with my beeper. I wasn't sure what time it was and I didn't want to miss my curfew.

"Do you know what time it is? I left my beeper in my purse in the car."

"Yeah, it's about 11:20. Are you gone get in trouble?"

"11:20? Hell yeah I'm gone get in trouble. Come on ... I gotta go!"

I knew I was dirt when I got home. Our talking and hugging was so special that time wasn't a factor. I enjoyed our time together but I realized that I may never see this dude again when Mama Betty finished with me.

"Oh shoot, my mama has beeped me three times since 9:15. Please hurry so I can get to my car."

I started to sweat under my arms even though the ride back to the car was only a few short minutes.

"Here you go Brooklyn. I am sorry for keeping you out so late but I really like you. Before you go can I have a kiss?"

"James, you tripping! I know I just said I have to go but here."

James full red lips grasped mine and we kissed. I felt his hand begin to rub my breasts and one go down between my legs.

"BEEP, BEEP, BEEP ..."

"Oh my God it's almost midnight! I have to go now! I will see you tomorrow at school, maybe."

I jumped out of his car and dropped my beeper on the ground. It broke in half but I grabbed it and put it in my purse. I felt like I was in the last quarter of the championship game. I didn't want to go home because I knew all hell was about to break loose.

"What am I going to say? I needed to get my lie together before I went in the house, I know I will tell her I got pulled over and the cop took me to some crazy police station and wouldn't let me leave. That sounds believable and I know she will believe me since I don't have a license."

I stood at the front door for about five minutes and finally I turned the door knob. Mama Betty was sitting on the couch waiting for me to come in the house. The look on her face told me to call 9-1-1 but I walked in and tried to hurry past her.

"Brooklyn, where in the hell have you been? I know you saw me paging you and you didn't even call back. What in the hell is wrong with you?"

"Mama, I got pulled over by the police and he wouldn't let me go."

Come on Brooklyn, drop some tears I thought.

"He searched my car and then put me in the back of his car. We drove over to a store near the highway and he made me sit there for about an hour. He went into the office next to the store and then he brought me in with him. They asked me all kinds of questions saying that my car matched the description of a car that was in a domestic violence call."

I couldn't tell if she believed me or not but she kept listening. I could see her nerves jumping and her veins popping out in her forehead.

"I asked them if I could call you because my beeper was going off but he made the comment that I was probably dealing. Then they told me no and since I didn't have a license they were going to run your name. They weren't sure who I was. Mama, I was so scared. They were all black men and one white man in the room.

I cried enough and then they let me go. As I was running out my beeper hit the ground and broke in half."

"Brooklyn, why didn't you get their names or badge numbers? Did anyone of them touch you in any kind of way? Did they try to hurt you," Mama Betty asked with a shaky voice?

"I didn't know to get that information and I was too scared because I thought I was going to jail. They didn't try anything even though one of the black men kept looking at me and winking."

I felt bad for lying but I couldn't dare tell her the truth knowing she would probably try to put me out again.

"If that car is going to get you in trouble I am going to take it and give it back to the dealership," Mama Betty yelled, "Thank God they let you go and didn't try something crazy like raping you or making you do something to them. Father, thank you for keeping my baby. I know you have your angels surrounding her and I praise you for it. Thank you Jesus!"

Mama Betty continued to pray as she left and went to her room.

Chapter twelve

The championship game was later that day and I hadn't missed a single practice. Sara and I had become real cool and she and I practiced in her apartments with some of the guys for the past couple of weeks.

"Brooklyn, you know scouts are going to be at the game tonight. Are you ready to show them what you got?"

I didn't really know they were coming tonight but I guess I had to wrap my mind around it and get ready. Coach told us that scouts from Texas Tech and Texas A&M called her and asked about me and Sara, but she didn't mention to us that they were coming.

"Well, I guess since they're coming I have to be ready. I will just do what I do and let my points do the talking." The grin on my face was wide and Sara burst out laughing while throwing me a hard pass.

"Dang, girl you on steroids or something? You throw like a dude. You almost knocked me down!"

"Naw, I've been lifting weights and trying to run at least a mile a day. But enough about that. What's going on with you and James?"

"Who told you about me and James?"

"Girl, the whole school know y'all seeing each other. He is the best on the baseball team and you are one of the best on our team so you know people are talking."

"Oh really, one of the best players on our team? Don't even front you know I am the best player on this team," I said while going in for a layup. "We just cool that's all."

"Whatever Brooklyn, I know you try to keep things real private but I know there is something special going on with you two. James has never talked to anyone since he's been here and now you are putting him on the map."

"BEEEEPPP, BEEEEPPP . . ." Coach blew her whistle.

"Come on let's get out of this gym before the boys' team come in here. What class do you have next," I asked Sara as we headed out of the gym?

"Chemistry, what about you?"

"I have honors English but I am going to head over to the field for a minute. If I hear that again I know where it came from, so mum's the word."

"I knew you two had something going . . . you can't hide that from me. Make sure you get back in the building before the bell rings, you know Mrs. Chong is crazy."

Sara was the coolest white chick I knew and I didn't mind telling her things because she really didn't have anyone to tell she pretty much stayed to herself.

I walked out the back door of the cafeteria to the baseball field and there I saw my baby pitching the ball to some scrubs.

As I walked to the gate, James saw me and came running, "Hey baby! What you doing out here?"

"Well, can I come see my man when I want too? How long you gone be out here? Don't you have another class before you go to work?"

"No, I will probably be out here until you get done with your classes. I am off today so I will be at the game tonight. Are you going to class?"

"Yeah, but I am feeling a little stressed and I need to release it before the game. Can you help me out?"

I knew that would make his smile light up and eyes buck. I wanted to hold off from giving James some but he was really nice to me and we got along really well. He understood me and we both loved sports. So why not? Plus I needed it.

"You ready now? I mean you sure?"

"Yep, at your place! Because you know there is a multitude of people at mine."

"That's cool! I will meet you at your car in about ten minutes. Is that cool?"

"Can you make it seven minutes? I really need to release some stress," I said as I winked and walked away.

"You got it baby girl!"

I had never been to James' house before that day but I could tell his people had some money. I walked in and looked at the pictures of babies and what looked like family members on his hallway wall. His mother was a beautiful lady with real light skin and long black hair. His father was a dark-skinned man with an afro. He looked like he was once a Black Panther, judging from many of his photos.

"Come on baby girl, my room is over here."

James looked at me with his puppy dog eyes which made me want to strip at the door. When I looked at him, my heart pounded and all the thoughts of us being together in crazy places flooded my mind.

"Come here baby girl and let me release some of that stress you got built up in you. Lie down and close your eyes. Just let me make you feel good, okay?"

I didn't want to say anything because I knew I would mess the moment up, so I laid down on his water bed and closed my eyes. All of sudden I felt my gym shorts coming down and his soft smooth hands rubbing my legs with one hand and pulling down his shorts with the other. Then in one smooth move he gapped them open . . .

I rolled over in the sheets and saw James lying naked next to me. I didn't know what time it was, but I knew my body felt good. I got out of the bed hoping his parents hadn't made it home and walked out the room to the restroom. I needed to shower before I went back to school for the game, so I pulled the shower curtain back and turned the water on high. I pulled my wild hair back and into a bun then stepped into the shower. The water added to the pleasure James gave me and my body shivered as I thought about our passionate moment.

"Baby girl, do you know what time it is," James asked busting through the door?

"No, what time is it?" I really lost myself in the shower and wasn't ready to get out.

"It's 4:30. Doesn't your game start at 5?"

"WHAT . . . yes it starts at 5! I can't miss this game or be late. There will be scouts there tonight to see me and Sara. I gotta go, now!"

I jumped out of the shower and ran back into James' bedroom. I hurried and threw my gym shorts on and one of his t-shirts over my sports bra. I grabbed my keys and flip flops and ran out of the door. I wanted to tell him how good he made me feel and give a long kiss but that became the last thing on my mind. I need to get to that school within ten minutes. Thankfully, I was only five minutes away.

"Brooklyn, what the hell is wrong with you? Where have you been? You almost missed the most important game of your life."

Sara was obviously pissed off as I walked into the locker room. I saw Coach shake her head in disgust.

"I went to James' house and fell asleep. I am so sorry . . . take the team through the drills for me. It will take me a few minutes to get dressed and then I will be right there."

Some of the other girls on the team were already on the court shooting and the other team was warming up as well. I saw how they looked at me, but I ignored them and tried to get my head focused.

"Excuse me Ms. Brooklyn, but where do you think you are going," Coach asked as I headed on to the court for the start of the game?

"I'm going out on the court, what's the problem?"

"I'm sorry, but you will not be starting today. You need to sit for a while and think about your actions and how they affect this team."

Was she serious? Not starting? I always started and the scouts were in the stands watching. What would they think if the star player of the team didn't start the game?

The whistle blew and we won the jump ball. Sara brought the ball up the court and passed it in to Meithy for an easy layup. The fans were on their feet and the game was on.

"Brooklyn, check in," Coach yelled to me where I sat near the end of the bench. It was near the second quarter and I needed to get some points and assists on the board. The ball was passed to me and I hit my first jumper. The crowd went wild. The coach from Taylor High called a time out. We jogged over to our bench for directions from Coach.

"Good job girls! Keep passing the ball and making them come after you. We are going zone instead of man-to-man. Look to Brooklyn to call the plays and yall do your thang!"

I had never heard Coach talk like that then put me out as the leader. That gave me more confidence and I knew then we had this championship game in the bag.

"Okay, right here and Cougars on three. One-Two-Three-COUGARS," we all yelled. As we headed back out to the court I scanned the crowd for James but I didn't see him anywhere.

"I thought he was coming. He told me he wouldn't miss this game for nothing," I thought as the ball was handed to me.

Ii dribbled up the court, looking into the crowd and before I knew it a stocky short girl stole the ball from me and scored.

"Oh no she didn't," I thought.

"Brooklyn, where are you? Get your head in the game," Sara yelled from the bench.

"My bad, my bad . . . okay y'all let's take this game home," I said as I ran back down the court. Meithy had the ball and was looking for me to pass it to, but just then I saw James walk in with some other girl. I got the ball and dribbled a little ways and got ready to pass it to Sara who had just come in the game.

"BLLRRPP . . . traveling," the referee called.

"Traveling? Come on man, I didn't travel. You blind or something?"

"BUURRPPP . . . TECH!"

"TECH? For what? Come on," I cried as I the referee headed over to the time clock table. I couldn't believe that jerk called a technical foul on me for making a remark. I looked back in the crowd and saw James hugged up with some girl at my game. What in the world was he doing? He's my man . . . tears began to roll down my face. As I went to the end of the bench, I noticed the scouts looking at me and whispering to each other.

"Jackie, go in for Brooklyn," Coach gently spoke as I sobbed. I couldn't stand that heifer. She wanted my position and now that I was messing up this was her opportunity to show off.

Coach kept me on the bench for the majority of the game. In the fourth quarter she asked me if I wanted to try it again and I declined after I saw James and the other girl leave together. The scouts must have left too. They were no longer sitting where I first saw them. This had turned into the worst day of my life.

Taylor High won the game 56 to 52 and they celebrated for what seemed like an eternity. I sat at the end of the bench with my head in my hands trying to understand why James showed up to my game with another girl. The team got in a line and went over to congratulate Taylor for a job well done. My face showed disgust as they received their trophy and the MVP for the game was named. I went back to the bench and covered my head with a towel.

"That should've been me," I thought as I gave the winner a half hand clap. I have to admit she was good, but had I been in the game should would not have been able to hold me, and that trophy would have been mine.

"Hey, Brooklyn! Good game . . . when you were out there you did the best you could," the new MVP stepped to me and said.

"How did this heifer know my name? Okay, Brooklyn she doesn't know you like that so ignore her and head into the locker room," my thoughts rang out.

"Let me tell you something little girl, you don't know me and if you ever step to me like that again I will break that trophy on top of your head!"

"Just like on the court, you all talk. Try to touch me and you will never use your fingers to play basketball or do anything else again."

This wench has lost her ever-loving mind. I snatched her trophy out of her hand and slammed it on the floor. Before I knew it she had grabbed the front of my jersey and tried to pull me to the ground.

"You better let me go . . . stand up and fight like a woman," I yelled. I took her head and put her in a head lock. My coach and her team ran over and tried to break us up.

"Brooklyn, what is your problem," my coach asked, "Are you mad and want to take your jealously out on another team?"

"Coach, you didn't see that girl come over here with her trophy and start talking mess to me? I'm a Rideaux and we don't take that off nobody!"

"I do not care what she said to you . . . you represent me and this school. You are not a hoodlum off the streets and you sure are not about to act like one here. Go into that locker room and clean out your locker. You are done . . . this team doesn't need an attitude like yours and we surely don't want any more of your drama."

"WHAT . . . I'm done? I am the best player on this team and y'all need me! This team won't get anywhere without me. You need me," I yelled as my face turned cherry red and eyes began to water again.

Coach looked at me, walked away shaking her head. I couldn't believe at that moment she had given up on me. I stood there in total astonishment as Jackie walked up to me with a smirk on her face.

"Sorry, Brooklyn. I guess you are no longer the best player on this team."

Everything in me wanted to haul off and slap the taste out of her mouth but I simply walked away . . . she was right.

Chapter thirteen

"Hey Big Mama, how are you doing?"

"Hey baby girl. You doing okay? I got a letter from your daddy today. He say you haven't written him in a real long time. Why not?"

"Uhmm, I was real busy with basketball and trying to fill out all those applications for college."

"Brooklyn that is no excuse. That is your father and he loves you very much. You need to let him know you love him too."

Big Mama never talked to me that way and I was almost offended. How could this man love me and he don't really even know me?

"Big Mama, I know. I will write him this weekend and mail it on Saturday. By the way, I am no longer on the basketball team. My coach kicked me off in our last game because I whipped this girl from the other school after we lost. So I am not sure if I am going to get a scholarship to go to college now or not."

"Brooklyn, what did I tell you about trying to fight and about your attitude? You know you needed that scholarship for school because your mama can't afford to pay out of her pocket and still take care of everybody. Didn't you tell me scouts may be at that game? Were they there when all this took place?"

Big Mama seemed worried that I would let this keep me from going to college. I knew she was big on education and I definitely wasn't going to let her down.

"No ma'am, they had already left but they did see the ref kick me out of the game. I don't care, Big Mama. I am not gone let a stupid basketball scholarship keep me from going to college. If

Mama Betty can't pay for it then I will get a job or a student loan. I am going to school; I gotta get away from this hell hole . . . I mean house."

"Watch your mouth Brooklyn Rideaux and as long as you have a plan then that's what will help you to succeed. By the way where is everybody? The house sounds quiet."

Our house was never quiet . . . especially on a Saturday morning. Everyone including Chrissy had to clean up. Mama Betty said she was old enough to pick up her toys now and she and Jazmine could straighten the knick knacks on the bookcase.

"They all in the front cleaning up. I came in to the bedroom to call you and let you know what happened with me and the coach before anyone else came and told you. I'm about to go back in the front and clean up. So I will talk to you later. Oh, please pray that I get accepted into at least three of my top five colleges. I should hear from them this week."

"Okay baby girl, I will talk to you soon, love you! Bye!"

As I hung up the phone I heard cussing and yelling coming from the living room. I immediately put the phone down and began straightening the bed as if I had been cleaning all along.

"You and your baby can get the hell out of my house. When you get to the point where nothing I say matters to you, then you need to go," Mama Betty yelled at Pearl. This was one of many fights those two had had in the last few weeks.

"Mama Betty, people around here walking on eggshells hoping not to set you off. Then when somebody mentions something to you, you blow a gasket. I am tired of that mess. I appreciate everything you do but I am tired of trying to please someone that can't be pleased."

Pearl was still in her pajamas with Jazmine on her hip. Her new glasses were beginning to slide off her face as she reached to push them up with the back of her free hand.

"If all y'all feel like Pearl then each and every one of you can get the hell out of my damn house. I am sick of breaking my back for some ungrateful people. I work two jobs every day and still have to come home to a dirty house? That shit is for the birds, like I said all of you can get to stepping. Where in the hell is Brooklyn? Brooklyn, get your ass out here too!"

Oh Lord, she was on a rampage and I was next. I heard her scream my name, but I didn't want her to know I heard her, so I grabbed my headphones off the dresser and quickly put them on. The batteries were out, but I jammed as if I was at the MTV Music Awards.

"Say my name, say my name," I sang as Mama Betty walked in the room. I was straightening the bed and bobbing my head when out of nowhere she walked over towards me and snatched my headphones off.

"Didn't you hear me calling your name, little girl? Bring your ass in this living room right now!"

"What did I do now? I am in here cleaning up like you asked me to and now you come in here cussing me out? Nobody can please you, I'm trying to do what you asked and stay out of trouble."

I hoped my teeth didn't get knocked out but I took the chance of siding with Pearl anyway.

Mama Betty turned around as she was heading out of the room, "Open your mouth again and watch what happens. Bring your tail in here NOW!"

"Betty these kids are trying to please you and make you happy. If they don't clean like you do you can't beat them into cleaning. Just get off of it and leave them alone," Madear yelled from her bed in the dining room.

"Madear, I work and take care of these kids . . . not you. So mind your goddamn business."

That was the first time I heard Mama Betty cuss directly at Madear. I waited and knew within a matter of minutes Madear would be in the living room on top of Mama Betty's head.

"Like I was saying, all of y'all can get your shit and get out if you can't do what I say. Better yet don't worry about it y'all can stay here and I will leave." I guess Mama Betty thought we were going to beg her not to leave at that moment but no one moved. It was almost kind of eerie because we didn't know the consequences of moving. Even Jazmine and Chrissy were still as Jazmine cried a silent cry.

"Man, I wish Michael was here," I whispered sitting next to Anthony on the floor, "Mama Betty would not be going off like this and for no apparent reason."

"Shut up Brooklyn, you are the reason why she is going off. Every since you got that car and met those little boys you been acting all fass and now she think everybody is acting up."

"Pearl, how in the hell can *you* call somebody fass, Mrs. Goody Two-Shoes? I am not the one sitting here with a baby on my lap and not in college. You know you had scholarships being thrown at you but oh no you wanted to gap your legs to whoever Jazmine's daddy is and now you have the nerve to talk about me?"

That raised the hairs on the back of Pearl's neck whenever me or anyone else talked about her having Jazmine. She knew she failed herself and whole lot of other people, but she was too prideful to let it show.

The low tone arguing between me and Pearl quickly came to an end when Mama Betty walked back in the living room with a duffle bag and her purse. She obviously was not joking when she said she was leaving and this time took steps to go.

"Betty, where are you going? You know damn well these kids and me cannot stay here and pay all these bills by ourselves. You need to slow down and try listening to what they are saying. They not trying to hurt you but rather let you know how they feel."

Madear had gotten up out of her bed and walked into the living room. She and Mama Betty had a cup of coffee together every morning and Madear was not about to let the tension in our house stop their tradition.

"Come in here for a minute and have a cup of coffee," Madear as she made her way to the coffee pot in the kitchen.

The aroma filled our little matchbox apartment and brought some much-needed peace. Mama Betty dropped her duffle bag on the floor at the small glass table in the kitchen and put her head in her hands. She had always been a strong woman and never really showed any signs of weakness. We all stayed out of the kitchen and went back to cleaning. We knew Madear was working her magic and we didn't want to get shot up again. I needed to enjoy that momentary peace.

I hadn't spoken to James in a few weeks since that night at the game and I hadn't planned on calling him ever again in life. My feelings were hurt, I was embarrassed and I was pissed. How could he come to the most important game of my life and bring another female?

"Beep, Beep . . . beep, beep . . . ," my pager went off in the middle of the night. I jumped up with beads of sweat popping off my neck and hoping the loud noise didn't wake Mama Betty. My eyes were blurry but I could still see the code, "1-4-3," it was him. He was using our code.

My heart began to beat faster as I wondered why this dude was calling me at 1 o'clock in the morning. In a way it made me feel good to know that I was on his mind in the middle of the night but what did he want?

"Did someone page Brooklyn," I whispered?

"You know who this is baby. I want to see you."

The voice on the other end of the phone came through deep and sexy. A smile came across my face as I squatted on the kitchen floor against the refrigerator.

"Do you know what time it is? I haven't heard from you since you embarrassed the hell out of me at the game and now you think you can just call me with this foolishness?"

"I am sorry about the game. I have been scared to call you because I wasn't sure what you would say or how you would react towards me. Brook, we have something really special and I don't want to let that go. We both leaving for college soon and I want to make sure we keep our bond."

His words were music to my ears; finally God sent my true love. I knew he was it because he woke up out of his sleep to check on me.

"Can you come over?"

"Come over where and when?" This dude was tripping but the thought of us lying together got my mind to plotting.

"Come over to my house. My parents are out of town so it will just be us tonight. I can have you back home before anyone gets up and realizes you're gone."

"Are you serious James? If I get caught trying to sneak out of this house I may have to come stay with you for real. My mama don't play that and she gets up early. Then my new cousins are sleep in the living room so they will hear me leave out the door and tell her."

The thought was exciting but how could I pull it off? This guy really loves me and, and he's willing to get back with me so I need to do my part.

"Listen, Brook. I will be waiting outside your apartments in ten minutes. Come to the front so I won't have to go through the gate. If you love me and really want us to work you will find a way out. Okay, ten minutes."

The sound of the dial tone pierced my ears and was loud enough to make Johnathan move. I gently hung the phone back on the receiver near the stove.

"Okay, Brooklyn. What are you going to do? He said ten minutes," I thought. My purse and shoes were already in the living room so I could quickly grab them and leave out the front door. Or I could leave out the patio door from the dining room but Madear would wake up and loud talk me. Before I knew it, I was out the front door and running down the sidewalk. It took me about fifteen minutes to get out the house but I figured if he really wanted to see me he would wait.

"James," I yelled as he was preparing to pull off, "where are you going?"

I ran up to his dad's car and knocked on the window. I was out of breath from running so fast and my hands were shaking from the cold air outside.

"Get in baby girl, its cold out there and you didn't even get your coat."

"You better be lucky I was able to get my shoes and my purse."

"I'm glad you came out baby girl that means so much to me."

"Well, I guess . . . I just hope you don't try to pull a stunt like this again. I mean my new cousins almost woke up and if Mama Betty would've gotten up then my ass would have been grass."

James pulled off as soon as my butt reached the seat and I barely had an opportunity to close the door. I could see his gorgeous smile out the corner of my eyes and I could tell he was really in love with me. I no longer cared about that other females he was with because I knew it was all about me. I mean, look, this dude leaving his house in the middle of the night to come and see about me. Now that is love.

"Come on Brook! We need to get out this cold. Come on, dammit!"

"Dang, what is wrong with you? I am coming. I needed to get my purse and your coat since it's raining now."

"Just hurry up," James said as he turned to walk in the front door. His house was like a mansion to me and I couldn't understand why they needed all those rooms when it was only three people in the whole house. I dropped my purse on the floor near the door and took off my shoes. The house smelled like pumpkins and cinnamon and the living room was cleaner than a hospital.

"Come in here baby. I want to show you something," James yelled from his bedroom.

I walked in slowly since the sleep was beginning to come down hard on me and it was dark in the hallway.

"Okay, I am tired and ready to go to sleep," I said as I walked in the door.

There on the bed James laid butt naked except for his gold teeth.

"What in the hell are you doing? I am trying to go to sleep. You need to put your clothes back on and get ready to go to sleep. I thought you just wanted to hold me?"

I was just about to be pissed off when James pulled out a gun from under his pillow.

"You better get over here and please me, bitch! Did you think I brought your ass all the way over here to go to sleep? Get on your knees now and get to work!"

What in the hell was wrong with him? Tears began to well up in my eyes as I headed to the floor. My legs and arms began to shake uncontrollably as fear filled my body. Thoughts of escape began to run through my head and I knew I had to get away or this man would kill me. Where in the world did he get that gun and why was he pointing it at me? The cold steel rested on my head and I was too afraid to move. I did everything James asked without saying a word, yet I cried the entire time.

"Go in the bathroom and wash your mouth out with some Listerine and wash your face. I don't want you getting in my car smelling like that."

My face was wet with tears and my eyes swollen from the constant crying. I slowly walked into the bathroom closest to the living room and closed the door behind me. The fact that a gun rested on my head with threats of death made me realize that I had to do whatever he said or I may not see another day.

"Okay, Brooklyn. This is your time to get out of here before he comes back and tries something else," I told myself while peeking out the door. I didn't have my shoes or my purse but I didn't care. I cut the light off and opened the door. The lights in the hall were still off and I could hear James in the room snoring. I tiptoed into the living, praying every time I took a step.

"Lord, please get me out of this house without him waking up and killing me," I whispered.

As I found my shoes and purse in the dark I heard James moving in the room.

"Oh Lord," I cried, "Please do not let him come out of that room."

I quickly grabbed my shoes and my purse. I wasn't sure how I was going to get home but I knew I had to get out as fast as I could. I tiptoed over to the door and unlocked as quiet as I could.

"Brooklyn, get your ass in here! What are you doing in there," James called as he jumped out of the bed?

"Oh Lord, please help me," I whispered as I ducked down by the front door to put on my shoes, "he is going to kill me!"

"Brooklyn, where are you?"

As tears flooded my face, a burst of courage filled my bones and I darted out the front door. Running as fast as I could, I felt one of my shoes come off but I couldn't stop.

"You better not let me catch you in the streets bitch," James yelled from his doorway.

I ran and ran. I wouldn't stop until I reached my apartment complex or somewhere near it, out of his sight. I darted through houses and flew down side streets. I was soaking wet from sweat and dew and could barely see where I ended up. I stopped to catch my breath and when I looked up my apartments were in plain view.

"Lord, I am so sorry. Please let me get into the house without anyone knowing I was gone."

I reached my apartment complex and remembered that the patio door was always unlocked and I should be able to sneak back in to the house. I looked down at my feet and both shoes were missing. My toes were bloody and swollen from running on anything that was in my way. I gently pulled the sliding door open and moved the vertical blinds to the side. My heart relaxed its fast beating as I shut the sliding door making sure I locked it tight.

"Excuse me! Where in the world do you think you're going?"

Madear stood at the corner adjacent from the restroom with her hand on one hip. I stood quiet not knowing what to say but hoping she would have mercy on me.

"You better hurry up and get in this house. Don't let me ever see you sneaking and creeping again. Ain't nothing out there this late but hoes and pimps . . . and you **ain't** one of them."

Chapter fourteen

S ince my life had been spared again going to college was
at the top of my list. Being accepted into a majority white
university was a major accomplishment for anyone that was a
minority but especially if you were in my family. The Rideaux's
were known as born hustlers. Very few went to college and some
went but never stayed or never went back. Mike was the first male
in our family to go to college. I believed Mike wanted to make a
better life for himself and staying around the house was not going
to do it for him. He was very ambitious and anything he wanted
he worked hard and got it. I loved that about my brother and I
was determined to follow in his footsteps.

"May I speak to Mike?" I could barely keep my composure
when asking his roommate for him that night.

"Hey Brooklyn, this BJ. Mike went to take the trash out. He
should be headed back in a second. Do you wanna hold on or call
back?"

"I will hold," I said full of excitement.

"What are you so happy about? I can tell you are trying to
keep from laughing! Did y'all win the championship game?"

My smile turned into a frown and I dropped the phone to the
floor. I didn't want to talk about the game, think about that game,
or revisit that night.

"Naw, I just need to tell him something. Is he back yet?"

"Yeah, here comes in the door now, hold on a minute. Mike . . .
Brook is on the phone for you."

BJ was just as big as his named sounded. He stood about
6-foot-5 and looked like he weighed at least 300 pounds. When I

first saw him I thought he was related to Shaq or Michael Jordan. Mike told me that even though he was as big as all get out he was really a punk. Some of the frat boys at their college wanted BJ to pledge their fraternity but he refused because he said he didn't want to be hit on.

"Hey Brook, what's up baby girl?"

"Hey Mike! Guess what?"

"What?" Mike sounded uninterested in my excitement so I decided to stop beating around the bush and give him the news.

"I got a letter today from A&M!"

"Okay, and what did they say? Did you show it to Mama Betty yet?"

"No, I wanted to call you first. I was a little scared to open it because I don't know if they turned me down, but right about now I need to know what the deal is."

"Okay, so go ahead and open it. Let's see what it says."

I took my time and slid my finger under the sealed flap on the envelope. As I pulled out the folded letter my heart began to race and my hands started to shake.

"Dear Ms. Rideaux, Thank you for your recent application to Texas A&M University. We received a high volume of impressive applications this year. This made admissions decisions even more difficult, and unfortunately we will be unable to offer you a space in this year's incoming class. I would encourage you to attend a community college or other school of your choice in the fall, and you would be more than welcome to reapply as a transfer student next year. I wish you the best of luck in your future endeavors."

Best regards, David Salberry, Admissions Director

As I read the letter the words seemed to jump off the page and slap me in the face. I couldn't believe the school that was my top choice turned me down.

"Baby girl? Are you okay?"

"Yeah, I'm good. I just don't understand it. I am in the top 25 percent of the class and my SAT and ACT scores were great. I took honor classes for college credit and I did a lot of community service. Why didn't they choose me?"

"Sometimes Brook they get so many applicants that they must go with the ones that are at the top. Somebody could've had scores a little higher than yours. And sometimes it's about who you know. If a kid had parents to attend there even if their scores weren't all that good they would accept an alumni's child before they accept someone off the street. Welcome to the real world, baby girl."

I didn't want to believe that the system was jacked up like that. I worked hard all my four years of high school to get into the best colleges when the time came and I didn't get accepted because some kid's parent went to college there and mine didn't.

"Mike, I'm about to go. I will talk to you later okay? Oh, tell Crystal I said hello and that I made up my mind. She will know what I am talking about. Talk to you later."

I hung up the phone and laid down on the sofa. Graduation was only two weeks away and I didn't know what school I was going to attend. I sent out applications for the best schools in Texas but I hadn't received any acceptance letters. I refuse to sit around here and be a bum like those people from the ward. Shoot, if Mike and Pete can go and do something with their lives then so can I.

"Brooklyn, let's go! I don't want to be late for the orientation. Did you put everything in the van? I can't make this trip twice today so you better have everything you need," Mama Betty yelled as she walked out the door. Her excitement filled the house but I couldn't tell if she was happy to get me out of the house or to see me go to college. Mike and Pete had both gone to school and were doing real good. Johnathan and Anthony were about to start the police academy and she knew they would be out soon. Pearl and Jazmine were still there along with Madear so her food budget was getting smaller and her cigarette butts were fewer.

"I have everything in the van. I am trying to say bye to Jazmine and Chrissy," I yelled back to the front room from the bedroom.

"You girls are the ladies of the house now. I will call and check on you sometimes to make sure you are doing your best in school. Remember, we are Rideaux's so we get things done and we don't settle for less. Y'all mind Mama Betty and Pearl. Help Mama Betty with Madear and keep doing your best in school."

Tears began to flow out of Chrissy's eyes as the two sat on Big Mama's bed. I sat down between them and put my arm around them both.

"Listen, I am going to miss y'all but I'm just down the street so I can come and see you on the weekends sometimes. Jazmine, you have to help take care of Chrissy if someone bothers her at school, you better get in their ass. Don't let anyone push her around. I am about to go but when I get to Prairie View and get my stuff settled in I will call y'all, okay?"

The girls wiped their faces and managed to pull out a smile. Chrissy stood up and kissed me on the cheek. Jazmine stood up and walked out of the room.

"Brooklyn, hurry up! It's late!"

I hugged Chrissy one more time and hurried out to the front. I gave Madear a hug and hit Pearl upside her head.

"Bye y'all, I'm going to be all I can be! Wish me luck!"

"Shut up Brooklyn and get out of here before you be all you can be right here in this apartment," Pearl said.

"Hey has anyone heard from Big Mama? She was supposed to ride down there with us."

"Here I am baby girl! It took me a little longer cuz you know I don't ride the freeway. Are you ready?"

Big Mama walked up to the open front door as I turned to ask about her. She wore one of Tommy Boy's baseball caps tipped to the side. Her oversized black and gold shades brought out her blonde curly wig under her hat.

"Dang, Big Mama! You shole looking phat, you got a date or something?"

"Naw, baby! You know I have to look my best when I'm rolling with you! Cuz you know we are both the BOMB!"

"Well, bye everybody! I love y'all and just know I'm coming back as a STAR-RA!"

∞

"Hey, you my roommate?" a girl with jet black hair and red glasses asked me as she walked into the dorm room where I was putting my things away.

"Uhmm, I guess if you are here in B6. My name is Brooklyn, what is your name?" I put my bag of shoes down and turned to shake her hand.

"I'm Tamara but you can call me Tammy. Where you from?"

"Originally, I was born in Louisiana but I was raised in Fifth Ward. What about you, where are you from?"

Tammy almost looked like she was from some part of Africa. Her skin was dark and her face was very bumpy. The only thing she had going for herself was her pretty smile that lit up the room.

"I'm from Chicago. My people just moved down here so I decided to come to school in the town where my people lived."

"So you are what they call a LOCAL?"

"Hell nah, like I said I am not from here. I just moved here because my dad is a professor here and the school bought us a house. I'm a Chi-town beauty, baby!"

We both laughed and boy was I glad. I thought what I said had offended her in some way but obviously not.

"I hope you don't mind but I took the bed by the door. If anything or if anybody starts trippin I need to be the first one out," I told Tammy as I hung up my clothes in my closet.

The room was considered a suite because it had three twin beds, three closets and one restroom that had to be shared with three other suite mates on the opposite side. I was really cool with the set-up because I was use to having a lot of people use one restroom anyway.

I prayed that the other three girls on the opposite side were clean and didn't have anything that we would catch.

"So Tammy, do you know who our other roommate is going to be? I mean, it doesn't matter cause I usually get along with anyone but I was just wondering if you had the heads up since your dad is a professor here."

"Girl, this is my first time over to this dorm. I came up here when we first moved to Prairie View but I only went to his office. You are the first person I have met so whoever she is I hope it's all good."

Just as Tammy finished her sentence a knock came on the door.

"I guess we are about to find out," I said as I dropped my shoes to the floor and headed to open the door.

"Hi, is this room B6? My name is Asha and they said I am supposed to be in here."

Asha was a very beautiful girl with long black hair. She stood about 5'10 and wore at least three inch heels. I felt like I was in the presence of super model and I found myself starring in awe.

"Brooklyn, move out the way and let the girl in . . . dang," Tammy said walking toward the door. She pushed me back and walked over to Asha and gave her a hug like they were ace boon koons. I stepped back and wondered why I didn't get that type of greeting. A hint of jealousy tried to pop up but I played it off and kept smiling.

"Come on in," I said, "hope you don't mind the middle bed and closet. Hey are you girls' hungry? I am starving; maybe we can go and get something to eat."

"That's cool with me but I think everything on campus is closed. I don't have a car so we might have to order something or eat some of these noodles my mama packed," Tammy said.

"Yeah, I don't have a car either," Asha said.

"No worries, I have a car and yall can just ride with me." That really made me feel important to know that none of my roommates had a car and they would depend on me to take them places at times.

"What's around here anyway? This place looks like a little hick town I've seen on television." With Tammy being from Chicago I guess the entire state of Texas seemed country to her. Her smart remarks were beginning to get on my nerves and I was hoping no one would catch on to my aggravation.

"I think I saw a Taco Bell and KFC on the highway as we drove onto the campus. It's about five minutes up the highway but that should be cool. Yall wanna go?"

"Sounds good to me," Asha said as she pulled her bag to the middle bed, "I will put these things up when we get back."

"Let's ride DIVAS," Tammy yelled as she walked out the door.

I grabbed my purse out the closet and placed my lock on the door hoping there were no thieves in the building.

"Lord, please help me to deal with this girl and not wring her neck," I silently prayed as I walked out behind her and Asha.

"Uhmm, excuse me ladies but where do you all think you are going? You need to sign out and leave your contact number here at the desk in case someone needs to get in touch with one of you," Greg the resident assistant called out from the front desk.

"Leave our number? Why we need to leave our number? We are going down the street to get something to eat and we will be right back!"

I could then tell Tammy was going to be a hot head who didn't take no mess. I wondered was everyone from Chicago like her and if so Lord help me if I ever move there.

"Young lady, I don't make the rules I just enforce them. By the way I am Greg your RA. If you ever have any problems or need anything I am here to help. I just have one request. Please do not let me catch you in the first or second floor rooms. Those rooms are for the boys and not the girls."

Uhmm, did I miss something? This dorm is co-ed? No one told me anything about that and I bet Mama Betty didn't know about it either.

"Ok, sir. Here is my cell number. I am driving so you can call this number if you need us for anything. Where do we sign out?"

I was hungry and didn't have time for all the extra drama. As we were headed out the dorm three tall, dark and handsome guys walked in with what seemed to be football jerseys. All three guys turned and nearly broke their necks looking at Asha and Tammy. Both girls had the looks, body and beautiful smiles. What about me?

"Did yall see those stallions," Tammy asked while getting in the backseat of my Hyundai Excel, "I know I can take that real tall one and make him my baby daddy!"

Asha laughed as she got in the front seat since her legs were so long.

"Girl, where in the world did you get this car with no bumper? I mean dang . . . you not embarrassed to roll around here like this?"

Tammy had just tapped dance on my last nerve and I was about ready to put her in check!

"No ma'am I am not embarrassed because half of yall fools around here aint riding in nothing. I can come and go as I please without having to bomb a ride."

The veins were popping out in my forehead and I was at my wits end with this chic who I barely knew.

"Brooklyn," Asha called after I put Tammy in her place.

"WHAT!" I yelled.

"You can't come and go as you please because you gotta sign out and get permission from Greg to do anything," she reminded me oh so gently.

I looked at Tammy through my rearview mirror and then over to Asha. What seemed to be two roommates already experiencing drama turned into a hilarious outburst of smiles and high fives. This year was going to be good and I was making sure of that. No distractions . . . I am about to be a STAR-RA!

"Yall wanna go through the drive-thru or you wanna go inside?"

"Let's go inside! There might be some cute guys in there that we can flirt with and get to buy our food," Tammy said.

"Shoot, that sounds good to me," Asha piggy backed off Tammy.

We all got out of the car and walked inside. I noticed that neither one of the girls brought a wallet or purse inside with them.

"I sure hope they have some money in their pockets because I am not about to foot the bill for all of them," I thought.

"Asha, here is five dollars. Can you get me a number one with a strawberry soda? I am going to wash my hands."

"A soda? What is that?"

"Asha, where are you from," I made it a point to get the 4-1-1 on people when I first met them but I forgot to ask Asha because of my overbearing roommate.

"I am from Philly. I came down here because my aunt came to this school. She pledged here and wanted me to be sure I came and followed in her footsteps."

"Ok, so a soda down here in Texas is a soft drink," I said sarcastically.

"Oh, a pop! I gotcha mama, go ahead I'll get it."

I walked to the back of KFC and stopped to tie my shoes. For some reason I felt like I was in elementary and began to giggle to myself.

"Do you always laugh at yourself," a deep voice came and stood in front of me?

I raised my head to see a beautiful specimen standing with his hands in his pockets. He looked to be Hispanic but I was sure there were not many if any Hispanics out in this country town.

"No, I do not," I said smiling as I stood up.

"You looked like you were having a good conversation with yourself. If you do that's ok I just need to know before I ask you for your number."

This guy was very bold and very direct. I thought he was gorgeous but I didn't know him like that to just give him my number. As I stood in front of him I could smell a fragrance that was so familiar. Derrick, I thought. It was the same cologne that drove me wild with Derrick and now this strange but sexy man was wearing it.

"I am sorry, my name is Sam. What is your name?"

"Hey Sam, I am Brooklyn but you can call me Brook."

"Does everyone get that privilege or am I special?"

"Everyone is special in God's eyes," I said sarcastically as I began to walk away. His brown puppy dog eyes followed me behind him and looked me up and down.

"Hey, Ms. Brook where are you going?"

"To the restroom to wash my hands before I eat. You wanna come?"

"Do you always have such a smart mouth," Sam asked with wide grin?

"It depends on who I am talking too!"

"Well Ms. Brooklyn, go and wash your hands. I will be right here when you get done. I want to know more about that smart mouth of yours."

I wanted to ask him how did he want to get to know more about it but I had to be a lady at least for now. I stood at the sink for a minute looking at myself in the mirror.

"You have to leave your past in the past. No one knows what you have been through unless you tell them."

That audible voice came piercing through my thoughts as if someone was there with me. The memories of my past haunted me often and kept me in fear of meeting a man like James again. For the past year I had stayed to myself and wanted no dealings with any guys anymore but this Sam guy seemed different.

"Hey, I told you I was going to be here when you came out. Did you have to do the #2 or something?"

"Boy, you are crazy! No I sure did not thank you! So do you go to PV too?"

"Yes, I am a junior in the psychology department. I take it that you go there as well but it is funny that I have never run into you before."

"This is my first year," I looked over at Asha and Tammy who had already sat down to eat.

"Oh, fresh meat I mean freshman! So what is your major?"

As my stomach began to growl, "I am an education major but I am going to have to let you go now because my stomach is in my back and I need to eat." I smiled as our eyes met and stayed glued to each other.

"That's cool, I understand. But can we continue this conversation later?"

I wanted to write my number down and give it to him but I had to stick to the game.

"Sure, give me your number and I will call you later," I said with one hand on my hip and the other hand held out waiting for the number.

"That's cute Ms. Brooklyn! Here it is," he said as he handed me what seemed to be a business card.

"So, you are an RA as well. Now, that's cute . . . ," I said as I walked away smiling.

Chapter fifteen

Being away from home was something I could definitely get used to, but I must admit that I missed Mama Betty, the girls and even my new cousins. For some strange reason when my guidance counselor set my classes up, she gave me two 8 a.m. classes. That meant I was up at six in the morning when everyone else was sound asleep.

"Hey Mama Betty, are you up yet?" I tried to remember to call home often and check on everyone.

"Hey, Brook. You doing okay? I am about to head out the door. What's wrong, you sound like something is bothering you."

"You remember when I used to wake up and just sit up in the middle of the night because my legs wouldn't stop tingling? Well, that is happening again and I can't sleep. Mama, it hurts," I softly cried to her so no one else would hear me.

"Brook, did you take some Tylenol like you normally do?"

"Yes ma'am. It just won't go away. Its time for me to get up anyway and go to class but I really haven't been able to sleep. Is everybody doing alright? How is Chrissy?"

"Yeah, everybody is good. Madear is a little sick but she is okay. Chrissy is in the hospital and that's where I am about to go in a minute. She had a seizure in her sleep day before yesterday and the doctors said it caused a mini stroke."

"Mama Betty, I am on my way home," I told her as I heard her hurt and pain through the phone.

"I don't think so Brooklyn. I am not paying for you to go to college and then run home every time something happens here. Remember you have to get it so these girls around here can see there is hope. Chrissy is going to be fine and Madear will too. Pearl is here and she is helping me out a lot. Brook, promise me that you will not come back home. I am depending on you to make life better for you and us."

Mama Betty and I didn't have many conversations like these so I took her words and allowed them to become my daily determination.

"I love you Mama Betty. I am about to get a work study job and I will send you some money when I get paid. I don't have classes on Friday except that one 8 o'clock class so I will be there this weekend. Tell Chrissy I love her and give Madear a kiss for me. I will call you later, okay?"

Mama Betty held the phone without saying anything. I didn't want to interrupt her thoughts because I could tell she was trying to get something out.

"Okay, Brooklyn. Talk to you later. Oh, I love you too."

Sam and I began to hang out more often and our relationship was starting to really take off. The conversations, the laughs and nights we shared together really had me falling hard for him. He was definitely different from Derrick. Sam wasn't trying to be a playa and he showed me that he loved me and didn't just talk about it. I wanted to tell Mama Betty about him but I knew she would just tell me to keep my head in my books and not worry about any boys. When Sam asked me to be his girlfriend I was totally shocked. I thought we were just friends with benefits but I guess he wanted more of me. I wanted to tell someone that really knew me . . . that understood me but who? Walking to class was never a problem for me even though I had a car. I actually enjoyed walking in the beautiful weather and seeing everyone dressed to impress on campus.

"You are their hope, the one to see your family through. Don't give up or let your past determine your future. Stay focused."

An audible voice that seemed to speak more often now came through piercing my thoughts again.

"I am the hope," I said to myself. "I am the baby of the family. I am the one that never got to really spend time with Tommy Boy and the one that tried to take my life. I can't possibly be the one that you chose."

I didn't know who I was talking back to in my head but the conversation continued all the way to the Delco building.

"Hey Brook, where you going so early in the morning," Greg called out as I reached the steps of the education building?

"I have an 8 o'clock class. Where are you going so early? Don't you have some lives to ruin with all your rules in the dorm?"

Greg was a cool guy even though I gave him a hard time. There were many times when I was hungry in the dorm and he would make sure to get me something to eat. I think there were some underlying feelings, but I knew he had a girlfriend and I had a boyfriend.

"Hahaha, Brooklyn! I have an 8 o'clock class as well. Plus I like the early morning weather. It helps me think and this is my time to talk to God. I get a lot from Him about my journey and the vision He has for my life," he smiled as we walked into the building.

"How do you know its God talking to you and you not talking to yourself?"

"I know because of what He tells me to do and when I do what he tells me to do things turn out better for me. I use to think I was talking to myself but I asked Him to make His voice distinctive. Now it's so audible and easily recognizable. It even pierces my right through my thoughts sometimes."

I dropped my books to the floor when Greg explained how he knew it was God talking to him. I couldn't believe that the very same experience he had I also had and the voice I heard was just as clear as Greg's voice.

"Wow, okay. Well I have to get into class. I will talk to you later."

"Brooklyn, just ask Him to make it distinctive to you so you will know for sure that it's Him, see you later," Greg said as he walked down the empty hall.

As I sat in class listening to my boring English teacher read a book that we could read for ourselves I thought about what Greg said.

"I will make my voice clear and you will know its Me."

"It was Him, it is God. Why do you want to talk to me? I am nothing and remember I tried to take my life not long ago. They said that is the ultimate sin because you can't ask for forgiveness. So why do you want to talk to me?"

"Who are they? I am God and there is no one like me. I've been talking to you but you didn't listen. Do you remember that day at Mike's musical and you were on the ground asking for forgiveness? Well, I heard you and that is when I started talking to you because you accepted my free gift to you."

"Brooklyn, baby where are you going," Sam asked as I walked down the sidewalk towards my dorm, "I thought we were going to look at apartments today?"

"Oh, hey baby! I am sorry. I was in a daze," I said as I turned around and gave him a hug.

"You sure were in a daze. Are you hungry? I know you didn't eat breakfast. We can go over to Alumni and eat if you want too."

"That's cool. I do want one of Alumni's famous waffles this morning," I said smiling.

Sam was known on campus as being one of the best guards on the basketball team, so no matter where we went in PV, someone knew him. As I was talking I looked around and Sam had walked away and was dabbing some other team members up and laughing. Their purple and gold windbreakers stood out in the crowd of people and they had everyone's attention. I went over to cook my waffle and I saw Asha and Tammy walk in.

"Hey, girl! What you doing in here so early," Tammy asked?

I looked at her and noticed something different. Her outfit was cute but it looked very familiar. Now I knew I wasn't crazy but that heifer had my shirt and shoes on like I wouldn't notice. Asha recognized that I noticed my clothes on Tammy and she gave me a shrug and slight smile.

"Tammy, are those my shoes and my shirt you got on," I asked as I placed my plate down on the table? I looked at the breakfast line and saw Sam watching me like a hawk. I gave him a real fake smile because I felt the tension rising in my nerves.

"Girl, I know you ain't trippin over this little raggedy shirt and played-out shoes. I saw it in your closet and just needed something quick to put on," Tammy played down the fact that she didn't ask me to wear my clothes.

"Tammy, do you have my cell number? Why didn't you call and ask me if you could borrow something? For it to be so raggedy you are shole wearing it like it's yours."

I tried to keep my cool and act civilized but this heifer was trying to get crunk with me in Alumni. Asha grabbed her tray and moved over to the table near the wall. She obviously felt the tension rising and knew that the mess was about to hit the fan.

"Listen, if I need to borrow something then I will. Don't try to check me in this place; you on the verge of getting cursed out."

Everything in me said "Brooklyn walk away," including my audible voice, but there was no way in hell this girl was going to clown me in front of hundreds of people that seemed to have their focus on us. I picked up my tray and turned around to get my now burnt waffle.

"That's what I thought," Tammy giggled to the girl standing behind me waiting on the waffle machine.

"SLLLAAAPPP . . . ," I took my tray and slapped Tammy upside the head. I jumped over the fallen chairs and got on top of her and punched her face until my hands hurt. Everyone yelled and screamed but no one tried to get me off of her. I kept punching even as I began to cry but I couldn't stop. She tried to get up off the ground but I sat on her and wouldn't let her move. Out of nowhere I was pulled up by my jacket and drug out of the cafeteria.

"What in the hell is wrong with you," Sam asked as he shoved me up against the wall outside of Alumni?

"Don't you know you will go to jail? If that girl is hurt bad Brooklyn she can press charges on you. What happened?"

"Sam," I said crying, "that bitch disrespected me and she got my clothes on. I told her all she had to do was call me and ask if she could wear them. Then she tried to get crunk with me in front of all those people. I am a Rideaux and you don't ever try to punk us especially in front of people!"

I sat down on the bench outside and tried to fix my hair. As Sam and I sat there, I saw her dad, the professor, walking up into Alumni Hall. He waved at me as he talked to one of his colleagues.

"Oh shit," I whispered to Sam, "that is Tammy daddy. Come on let's go!"

"Do you think she still in there? I hope she got herself up and got out because you whipped the hell out of her. Y'all live together Brooklyn, what are you going to do when you go home?"

"Can I stay with you for a little while until this flies over? You know this will be in the 20 questions and everyone on campus will be talking about it. I need to lay low for a minute."

"That's cool . . . come on let's go get you cleaned up."

My first year went by so fast and I was already back for another try at this college thing.

"Hey Mike, what you doing?"

"Hey Brook, how was it? Isn't it the best feeling in the world to know you have completed a full year of college and now you already back?"

"Yeah, it feels good. I am just glad I am back. Mama Betty was getting on my nerves about having a curfew while I'm home and not going to certain places. She never did that to you Mike when you came home."

"Brooklyn, you have to understand that you are still the baby. I am a man and you are a girl. Mama is going to be like that with you even when you get married and grow old. You just better be lucky Tommy Boy ain't there because it would be worse. By the way have you heard from him lately?"

Tommy Boy was up for parole and the rumor was he could be home any day. I was a little excited but for me I didn't know what was missing. I knew we talked through letters and mail but I didn't really know him so I wasn't too enthused about him coming home

"Naw, they say he up for parole and he sent some letters to the house but I never really read them. They all say the same thing, Mike, I know he loves me but we never had a relationship so I just put them up somewhere."

"Brook, all I can say is that's your daddy. You have to respect him," Mike turned serious, so I didn't say anything else. I held the phone until Mike broke the silence.

"Listen Brook I will talk to you later, okay. I love you baby girl."

"You too . . . bye," I hung up the phone and walked into the bathroom.

"He really does know you and love you, Brooklyn," the audible voice came back. I hadn't heard it in a while and I was surprised that it came through so clear. As I sat in the bathroom, my place of refuge in our house, my hands and legs began to tingle. I went to the medicine cabinet and got out two Tylenols and filled the cup on the counter with water. The pills were difficult to take as they always are because of the time I tried to take my life. All

those pills made me sick and what they did to me in the hospital never left my memory.

"Let the past be the past and move toward the prize I have in store for you," that audible voice came piercing through again.

I closed my eyes and prayed, "Lord, please take this pain away."

Chapter sixteen

Asha and I were still roommates our sophomore year in the new apartments the campus built. I felt a little grown now that I had my own place and was out of the dorms. Sam had moved in with one of his teammates in a duplex off campus and he loved it. A little part of me worried about it because of all the girls that I knew were interested in him that would probably pop up at his house. I didn't want him to know that I was a little jealous, so I made sure he was with me as much as possible. Tammy had moved back home with her parents and was attending Blinn College. I felt a little bad about Tammy leaving since it was mostly my fault. I hoped we would have a relationship like me and Asha. For some reason since that fight she and I got a lot closer and realized we had a lot in common.

"Asha, are you going to the rush?"

"Girl, you know I will be there. Both of them are having rushes so which one are you going too," she said sarcastically.

"You already know that it aint the one you going to!"

We both smiled and looked at each other with a distinct look. Asha was the type of girl that loved how she looked but she was cool and down to earth once you got to know her. Our apartment was a two bedroom with a kitchen that separated our bedrooms. It was cool because there would be nights that Sam would stay over and we needed our privacy. Asha didn't have a boyfriend that I knew about. Most of the Kappa's were trying to talk to her but she tried to keep her head in the books. Her goal was to be a pediatrician and she knew that she couldn't mess up her grades by letting boys get in her head.

"Asha, I am so pissed at Sam. He came over here last night and left in the middle of the night because we got into an argument. Did you hear us?"

"No ma'am. You know when I am sleep I am sleep. What were y'all fussing about now?"

Dang, do we fight that much? I guess it didn't mean anything to Asha to hear about another argument?

"That damn cell phone of his rings in the middle of the night and he swears up and down that he doesn't know who it is. I am not stupid. It's probably his ex-girlfriend trying to find out where he is. I really want to whip that heifer since she can't seem to let him go and move on."

"Brook, why do you think you have to whip her? Can't he just tell her to step off? Hey come over here in my room and let's smoke a black. It will relax you honey."

For Asha to be so preppy and pretty she would pull out a black and mild in a heartbeat and start smoking. I think I liked that about her; she was just real like that. I went in her room and plopped down on the bed. I was almost in tears because I was so mad at Sam and how he hadn't called me all day to apologize.

"Yeah, he does need to get that trick in check before I do," I went back to our conversation, "I mean I am not the one to fight over boys. Do you think I should call him?"

"Do you love him Brook?" Asha asked as she exhaled smoke from her nostrils.

I wasn't sure if I loved him or not. I knew that he was a good guy with his head on straight headed for an awesome life and great career. Sam's major changed to chemical engineering and he always talked about owning his own chemical plant someday. He was extremely smart and talented on the court too.

"I don't know . . . I guess I do. Shit, Asha I think I am in love with this dude," I said as I put my head in her pillow.

"Now I'm confused. Is that a bad thing? I thought falling in love was something beautiful and full of excitement. I've never felt that way about a guy before and I can't wait to experience it for the first time, Asha said full some sort of anticipation.

"Okay, missy come back from lala land into reality. Falling in love is wonderful when it's effortless. We fight and argue a lot. I keep saying that I don't want to have sex with him because of my faith but then I turn around and do it anyway. Then I feel guilty and start crying right after and he then feels guilty."

"Yeah, that's a bit much Brook. You need to either do it or not. Stop playing with his head."

Just then a knock came on the door. We hurried and put out our black and mild's and sprayed the room with Lysol.

"Who is it," I asked while Asha fumigated her room?

"It's me Brook, can I come in?" Sam must've fell and bumped his head for showing up at my apartment without calling.

"Who is it Brook," Asha called from her bedroom? I could smell the Lysol coming into the living room.

"Its Sam," I whispered, "should I open the door?"

"Stop playing Brooklyn. Open the damn door!"

I rolled my eyes and opened the door. Sam stood at the door with a vase full of red and yellow roses. My mouth dropped and my heart melted. I wanted to be hard, but I couldn't let this moment pass us by.

"Baby, I am so sorry. I know I upset you and I don't ever want to do that again. Brooklyn, I love you!"

I grabbed the vase out of his hands and placed it on the table in the living room. My hands were shaking and I became real nervous. I wanted to yell back that I was in love with him too but I kept quiet. I took his face and kissed him slowly. I forgot to close the door and my neighbor across the hall began to whistle. We stopped kissing long enough to laugh and close the door.

"Sam, I hate fighting with you. I want our relationship to be effortless. I don't want to compete with you or have constant disagreements. Let's just love each other."

"So does that mean you love me too," he asked as he picked me up and walked into my bedroom?

As I lay across the bed Sam closed the door and locked it. He took his jacket off and threw it on the floor. The light was on and the ceiling fan was going real fast making a ridiculous loud noise. Sam pulled his polo over his head and showed his bulging six pack abs. My body began to get warm as I watched his every movement and laid in silence visualizing what was about to happen.

"Brook, I want you real bad but I don't want you to start crying. I love you and I know we can be together effortlessly . . . just let me love you the way I know how."

"Sam," I started.

"Shhh, don't say anything. Let me do the talking tonight. I want you to feel, hear, and know how much I love you."

He pulled me up and began to kiss my neck and face gently. His lips were cold but immediately warmed up as he touched them to different parts of my body. My hair had come out of the ponytail and was hanging on my shoulders. I reached for my rubber band and Sam moved my hand away.

"Leave it down," he whispered. He stood up and pulled the switch to turn the light off.

"What about Asha? She might hear us."

"It's about to get hot in here so I am going to leave the fan on. Plus it will be loud enough so she won't hear anything. Take your robe off so I can feel you."

The moment felt surreal and I wanted to make sure I didn't miss out on any emotion. Finally, a man that really did love me. Sam held me tighter than ever before and he whispered in my ear with every stroke.

"I love you Brooklyn, I love you baby."

This was it for me and I knew God had finally sent the love of my life, this was my husband.

"Mama Betty, I am headed to the emergency room. I can't see out of my right eye."

"WHAT?! What is wrong with your eye," Mama Betty sounded furious and worried at the same time? I didn't want to tell her because I knew she had been back and forth to the hospital with Chrissy.

"I am not sure. Sam is driving me up there and when they tell me something I will call you back. Don't worry, I am all right." I needed to reassure her that I would be fine, but in a way I wasn't sure if I would be.

"Yes ma'am, can I help you," the lady at the front desk asked as we entered the emergency room?

"My girlfriend lost the sight in her right eye," Sam interrupted, "we would like to see a doctor please."

"I'm sorry but I need you or her to fill out these papers and take a number. Someone will be with you in a minute."

"Ma'am, she can't see anymore. This all just happened this morning when she woke up. Can we please see someone as soon as possible?" I don't think I had ever seen Sam get that tense and I really felt sorry for the lady because she really was just doing her job.

"Sir, I understand your needs but there are about thirty other people here with needs as well. Please fill out these papers and bring them back when you're done. I will try my best to get you in to the doctor as fast as I can."

Sam took the clipboard and led me to a seat near the front desk. I looked around out of my good eye and saw that there were a lot of people waiting to be seen and I knew we couldn't just skip all of them.

"Brook, can you see to fill out these papers? If not I will put down as much as I can and then you will have to just tell me the rest."

"I'm good baby. I can see out of my other eye." I took the clipboard and tried to begin reading the small black print on the paper. Each time I squinted, the pain in my right eye became more severe and irritating.

"Sam, here it hurts too bad. The rest of them just need my signature so you can sign my name." I laid my head in his lap after he took the papers to the front desk. He rubbed my back and I prayed that they would call me in real soon.

"By my stripes you are healed. Speak healing in your life," the voice came out of nowhere.

"What stripes," I thought?

"Brooklyn Rideaux, Brooklyn Rideaux," a nurse called from the back.

"Yes, I'm here. Sam come on. Can you get my bag please?" I looked up at him and he looked nervous.

"Baby, I will be here when you come back out. You know I don't like hospitals that much."

I remembered Sam and I talking about him having to go to the hospital a lot when he was young and get several shots. I didn't know he still had distaste for hospitals though.

"Okay, I will be right back."

I walked to the back with the nurse and she immediately began hooking me up to a machine.

"Ma'am," I asked nervously, "what is all this for?"

"You said on your paperwork that you can't see out of your right eye and this happened all of a sudden, right?"

"Yes, I woke up this morning and I couldn't see and there is pain every time I move it to the left or right."

I thought it was because of my disposable contacts that I slept in them and wore them for weeks after they should've been thrown away. I knew Mama Betty didn't have the money to buy any more so I tried to keep those as long as possible.

As she was hooking me up to a huge machine in the small room, she asked, "Have you been hit in the head or eye recently? Or have you had something like contacts in your eye for a long period of time where an infection could've formed?"

"No ma'am," I lied.

"Okay, this is an MRI machine that will take a picture of your brain and any activity that is going on in your brain. The doctor will need to see this to determine what the problem is. You will hear a lot of noise but be very still and when it is finished in about twenty minutes I will pull you out. Do you want some cover?"

"Yes, how long will this take again? My boyfriend is sitting in the waiting room. Can he come in here too?"

"No, sweetie. I am sorry but only the patient is allowed in the room. Here is a blanket in case you get cold. Remember, try not to move."

The pain in my eye got worse and I tried to go to sleep and ignore it. All I could think about was me getting out of here and them giving me an antibiotic to take the pain away. I hope Sam was okay sitting out in the lobby looking at all those sick people.

"Okay, Brooklyn, we're done," a male nurse said as he pulled me out of the machine. "Are you okay? I'm going to take you back out with your husband and the doctor is going to review the results. As soon as we know something we will bring you back and you can talk to the doctor. Here let me help you up."

"Thank you God for speaking to me through this nurse"

I walked back out to the waiting room where Sam had fallen asleep in the chair. They moved him out of the emergency part and put him in a room right outside the MRI room.

"Baby," I gently spoke, "I'm back. They did an MRI and now I have to wait for the doctor to review the pictures of my brain. Are you hungry?"

It was still early and I knew we really didn't get much sleep the night before. I still had visions of the yellow and red roses in the vase on our table and my body still quivered from the lovemaking. Last night was one of the most special nights in our relationship and plus he told me he loved me.

"Brooklyn, hi, I am Dr. Roshan. I had a chance to review your MRI results. Would you please come to the back with me so I can discuss them with you?"

An older white man with thinning silver hair came out of the back and into the waiting room. He walked bent over and his head sort of shook as he talked. I could see my chart in his hand and the pictures of my brain as well.

"Hi, is it okay if my boyfriend comes back with me?"

"Sure, that's up to you."

"Sam, you wanna come?"

"Yeah, I need to know what to tell your mama when she gets here because you will probably be sleep."

We walked into a large office that reminded me of the dean's office at PV. I was scared to hear what the results were even though it couldn't be anything serious. Unless it was arthritis, nothing really affected anyone in my family's health.

"Brooklyn, I reviewed your MRI and you have lots of what we call lesions on your brain. These lesions have plaque on them that is causing some concern. What I am saying is your nerves are being affected and that is why I believe you lost your vision. This is something we see in patients that are suffering from a neurological occurrence called Optic Neuritis. I want to do one more test that will conclude if my prognosis is correct but it is a little painful. I will have to go in your spine with a needle and take out some of the fluid. I will then see if what I saw on the MRI is the same as what I see in your spinal fluid. If I do, then I am ruling out what I initially thought as lupus and diagnosing you with multiple sclerosis."

My head dropped and I began to cry. Sam pulled me close to him and held me while I bawled.

"Sir," Sam went on to ask, "what about the pain right now? Does she have to get the procedure today?"

"Unfortunately, she needs to have the procedure today. In the event that she leaves here and is not treated for the problem, things could get a lot worse. I am not a neurologist but my partner is and I will have her do the procedure and come in to talk to you. Oh, does Brooklyn have family here? If so, you may want to get them on the phone and ask them to come here as soon as possible."

Dr. Roshan walked out of the office really slow still looking through the pictures of my brain. I kept my head on Sam's chest because I couldn't believe what I was hearing. Sam had picked up his cell phone and was already talking to Mama Betty, telling her what the doctor said. He told her we were at Cy-Fair Medical center right off 1960. We both got up and walked back into the waiting room.

"Sam, am I dying?" I asked as we walked back into the waiting area.

"Nawwwww, Brook. You not dying, stop talking like that."

Within the next hour Mama Betty and Pearl walked in the room. Sam and I both had fallen asleep waiting on the doctor to come back with his partner.

"Brook, you all right?" Pearl asked as she looked at me with the patch the nurse put over my eye. I sat up startled when I heard her voice. "Hey y'all," I said as I sat up, "y'all got here fast. Where are the girls?"

"We left them home with Madear and Mrs. Mo. So what did the doctor say," Mama Betty asked as she sat in a chair next to me?

"They did an MRI and he said he needs to do another test where he takes fluid out of my spine to see if it's the same as what he sees on the MRI."

"A lumbar puncture," Pearl said. She was now in nursing school and knew all the medical terms and lingo from the doctors.

"Brooklyn Rideaux," a different female doctor called my name. She really looked too young to be a doctor but I was in too much pain to question her credibility.

"Yes, I'm Brooklyn."

"Hi I'm Dr. Phim, Dr. Roshan's partner. He showed me your MRI and I have to agree with him in regards to the prognosis. I am ruling it to be either lupus or MS, but once we do the spinal tap we will be able to see for sure."

"What is a spinal tap? He said he needed to get fluid out of my spine."

"They are the same thing, Brook," Pearl said.

"Yes, they are the same thing with different names. So, do you think you're ready? The place we have to go is actually across the street. You can drive over there in a matter of seconds. The name of the center is Phim Neurological Diagnostics. You can go in and tell them that it's an emergency appointment and they will get you ready."

Sam took my hand and started caressing it like I was a baby. He put his other arm around my waist and we all walked to the car.

☙

"Hi, my name is Brooklyn Rideaux and I was sent over from the emergency room by Dr. Phim."

"Yes, they just called about you. Okay I need you to fill out these papers and I will get the room ready. When you're done just leave them on the counter and ring the bell. Thanks."

The overly happy receptionist had long blond hair and crystal blue eyes. She reminded me of some actress but I was in too much pain to try and think about her name.

"Brooklyn, can you see to fill out the papers?" Mama Betty asked.

"Yeah out of one eye. I will fill out as much as I can but you can sign my name."

Before long my eye began to hurt worse and I just knew that I was going to pass out.

"Sam, can you ask them if they can give me anything for the pain in my eye? It is hurting really bad."

"Sorry, ma'am but I overheard you ask your husband for something for the pain, but unfortunately we have to wait until the spinal tap is done before we can give you pain medicine. But we are ready for you to come on back. You can only bring one person back with you."

Sam told Mama Betty to go with me and he would wait until they were finished. I really wanted him to come back but I guess he was being respectful.

"Okay, Brooklyn you are going to feel a lot of pressure. Just squeeze your mother's hand and it will be over soon. Ready one, two, and three . . . big stick."

"AAAHHHHHHH," I yelled. The pain felt like a ton of needles going through my back. I squeezed Mama Betty's hand

and yelled at the same time. I tried to be dignified but the pain was too unbearable.

"Okay, okay we are done. I know that hurts and I am so sorry. I am going to take this into the lab and process it. Nurse Jane will clean you up. I need you to lay flat on your back for 30 minutes without moving. The blood and fluid needs to form together again so lay still and don't move."

Nurse Jane cleaned my back and gave me two pillows, one to go under my knees and the other to go behind my head. I could not stop crying and eventually I fell asleep.

When I woke up, Dr. Phim and Dr. Roshan were talking to Mama Betty. I tried to pretend like I was still sleep so I could hear what they were saying.

"Mrs. Rideaux, Brooklyn has multiple sclerosis and currently there is no cure for it but research is being conducted daily in hopes of finding a cure. There are medicines that she can take to stop the progression of the disease and by looking at her MRI we need to start her on it quickly. She will be set up with a nurse initially because the medicine comes only in an injection. The nurse will come out and show her how to inject herself and what to do in order to overcome some of the symptoms from the medicine. It would be helpful if you or her boyfriend were there as well as a support. Again, I am sorry," Dr. Phim said with one arm around Mama Betty.

"Multiple sclerosis, what in the world is that? Is that the disease that Jerry Lewis has?" I thought to myself, "And there is no cure? What am I going to do? I am only 20 years old. How could this be happening to me?"

Chapter seventeen

I ended up staying in the hospital for seven days and missing a few assignments. Asha came up to the hospital and brought me lots of fruit and flowers. Plus she had to give me all the 4-1-1 in PV as well.

"Chile, I know you heard about the rushes that are coming up, right? Everybody and they mamas are talking about going so you know it's going to be packed. I hope you are home and feeling better by then because you already know we have a place on both lines."

Asha had been approached several times by girls in the sorority that she was interested in joining. I hadn't been approached, but I wasn't really worried because I knew they liked me. One of the girls in the sorority I wanted to join was in my ballet class. Neither one of us knew what we were doing in the class so we hung tight.

"So when is the rush and are they having both of them on the same day?"

"Yeah, I heard they knew of some girls that wanted to be down with both sororities so they put the rushes on the same day to see where those girls would end up. That's crazy, as small as PV is you would think they need to stick to one and pursue that," Asha giggled as she plugged up her flat iron.

"Girl, I know! Oh, thank you so much for bringing your flat iron. My hair looks a mess. I been laying up here doped up and haven't done nothing to it. Have you seen Sam around the yard?"

Sam hadn't really come to the hospital to see me but I understood why so I didn't make a big deal out of it.

"Naw, I heard his team went out of town. Some of them are supposed to be trying to qualify for the Olympics. Is Sam trying to qualify?"

"He hasn't mentioned anything like that to me so I doubt it. Man, I am so ready to get out of here and continue with my life. I have one and a half years of school left and then I start my student teaching. I am so ready to start working and making my own money."

Asha came from a pretty wealthy family who had a lot of dealings in the oil industry. Money was the least of her worries so she never talked about being without any. Her parents bought her a car after our freshman year, they paid for her school out of pocket unlike me with my many student loans and she always shopped on their credit cards. That was the life . . . living in a house with both parents and no worries.

"Don't forget how much it is going to cost for you to pledge. You can't write a check so you have to bring a money order. I think for y'all it's going to be around $700 and for us its about $900."

"Why is the price different?" I asked as she oiled my scalp before flat ironing my hair.

"Well, you have the best, the first and the only sorority worth something, so that's priceless!"

I could have thrown up at the very thought of what she was saying.

"The first, true, to organize but the first real sorority came after two ladies decided they were not only beautiful but had the need to live meaningful lives by serving their communities."

This was about the hundredth time that Asha and I had this conversation. Our decisions about the sorority of choice were evident and there was no wavering with us. We normally would laugh and keep going with another conversation but this time something seemed different.

"Brook, how are you doing really? I know you are putting on your hard hat and trying to be big about this disease but how do you feel for real?" Asha had stopped flattening my hair and was now sitting next to me on the adjustable hospital bed.

"Honestly, I don't know how I feel. I am sort of numb. Some days I want to cry and then some days I just ask why? Then this quiet but loud voice comes to me and makes me feel so much better. I am scared I guess, real scared. There is no cure and when I looked it up on the internet people don't usually die from it but they live disabled lives. I want a husband and kids and to live a normal life. That is what I am most scared of; not being the mother like Mama Betty was for all of us. If I can't give my kids anything material I at least want to give them me. Take that away and what do I have left?"

Surprisingly, I didn't cry. I gave it to her straight. The last couple of days I had nothing but time to sit and think about how I felt about everything. My thoughts were seemingly positive but there was a definite fear of what my future would turn out being like.

"I understand," Asha said.

In the midst of our silence, the nurse and Dr. Phim walked into the room.

"Hi Brooklyn! How are you feeling?" Dr. Phim asked as she looked through my chart. The nurse that came in with her, grabbed the arm cuff and began taking my blood pressure and getting the rest of my vitals.

"I am okay; just want to know when I can go home. So Doc when will I be out of here?"

"Well, Brooklyn you are doing well. I just need to check your vision to make sure you can see clearly again. You have taken approximately 1000 mg a day of solumedrol and it seems to be working. Here look at this board and tell me if you can read these letters."

"Can you come closer? Because I am not wearing my contacts and I don't have my glasses."

"Sure, okay can you read them now?" Dr. Phim walked toward the bed as I sat up and tried to focus.

"E-A-F-G-O," I read quickly. "Do you want me to keep going with the rest of the letters?"

"No," she said laughing, "I think you have proved that your vision is back to normal. I am going to prescribe you this same medicine in a pill form and when you go home you are to take it for the next week. Also, Brooklyn I have to prescribe you an injection for the MS."

An injection? I don't have diabetes, I have MS and the only way it can be treated is through an injection?

"What do you mean an injection? I have to come back up here and let somebody poke me? How often do I have to do that?"

I wanted to be kind and polite but now I was mad. There has to be a pill or something that I can take to control this mess. I am not coming up here for a shot every day.

"Well, fortunately Brooklyn you don't have to come to the hospital at all. You will give yourself the shot every day. I am going to send a nurse to your house to show you how to do the injections and then from there you or someone close to you will administer the injection."

My head dropped and Asha slid over and held me. Just then Sam walked in the door and saw me crying.

"Good afternoon Doc. Is everything okay?"

"She just found out that she has to give herself a shot every day for the MS," Asha told Sam.

"It's a very small needle and she probably won't even feel it. There are side affects like flu symptoms after the injection is taken so she will need to take Tylenol or Advil to combat them. The best time to take it is at night right before bed. That way she can sleep through the pain and in the morning she will be fine."

"Brooklyn, don't worry baby," Sam said as Asha moved and he took her place, "You will be all right and I am here to help you. I will always be there to help you."

I looked up at Sam and saw his eyes fill with tears. This man must really love me if he is willing to stay with me knowing I have an incurable disease.

"Doc, when does baby girl have to begin taking this medicine? Are there supplies that she needs to buy and we keep at home?" Sam began to throw his questions at Dr. Phim.

"There are no supplies you all have to buy and she needs to begin as soon as she leaves here. You see Brooklyn, your MRI showed me that you are in the beginning stages of MS called relapsing/remitting. If we begin to treat you now and you get the medicine into your system, you have a very good chance of this disease not progressing as rapidly as it would if you don't begin treatment immediately," Dr. Phim commented as she walked over to me.

"Asha, call Mama Betty and let her know what the doctor has told us and tell her I will call her once we get back home, please. Brooklyn, we got this, it doesn't have us," Sam instructed Asha and me. "Thank you Dr. Phim. So is she ready to go home today?"

"Actually yes she is. Her sight has gotten a lot better and the solumedrol took away the inflammation in her eye. Brooklyn," Dr. Phim said as she touched my shoulder and looked me in the face, "please go home and rest for the next couple of days. You have been through a lot and your body needs to recuperate. One other thing, you will notice that you have gained some weight. It is the fluid and when you get back to your normal routines it will go away, so don't worry. Sam, make sure you guys call my office and schedule a follow-up appointment within the next couple of weeks. Take things slow Brooklyn, okay? The nurse will get you guys her discharge papers and you are free to go."

"Thank you so much Dr. Phim, I really appreciate all your help and encouragement."

"No problem Brooklyn. That is what I am here for."

Dr. Phim and her nurse walked out of the room and Asha began gathering my things.

"Girl, let's go! It's time to get you out of that hospital gown and into something decent. I am going to put all her stuff in the car, Sam. Mama Betty wasn't home so I am sure she will call you back later.

"Thanks Asha, I love you girl," I said as she picked up my bag and headed out of the door.

"I know girl and yes, I kept the apartment clean too so you don't have worry," she laughed.

∞

School was in full swing and people were looking tight as ever on the campus. I was a little embarrassed because my face was so fat and some of my clothes didn't fit me right in the right places. The entire campus seemed to be buzzing about the rushes that were planned and who they each already wanted. I wasn't sure if they all of them liked me but I did know that I was cool with a few of them.

"Hey Brook," Regina called from across the yard, "you going to the rush tonight, right?"

I couldn't believe this extremely ghetto girl would shout that out across the yard knowing it would get everyone's attention.

"What in the world are you talking about?" I tried to play it off.

"You know the rush is tonight? Girl, you know I'm gone be there. Wait a minute, which one are you trying to be down with again? I heard those pretty girls want you but I ain't sure you fit with them. You got a little hood in you," Regina said as she came a little too close to me.

"Uhmm, well I didn't know anything about a rush and I am definitely not interested in going. Okay, gotta go!"

I walked away as fast as I could and I was looking back I ran into Kathy, the president of the coldest sorority on the yard.

"Hey Brooklyn, what are you running from? It looks like you just saw a ghost or something!"

"Hey Kathy, no I am trying to get away from ghetto Regina. What's going on?"

I always tried to keep my cool whenever I talked to one of "them" even though I was nervous as hell.

"Nothing much chile, headed to class. So I will see you tonight right?"

Okay, Brook . . . should you play crazy or assure her that you would be there?

"Where is my audible voice when I need it?" I thought.

"Yeah, I will see you tonight. What time does it start?"

"You need to be there at 6:15 but it doesn't start till 7. Listen, this conversation is strictly confidential and I better not hear it from anyone else."

Dang, I had never seen Kathy get so serious with me like that before. As she walked away my heart began to palpitate and I went over to a bench and grabbed a seat. I wasn't sure if I was nervous because of how and what Kathy said or if I was experiencing side effects from the injections. As I sat on the bench I noticed that I was near my sorority of choice tree in the courtyard.

"Oh Lord, please don't let one of them say anything to me because right now my heart is going crazy and I am almost out of breath," I thought.

"Hey Brook," a girly voice came from behind the bench. As I looked around I didn't see anyone except a group of fake cops.

"Brook, you better get up from by our tree," that same sweet voice came again.

"Whatever," I said, "why don't you come from around that tree and show your face?"

I was all geared up to put a beat down on someone and out steps Sam. Dressed in his basketball uniform and sneakers, he darted out from the tree and hugged my head like a head lock.

"Boy, you almost got beat down. Don't play with me like that. I thought you were one of these girls around here who already know what's up."

"Hey baby girl," he said as he kissed my forehead, "calm down! Aint nobody trying to fight you. Why you sitting over here all by yourself? Are you feeling okay?"

Sam looked totally confused. I didn't want him to get worried so I tried to ignore his question by changing the subject.

"Hey, guess what? I was approached by the president and she told me I needed to be at the rush tonight early. I don't know if I should be excited or scared."

"Well, this is all I've heard you talk about since you came down here so there should be some excitement. While you are at the rush I am going to be in the science lab studying with my group. I will just come by the house when you are done."

"That's cool. I think I am about to go home and lay down. I don't think my professor is here today anyway, so I'm going home. What do you have going on for the rest of the day?"

"Huhhh? Oh, I have to go to the science building and study," the way that came out of Sam's mouth I knew something wasn't right but I didn't feel like debating or hounding him about his whereabouts.

"Whateva Sam. Just be to the house tonight when I get out of the rush so we can talk. I need to see where your head is at."

"Okay, baby girl. I will catch up with you later."

Sam saw one of his buddies across the yard so he ran and caught up with him. In a matter of minutes all I could see was his purple sweat suit in the wind. I could not get out of my head the way he answered that question and something in my stomach told me he was lying. I would normally get into my private eye mode but my body wasn't allowing me to pursue anything. I slowly got up off the bench and headed to my apartment. I wondered if Sam and I would be together long or if this was just a fling.

*"For God so loved **you** that he gave His only son for you . . . ,"* the familiar voice spoke as I hiked through the campus.

"You can't have any other gods before Me, Brook. I love you more than you know."

Any other gods before Him? What was he talking about? I am a Christian and not trying to test the waters on any other religions! I kept walking still trying to figure out what that voice meant and wondering why my audible voice would leave me sometimes confused.

"Hey Brook, I see you made it right on time. Okay, go over there and start pouring that red punch into those red cups," Kathy said as soon as I walked in the door. I felt a little uncomfortable because I had never attended a rush before and I wasn't sure if my black dress with little white flowers was alright or if I was overdressed. I looked around the MSC ballroom and there were several other girls who were there early as well. Some faces looked familiar but I wasn't sure of any names or anything. I grabbed the white gloves that sat on the table next to the punch and began pouring it into the cups. I knew enough about what to do and what not to do from Mike's girlfriend, Crystal, who was a member of this sorority already. She told me often to be sure that's what I wanted and not to waiver. I took her advice and that was why I was invited to come early. They saw my sincerity and work on campus so I was obviously a natural fit.

As the time progressed I poured what seemed to be about a hundred cups of punch. A little bell was rung by Kathy to get everyone's attention.

"Good evening ladies. Please take a seat and if there are no more seats please stand around the walls in an area where you can hear us clearly. Make sure you received a packet as well. I believe we may have run out since we only printed 300 and there seems to be more people here tonight. So if you didn't get one raise your hand and one of the sorors will come around and get your name and number. My name is Kathy and I am the current president for this chapter. This semester we will have an intake and many of you will not be a part of it."

"Dang," I whispered to myself, "she aint playing. Lord, thank you that I was invited."

The rush went on for another thirty minutes with Kathy explaining how the process would work. Crystal had already hipped me to the game so I was already clear about everything.

"Ladies that is all for the evening, please enjoy some refreshments and I probably won't see most of you later! Goodnight!"

"You better not drink any of that juice or even touch that cup," I heard one girl whisper to her friend, "they don't want you to touch anything red."

I smiled as I went over and put the white gloves on again and picked up a cup. The two girls looked at me with bucked eyes because they knew nothing about the gloves. As I walked away smiling I saw Sam running into the building, looking around.

"He better be looking for me and not one of these chicken heads in here," I thought.

"Brooklyn," I heard him yell, "come here quick."

I dropped my cup in the trash and placed the gloves back on the table.

"Sam, boy what are you doing here? You know you can't be at this rush!"

Sam grabbed my arm and pulled me to the side, "Brooklyn, I need to take you home, right now."

My heart began to palpitate again as I looked at him with fear in my eyes.

"What happened Sam?"

"I will tell you in the car but we have to go now."

I looked over to see if I saw Kathy and she looked at me and waved. I guess Sam or someone had already told her so she was cool with me leaving.

Asha was waiting in the backseat of the car with one of Sam's teammates. I ran and jumped in the front still not knowing what was going on.

"Asha, Sam, somebody tell me what is going on?"

"Brook, something is wrong with Madear and Mama Betty told me to bring you home right now."

I put my head down and prayed to the voice I always hear, "Please let my grandmother be okay and keep her with us."

Cars were everywhere and parked in every direction when we arrived to the house. Mama Betty and Pearl had moved down the street into a townhouse that was a lot bigger than the matchbox apartment. Madear's room was upstairs so as I entered the house I headed up the stairs. I didn't speak to anyone but was focused on seeing my grandmother.

"Brooklyn," Pearl called, "where are you going? Somebody stop her, please."

My new cousin Anthony grabbed me as I headed up the stairs and sat me down on the step.

"She's not there Brooklyn, she's gone. She's gone baby girl."

"Anthony don't tell me that," I cried and held him, "don't tell me that."

Sam came in the house behind me and sat down next to me and Anthony on the step. I put my head on his shoulder and cried like a baby. Anthony got up and walked back into the living room. The entire family had come but I didn't see Mama Betty.

"Where is my mama?" I asked Sam.

"She is upstairs Brook but they don't want you to come up there right now."

"I want to see my grandmother and my mama!"

I jumped up and ran upstairs to Madear's room. Her body lay in her adjustable bed stiff and cold. Her eyes were shut and her mouth was wide open. I looked at her skin and it looked smooth and her silky gray hair was pulled over to one side. Mama Betty held her hand and whimpered while talking to her.

"I know this isn't you Madear. But I wasn't ready for you to go."

"Mama," I said.

"Brooklyn, go back downstairs. You don't need to see this right now. My mama is gone and she not coming back."

Chapter eighteen

Mama Betty wasn't herself since Madear passed away. Even though it was a burden lifted, I would find her in Madear's room laying in her bed crying. I didn't know what that could possibly feel like, so I would act like I didn't see her. After Mike graduated from college he stayed to coach football in a nearby town. His initial goal was to come back and teach, but since the school knew he loved football and was real good they offered him a job.

"Hey baby girl, how are you doing? How is Mama Betty and Chrissy?"

"Mike, when you coming home?" was all I could muster out. "Mama Betty just ain't the same since Madear passed and she needs some help. Pearl moved out and got a place with her boyfriend, I am going back to school this weekend and the new cousins are doing what they do best . . . nothing. You are finished with school so you can come down here and coach at one of these schools."

Mike obviously heard the seriousness in my voice since he became very quiet.

"Brooklyn, remember when I left I said I was going to make a better life for myself so I could come back and take care of you guys. Well that is what I am doing. I got this job as an assistant coach and one day I may be the head coach but I have to do what I need to right now. Listen, Mama Betty is tougher than you know. She has been through a lot of things even before you got here and she will make it through this too. Just give her the space she needs. While you are there help with Chrissy and keep the house clean. I will be there to check on her in two weeks when the team comes to Houston to play."

"But Mike," I started to say.

"Brook, trust me. Everything will be fine. I love you and will talk to you later."

Mike hung up the phone in a hurry and I was left with the weight of the world on my shoulders. I wanted to comfort Mama Betty like Madear did, but I couldn't. Sam and I were supposed to meet for lunch that same day but he didn't call me. I walked in to check on Mama Betty and let her know I was about to leave for a little while.

"Mama Betty, are you going to be okay? I was about to go have lunch with Sam. Do you want me to bring you anything back?"

Mama Betty didn't acknowledge that I was talking to her. She lay in Madear's old bed in a fetal position and had fallen asleep. I wanted so bad to get in bed with her and just lay there beside her. But I needed to give her some space like Mike said.

"Okay, I'll be back. Chrissy is with Pearl and Jazmine so don't worry about her and I will bring you something to eat."

As I turned to walk out the bedroom Mama Betty spoke, "Thanks Brook, I love you."

"Sam, where are you? I have been waiting at this restaurant for thirty minutes." I was highly frustrated and hungry. Sam told me to meet him at Chili's by the highway at 2:00 and he is nowhere to be found.

"Uhmm, I am on the way. Go ahead and order your food. By the time you get it I will be there."

"Where are you and who is that I hear in the background?"

"That is the radio and I am on my way, damn!"

"Excuse the hell out of me, you told me to be here at a certain time and I am here. You need to get your butt up here like you said."

I hung up the phone in his face. I wanted to get up and leave but I promised Mama Betty that I would bring her something to eat and I didn't have any money. There was this gut feeling that I kept getting about Sam and someone else but I couldn't put my hand on it.

"Hi, my name is Sheila and I am your waitress today. Can I start you off with a drink?" A young girl with a lip piercing and nose ring came over to the table. She had jet black hair with red highlights and lots of gel. Her face looked extremely pale and her black lipstick was starting to peel. On top of me being pissed off with Sam, they have sent Dracula's sister over here to bring out my food.

"Uhmm, no thank you. I am waiting on someone," I said while looking at the menu. I didn't want to continue to look at her, knowing I would soon be eating and the memory of her chapped black lips would be in my head. I sat in the restaurant waiting on Sam for another hour. After three glasses of water I couldn't take it anymore.

"Ma'am, I am going to leave, but thanks for your help," I told the waitress while walking to the ladies room.

"Brooklyn, sometimes what you feel deep in your gut is true. Ask the Father for wisdom," my audible voice came back. This time I was talking back.

"So, what do I do?" I said in my head.

"Pray and listen to what the Father tells you. Then be obedient."

Wait a minute how many people are in my head talking to me? Okay, please don't let me be going crazy.

I washed my hands and walked out the door. I was confused but yet at peace with what the voice told me. I got in my car and saw Sam driving up to the restaurant as I drove out. He stopped and waved for me to let down my window. I had every mind to keep going and act like I didn't see him, but we were right next to each other going in opposite directions. I reluctantly let my window about a fourth of the way down.

"What?" I said, highly pissed off.

"Where are you going? I thought we were going to have lunch," Sam said acting as if he was early.

"You have obviously lost your mind having me wait for your ass almost two hours. You know what Sam? Don't worry about it, okay? And as a matter of fact don't worry about calling me anymore. You think I am a fool but you just met your match!"

Sam looked shocked. I wondered if he was going to try and shoot back but he never did.

"Baby girl, I am so sorry. Can you please pull back in because I really need to tell you something? And can you please let your window all the way down so you can hear me?"

"Sam, you are full of it," I said as I let my window down, "tell me what you need to tell me right now."

"Brooklyn, please. Pull back in the parking lot. We don't have to go back in if you don't want to."

I was hungry and didn't have any money. My stomach said go back in but my head said shoot him the finger and keep going.

I pulled back into the parking lot and parked my car. Sam pulled his old blue Chevy in the space next to me and got out the car with a huge smile and flowers.

"Where in the hell does he think he going trying to suck up with flowers?" I thought.

"Baby girl, get out of the car and give me a hug!"

"Sam, where have you been? And who are those flowers for anyway?" I said as I got out of the car.

"Baby girl, I just wanted to let you know how much I love you. You have been through so much this year and I wanted to surprise you!"

I smiled but that gut feeling wouldn't leave and I knew he was lying.

"It took you two hours to get some flowers to surprise me? Sam, that is a lame lie and I am not trying to hear it!"

"Damn, Brooklyn! Take these flowers and these papers. You make it very hard for anyone to do anything for you." Sam was obviously pissed off but I didn't care. I needed him to understand that I wasn't just some random girl and he couldn't do and say whatever he wanted. I took the flowers and laid them on the front seat in my car.

"What are these papers?" I asked.

"Open it up baby girl," Sam said while managing to crack a smile.

"Apartment lease? Who is this for?"

"Me and you, for next semester. I know we spend a lot of time together and it doesn't make sense for us to pay two rents. I went over to the apartment complex today and got us a two-bedroom place. You don't have to worry about anything because I can handle the rent. Well, you might have to pay the phone bill or something but that's it."

I couldn't believe that Sam had gone to get us an apartment without talking to me about it first but I was happy. A man wanted to take care of me and stay with me knowing about the disease? That made my heart turn flips and no one could tell me that he wasn't in love with me.

"Sam, I can't believe you did all this for us! I love you so much!"

We stood in the parking lot hugging and kissing as people watched us. I didn't know how I was going to break the news to Mama Betty that Sam and I would be moving in together but I knew I had to soon. I didn't want her to tell Big Mama or Mike so I thought about waiting until after we had moved.

"Sam, how am I going to tell Mama Betty? You know she is totally against people living together before marriage. I don't want to stress her out, not now since she is still going through with Madear's death. And then if Mike or Big Mama finds out you know they gone trip."

"I thought this was something YOU wanted? Listen Brook, you know we love each other and will probably spend the rest of our lives together so why not get started now?"

Sam was dressed in nice pair of khakis with a striped polo pullover. It looked as if he had been out on a date or something, but then I remembered this was how he dressed, preppy. I dropped the paper through my driver side window and planted a big kiss on his lips. Nothing seemed to matter at this point except Sam and I being together. I loved my family but I came to the conclusion that I couldn't live for them. I was coming into my own and I had to make my own decisions.

"Baby girl, I have to go by one of my classmate's house to study so I am going to hit you up later okay?"

"Sam, damn you just got here!" I knew his major was difficult and required a lot of work, but how much studying did he really need to do? That gut feeling came back and I knew he was lying.

"Okay, call me when you get done," I said as he held me in his arms. I held him tight and didn't want to let him go.

"Sam," I said looking up into his eyes, "You love me right? And you not just saying that right?"

"Of course Brook I love you. I don't just go around telling people that because I have nothing else to say. I really love you, baby girl." Sam grabbed me tighter and began to kiss my neck. I rested my head on his and thanked God.

"Hello," I walked out of class as my professor had just begun her lecture and answered my cell phone. Dr. Roacha was one of the longest standing education professors at Prairie View and Asha and I loved her. She lived in the small town so many of us considered her a local, but she was the coolest and smartest around. I gently closed the door and walked out into the hall, "Hey baby girl, this is Tommy Boy!"

Tommy Boy? How in the world was he able to call me in prison?

"Hey Daddy? What are you doing calling me all the way from prison?"

"I am home baby! Your daddy is home. When can I see you, huh? I missed you and want to spend some time with you!"

"Daddy, I am in school. When did you get home and where is Big Mama?" I was so surprised and shocked that I never went back into the class. I wanted as much information as I could get from him just in case we never talked again.

"I got home last night and Big Mama is in the kitchen cooking. That is why I want you to come over tonight. She is making a big meal for the whole family. Where are Pearl and the baby?"

"Why didn't you call me when you got home? I would've tried to get down there last night. I can't leave the campus because I am doing something with a group of girls tonight and tomorrow night. Are you staying at Big Mama's house?"

I hadn't seen my dad in almost ten years and I wondered what he looked like. As I got older I stopped wanting to go with Big Mama down to the prison to see him. I was tired of the drive, the wait and being frisked by the cops. As I sat talking on the phone Sam's ex-girlfriend walked by me in the hallway and rolled her eyes.

"Hold on a second, Daddy. Tisha, you got something you want to say?" I asked as I jumped up off the bench and headed her direction down the hall.

"Who you think you talking to, Brooklyn?"

"I am talking to you, heifer. You come down this hall rolling your eyes. If you got something to say then say it!"

Tisha and I had been at odds with one another since Sam and I got together. Come to find out they were still dating and Sam told me when we met that they were done. I would not have talked to Sam if I had known that he and Tisha were still dating. There are a lot of things I do that's not right, but messing with another woman's man was not one of them.

"Brooklyn, I don't have time for this mess. You are crazy!"

"You right, I am crazy and if you roll your eyes again I will show you how crazy I am!"

I totally forgot my Daddy was on the phone listening to everything that was happening.

"Hello, Daddy?"

"Brooklyn, what is going on? Are you about to fight somebody?"

"Nope, not anymore."

"Listen, if you don't remember anything else I tell you remember this: men come a dime a dozen and past girlfriends ain't never worth losing your respect behind. You have to learn to be wise as a serpent but humble as a dove. You got that Brooklyn?"

I held the phone and didn't respond. I wasn't sure how to take everything that he said, but I had to take it as him trying to impart some wisdom.

"I hear you Daddy. I am going to try and make it out there this weekend. I just know I can't leave the campus until Friday evening. But I am in class so I will call you when I get done or later this evening. Okay, bye!" I know I kind of gave him the cold shoulder, but there was nothing there. I never had a real relationship with him and like the saying goes, "You can't miss nothing you never had." Before he was able to say anything I hung up the phone. My mind was still on Sam's ex-girlfriend walking by me rolling her eyes. I really didn't like her whether she was Sam's ex or not. Tisha was a little shorter than me with long black hair. Everyone said she was from some part of Africa and she came to the U.S. about a year ago. People that I saw from Africa didn't look anything like her, but she was from the eastern part of Africa. Her skin was caramel and smooth. Her big brown eyes were garnished with super long eyelashes that fluttered every time she spoke. Not only was she beautiful but she was smart as well. I was told that she was a pre-med major and eventually wanted to be a doctor.

"Sam, you better get your girl before I break her neck. If she comes by me one more day and rolls her eyes I am going mucho loco on her," I demanded on Sam's voicemail.

∽

"Brooklyn, are you going to work in the morning? Well in a few hours," Asha asked as we both reached our rooms about 4 that morning. Sam was in my bed knocked out with the television on blasting a weight loss infomercial. Asha stood by her door waiting for an answer. Her long black hair was pulled up into a wet ponytail and her face was painted green.

"Naw, I am too tired. I am going to sleep all day if I can. Can I come take a shower in your room? I don't want to wake Sam up. Look at him girl he over there knocked out like he has been working on the railroad!"

"You know you crazy. Give me about fifteen minutes since I need to wash my hair."

I took off my clothes and tied my hair in a bath towel. I wanted to lie next to Sam, but he slept so light and I didn't want to wake him. I knew Asha was going to be longer than fifteen minutes so I tiptoed around my room.

"Baby, you okay? Did you just get home? What time is it?"

Sam was obviously delirious and spoke almost gibberish as he looked around and questioned me.

"Shhh, go back to sleep. I am okay, just tired and achy."

"Come here and lay down next to me. I want you to rest before you have to get up in a few hours. Well, are you even going to work tomorrow?"

"I am not sure," I whispered as I stumbled around in the dark, "DANG . . . Ohhh . . . Ohhh!! I hit my knee on the dresser, shoot!"

"Come here Brooklyn and lay next to me. Where is Asha?"

"She's in her room taking a shower. I am waiting until she finishes and then I am going in there to shower."

"Why?" Sam asked.

"I was trying not to wake you up. But since you are up and I am here I might as well go on in there now. Go back to sleep, I will be out in a minute."

"Before you get in come here and let me get you a little dirtier . . . !"

Sam turned the lamp on next to the bed and smiled a huge smile. I was a little hesitant since I had told him that I didn't want to have sex anymore until we got married. I still hadn't told Mama Betty about our plans to move in together and he hadn't told his mother either.

"Sam, go back to sleep. I am too tired and my body hurts," I said as I headed into the bathroom. I turned the shower on full blast and waited for the hot water to join in.

"Brook, moving in with Sam is not the thing to do. It's not time."

I stepped in the shower and closed the curtain behind me. I was hoping Sam had forgotten about his advance and gone back to sleep.

"Just trust in the Lord for the love you desire . . . His is unconditional."

I closed my eyes and sighed. I knew who that now familiar voice was and something inside wouldn't let me ignore it.

Chapter nineteen

The apartment was huge and had more than enough closet space for all of mine and Sam's clothes. There were two large bedrooms, a nice remolded kitchen and one huge bathroom.

"Brook, the movers want to know where to put your boxes of shoes; in the guest room or in our bedroom?"

"Tell them to bring them in here," I yelled out to the living room from our bedroom. I had already begun hanging my clothes in our closet and noticed that Sam would have to use the other room for his things.

Sam and his friend Utah were helping the movers unload the truck for the second time. I didn't realize how much stuff Sam and I had combined until it all came together in one house.

It's not too late to get your own place . . .

"Brooklyn, come look at the refrigerator. I think it's brand new," Sam said as he brought another box with purses into the bedroom.

"It is brand new. I called the apartment people and told them we needed a new one because the one in here looked a mess."

Sam put the box on the floor next to the door and kissed my forehead.

"That is why I know you will always be my baby girl!"

Sam and Utah headed out to get us all something to eat after the movers finished their last load.

"Brook, you want pizza or sandwiches?"

"Pizza, with extra cheese," I yelled out into the kitchen. Sam was still admiring the new refrigerator and telling Utah all about it.

"See man, my baby called the people and had them hook us up on a new refrigerator. She is the bomb when it comes down to handling business."

"Oh yeah, well what about Tisha?" Utah asked.

"Man, let's go. Brook might think you're me or something. Brook, we're gone! I will be back in a minute."

Utah was one of Sam's team mates and they hung tight. Utah was a kinesiology major and wanted to coach track and basketball one day. He was on the basketball team, track team, and the baseball team for the school. I wondered how he did all that with the seasons overlapping, but Sam said he was so good that the coaches let him have things his way. As the guys were headed down the stairs I overheard their conversation about me and Tisha.

"Say dog, you not still messing with Tisha are you?"

"Man, do you see how beautiful Tisha is looking lately? And she wants me. I know it ain't right but I still cut for her."

"Dude, you crazy," Utah said as they got into his truck, "if Brooklyn finds out about that you know your ass is grass."

"That's the point . . . she ain't gone find out."

Asha and I crossed at the same time and probated together. It was the best feeling in the world to be part of an organization that was all about service and helping in our communities. Even though we were best friends and on two different lines that didn't change who we were.

"I see you Asha in your pink and green. Excuse me while I go throw up, but you look good!"

"Whatever Brook, where is your paraphernalia at anyway? We just crossed and you know people dying to see you in your symbols."

"I know girl but that ain't me. I got some stuff but I ain't tripping about showing off with my clothes. Wait until our first step show, our first community event, or our first party. Then I will let y'all have it!"

Asha and I walked across campus together and all you heard were her sorority calls.

"Is that a cat dying?" I asked as we laughed.

"And when your line sisters see you the cows will start mooing! Anyway, how is the new apartment? Did you all get everything moved in and put up?"

"Yeah, it's all put up. Asha last night when I was laying on the couch watching television I ran my hand across the rug and found an earring back. I knew it wasn't mine because I don't wear those kind of backs on my earrings. Girl, if that punk has had someone in my house its gone be on like Donkey Kong."

Asha eyes grew real big and she lowered her head.

"Oh hell no! Tell me what you know Asha and don't play with me!"

I knew she knew something because her eyes widened, her head dropped and she got real quiet.

"Brook, my line sister told me that she saw Sam and Pat together at the science building late one night. I didn't believe her because that girl is ugly and I know Sam wouldn't mess over you with her. But when you said you found a back on your floor it confirms the other stuff my line sister said."

"Asha," I said in a low melancholy voice, "What else did she say?"

"Brooklyn, promise me first that you not gone go and look for this girl?"

"What else Asha?" I yelled as we approached the MSC.

"Pat told my line sister that she was at your house when you were at a sorority meeting. Sam asked her to come over and study with him. That is all I know seriously."

"Call your line sister and ask her and Pat to meet us at the library. Asha? If you my girl I know you will do this for me."

Asha hated confrontation but she knew that I was serious. She took out her cell phone and called one of her line sisters and played everything off like a pro.

"Hey girl! What are you doing? Hey can you and Pat meet me at the library? I need to show you something. In about ten minutes, okay? Cool."

As Asha called her people I called Sam on my cell phone.

"Hey baby, what are you doing?"

"Nothing, sitting here at Utah house playing the video game. What's up?"

"Can you come get me from the library on campus? I rode with Asha but she is about to go with her line sisters somewhere."

"Yeah, give me about ten minutes. Where are you going to be?"

"On the second floor by the video room."

Sam was the type of person that did not like confrontation either, but I knew the gut feelings I was having were about to prove themselves to be true.

"Asha, let's go up to the second floor and wait for both of these fools to come. I just hope they don't see each other outside and figure out what's going on."

Sam arrived first and walked over slowly towards me. He looked at me with a suspicious look as if something was about to go down but I didn't give him a hint.

"Hey, baby! Thanks for coming to get me. I'm almost done here on the computer and then we can go."

Asha was on the other side of the room by the videos waiting for Pat to come up. We gave each other eye signals when we knew one of them had arrived or someone else was coming on the floor.

Our library was huge and often times there were classes held on the first and third floors but the second floor was always empty. The video room was used occasionally by professors, but today it was empty. Sam sat in the seat next to me and started rubbing my back while I pretended to be looking up something on Yahoo.

"Brook, how much longer you gone be? I have to go study today and I want to wash the car before I go."

"Just a little bit longer honey," I said and just then Pat got off the elevator. She didn't see Sam and me sitting at the computers, but she spotted Asha's loud pink jacket. Sam looked around the library and spotted Pat. He immediately began to fidget and look away.

"What's wrong with you? Why you so fidgety?" I asked him in a sarcastic tone.

"I told you I need to go study and wash the car so I am ready to go."

As Sam mumbled on Asha and I looked at each other and gave the okay to meet.

"Oh, hey Asha," I said as she and Pat walked over to Sam and I at the computers. "What are y'all doing in here on the second floor?"

"Hey Sam," Asha said with a sour attitude. "You know my girl Pat don't you?"

Asha was a pro and she handled everything better than I could have imagined coming from her.

"Asha, what's going? Why did you ask me to come up here?" Pat began to look scared.

"Pat," I interrupted, "do you know my man, Sam?"

"Your man Sam said y'all were over!" Pat looked at Sam confused and her lip began to quiver.

"Brook, what in the hell is going on? I thought you needed a ride home?"

"I do right after we get down to the bottom of this foolishness. Pat are you and Sam sleeping together? Or have you ever been to my house? Because I found your earring stud on my living room floor."

"Yeah, I went to Sam's house and we are sleeping together. Like I said Brooklyn, Sam told me y'all were done with each other. So if I want to go to *his* house I can and it's not your business what we do when we're there."

I looked over at Sam and he had put his head down and was rubbing his temples.

"Sam, is this true?" I asked.

"What do you mean is it true? I don't have to lie to you and like I said what we do is our business. Asha, you supposed to be my girl and you brought me up here for this mess? I can't believe you!"

As Pat began to walk away I hurriedly reached over and grabbed the hood of her sweat jacket.

"No ma'am we are not done," I said as she fell to the ground. Pat was a short girl with big hips and a big butt, so when she hit the floor it took her a minute to readjust and get up.

"Brooklyn, what is wrong with you? I know you not trying to fight this girl."

"Sam, the best thing for you to do right now is sit your ass down or leave. Go pack your shit from that apartment and leave. You sorry punk, all this time you been telling me you studying and I actually believed you. You have been over to this slut house banging her. You are sorry and I can't stand to look at you."

My words came out like fiery darts. He looked at me in total astonishment that I had actually found out about him and Pat.

"Brooklyn, who do you think you are pulling on me," Pat said as she lunged for me and knocked me to the ground?

I wasn't expecting her to come after me, but when she did she pinned me to the ground and tried to sit on me.

"Pat! Pat," Asha called as she tried to break us up. Some sort of way we managed to get on our feet and fought toe to toe.

"If he was your man then you should have kept him on a leash," Pat said.

I grabbed her head and swung it to my knee. She fell on the ground between two computer desks and began to yell and curse up a storm. By now the fight was in full swing and the students from the other floors had gathered to watch. I pulled Pat from between the tables by her leg and began to kick the life out of her.

"Don't you ever disrespect me by coming to my house again? I don't care who invites you, don't bring your fat, nasty whoring ass to my house."

I was so mad tears began to run down my face and I couldn't stop kicking Pat in her face. Even after the security came and tried to pull me off I still kicked and fought trying to leave my mark on her face. One thing I did learn in the ward was if you fight; make sure that person never comes back again for seconds. Many of the Rideaux clan had gone to jail for leaving their marks on people and it looked like I was headed down the same road.

"Someone call campus police and the ambulance," the security guard said as he pulled me off and to the side. He took out a plastic tie and wrapped it around my wrists, behind my back. I looked around after I regained control and saw Pat on the ground with a bloody face, Asha sitting by her side crying and Sam nowhere to be found.

"Hello, Mama Betty? I need you to come to Prairie View today. I am in jail . . ."

Chapter twenty

" **A**ll I'm going to say is don't follow the path of your daddy, you hear me? You down there living with that boy and now fighting people behind him? Come on Brooklyn, I know I taught you better than that."

Mama Betty was highly disappointed in me.

"After all you've seen me go through with Chrissy being sick and Madear passing I would think you would try to stay out of trouble."

I knew the ride home was going to be a long one, especially now that Mama Betty knew Sam and I lived together and she hated the idea, but I was grown. I didn't want to go back to the apartment so I asked if I could come home for the weekend. I knew she wouldn't say no, but I wanted her to know I was trying to be respectful by asking.

"Brooklyn, what are you trying to prove by living with this boy?"

"What do you mean?" I said in a low monotone.

"Just what I said! Why are y'all living together? What happened to the apartment you and Asha had on campus?"

I wanted to scream to her if you were involved in my life then you would know what's going on with me but I kept quiet.

"You know Jazmine and Chrissy are looking up to you and now I have to come down to Prairie View and bail you out of jail? What does that say to them Brooklyn? Do you want to end up like your daddy and the rest of the Rideaux clan? I worked hard night and day to provide a stable life for you and Pearl and Mike but what do I get in return from you? Heartache, that's what. None of my other kids have disappointed me like you."

Her words shot through my chest like a steel bullet. I was the only one that did this and the only one that did that. I was tired of being pushed to the side and then blamed for everything.

"Mama Betty you know what? All my life I have tried to please you and make you happy. But the reality is you not happy with yourself so you want to take your hurt out on me. I thank you for being a mother and father to me and doing everything you have done but I am not your trash dumpster. You cannot just dump all your pain and hurts from your life out on me."

Tears were flowing down Mama Betty's face as I she kept her eyes on the road. I wanted to cry too, but that is what she expected and since I was now a grown woman I had to act like one. The ride was silent until we reached the house and Chrissy and Jazmine ran out. My hair was pulled back in a messy bun and the clothes I wore smelled like cigarettes from the holding cell.

"Ooh, Brook where you been looking like that?" Jazmine asked as she stopped before hugging me.

"She been in jail, Jaz. She was fighting some boy in Prairie View," Chrissy tried to whisper.

She had just gotten out of the hospital again and was walking slow. She had a little limp in her leg that kept her from getting to me before Jazmine and you could see the frustration. Both girls were getting taller and Jaz was starting to look more like the Rideaux's.

"Be quiet, Chrissy. You don't know what you talking about so go sit your tail down somewhere!" I had never talked to Chrissy like that before so both girls were shocked at my response.

"Dang, Brook I'm just asking. You don't have to be rude to me, you the one down there fighting and going to jail not me."

"Both of y'all go in the house before I whip some ass out here today." Mama Betty interrupted, "as a matter of fact make sure that room is clean because Brook will be here for a while."

"FOR A WHILE," I thought, "she really has lost her mind. Sam may have to leave but I am going back to my apartment."

The night seemed different without Sam being with me. I wanted to call him and check on him, but I didn't want to seem desperate and stupid. Shoot, he hurt me. He slept with that hood rat in our house. He needs to call me and make things better. I sat on the floor in the living room watching *In the Heat of the Night*, one of Madear's favorite shows, while everyone else was doing their own thing. Jaz had gone home and Chrissy was sleep. Mama Betty gave her the medicine the doctors sent home but she had to sleep with it in injected in her stomach overnight. I really felt sorry for her because she was only a kid and having to experience so much pain at a young age. Mama Betty was sitting at the dining room table balancing her checkbook. All these years of being in a noisy house and with so many people running in and out this scene seemed surreal. A quiet house, no phone ringing, no Rideaux fighting . . . what's really going on? Mike had moved back to Houston and was living with his fiancé in a nearby apartment. It seemed like I never saw him or talked to him either since he got engaged. I just knew the love we had for one another and the friendship we had no one could come between. So much for dreams.

"Hello," I said as I grabbed my phone off the coffee table. The vibration noise seemed to echo in my sleep and I thought I was dreaming.

"Brook, you sleep? This is Sam."

I looked over at the clock on the VCR and it read 1:34 a.m. Mama Betty had turned off all the lights in the house and cut the loud ceiling fan on that seemed to follow us from house to house.

"Hey Sam, no I'm not sleep. What's up?"

"I just wanted to hear your voice. I miss you baby girl. I don't like the fact that we fighting and not communicating like we use too. I love you Brook and I am so sorry for everything I did."

I began to hear a whimper in Sam's voice and then a totally complete silence.

"Hello," I said beginning to worry that the phone had lost its signal.

"Yeah, I'm still here. I just don't like it Brook, I want you to come home today. I am so sorry," Sam said as he began to louder.

"Baby, don't worry. It's going to be okay. I mean we will make it through this. I love you Sam but you did hurt me. I can't believe you brought that "thang" into our house. Why did you do that to me?"

"Baby girl, I know I was stupid. I am so sorry and I promise I will never hurt you like that again. Will you come home, please?"

"You didn't even come up to the jail and try to get me out. I had to call Mama Betty and now she pissed at you. You have to show me something different Sam because right now I don't trust you at all."

"I know baby girl. Listen get your things together and I will be there first thing in the morning. Will you come back with me?"

I held the phone for a minute before I answered.

"Brook, trust in the Lord with all your heart. Stay home and let the Father heal you."

I wanted to obey that comforting voice but I also wanted to be loved again by Sam.

"I love you unconditionally and there is no greater love than my love for you. Come back to me and I will make you strong again."

"Brook, so are you coming home with me baby?" Sam asked again.

My heart tugged for the one who loved me first . . . but . . .

"Look at everything I did for you honey!"

As I walked in the apartment I was a little nervous because visions of Sam and that girl making love ran through my head. My body tensed up and I began to get angry all over again. The living room was filled with yellow, white, and red roses in different colored vases. My smile widened because I had never seen so many roses before in one place.

"Are those all for me?"

"Of course baby girl! I wanted you to know how much I missed you and love you. The yellow roses are for our friendship, the white ones are for purity because from here on out I will not mess up like that ever again. And I know you know what the red ones mean."

Sam took me throughout the apartment showing me the roses and how he had cleaned up the house. I was really impressed because it all looked good even though I wanted to seem uninterested.

"This looks nice Sam," I said softly as we walked toward the bedroom.

"Open that box baby girl!"

A red velvet box lay on the bed next to the neatly arranged pillows. I felt like running to the bed and snatching the contents out, but I stayed put at the door.

"Well, aren't you going to go open it?"

"Sam, I really hope you don't think you can just buy me things and I come running back into your arms. I am worth more than flowers and jewelry and you need to understand that."

"Brooklyn, I do understand that sweetie. I just wanted to show you how much I love you. You do know that I love you with all my heart right?"

"Do you really love me . . . I mean unconditionally?"

"Uhmm, have you looked around here? I went out and did all this for you and you asking me do I love you? Hell yeah I love you. Now will you please open the box?"

I walked as slow as I could to the bed and picked up the box. I knew it wasn't a ring since the box was long and rectangular but my heart was still filled with excitement and seemed to skip a beat.

"Oh my God! Where in the world did you get this from? Where did you get the money for this baby?"

I sat down on the bed starring at a beautiful white and yellow gold swirl link tennis bracelet with begets and round diamonds. My mouth stayed open as I sat on the edge of the bed with the red box in my hand. Sam came over and took the box and sat it on the nightstand.

"Now, do you believe I love you? I am so sorry baby girl and I promise I will never hurt you again."

He grabbed my face and began to kiss me softly. I melted like putty in his hands.

"Sam, promise me you won't hurt me again, I need you there for me and not anyone else," I said in between each kiss.

"Shhh, come here," Sam said as he pulled me closer to him and laid me down on the bed.

"Brook, you are the only one I want and I am not going anywhere."

"Shhh," I said, "and kiss me!"

"Sam, where are you going?"

"I have to go to the campus for a little bit but I will be right back. Stay in bed and get some rest. I put your things up so all you have to do is rest today."

"Why are you going up to the campus?"

"I have to pick up some papers from coach. Don't worry Brook I will be right back."

Sam kissed my forehead and walked out of the room. My stomach immediately felt the butterflies that I initially felt when I found out about him and Pat. I almost didn't want to show my face on campus because I heard she went and pressed charges. Maybe if I stay low key then all of this mess will fly over.

"Lord, please don't let him be cheating again," I whispered.

"Brooklyn, you are worth so much more than a diamond bracelet. I want to give you all your hearts desires. Just commit your ways to me . . ."

That voice always seemed to come at a time when I needed comforting or was about to make a serious decision. I knew in the back of my head that Sam was still trying to cover something up. I just felt it in my heart.

"Hey girl, what are you doing?"

I called Asha to see what she was doing. I knew she had gone home for the weekend to vacation with her family and I wasn't sure if she was back.

"Hey girl, how are you? I haven't heard from you since you and Pat fought in the library. Are you okay? Are you and Sam back together? Lord, I hope not because that dude lost his mind bringing somebody else into y'all house."

Asha started going off and I tried to stop her before she went too far. She was my girl but sometimes she took things too far too fast.

"I'm good and yes we are back together. Girl, you should've seen this house when I got back. The house was clean like he had Molly Maids come over and then there were roses all over the place. Red ones, white, and yellow ones. Then he took me to the bedroom and there was a red box sitting next to about a hundred pillows. Do you know he even went and researched what each flower's color meant and got just the right colors for our situation? I am still in shock."

"Are you serious? And what was in the red box? Please don't tell me this dude proposed to you?"

"Naw, but I have a real good feeling its coming soon! It was a beautiful diamond tennis bracelet. It came from Zales so I know it is the real deal. I told him he better not think he could just buy me with diamonds but shoot that did the trick to keep me around a little while longer!"

"Girl you a mess. So what are y'all doing for Christmas? It is literally right around the corner."

"I know . . . all my family is going to my mama house and I think Sam is going to see his sister in D.C."

"Wow, y'all not gone be together? I can't believe it! I think we are going to Colorado for our annual ski trip. I am almost tired of traveling. I am really ready to have Christmas at home for a chance. It's okay traveling with the family but I want to see what it is to be at home with the family. You know what I mean? Spend some quality time with the family like y'all do. My daddy is always working and even when we go on trips he seems to have to work and my mama is off somewhere drinking."

I could tell Asha needed to vent since she went on and on with what was wrong with her family. Even though I was a little envious of how much money they had, I didn't want a family that spent no time with each other. We were probably poor and fought a lot but one thing we had for each other was love.

"Hey listen, if you don't want to go with your family you can always come home with me. Sam will be gone so we can go shopping at the Galleria and hang out in Midtown."

"Man, that's awesome! I will talk to my daddy today and let him know that I do not want to go to Colorado. My mama will probably be happy that I spoke up because she actually hates the trips. She can't bring her 'special' liquor with her and that makes the rest of our lives hell when she has to get a substitute."

"Girl you are crazy. Hey I gotta go; I think I hear Sam coming in the door."

"Where he been this early in the morning?"

"He said he had to go to the campus to pick up papers from his coach."

"Up to the campus? Are you serious Brook? Is he starting that mess again?"

"Listen, I am not trying to even think about it because if he is messing around still, who got the diamonds?"

"You right, baby. Well I will talk to you later . . . love you chica!"

"Love you too, call me and let me know what your dad says, okay. Bye!"

I hung up the phone with Asha in a hurry even though I knew Sam wasn't coming in the door. I didn't want her and anyone else thinking he was still cheating even though I was.

❀

"Mama, what time is everyone coming tonight?"

"Well, you know we open presents at midnight so they will probably be here around 11. Make sure Chrissy has her clothes on right and cut the lights on outside."

When I got home that night Mama Betty was making egg nog and had just put a cake in the oven. Big Mama had made it to the house too, and was mixing some sort of batter in a large mixing bowl.

"Hey Big Mama, what are you making? Is this for tonight? Can I lick the bowl?"

"Hey Brook! You know this is my special banana pudding that everyone loves. Yes, you can have the bowl baby girl. I am almost finished. Here, hand me those bananas and that chopping board."

This was Christmas! Cooking, laughing, and the O'Jays in the background singing Christmas carols. I was so ready to see all my family I hadn't seen in a while and open all the gifts. Asha was coming over later, Sam was gone and Christmas Eve night was in full swing. The doorbell started to ring one after the other and before long the house was full of Rideaux's and other family members. It was close to midnight and everyone had made it to the house.

"Ding, Dong . . . Ding Dong!" The doorbell rang again for the final time. I looked around and it seemed that everyone was there that was coming, including Asha.

"I'll get it," I yelled to Mama Betty who yelled out for someone to get the door.

"Who is it?"

"Telegram for Ms. Brooklyn Rideaux!"

What in the world is a telegram and who knows where I live? I opened the door feeling safe since the whole crew was at the house and a white man dressed in a tuxedo and top hat stood with red roses smiling from ear to ear.

"May I help you sir?"

"I am looking for Ms. Brooklyn Rideaux, is she here?"

"I am Brooklyn," I said and at that moment Sam stepped out from around the corner. The white man in the top hat handed the flowers to him and began to sing. I had never heard a white man sound so much like Brian McKnight in my life. As he sang Sam smiled and got down on one knee. I couldn't understand why he was in Houston and why he was at my door on one knee, but I was excited to see him.

"Mama Betty, Big Mama come see this," Pearl yelled back into the house as she came to the door. Everyone including Tommy Boy who had just got to the house came to the door to see all the commotion.

"Brooklyn, I love you so much and I want to spend the rest of my life with you. Will you please be my wife?"

Chapter twenty-one

"Hell to the naw," Tommy Boy hollered out after I accepted the proposal, "I don't know this fool. Ain't this the one, Betty that had Baby Girl going to jail behind him? Hell naw, she ain't marrying this fool!"

Tommy Boy was showing his true Fifth Ward/New Orleans culture now that someone was interested in taking me off his hands.

"Tommy Boy," Sam began to interrupt.

"That is Mr. Rideaux to you son," Tommy growled.

"Yes sir, I have made my mistakes with Brooklyn and I am sorry for them but I love this girl with all my heart. I mean, look at the diamonds I have put on her wrist and hands."

"Listen to me you little punk. My baby cannot be bought and just because you put those little cubic zircon diamonds on her don't mean nothing. My baby is worth more than some funky piece of jewelry. Now you listen, I haven't been here with Brooklyn to show her what a real man looks like and I blame myself for that, but I am here now. I am not going to sit back and watch you destroy my baby's heart with your cheating ways, you dig?"

Tommy Boy was in rare form and wasn't backing down to Sam. Even though he stood a little shorter than Sam you would think he was a giant by the way he spoke to him. It felt good to have my actual father try to take up for me. I always had to fight my own battles but now having someone say the same things I heard the audible voice say to me was amazing. I wondered if this was how Tommy Boy handled the dudes in the hood. If this was his way of getting what he wanted.

"Tommy Boy, I love Sam and I know he is the one for me. I appreciate you trying to be there for me but I am grown now and this is my decision."

The room got so quiet you could hear a pin drop. No one had ever in life stood up to Tommy Boy the way I did. He was the "Don" and in the past whatever he said was it; no questions asked.

"Brooklyn, you listen to me. I am your father . . ."

"You mean my daddy . . . ," I interrupted.

"Little girl . . ." Tommy Boy stopped in the middle of his sentence and walked out of the door bumping into Sam on his way out.

"Congratulations Brook, I am so happy for you and Sam," Mike interjected. He was my real father and to know that I had his approval made me feel that much better. He came over and shook Sam's hand and gave him the "man hug."

"What's up bro! Now we can hang out for real with the frat and chill!"

Sam squared his shoulders and hugged Mike back. His approval not only meant a lot to me but it meant more to Sam.

"Big Mama, look at this ring! I am getting married! Can you believe it?" I said sitting next to her at the table. Everyone continued to party and enjoy the music while we chatted.

"Brook, marriage is a big step. Make sure this is something you truly want and if you're sure than I am here to support you all the way. I love you baby girl."

"Thanks Big Mama. I think this is what I want, though. Sam has changed and I know he will take care of me and not let other women come between us anymore.

"As long as you know baby girl," Big Mama said as she got up from the table.

The music was loud and the laughs and smiles chimed right in. Before long the gifts were opened and all the family was leaving. I was unsure if Tommy Boy would try to talk to me again before he left, but he didn't. He helped Big Mama pack up her things and got in his car and left. I was a little upset but when Sam came asked me if I was ready to go, my mood changed.

"Baby girl, you ready?"

"Where are we going? I thought you were headed to D.C. to see your sister."

"I told you that just so you wouldn't get all nosey about my plans to propose to you tonight. Everyone is flying down to my grandma's house and I want you to come with me. This is the perfect chance for you to meet the family and for them to get to know you. So what do you think?"

I didn't know what to think. Everything was happening so fast. Proposal and meeting the family. What next, some kids?

"Can we talk about this in the car? I am going to say bye to Mama Betty and Chrissy. I will meet you outside."

"Okay, its late Brook so don't take forever," Sam said as he walked out the door.

Who in the Sam Hill does he think he is talking to?

"Mama Betty I am leaving now. Sam asked me to go to his grandma's house with him later to meet his family. I told him we would talk about it in the car. What are y'all doing tomorrow?"

"Meet his family? Already? Well I guess since y'all about to get married. Uhmm, that's fine Brooklyn. We will be here cleaning up and eating. So go ahead and leave your family to be with his family. What about Asha? I thought you invited her over for Christmas with us and now you leaving?"

"Asha will still come over. I guess you didn't notice that she left with Anthony. Trust me; she will be here for Christmas dinner with her new Boo! I'm gone. I should be back in a few days so I am going to leave my car here, is that okay?"

"As long as you leave the keys."

What's the deal with Mama Betty's attitude? So what I'm leaving the family to go with Sam. Big deal, we are about to be married.

"Why do you need my keys? No one should be driving my car while I am gone."

"In case I need to move it for something, so if you want to leave the car leave the keys."

"Don't even worry about it," I said as I walked to the back to hug Chrissy. My heart was beginning to race at the fire Mama Betty brought in me. It was almost impossible for her to be happy for me. Nothing I did seemed to matter and I was just about tired of her games.

"Bye Chrissy, I will see you later. Me and Sam about to leave."

"Why you leaving? I thought everybody was coming back for dinner," Chrissy slowly said. The IV that was coming out of her stomach made her move a lot slower and talk slower. I hated to see her get the medicine, because it made me hurt inside. Just to see everything that she was going through at such a young age made me appreciate my life all the more.

"I love you sweetie, but I have to go. I will call you tomorrow, okay? Are you happy for me? You know now that I am going to get married?"

"Yeah," she said softly, "just don't have a lot of kids." Chrissy smiled as she blew me a kiss and turned over in her bed. I grabbed her kiss out of the air and put in on my heart.

"I won't."

"Brook, get up! We late!"

Sam jumped out of the bed and ran to the bathroom. I heard everything he said but I couldn't move. I had taken my medicine when we got home and my legs and hands were numb.

"Sam, I can't move my legs. And my hands are numb, too."

"Girl, stop playing and get up. I told my mama we would be there by noon and it is already 10. It is going to take us at least three hours to get to Dallas. Now come on Brooklyn, we gotta get out of here."

I wanted to scream at him but he wouldn't understand how my body was feeling. I guess this was the beginning of my life as a wife and no understanding from my husband. I grabbed both of my legs and threw them over the edge of the bed. I rubbed my hands hoping to get the pins and needles feeling out as I struggled to get up.

"Lord, please help my body. I don't need this to stop me . . . not now," I whispered as I managed to get up.

"What did you say Brook?"

"Nothing, I was praying."

"Oh, well pray fast cuz we got to get out of here in ten minutes. And I do mean ten!"

I was determined to put an end to Sam's abrupt tone and attitude before we walked out of the door.

"Let me tell you something before this goes any further, you had better watch how you talk to me because I am not having it. Not here, not at your mama house, not anywhere."

"Brook . . . whatever! Just hurry up!"

Sam obviously thought I was just talking out the side of my neck but I was so serious. So serious that the three-hour drive seemed like ten hours with all the silence.

"Brook, you gone ride all the way here and not say anything to me? As long as you drop it before we get to my mama's house. I will not bring a rude girl to meet my people so you better let that attitude go before you get out this car."

I could not believe my ears. Where did this person come from and what did he do with my baby Sam? I was not going to let him talk to me that way and I did nothing about it.

"SSSLLLAAAPPP . . . who do you think you talking too?"

Before I knew it and without thinking I had reached over and slapped the mess out of Sam. He was shocked but kept driving and I looked over at his red face and his flared up nose. I wasn't sure if he would pull over and put me out or beat me once we got to his mama house but he didn't say anything else the rest of the way.

"Hey Mama! I missed you guys! Hey Grandma! You shole looking good," Sam happily said as he jumped out of the car once we reached his parents house.

"Hey baby! You getting taller and looking more and more like your father!" Mrs. Johnson was a short plump lady with chocolate colored skin and long gray hair. She walked off the porch of their gray two story house and gave Sam a huge bear hug. Sam's grandmother stayed rocking on the porch in her rocking chair while looking over her slim glasses.

"Sam, where is your special lady?" Mrs. Johnson asked.

"She is in the car. Brook, get out the car and come meet my mama and grandmother."

Sam walked over to my side of the car and opened the door for me. I could still see the pissed off in his face as he forced a smile. He grabbed my purse and held out his hand.

"Baby, come here. This is my mother and over there is Grandmother."

I wasn't sure if I should try to hug his mom or give her a handshake so I waited for her to initiate body language.

"Hi Mrs. Johnson," I said smiling from ear to ear, "you all have a lovely home."

"Hi there Brooklyn," as she walked up and gave me a huge bear hug as well, "we have been waiting for you guys to get here. And look at her Sam, she is beautiful, "she said to Sam as she let go of her death grip.

"Mrs. Johnson, I have heard so much about you and Grandmother. Sam has told me about all the good cooking you do around here and I can't wait to taste it!"

"Mama, where can I put Brooklyn's bags? She packed like she was moving down here or something. I told her we would only be here for a few days so she brought a few bags!"

"Boy, didn't I teach you about women? We always over pack because we never know where we may end up. Anyway, dear you can put her things in the guest bedroom and you put your things in your old room. I hope you two didn't think you would be sleeping in the same room in my house!"

She laughed as she and Sam walked in the house. I grabbed my small duffle bag out of the car and hurried behind them. As I walked into their house it reminded me a lot of the house Papa built for Big Mama. Not because it was small but it seemed to have so much love.

"You two go on in and wash up. I will be serving dinner here in a little while. Sam . . . honey are you alright? You seem disconnected from something. Is it that drive that wore you out?"

I wanted to get down on my knees right then and there and begin to apologize to Sam for slapping him. I knew that wasn't right, but he made me mad and I didn't know of any other way to hurt him like he hurts me with other women.

"No, mother I'm fine. I guess it was the drive that has gotten to me," he said as he looked over at me with a smug face.

"Brooklyn, come in the back and let me show you where everything is," Sam said as he motioned for me to follow him.

I reluctantly walked to the back with him bracing myself for a needed knock out.

"Brooklyn, if you ever in your life put your hands on me like that again I will kill you. I don't know who told you it was okay to fight or hit a man but you better be lucky I'm not like most dudes who would've put you out or kicked your tail. Do you understand me?"

There really wasn't much to say for my defense. He was absolutely right and I was so thankful he didn't knock me out.

"Brooklyn, just because your mother fought your daddy and your aunt fought her husband doesn't mean you have to become a product of your environment."

My comforting and sincere voice began to speak to me again before I answered Sam.

"So what does that mean?" I thought.

"It means you have the power to control your actions and you don't have to lose control just because you have seen others lose control. Be not conformed to this world but transformed by the renewing of your mind."

Chapter twenty-two

Meeting Sam's people for the first time was cool. They were definitely a little country, but I could get used to them. I really loved the fact that they ate a lot and all sat together when dinner time came around. His mother treated me like I was her daughter from the first day I was in her house. She fed me well and even mentioned that I needed to put on a little weight.

"Mrs. Johnson, I really appreciate you all cooking me all this food. Maybe you will meet my mama and Big Mama one day and y'all can cook together."

Mrs. Johnson looked at me like I had said something wrong. She shook her head at Sam and his grandmother and walked back into the kitchen.

I was so happy Sam didn't mention our little dispute to his mom. As a matter of fact he acted like nothing had happened. My heart was extremely heavy knowing that I had hurt him and he still shielded me from what could have been some crazy drama from his mother.

I remembered hearing stories of how Tommy Boy and Mama Betty would often fight and seeing Pearl fight with Jazmine's father. Mike once told me that Aunt Sheila and her husband would fight so bad that they both ended up in the hospital.

"Their past experiences do not have to be your present realities."

"Sam can we talk about what happened?" I asked on the drive back to Hempstead.

"There is nothing to talk about. I told you if you ever put your hands on me like that again I am going to hurt you and I mean that!"

I felt like I was a child being scolded by her father, so I kept quiet as long as I could. His matter-of-fact tone really got my attention and I was a little intimidated.

"Baby, I am so sorry. I am not sure why I felt the need to put my hands on you. All I know is I love you and I will never do that again."

I waited for a response but Sam stayed focused on the road and showed no emotion.

"Did you hear me?" I asked, touching his forearm.

He moved it off the console and began rubbing the back of his head. That notion hurt and the rejection that I felt again from him was evident.

Sam broke the silence and said, "Brooklyn, what do you want me to say? You know what pisses me off? Everything has to be your way. Do you want me to say what happened is okay? Well it's not okay and I am not going to tell you it is."

By now his emotions were in full force and his true colors were showing.

"How would you like it if I just reached over and slapped you?"

Out of nowhere Sam's huge hand came from the back of his head and landed across the back of mine. The slap was so hard that my head went forward and hit the dashboard. For a minute I thought I was unconscious until I heard the music on his radio go up.

"Now, how did that make you feel? You didn't like that did you? So like I said, don't put your hands on me again."

I could not believe what had just happened. Sam knew my intention was not to hurt him but yet he felt it necessary to put his hands on me.

"Listen Brooklyn," Sam said as we pulled into our apartments, "I know you grew up with very dominant women in your family, but as you know all of them are single to this day. You don't have to be like them or act like them. You know I was really hoping you were different."

His words hit me like a Mack 10 truck and what little confidence I had left was crushed. I wanted to say something back to him and give him a piece of my mind but my head and heart were both in pain.

I was only three weeks away from graduation and I had not passed the certification test to become a teacher yet. Sam had already graduated and was working for an engineering firm in Houston. He was happy with his job and the people he worked with, which often made me a little jealous. I had begun my student teaching at a school in Houston that had no black teachers on campus. The principal of the school was an older white lady who had been there for over 25 years and my teacher supervisor was a little white lady who was very young and rich. She and her husband lived in the suburbs of Houston and only came into the inner city for work. I had taken the teacher certification test already four times and was unsuccessful with very little hope. I was scheduled to take the next test right before graduation and I had not prepared for it at all. I found out about a review session that was being held on campus for two weeks and there was no way I was going to miss it.

"Sam, hey are you busy?" I called him at work while I was on my way to register for the upcoming review session.

"Hey Brook! I am but what's up?"

"Dang, how are you doing? Sometimes I just want to check on you and see how things are going."

"That's not why you called me. You would have sent me an e-mail to check on me, now what's up?"

"Whatever, hey I am going to register for this review session that is being held on campus but I need the money. Can you transfer it into my account right now? I need to write them a check but I don't have the money to cover the check."

Sam got quiet as if he was thinking about whether or not he was going to put the money in my account. I really didn't like asking him for anything because I was often drilled or questioned about what I was going to do with the money. I hoped and prayed that this didn't turn into an argument.

"Brooklyn, what happened to the money I gave you last week?"

"I spent it!"

"On what?" he said roughly.

"Stuff," I replied, "listen, are you going to put the money in my account so I can take this review session and pass the test and get a real job? And not have to ask you for anything."

That part I whispered but inspector gadget still heard me.

"Brooklyn, I don't mind giving you the money I just don't want you to waste it on a review class that won't help."

"What are you trying to say? You saying I'm dumb or something? You know what Sam, I hate that I even called you for help. Don't worry about it I will get it from somewhere else."

I hung up the phone angry as hell because he knew I didn't have anyone else to get the money from except him.

Knowing the material for the test was no problem for me but when it came to me being in the room sitting at the desk and actually taking the test, some sort of fear would come over me.

"Brooklyn, I did not give you the spirit of fear, but power, love and a sound mind. You can do all things through Christ that strengthens you."

The Father kept reminding me of all that he put in me but it never seemed to come out when I got ready to take any test.

"Is there a Ms. Rideaux here?" the instructor called out as I was walking into the room.

"Yes, I am here," I gasped as I grabbed the first seat near the door. I looked around to see if there was anyone in the room that I knew, but I didn't recognize anyone.

"Ladies and Gentleman, I am Mr. Tyler and I will be your drill sergeant for the next two weeks. Everything I tell you and give you will help you to be successful on the test. Passing this test will enable you to become a teacher in the state of Texas only. I have 30 years in this profession and I am well equipped to give you everything you need but I can only do my part and the rest will be left up to you."

As Mr. Tyler continued with his dissertation I began to daydream and slip into a nod.

"Excuse me Ms. Rideaux, if you are coming here to sleep, then I will excuse you now and wish you the best of luck. But according to your record of how many times you have failed this test you need to be here and AWAKE!"

"Oh no he didn't! Did this dude just call me out in front of all these people I do not know and put my business in the street? I do not have to take this . . . I paid him to be here. I'm out," I thought.

"You need this Brooklyn and you cannot afford to walk out of this session. Remember what your dad told you, be wise as a serpent and humble as a dove."

"Ms. Rideaux, are you leaving?"

This dude was still pressing my buttons and everything in me wanted to walk clean smooth up out of that classroom.

"No sir, I am sorry I just got back from out of town. I'm awake, I'm awake," I said while wiping my face and sitting straight up in my seat.

"Thank you, now is there anyone else in here that feels they do not need to here and that this is boring? If so you too can leave now. If there is no one then we can continue."

After sitting for four hours and taking as many notes as I could, the class ended and Sam was blowing my phone up.

"Brooklyn, why haven't you answered your phone? I have been trying to get in touch with you to let you know I would be getting off work late tonight."

"Why are you getting off late? I thought we were going to the movies tonight."

"I know, I will make it up to you but right now I have to finish this report by the morning. You understand right?"

"Hell naw, I don't understand! I don't understand why when we have plans to do something you always have something to come up. Sam I'm tired of this and I hope to hell that you are not cheating again because this time I ain't fighting no heifers . . ."

I was livid and Sam knew it! I hung up the phone without saying goodbye and drove home in silence. I needed to talk to someone but there was no one available. Mama Betty was dealing with Chrissy, Pearl had Jaz and Mike was with his wife and Asha was with Anthony Who could I vent to before Sam reached the house and I go off?

"Brooklyn, I am always here. I promised you I would never leave you nor forsake you. I want you to talk to me."

"Okay," I said sounding and looking real crazy talking to myself, "you want me to talk to you but you know everything. I am scared about this test. If I don't pass it then I won't have a job. Sam is cheating again and I know it. What is wrong with me? I have been there for him and tried to please in every way I know how but it's not enough. So what do I do?"

I began to cry as I talked to the Father. I know I sounded stupid but my heart was heavy and I needed the one who created me to fix me.

"That's the problem; you are trying to please him instead of trying to please me. I am your source, strength and I am not like man . . . I cannot lie. Trust Me Brooklyn, I promise I won't let you down."

I wanted to trust the Father and I remember reading the word and it saying just what he said to me; that He would never leave me and if I would just trust Him then he would direct me and make my paths straight.

"I trust you Lord, please tell me what to do. Please take these feelings of rejection and loneliness away. If Sam is not the man for me, move him out of my life."

The day of the test came way too fast and the review session ended just as quick.

"Ms. Rideaux I am still baffled by how you couldn't pass any of the previous tests. You are extremely bright and you know most everything I am telling the students in this class. You could actually be the instructor," Mr. Tyler said as he let us out of our last session.

"That is why I came to this session Mr. Tyler. This was my last hope and even though the information didn't change the delivery and the deliverer did. I appreciate you for being so tough and letting me know that everything I need to succeed is already in me. You did your part so now I am about to do mine."

Mr. Tyler held out his hand for me, but I grabbed his waist and hugged him like he was my father. He seemed stunned and stood still but then relaxed and hugged me back.

"Good morning, today you will take the Professional Pedagogy test for Texas teacher certification. As soon as you get your test please read the directions and you may begin. You will only have five hours to complete the test and once your time has expired I will collect your tests and you may leave."

I was all too familiar with those words but for some reason the nervousness that I use to feel I no longer felt.

"Remember I did not give you the spirit of fear. Look around you at all the posters on the wall."

Ironically, the teacher that used the class on a regular basis forgot to take her motivational posters off the wall. I sat next to the far right side wall and all the posters spoke directly to me.

"It's only impossible if you don't try," "Look to the future this job is already done . . . you have the victory . . . ," did God himself come in here and put these posters where he knew I would be sitting?

"Okay, Brook, this is your day! You know the information now put it back on paper. Remember I can do all things through Christ that strengthens me. Its mine . . . I got this!"

It took me the entire five hours to answer 120 questions but I did it with confidence and hope. Before I got up from my seat, I whispered a short prayer of thanks to God and handed my test to the moderator. I had the biggest smile on my face, which seemingly surprised the moderator and she asked me to wait while she checked my work. Did she think I had cheated or something? Whatever. This was it for me and nothing was going to take my victory away!

Chapter twenty-three

Mrs. Smith came into the class with her thin red glasses pulled down over her nose and looked out at the students' work on their desks. I was a little nervous seeing her in the class where I was doing my student teaching because it usually meant one of two things: I was being let go or I was being hired. Everyone knew that I had graduated and my student teaching would end that week, but no one had mentioned anything about hiring me. I went to several job fairs in Houston but I still had not heard anything.

"Ms. Rideaux can I speak to you for a minute?"

The kids began packing up their things to go to physical education and computer class as I walked over toward Mrs. Smith.

"Boys and girls you can finish your math work when you all come back from your classes, okay, let's go!"

I walked all the kids to the door and went back into the classroom to speak with Mrs. Smith. She was standing next to my supervising teacher and they both were smiling ear to ear.

"Brooklyn, the district has not given me permission to hire you here because we only have a half position for a teacher."

When I heard those words my heart began to beat faster than normal and sweat beads began to form on my nose.

"But," said my supervising teacher, "We want to offer you a position here as a third grade reading and fourth grade math teacher! That is a lot of work but we need your enthusiasm and hard work here and we know you can handle it. So what do you think?"

"Oh God, I was so nervous and I just knew that you were going to tell me today was my last day. I am so happy, yes . . . yes . . . yes! Where do I sign up for my e-mail and where will my class be?"

We all embraced and laughed as the other fourth grade teachers walked into the class with a small cake that said "congratulations" in red icing. Everyone was all smiles except one teacher, Ms. Eastly. She had it out for me and I am not sure if since I came on board made her feel any better. Oh well, it's not about her, it's about me and I was loving it!

"Thank you all so much! You all are so sneaky, you already knew about this and kept it a secret! I really thought I was going to have to apply to McDonald's if I didn't know something soon. Thank you all so much!"

We sat and ate cake and talked until the kids walked back into the classroom.

"Congratulations Ms. Rideaux," all the kids yelled in unison.

"You kids knew too, and didn't tell me anything? I'm going to get y'all!"

Smiles and laughs roared out in the classroom as I celebrated with the kids.

"Brooklyn, all you have to do is trust me and I will make sure you're taken care of and all your needs are met."

"Thank you Father," I whispered in the midst of the celebration.

Planning a wedding and trying to buy a house was a monumental task. I moved out of the apartment with Sam and moved in with Mike and his wife in hopes of saving money for the wedding and our new house. Everything was happening so fast and all the drama from Sam and other women had subsided for what I hoped was forever.

"Ms. Rideaux, can you and your fiancé come by the office today to pick out cabinet colors and carpet type? We are scheduled to begin putting everything in the house in about two weeks so we want you all to come in as soon as possible. Please give us a call back here at Pulte to schedule your appointment."

I was about to buy a house and get married all in the same year. Sam wasn't showing as much emotion and excitement as I was, but this was big for a little girl from Fifth Ward.

"Hey Mama Betty, how are you doing?"

"Hi there Brook, all is well over here. How is the planning and house coming along? I thought you would ask me to come with you to pick out flowers and decorations or something, but I see you got somebody else to do that."

Mama Betty wanted so much to help me plan my wedding but she never said anything to me until after I had already asked someone else to help. I didn't think she knew anything about planning a wedding, so I asked a long time friend of the family, Juanita, who had planned several of our church members' weddings in the past.

"I didn't know you wanted to help. I thought you were good just watching the ceremony and looking pretty like all mother of the brides do."

"I am not sure who gave you that idea, but that is not me. I wanted to be involved but that is too much like right. Anyway, have you decided who will walk you down the aisle?"

"Well, I talked to Mike and he said Tommy Boy should do it since he is home, but Mike has been like my dad all my life. But, out of respect for Tommy Boy, I guess I will ask him."

"That is the right thing to do Brooklyn and plus if Big Mama didn't see her son walking you down the aisle she would pitch a fit."

"Yeah, well I am getting off early today to go try on my dress for the second fitting; do you want to come with me? I have to be there for 5 o'clock."

Mama Betty was really the only person I wanted to see my dress. I had everything in my head of how the wedding was going to look. Ever since I was a kid I had everything mapped out and I really didn't want some strong personality person in the way trying to change things.

"That's fine Brooklyn, I will meet you there. What's the address?"

"I don't have it with me so I will just come pick you up. Can you please be ready by 3:30? I know we may end up running into traffic going into the Galleria area so I want to leave early."

"I will be ready, see you later!"

Sam was still living in the apartment that we had together so often times I had to go by myself to the homebuilders for our concerns or questions with the house. His schedule at work plus the distance he had to drive to get to the north side of town would always put him in traffic and cause him to miss our appointments. We decided that since I was over on that side of town I could speak for him to the builders if there were any problems.

"Sam, hey the builders called and they want us to come and pick out the carpet and the cabinets. Will you be able to make it out here this week so we could go together? I know what you like but I would like for us both to be there since this is our first home."

"Brooklyn, I thought we already agreed that you would handle things since I am not as close as you are? Can you handle that small task without me? Dang."

"Who do you think you are talking to? I asked you a simple question that needs a simple answer and now you want to get an attitude. Don't worry about it because I can not only handle that but obviously a whole lot more than you."

"Brooklyn, whatever! Say what you want to say. Like I said, handle that without me please."

Sam hung up the phone without me being able to get another word out. Lately his attitude was horrible and he was often rude. I was really hoping that this isn't what marriage was going to be like because if it was I didn't want any part of it.

"HONK, HONKKKKKK, HONKKKKK . . . Mama Betty you ready? Come on before traffic starts to build up," I yelled as I pulled into the driveway of her house. Not long after Madear passed and Pearl, Johnathan and Anthony got their own places Mama Betty found a rental house that was just right for her and Chrissy. I admired the faith and "bounce back" that Mama Betty had in her. No matter what came her way she always had faith in God and overcame all her obstacles.

"Girl, you act like the store is about to close. Unlock the door so I can get in," she growled as she came out of the house.

I opened the door and put on a fake smile so she wouldn't detect anything with me. Mama Betty liked Sam but like she said, I was her baby girl and if anyone ever did me wrong then she would hurt them.

"Mama everything is coming along really good and we only have a couple more weeks before we close on the house and before the wedding. I am getting a little nervous."

"Girl you will be fine. That is just apart of growing up. You've done a 180 with your life Brook and I am proud of you. You've graduated from college, building your first home and you're about to get married. You managed to do all this without getting pregnant and without dying. I thank God for keeping you and delivering you from those streets."

"Don't cry mama. I know it had to be God because even after I accepted Him into my life I still did some crazy stuff and he was always there."

Mama Betty took out a piece of balled up Kleenex that was in her purse and wiped her eyes. She handed me the used Kleenex when she was done and I did the same. The ride to the bridal store became an intimate interaction between mother and daughter that was way overdue.

"Brooklyn, so what do you think about Sam's people? Are they anything like us?"

"Well, they are all nice. His mother kept feeding me while I was there and telling me that I needed to gain some weight," I said while breaking out into a loud laugh.

"Did you tell her that the Rideaux's don't get big and we all look good?"

"You know I did and I don't think she liked that too much!"

"Well baby girl it is what it is," Mama Betty said laughing.

∞

"Hi Ms. Rideaux, are you here for your final fitting of your dress?" the sales associate asked with a smile.

"Yes ma'am and I brought my mother with me. Is it okay if she comes into the fitting room with me?"

"Of course, mom can come right on in with you. I am going to run to the back and get your gown. I will be right back and there is coffee on the table if you ladies would like a cup."

"Thank you so much," I said as we laughed at how she mimicked the little Energizer Bunny.

As I pulled the puffy Cinderella gown over my head and began to look at myself in the mirror the memories of Sam and Pat sleeping together surfaced. I wanted to forget about them and all the other girls Sam told me he had been with, but that fear stuck out from the back of my mind.

"Brook, you okay? You look so beautiful," Mama Betty said as she came over and started straightening out the gown.

"So Ms. Rideaux, what do you think? I think out of all the dresses you tried on this one has your name all over it," the little Energizer Bunny said.

"Mama, what do you think?" I asked as I turned around to see where Mama Betty had walked away to.

"It's beautiful," she said looking at me through the long glass mirrored door. "It's beautiful."

"Whenever the mother cries and calls a gown beautiful that is the one you need to go with," the store manager said as she came over and handed the energizer bunny a diamond tiara.

"Now, let's finish the look of a princess," she said as she placed the tiara on my head.

I paused and took a long look at the beautiful gown and tiara in the mirror.

"Mama, I think I'm ready."

The weather in the summer months in Houston was very unpredictable. The builders gave Sam and me an estimated time of when the house would be ready and when we could close. The hurricane warnings and heavy rain had a different story. We were scheduled to close three weeks before the wedding and get everything moved in just in time for his family to arrive.

"Sam, is your family still coming this weekend? I mean we will close on the house this Friday and the wedding isn't until next Saturday. Can't they wait a week?"

"How are they going to wait a week Brooklyn when most of them are flying into Texas from up north? Please don't start acting like you are all that since we getting this house. They are my family and they are coming this week."

All this talking crazy to me was about to tap dance on my last nerve and Sam was about to get a mouth full.

"If this is going to be your husband then you have to defer; submit to him even if you think he is not right. I will honor your obedience."

"Sam are you sure this is what you want? I mean we about to buy a house and get married in less than a week. There ain't no turning back, this is it for both of us and once we sign those papers on this house, it seals the deal."

Sam looked puzzled. He rubbed his unshaved chin.

"Did you hear me? Do you want this or not?" I asked.

"Brooklyn, listen I am tired of having to prove to you over and over again that I love you. If I wasn't sure about us then that house would not be built and we we you would not have that four-carat diamond on your finger. Of course I want to be here, but don't think you are going to be running things because I ain't having that shit."

Even though he was still talking crazy, I loved the way he took charge. He really did love me and that was all that mattered.

We made it to the title company right on time for our appointment and I was hoping nothing had changed. I had my mind set on moving into my new house before my wedding so we could at least be a little right with God.

"Sam and Brooklyn, congratulations on your new house! Here are the keys and I see you guys are ready to move today with the U-haul truck waiting outside!"

"Yes ma'am, thank you! We really appreciate it! Come on Brooklyn, baby girl, let's go move into our new house!"

"Sam, did you really bring a U-haul up here? I can't believe you brought a truck to this closing, that is so tacky," I whispered to him as we headed out the front door.

"Brooklyn, there is nothing you can say to me today that will take away how happy I feel. I am going to my apartment to meet Utah and I will be over to the new house later. Go ahead and go over there and start cleaning up. Call your mother and ask her to come and help you out."

He totally ignored every word I had to say and didn't allow my attitude to affect him.

"Whatever!"

"Thank you all so much for coming to our new house tonight! I also want to thank Ms. Williams, one of my student's mothers, for taking on our rehearsal dinner at the last minute. As you all can see, everything looks great tonight! So thank you so much Ms. Williams. Juanita, please come in here and let everyone know about tomorrow. Juanita is my wedding coordinator that you guys saw at the church tonight. She is a long time friend of the family and has been doing weddings for a while. She did a great job at the church so let's give her a hand."

The house was full of Sam's family, our wedding party and even the new neighbors that we invited to come to the wedding were all there. Everyone was having a good time and laughing when Juanita interrupted.

"Thanks Brook, ladies and gentleman please make sure you are at the church tomorrow at 1 p.m. We will be taking pictures at 1:30 and I need everyone dressed and ready to go on time. Also, we will have a few pictures after the wedding, so do not leave until you all are dismissed to the reception hall. When you get to the reception there will be tables reserved for the wedding party. Also, the dinner is a buffet style for the guests, but you all will have a server come and serve you as well as the immediate family."

Juanita was a no-nonsense lady who was fresh out of the military and she didn't take anything off no one. I asked her to be my coordinator because she was extremely organized and professional. She had been in the military for ten years and decided to retire and come back to Houston. I admired her so much because she kept her mind focused on her goals and she achieved them. I had not seen too many people from the ward come out with achieved goals. She had already gone down the path that I was headed on with my life. My career was started and my life was on the right track.

"Thanks Juanita! Sam baby is there anything you want to say to your guys before the wedding?"

I looked around for Sam and he was standing against the wall talking to one of my bridesmaids. They were laughing and cheesing with each other and totally ignoring Juanita and me.

"Uhmm, excuse me! Sam did you hear me?"

The room grew still and silent as I walked over and stood next to Sam and Stefany.

"Baby, did you hear me?" I said trying to crack a fake smile.

"Excuse me sweetie," he said to Stefany. "Yes I heard you. What's up? Naw, I don't have nothing to say but thanks to everybody and to my boys for coming out and sharing this day with me. Oh yeah and thank you mama for coming down too. Look at this house! Don't y'all like it? Man 4,000 square feet and it's just me and Brook. This is a blessing. For real I thank everybody for coming out and sharing this special moment with us."

Sam's mother got up off the couch and headed over to give him a hug. They embraced for a minute and tears began to flow. I had not seen Sam shed a tear since I found out about his cheating and especially not in front of his boys.

"Again, thank everyone for your support and for being a part of our special day," I said as I walked over to Stefany.

"Listen," I said to her, "if I ever see you and my man hehe and hahaing again, especially in my house, it's going to be on in your world. I asked you to be a part of this day because I considered you a friend just like the other six girls, but you have embarrassed me in my own damn house."

"Brook, that conversation wasn't about anything. We just kicking it. You are too uptight right now because of the stress of the wedding. Just chill, girl. You letting this wedding get to your head."

Stefany had been a friend from Prairie View and I thought her to be a cool person. I remember there being rumors about her and Sam hooking up before he and I got together. I never confronted them about it, but seeing them tonight made me wonder.

"Maybe you're right. I am stressed and I need to get some sleep so I can be ready for tomorrow. Okay, girl thanks again for being here to share this most special day with me."

"You got it girl, listen I am leaving so I can be ready for tomorrow. I will see you at the church okay?"

"Okay girl, see you later."

Stefany got her purse and walked toward the front door. Sam looked over at her and motioned for her to come to the kitchen and I followed behind her.

"I thought you were leaving, Stefany," I said as I walked in the kitchen behind her.

Sam looked shocked and walked out of the kitchen.

"Say, Brook, Tony got us a ticket to Vegas and we about to head out. We will be back tomorrow," he off handedly said.

"Vegas, Sam we are getting married tomorrow. You can't go to Vegas tonight. Plus all your family is here and we need to get some rest so we can be ready."

"This is my bachelor party! I have to have a bachelor party and my boys want to take me to Vegas. What's wrong with that?"

Mama Betty walked into the dining room with a look on her face that caught our attention.

"Brook, I have something special for you and your girls tonight. Come on and get everybody together so we can go."

Mama Betty was trying to save Sam from a beat down before our wedding and save me from going back to jail.

"Sam, leave a number where you can be reached besides your cell and go have a good time," Mama Betty said.

Sam walked out with his groomsmen and got into an SUV and left me standing there with my mouth wide open in disbelief.

"Okay ladies, the men are gone and now its time to have fun! Get your bags and let's go. Meet us at the Doubletree in the Galleria in one hour. Brook, you and Stefany can come and ride with Pearl and me."

"That would be good, but Stefany said she was tired so she left early."

My mind began to run races around the thought of Sam and Stefany messing around. We had come too far with our lives to deal with drama from another woman and now that he was about to be my husband I was taking no prisoners. A homicide would be committed if I found out anything else about Sam and another woman.

The weather report called for a 100 percent chance of rain for the day of my wedding. I had never seen a forecast for 100 percent chance of rain and I was really beginning to get nervous.

Asha had ordered her dress while staying in Atlanta and when she picked the red satin dress up from the boutique it had water stains in the front of it. The wedding started in three hours and Asha, my maid of honor, did not have a dress.

"Asha, what did the people say about the dress? Did they order you another one and have it shipped here?"

"They said there was only one other dress in the U.S. and it would take four days to get it here. I did tell them I needed it in two days and they said they could do a rush order. The only thing is we have to go to Sugarland to pick it up and they don't open till noon."

On the day of my wedding everything that could go wrong was happening and on top of all that, Sam was nowhere to be found. He left the house at 9 p.m. to head out to Vegas and no one had heard from him since. His plane was supposed to come in at 6 a.m. this morning and he should've been back home by 9 a.m.

"Okay, well come on let's go ahead and head out to Sugarland now and get the dress. I have to meet my stylist and makeup artist at the church by 1 and you guys have to be there by 1, too."

I began to get a migraine headache and so I popped three Tylenol pills. That old pain and difficulty of swallowing pills never seemed to go away.

"Brook," Asha broke the silence while driving to the boutique, "are you ready to get married? Do you think Sam is ready? I mean I know you know about all the stuff that he has done and are you sure you can move on and let all that go?"

Asha came across very compassionate and sincere.

"Well, I can't speak for Sam but I know I am ready. We have been through a lot but I love him and I chose to stick by him so now is my turn. Look at this rock on my finger! Don't you think if he spent this kind of money for me on a ring he ready to be married?"

Deep down inside there was doubt about Sam and I, but no man had ever showed me such a good life like Sam. Everything that I wanted he got, with some interrogation, but he still did whatever I asked him to do.

"I guess you're right, Brooklyn. I am just looking out for you and I don't want to see you hurt anymore," and she quickly dropped the subject.

The rain came down just as predicted. The church we decided to marry in sat back off the road and the circular parking lot was filled with water.

"Brooklyn, have you talked to Sam this morning?"

Mama Betty sent Chrissy in to ask me if I had heard from Sam. Chrissy and Jazmine were the ushers for the wedding and they both had grown into beautiful girls.

"Chrissy, tell Mama Betty no I have not heard from him and to please ask Juanita to get my cell and call him. I do not want to worry about anything right now."

"Brook, you look so pretty," Chrissy said as she walked out of my dressing room.

"Thanks baby so do you," I said. Even though she walked with a limp she was still a beautiful girl with a beautiful smile.

"Okay, I need everyone to line up like we did last night. As soon as the music begins I need everyone to be in place and ready to walk down the aisle."

Juanita had everyone in place before time and everything was on schedule. A few of the senior ladies from the church came into my dressing room and prayed with me before I went into the lobby for grace in our marriage. The music played and everyone was on the way down the aisle. There was no turning back and this was it for me. I peeked through the window of the church doors and I didn't see Sam standing next to the pastor.

"Juanita, where is Sam? Why is he not standing down there at the altar with the Pastor?"

"Uhmm, Brook. I was trying not to tell you this, but Sam just arrived. He and his best man are still getting dressed."

"Why did you start the wedding if he wasn't here?"

"He called me and asked me not to tell you but he was on his way and needed everything to be in place when he got here."

"Oh no he didn't! He can't tell anybody anything when he coming to his own damn wedding late. I can't do this, this is not gone work," I told Juanita as she handed me a soft white face towel. I dabbed my face hoping not to mess up my makeup. I looked back through the church doors and Sam had made it to the altar with his best man.

"See Brook, everything is going to be fine, here's there."

"I see but where is Tommy Boy? He should be here now so we can walk down the aisle."

"Brook, Mike is going to walk you down the aisle instead. As soon as he finishes singing this last stanza he will be here to walk you down."

"WHAT? Where is Tommy Boy?"

"He got into some trouble late last night and is not going to make it today. Come on sweetie, here is Mike. Let's get you down the aisle."

Mike came and grabbed my hand and the male ushers opened the doors. Everyone in the church stood as the music began to play and Elle, my sorority sister, began to sing.

"Brook, you are beautiful. Don't worry about anything. Let's just get down this aisle," Mike whispered as he walked beside me.

The church was packed and I did not want the guests to know what was going on with me, so I faked a smile and held back the tears. The red and white decorations in the church formed an elegant ambience and the mood was that of love. Everything that Sam and I had been through was for this moment and now the time had finally come and in an instant I was his wife.

"I now pronounce you husband and wife. Sir you may salute your bride!"

Chapter twenty-four

July 27th was the best and worst day of my life . . .
I woke up early that morning almost not realizing where I was. I quickly remembered we stayed at the Doubletree Hotel in the presidential suite given to Sam and me as a wedding gift from one of Mama Betty's church members.

Oh my gosh . . . last night was amazing and beautiful. I could still feel the tingle in my thighs from our night of passion. "I's married now" played over and over through my mind! The things that Sam and I did last night were ONLY what married people should do and we were fully indulged.

Our wedding day was so tiring and emotionally exhausting that I forgot to eat that whole day. All I wanted to do was get out of that Cinderella wedding gown and those high rhinestone heels and slip into my wedding night lingerie for Sam. When we arrived at the hotel we were treated like royalty. A private honeymoon suite overlooking the city skyline was to die for and there on the balcony was a table set for two. The burning candles smelled like sweet jasmine and vanilla and its aroma filled the room. A line of fresh red and white rose petals marked a trail out to the balcony from the front door and covered the ground. When Sam saw the room, the biggest smile came on his face as he grabbed my hand and led the way. I was in heaven! We sat down at the small table on the balcony and before we knew it there was a knock at the door.

"Room service," the voice on the other side of the door yelled.

Room service? That's what I am talking about . . . we're royalty! Being at a nice hotel like this was not the norm for me or Sam so this was a special treat. Sam jumped up and rushed to the door like he was in a hurry to get this guy out of the room.

"Good evening sir, I am Marcel and I will be taking very good care of you during your stay here at the Doubletree."

He came with a small cart that had two silver plated serving trays with dome-size lids. I was hungry but I didn't want to seem greedy. Sam ate at the reception but because I was doing more talking than eating I didn't have much of anything. Our server arranged our meals and left shortly thereafter. Sam slid his hand across the table and gently grabbed mine.

"Brooklyn, all my life I have waited for a woman like you to complete me. Today when I said those vows I meant every word. You are all I need baby girl and I don't want to ever lose you!"

Those words came out of his mouth like butter. His words took my breath away and I began to feel a tear roll down my cheek. Sam leaned in toward me and pulled my lips to his. As he pulled me toward him he whispered over and over . . .

"I love you, I love you, I love you!"

A "man" had never told me those words and meant them before and boy did it feel good. To know that I had someone in my life who was in love with me no matter how I performed was amazing. As Sam began to kiss me I heard another knock at the door.

"Damn, who is it trying to ruin my wedding night already? Don't answer the door baby . . . they will come back," I managed to say in between each kiss.

"Just a minute . . . I'll be right there" Sam yelled to the person on the other side of the door. You would swear I had just lost my best friend. The look on my face told Sam that I was not too happy about him going to the door. As Sam chatted with the doorman, I began to gulp down some of the food our server brought in. Sam walked out into the hall with the bellman and the door closed behind him. I wanted to get up and change into my wedding night lingerie but either the food was too delicious or was too hungry. Sautéed shrimp in a creamy lemon butter sauce over fettuccine, crisp garlic bread and bottle of Don Perignon champagne sat on the table in front of me and I couldn't help but dig in. My baby did all this for me . . . what a true blessing from God! Thank you Jesus!

"Brooklyn, seek to please me first and I will give you the desires of your heart."

"Father, are you happy with me? I mean I am in a serious relationship that I hope pleases you and I know I am going to need you to make this work. Please change Sam and let him be the man you purposed him to be."

"Baby girl, did you eat already? I want to show you something," Sam said as he burst back in the room and cut my conversation with the Father.

"I am not finished, but I ate some, what's going on? I can't go anywhere in this big ole' gown."

"Come back in the room, we not leaving I just want to show you something."

I covered the delicious shrimp and pasta back up with the dome lid and lifted the huge gown out of the chair as I got up. "What's up baby?" I asked as I sat next to Sam on the bed.

"Like I said Brook, I love you and I want you to know that I am not going anywhere. Here I bought this for you."

Sam handed me a black velvet ring box and motioned for me to open it. I smiled from ear to ear and slowly opened the small box still wondering if I was really in heaven yet.

"Oh my God Sam! What is this? Why did you buy me another ring? I mean don't get me wrong it's beautiful. Where are you getting all this money from?"

The box held a platinum past, present, and future princess cut diamond ring with the words "our love is forever" engraved inside.

"Do you like it baby?" Sam asked as I sat on the bed speechless. I didn't know if Sam was trying to buy me because of all the drama he had put me through or if he genuinely wanted to see me happy.

"Baby, I love it! It is beautiful! Thank you so much," I said slipping the ring on my right hand, "you didn't have to do this but I am glad you did."

Sam pulled me close to him again and kissed my neck while caressing my back. His huge hand began to rub my thighs and the other unzipped my gown. I managed to slide the Cinderella gown off and to the floor.

"Baby girl tonight I want to make you my wife . . . tonight I want to show you how a husband is supposed to love his wife!"

I couldn't believe it! I was finally going to a tropical island! I had seen those places on television and never thought I would be there but now it was going to be my reality. Sam had not really told me exactly what island we were going to but as long as it wasn't Galveston, I was good. I knew we were only staying for a few days but I wanted to be sure I did everything the island had to offer and enjoy my new husband.

Sunday morning Sam and I got up early and were determined to go to church after our wedding day. We had seen so many couples go MIA after their weddings and we wanted to be different, so we headed to church early that morning. Man, it felt really good to be sitting in church with my husband. Something about me being able to call Sam that now made me feel real special. As I sat in service listening to the pastor I couldn't help but wonder how Sam was feeling. Was he as excited about our new life as I was? Did the mere fact of me being his wife make him feel real special too?

"Lord, please help me to focus on what the pastor is saying in the service."

As I sat there my mind continued to wander to the new life that Sam and I would have and how wonderful it would be. I guess I was in lala land for a while, because before I knew it the service was over and everyone was headed out. After service we chose to visit one of our favorite restaurants instead of cooking at the new house. Sam wanted to get some rest before we left for our honeymoon the next morning and I understood because I was tired too. We arrived at the restaurant for lunch and I was a little slow getting out of the car. Our long night and passionate lovemaking had worn me out, literally. This restaurant was known for having an overflow of people on Sundays and Sam did not want to wait in line or look for a seat. I looked up to see where he had gone and he was already standing at the door with the ugliest look on his face.

"What's taking you so long? You know how this place fills up quick and I am hungry, so hurry up," he yelled back to the truck.

Those words hit me in the face and embarrassed the hell out of me. An older couple was walking through the parking lot at the time and their noses turned up when they heard what Sam had to say. Sam had not used that tone with me since college and now he decided to let it show up again and in public.

"Dang . . . I'm sorry," were the only words that could flow out of my mouth. I couldn't understand how he could flip so quick from being a saint in church to showing so much disrespect.

"Brooklyn, you over reacting! The man is just hungry and ready to eat . . . quit tripping," I had to remind myself.

As we got our food and headed to find a table we saw our favorite waiter, Malcolm. This guy was a very hard worker and he always took real good care of us. I told Sam that whenever we started our business I wanted to come back and get him to work for us. When Malcolm saw us looking around he waved his hand to summon us to the area he worked. Big smiles came over our faces as we hurried to be seated in his section. The meal was good, but our communication was dry. I am a talker and especially with my new husband I felt that we should have lots to talk about. You know our new life together, planning for a baby and how we were going to make money, etc. Obviously talking wasn't happening today since we barely even asked each other how the food tasted. This was crazy so I broke the silence.

"How is your food honey?" I knew this was a one word answer but I needed something to be said.

Sam looked up at me and said, "good," faster than I had ever heard. Did he not want to talk because he was so hungry? Let me try again.

"Baby, when we come back from the honeymoon I wanted to see if we could go look for a television for the living room. Remember we talked about buying a big screen and I know of a place that has them on sale."

Surely, talking about electronics would spark his attention.

"I don't care," was all that I got out of him.

You don't care … since when? Did I do something to him? Did me getting out of the car too slow really make him this mad?

"Think Brook . . . what is it that I can do to make him feel better or listen to me? Okay, next time I am going to get out of the car faster so we won't have this confrontation anymore," I said to myself.

I raised my hand and asked Malcolm for the check. I knew this wasn't going anywhere so I wanted to go home.

When I asked for the check Sam asked, "What are you doing?"

I said, "I am done and I am full. Looks like you are done, too. So we can get ready to go. I mean come on dude, what is all this attitude about? I did not get married to have to deal with so much drama for the rest of my life and yes, this will be for the rest of my life because divorce is not an option!"

Malcolm brought the check and sat it on the table next to Sam. He grabbed the check and analyzed the prices to make sure that the restaurant didn't add too much to our bill. I needed to go to the restroom so as he prepared to pay I began to get up and head to the ladies room.

"Where are you going Brook?"

"To the ladies room, I'll be right back!"

"Who is going to take care of this bill? I hope you don't think that every time we go out to eat that I have to pay?"

"What?" I could not believe my ears. Is he trying to argue already? The bill could be paid by either one of us, it really didn't matter to me. Okay, so do I go off on this sucker in this restaurant or do I get the check and head to the ladies room? Since this was Sunday and I had just kind of heard the word from my pastor I decided to put the little I did hear into action, so I walked away. I went into the ladies room and sat down on the toilet.

"Lord, what is really going on? This is not how things are supposed to be. We just got married and already we are fussing and about nothing."

As I sat there praying tears began to flow like a river from my eyes.

Why in the world is this happening? If I could've sat on that toilet for the rest of my life I probably would've. I knew that I could not go back into the restaurant with my eyes red and make-up smeared so I got up off the toilet and went to wipe my eyes and clean my face. As I looked at myself in the mirror I could see the hurt but I quickly looked away because that was not supposed to surface anymore. Sam promised that things would be different once we got married. I am not about to go through all that drama like I did before we got married. Every day fighting and fussing. Moving in and out of the apartment. Just chaos and drama and that saga in my life was now over because we are married and he promised that he loved me.

"*Okay Brook, pull yourself together and put a smile on your face. Remember you are royalty, a child of the king.*"

I walked back out into the restaurant and headed to the counter to pay for the check. I could've gone back to the table to pay for it but I didn't want any questions from Sam. The cashier asked me how I wanted to pay and I told her debit. As I began to search my wallet for my card I saw Sam walking out of the door out the corner of my eye. The first thing that came to my head was did he or I drive? Oh Jesus, he drove his truck. If this sucker is trying to leave me here at this restaurant there will be some major consequences and repercussions. I quickly gave the cashier my card and gave her a look like "can you please hurry up?" She handed me my card and the receipt and I rushed right out the door. As I got outside I looked around for Sam and the truck but I didn't see it. I started to get very heated so I walked over to where we were parked. No truck and no Sam.

"This butt face punk. I know he didn't leave me at this restaurant!"

I took out my cell phone and got ready to call him. Just as I began to dial his number, he pulled around the corner.

"Sam, why did you leave without me?" I asked in a matter of fact tone.

"Brooklyn, get in this truck and close the door. I don't have time for that mess. It's time to go."

"Listen, who in the hell do you think you talking too? You have this funky ass attitude and I have not done anything to you. We just got married Sam and already you acting an ass!"

I was really trying to keep from giving him a good tongue lashing, especially since we had just gotten out of church but he was tap dancing on my last nerve and I was sick of it.

"Whatever Brooklyn, just close the door."

I closed the door and sat real still and quiet in the truck. Things were starting to freak me out and I had heard of people snapping due to stuff built up in them. If that was what Sam was going through then he had better get it together before we left for the honeymoon.

White sand beaches and beautiful clear blue water was just like I saw on television. Everything a twenty-two year old could ask for, along with the man of her dreams.

"Sam, this place is the bomb! Where did you find this location?"

"I searched several places on the Internet and this was the one I thought you would like the most. So do you like our room? I made sure that this villa was close to the beach so we could just walk right out onto the beach."

I couldn't believe that God had given me all this luxury at such an early age. I felt like I was the one to break the curse of abuse and singleness among the women in my family. I was not any longer allowing the enemy to travel through generations and destroy families and children . . . it was over!

"Sam, are you ready to go and sit out on the beach? Maybe we can talk to the concierge and see what activities they have today! Come on baby let's go see what is out there for us to do!"

"Brooklyn, we just got here. Let's lie down for a minute and then go out later. I mean we are here for five days so there is no need to rush."

I did not come all the way from Texas to a remote island to sit in a room. The weather was gorgeous and the day was early. I wanted to try on my new bikini and get in the water with my auburn colored braids glowing in the sun.

"Come on Sam this is our honeymoon! We need to get out and enjoy it together."

"Brooklyn, I am about to sit right here for a minute. Just be quiet for a change and enjoy your husband."

"Sam, don't come down here with that mess. You have done a lot of beautiful things for us and I want to share it and enjoy it all with you. But that attitude of yours has got to go. I am going in the bathroom to change into my bikini and shorts and I hope you will be ready when I come out."

I walked away and left Sam sitting in the chair puffing on a cigar he got from one of his groomsmen. I didn't understand how a person could come all the way from the United States to a beautiful island and do the same things they did at home. Pshhhhh, not this chic! I was about to hit the beach.

My bikini fit tight in all the right places and my straw hat and chocolate Dolce Gabana shades sealed the deal.

"Damn, Brook baby you look good. Where do you think you are going? You are not leaving out of this room like that, so you may as well put on some shorts or something."

Sam was obviously starting to get jealous at the thought of another man looking at me. I had to admit I did look good and if I was to walk out of the room with that bikini on it was a chance that I wouldn't return.

"Then come with me," I said as I sat on his lap and began to slowly move to the left and right, "if you don't want nobody looking at me then you better come to protect me."

Sam wasn't budging and I was getting extremely frustrated. I jumped up off his lap and headed toward the door.

"Brooklyn, I said you are not leaving out of this room with that mess on. You better take your tail back into that bathroom and put some clothes on."

Who did he think he was talking too? I had had it with these sudden outbursts of rudeness and disrespect. For some reason Sam forgot that I was grown and the more he said no the more I said yes.

"Bye Sam. I will be down at the bar by the pool."

Sam jumped up out of his chair and just as I opened the door his huge hand came over and slammed it shut.

"What is your problem?" I yelled.

"Didn't I tell you that you weren't going anywhere looking like that?" Sam grabbed my face with one hand. "Go in there and put some damn clothes on before things get bad in here Brooklyn."

"Sam you had better let me go before I beat your ass. You don't run me or anything else."

I slapped his hand down from my face and walked back into the bathroom. He stood at the door as if he was guarding it to keep me in.

"Father, I did not come all the way down here for drama. HELP me!"

I grabbed a pair of sweat pants and the only sweater I brought out of the bag. All my shoes were in the room with Sam and I was hesitant to walk back in there with him.

"Brooklyn, hurry up. Let's go eat," Sam said from the other side of the door.

Had he really lost his mind? Hurry up after he had just talked crazy and disrespected me again? I wish I would.

After several minutes I walked out of the restroom with my bikini but this time with a floral wrap around my waist. I placed my straw hat on and grabbed a different pair of shades off the counter and headed to the door without saying a word. Sam was still standing around in the room as if he was waiting for me to come out. I put my shades on and opened the door.

"Let me go you fool," I yelled as Sam grabbed my arm and began to pull me back into the room.

"Sam let me go right now!"

I didn't weigh but a buck o' five so it seemed as if he was handling a rag doll and that is exactly what I felt like. He pulled my arm and threw me on the floor in front of the door. My hat and shades both flew off and landed near his feet.

"I told you to change, but you want to be ignorant! So since you acting like a child then I am going to treat you like one."

Sam began unhooking his belt on his pants and holding me down on the ground with one hand.

SWOPPP, SWOPPP! "Sam stop hitting me! Stop it right now!"

Was this man whipping me? Had he snapped and lost his mind? This was the man that put the diamonds on my fingers and brought us to this private island and now this?

"Now get up, I told you to stop playing with me. Go in there and change clothes and then we can go get something to eat. When I come back in here *you* better be ready."

He walked out the door and I laid on the floor crying like a baby.

"Lord, what is wrong with this man? This is not who you gave me? What happened? Why did you let me marry this fool?" I sobbed as my cries got louder and louder.

"Sometimes people ignore the warning signs to get what they think they want."

"How did I get myself in this mess? Help me to get out of this Lord, please!"

I began to hear footsteps coming back toward the room so I hurried and crawled into the bathroom. Seconds later Sam came in the door with another woman.

"This is the villa that I bought, what do you think?"

"Sam this is very nice and you did all this yourself?"

Who in the hell is that in my room with my husband? I jumped up off the floor and turned the faucet on full stream.

"Uhmm, Sam do you have someone here with you?" the female voice asked him as I listened with my ear to the door.

"That's just my wife. She is changing her clothes so we can go eat. Would you like a drink while we're waiting?"

The nerve of this bastard bringing another female into our room right after we had an altercation. He knew if we were in Houston and he pulled a stunt like this the Rideaux clan would be on his ass.

"GGGRRHH," I said as I walked out and into the living area, "Sam honey who is this?"

"This is Daisy, she is the concierge here at the hotel and she is the one that set this trip up for me. I wanted her to meet you and see how nice everything turned out."

This dude had flipped the script again. I felt like I had married Dr. Jekyll and Mr. Hyde. Did we not just have a huge blowup and did he not just call himself whipping me like I was his child?"

"Hi Daisy. Nice to meet you but sorry you have to go. Sam and I have a few things to discuss and then we are headed to dinner. Thanks for everything," I said as I shoved her toward the door.

"Uhmm, okay. You guys enjoy your stay."

Daisy, Deborah or whatever her name was sashayed out the door and turned to wave at Sam.

"So does she do personal visits to all her guests' rooms? You know what Sam I didn't sign up for this and I just remembered it's not too late to get an annulment. We technically have been married less than a week and you already putting your hands on me. I want an annulment when we get back to Texas."

I was straight forward and direct with him. I didn't want him to know how he had hurt me and crushed my spirit.

"Brooklyn, I ain't going nowhere and guess what? You are stuck with me for the rest of your life. We ain't getting an annulment or a divorce; like I said at the altar, till death do us part."

Chapter twenty-five

We arrived back in Houston to our new house full of ants. Mama Betty had left my wedding cake sitting on the counter instead of putting it in the freezer like I asked her to do. I saw the look on Sam's face and I knew this could possibly turn into something bad. The ride on the plane was tense and Sam had very little if anything to say to me. I stayed in the villa the remainder of the honeymoon not wanting anyone to see the bruises on my legs. Sam never apologized and acted like nothing happened. He went on excursions without me and even had dinner with that little concierge that set the trip up. I remained distant and quiet because I didn't want a repeat episode of what happen on our honeymoon. So I took my bags into the bedroom and got in the shower. I was hoping Sam wouldn't come in while I was there because I needed some peace. It seemed that was the only time God and I could have a real conversation with each other. As I bathed and let the water hit my back I cringed due to the stinging from the whelps that Sam left.

"Lord, if this is love I don't want it," I cried as the shower water mixed with my tears.

"The love I have for you is unconditional. You don't have to do anything . . . my son did everything."

"I know he did everything on the cross for me but why do I have to deal with this pain and abuse?"

I took one of the fastest showers I had taken in years and rushed to get in the bed. I needed answers so I picked up my Bible and began reading.

"Brooklyn, can we talk?"

Sam came in to the room soon after I got into the bed and sat at the foot of the bed.

"What do you want to talk about?" I asked while continuing to read my Bible.

"Can you please put that dang Bible down and listen to me for a minute? Listen baby girl, I am sorry about everything that happened on our honeymoon. I love you Brooklyn and that is that. Just like you have some issues with being controlling, so do I. So do you forgive me?"

Sam really didn't sound apologetic at all and I kept a quiet nonchalant look on my face while listening to his sad story.

"Brooklyn, are you going to say anything? I mean I am pouring out my heart to you right now and you act like you don't hear me."

Just as I pulled myself together enough to respond to his apology, his cell phone rang. Sitting starring at me and pretending he didn't hear the phone pissed me off all the more and I reopened my Bible and began to read.

"Sam you not gone answer that phone," I said after about five rings.

"I don't have to get that right now, I will call them back. So are you going to answer my question?"

"I hear what you are saying but it is hard for me to accept that when my back and legs are bruised up. I care about you Sam but I am not going to let that shit happen again."

I felt tough and like the time had come for me to speak up. If anyone in my family found out that Sam had beaten me like that he would be dead in a heartbeat. I thought about calling Big Mama, but I knew word would get back to Tommy Boy and he would send someone to hurt Sam.

"I hear you Brook and I promise that won't happen again."

Sam slid to the top of the bed where I was and closed my Bible. His smooth hands gently caressed my breasts and his soft lips touched mine. I believed in my heart that he was sorry after he promised not to do that again so I dropped the issue and kissed back.

"Hey married lady! How are you doing? You pregnant yet?" Asha sounded excited when she called me from Australia.

"Hey girl! Pregnant? Have you lost your mind? We just got married and we are not ready for kids yet," I was not as excited as she was. And since she and I were close she knew something was wrong.

"What's up Brook? You not sounding like yourself."

"Girl, you know! We just built a house, got married and now about to go back to work all in three months. I guess it's taking a toll on me. So how are you out there in no man's land?"

Asha took a job as a chemical engineer for a major oil company and they moved her all of the world. She had been in Europe, Africa, Asia, and now Australia. I was so happy for her but also jealous to a certain extent. She didn't have to put up with the mess that I was dealing with and it seemed she had no care in the world.

"Brook, that sounds good but what's really going on with you? You know Anthony is coming out here this weekend. Girl, I didn't know your cousin was so funny and fine. Anyway, you and Sam okay?"

I wanted to blurt out "he beat me" but I couldn't let her know how unhappy I was really.

"Yeah," I said after a brief pause, "we good."

"Okay honey. You know if you need anything, hit me on the hip. I love you and I will check back with you later. Bye!"

"Bye." Reluctantly I hung up the phone. If I had just told Asha what was really going on then maybe she would have sounded the alarm and freed me from this hell hole. Did I really feel like I was trapped? Naw, I'm in control . . . I'm Brooklyn Rideaux.

The summer had come to an end and I was heading back to work to teach the kids. There were so many things I needed to do and research ways to make learning fun for the kids. Our new house was large enough for us to turn one of the rooms into an office and that is where Sam did most of his work for his job. I decided to look online for strategies to make learning fun for the kids and as I logged in an instant message popped up.

"Hey baby, you working hard tonight?"

Who is this delicious101 sending me this message? I ignored the pop up and continued to surf the web.

"Sam, are you ignoring me tonight? I miss you baby and want to see you," the message popped up again.

I couldn't believe what I was reading and that this person actually knew my husband's name. Being the detective that I am, I needed to find out who this hoochie was and why she was contacting my baby.

"No, I'm not ignoring you, just working. So when are we going to see each other again?"

The instant message came back as quick as I could close out the other one. "TONIGHT!"

"Where?" I typed.

"Is your wife home? I could come by there again!"

My heart raced and my face turned red.

"No this half of a man did not bring this tramp to my house! We just got the house so when did he have time to bring a hoe over here?" The questions flooded my mind and I played right along with her requests.

"No, she is at her mother's tonight for a while. Can you come in an hour?"

"Gotcha . . . ," delicious101 replied.

I shut the computer down and got my mind and body ready for war. I knew Sam would be home in a half hour, so that gave me time to sweet talk him and make sure he didn't leave back out. I went back downstairs and put on a pair of PV Alumni sweat pants and an old t-shirt from a Majic 102.1 promotion. I found my old Nikes in the garage and I slipped those on as well. I put my hair up in a scrunchy and all the makeup I had on from that day I washed off. I was ready for anything and I didn't care at this point what the consequences of my actions would be. I sat in the living room with a glass of red wine as I waited on Sam to come home.

"Hey baby," he said as he walked in the door, "I am hungry. Did you cook anything today?"

"Yes honey, your plate is in the microwave."

I didn't show any emotion as Sam came over and kissed me on my cheek. I kept my face toward the big screen TV and waited for him to sit down and eat.

I had moved my car in the garage and turned the porch lights off so it would appear that no one was home. Moments after Sam sat down the doorbell rang. My heart began to race again and I could feel the tension building in my shoulders.

"I'll get it baby . . . you keep eating!"

"That's why I love you Brook, you got your man's back."

I smiled at Sam and walked to open the door. I kept the porch light off not wanting to scare the tramp off.

"It's me Sam, Delicious. Open up before someone sees me out here!"

I popped my knuckles and opened the door. Delicious wore a long black trench coat with red stiletto high heels. She had turned her back to the door and began to untie her coat. Before the coat hit the ground I grabbed her by her long horse hair and pulled her into the house.

"What the hell is going on?" she screamed as my grip grew tighter and tighter.

"Sam, Sam, what is going on?" Delicious yelled as I drug her into the breakfast area where Sam was sitting.

"Brooklyn, what in the hell are you doing? Who is that?"

"What am I doing? I'm about to commit a murder tonight. And please do not act like you don't know who this is. Who is she Sam?"

I was waiting for him to lie because my grip got tighter and tighter on Delicious head and she was soon going to fly into our glass table.

"I don't know who that is Brooklyn, you bringing some random woman into our house talking about committing a murder. Who is she?"

I turned Delicious around to face Sam and when he saw her face his mouth dropped.

"Delicious?"

"You damn right its Delicious! So you been fucking this bitch Sam even after we got married? You ain't shit and trust me, Tommy Boy and the entire Rideaux clan will know about this tonight. So if I were you I would take you and your tramp to a hiding place because both of y'all going to hell early."

I let Delicious' ponytail go and went into the bedroom. I grabbed my cell phone and began to call Uncle Kenny, the chief of the Rideaux clan. He always told me whenever I couldn't get to Tommy Boy to call him, and today was the day.

"Girl, who told you to bring your ass over here? You know I am married and I told you I will let you know when you can come."

"You told me to come in about an hour so I did. Why is she here?"

"Damn, that was Brooklyn signed in as me and you must've seen my name and thought it was me."

I heard their conversation from the bedroom and I grabbed my police flashlight from under the bed. I was determined to make them remember that night since I couldn't get a hold of Uncle Kenny.

"You damn right it was me and why in the hell are you messing with this slut anyway? Don't worry about it because we have only been married a few months and when I said till death do us part I meant that!"

I gripped the flashlight in my hand and began to slowly walk toward Delicious. She would be the first one I took out and as I made my way to her, Sam moved her behind him and stood in front of her.

"Listen Brooklyn, baby, you need to put that flashlight away before somebody gets hurt."

"That is my intention and you have the nerve to try to save this hoe in our house?" I swung the flashlight at Sam's head and missed by an inch. He ducked and I ended up hitting Delicious in her right ear. She flew to the ground and blood gushed from her head.

"Got damn Brooklyn, look at what you did! This girl could be dead!"

I dropped the flashlight and called the police from my cell phone.

"Hello, we need an ambulance and police to come. We found a trespasser in our house and I was able to knock her to the ground. Please come quick because she is bleeding."

I hung up the phone and threw it on the sofa in the living room. I went and picked up my glass of wine and sat back on the couch waiting for the police to arrive. Sam had gone into the kitchen and got several wet towels and some ice for the hoe's head. Unfortunately, she was still alive, but couldn't seem to pull herself together before the cops got to the house.

The police knocked on the door and I ran to answer it. Sam finally left Delicious sitting up against the wall in the breakfast room to come to the door with me.

"Ma'am did someone call for assistance?"

"Yes, I did. When my husband and I returned home there was an intruder in our house. She tried to attack my husband and I was able to grab a flashlight and hit her with it before she hurt him! Officer she is in the breakfast room on the floor, please help us."

My face was full of tears but no obvious signs of abuse as I could see the cop checking me out.

"Sir are you her husband? Can I come in please?"

Sam nodded and moved out of the way to allow the officer in the house. The officer walked in to where Delicious was sitting and radioed for an ambulance to come to our address when he saw the gash on her head.

"Ma'am did you say you hit the intruder with a flashlight? Looks like it had to be a heavy duty flashlight," the officer commented.

"Ma'am can you tell me why you were in these good people's home? Do you know them?"

I gave Delicious a look that made her cringe. If she said the wrong thing I would make sure she never spoke a word again.

"Brooklyn, this is not you . . . this is not who I called you to be."

"Father," I thought, "not right now!"

"I am so sorry this happened to you tonight. This lady will be taken into custody for burglary and trespassing and I will need you both to come down to the station within the next 48 hours and file a statement. Was there anything missing when you noticed the intruder?"

"Yeah, my husband," I wanted to say.

"No officer as far as we can tell nothing is missing," Sam interjected after seeing the expression on my face.

"Okay, well the ambulance is outside so I will take the intruder with me. You all lock up and have a good night."

The officer walked out of the house and I locked the door. Sam hurried over and picked up the flashlight off the ground and held it in his hand.

"So you think you Billy Bad Ass now right? Well let me see how bad you gone be when I whip your ass. Who do you think you are hurting that lady?"

I stood there waiting for Sam to try and put his hands on me again. I didn't respond to his accusations but instead I braced myself for what could be a long night.

"You know what Brooklyn, you ain't even worth it."

Chapter twenty-six

No one knew what happened with Sam and I and I wanted to keep it that way. Our relationship was our business and plus if the Rideaux family got involved, things would be worse than what they were now.

There was no voice of reason that I could talk to about Sam. I thought about talking to the pastor of the church we went to, but he only wanted to talk when Sam wasn't around. I was not about to get caught up in that foolishness so I remained quiet, again.

"Hey Mama Betty, how is Chrissy?" I asked after calling one day out of the blue.

"She is good Brooklyn. How are you and Sam doing? I haven't seen or heard from you guys since the wedding! You having fun?"

"Uhmm, yeah I guess. Y'all have been on my mind for a while and I thought I would give you a holler."

I wanted to pour my heart out to Mama Betty, but there was no way she would let me stay in this house.

"So how are y'all enjoying that huge house? Do you even go upstairs Brooklyn? I told you that was too much house for just the two of you but if you like it I love it!"

"Well it does get lonely every now and then but I'm starting to adjust. I spend a lot of time at work when Sam isn't home so it's okay. Mama Betty is everything okay with you and Chrissy? It seems like you want to tell me something."

"Well Brooklyn, I wasn't trying to bother you with my problems but we got an eviction notice on the house today and I have seven days to be out or to pay the past due amount."

Mama Betty was a woman with almost too much pride for her own good, so for her to come out tell me she needed something really meant she needed it.

"How much are you behind with? I know Sam and I don't have the money since we just put all we had into the house and the wedding."

"Well I need $1,500 just to catch up. They cut our hours at the job so my checks aren't the same."

"Dang Mama! Did you call Mike or Pearl? What did they say?"

"They told me to call you. You guys have that big house over there and it's just you and Sam. Maybe Chrissy and I can come stay with you guys for a little while. At least until we can get our own place."

I knew Sam wasn't going to even hear that, especially since we just had the cops out and his mistress at the house. I paused and held the phone because I did not want to give an answer without talking to him first.

"I know you all are newlyweds but this will be a very temporary thing. So can I come and stay with my baby?"

"I need to talk to Sam. I will call you back."

I was very dry and didn't want to show any emotion what so ever. I loved my mother but I was not sure how Sam would take the message so I waited a couple days before I asked him.

"Good morning honey! How did you sleep last night?" I asked Sam as we began to get dressed for work.

"I slept okay. I had a dream about your mother and it was crazy but other than that I slept fine."

Oh Lord, what kind of dream did he have about Mama Betty? Does this dude have ESP? Did he already know I was about to ask him about Mama Betty moving in with us?

"That is so weird because she and I talked and she told me that they are having some financial problems. She is about to be put out of her place and wanted to know if she and Chrissy could come stay with us for a little while until she got back on her feet."

As soon as I asked Sam that question I walked into the kitchen and began making us some coffee. I didn't want to see his reaction to the question and didn't want to get knocked out either, so I waited on a response from a distance. For a while the house remained quiet as Sam and I continued to get dressed for work until he finally broke the silence while walking out the door.

"Brook, have a good day. I will see you this evening."

Huh? Did he totally forget that I asked him about Mama Betty or did he just not want to deal with it?

"Okay, babe! Talk to you later," I said sounding confused.

"Oh, and by the way Mama Betty and Chrissy can stay but for only thirty days," Sam said and the front door closed behind him.

Thirty days? What kind of ultimatum is that? Who does he think he is giving me an ultimatum with my mother and sister? This is my house as well and if I want to bring someone in then that is up to me. I didn't know if I should call Mama Betty right away and tell her what Sam and I agreed on or not. I knew she would be happy with having a place to go, but I was not sure if she would be too fond of the thirty day limit. I didn't want to seem like I didn't love my mama or didn't want her to stay with me. I just couldn't understand why she and Chrissy couldn't stay with Pearl or Mike especially since Sam and I were secretly having problems. So I got over it and I was pretty much okay with her coming because we had a pretty good relationship and I was her baby, technically. So if there was anything I could do for my mama I was going to do it and not be worried about the thirty day rule.

"Okay, boys and girls. Today we are going to take a little journey in our minds! I am going to place a photograph on the overhead and turn the lights down. You will hear soft music playing in the background and I want you to try and relax. Focus on the picture and get three things in your mind about what the picture reminds you of, makes you think about, or what you totally dislike about the picture."

I placed a picture of a woman holding a baby sitting inside a barn. The worn clothed lady gripped her baby in fear while sitting next to a pig's slop bucket.

My kids got all into the fact that there was music playing and the lights were off that one or two of them fell asleep in that short amount of time.

I loudly cleared my throat, "Okay, now I would like some volunteers to tell me what the picture reminds you of or what it means to you?"

"Ms. I am not trying to be funny but she looks homeless. Like she just had that baby and she scared somebody was going to take it away or something."

"That is a very good observation, Marcus. She does indeed look homeless possibly and definitely scared. Anyone else?"

Just as I asked for more volunteers my cell phone rang out loud. I normally place it on vibrate when I first get to the school but I guess with Mama Betty and Chrissy on my mind I forgot.

"Okay, guys talk to your partners at your group and discuss the picture for just a second."

I stepped out of the classroom and looked at the caller i.d. to see if I wanted to answer my phone.

"Hello?"

"Brooklyn, where are you?"

Sam was yelling through the phone and seemed to be throwing a fit about something.

"Sam, I am at work. What is the problem? Why are you hollering?"

"Brooklyn, why didn't you tell me that your mother was moving in today? I just told you this morning that it was okay for her to come. I came home and I see a U-Haul truck in my yard. Did you give her a key to our house?"

"No, I did not give her a key to our house. Where are you? Is she at the house now?"

I heard what sounded like working men in the background and I really couldn't make out what they were saying but I heard the word boxes and I knew that she was there to move in.

"Brooklyn, you better call your mother right now and tell her we did not say anything about moving in today. And how did she get into my house?"

"Sam, I am at work. I do not know how she got in the house unless she went through the side garage door that *you* never lock. I mean why are you home in the middle of the day anyway? You talk to her and figure it out. Like I said I am at work."

I was highly pissed off at both Sam and Mama Betty when I hung up the phone.

"Mrs., you okay? We heard you telling somebody off and we didn't know what was going on. Do I need to go hurt somebody for messing with you?" Marcus asked. He was only in the fourth grade but he resembled a mini-giant. He stood about a 5-foot-6 and was already showing facial hair. I asked the other teachers if he had failed a few grades and they all told me he was just very mature for his age. His mother was a short white lady that was very quiet but his father was from Africa and was supposedly a warrior back in the day. I could definitely see the "warriorness" in him and as the years went on I could see him being a wrestler or something.

"No, Marcus I am good. I just had to take care of some business. Okay so boys and girls tell me what you think about the picture."

"Mama Betty, what is your problem? I never told you what Sam said about you moving in with us and now you show up with a U-Haul? Why didn't you at least call me first?" I yelled as soon as I walked in the door.

When I got to the house after work Mama Betty and Chrissy were putting their things away in the closet and dresser in the upstairs bedrooms. Sam was nowhere to be found and the kitchen was a mess with boxes of food and dishes.

"Brooklyn, who in the hell do you think you are talking to?" Mama Betty growled as she walked down the stairs into the kitchen where I was standing.

"Mama, I never told you what Sam and I discussed so how could you just move into our house and then try to do it while we are at work? You didn't think to even call me and ask what he said."

"I know it wasn't the right way Brooklyn, but the sheriff came and put us out. I had literally two hours to get my stuff and get out of the house. I didn't know where to go or where to tell the man to take me so I came here."

"Mama but you still should have called me. You know I have my cell on me all the time. It's like you broke into our house. We didn't know you were coming and we didn't give you permission to come either."

I hated having this conversation with my mama knowing the situation she was in but I had to say something. I needed to make sure Sam was okay and still find out why he was home from work in the middle of the day.

I went into my bedroom and popped three Tylenols and gulped down a large glass of faucet water.

"Father, what is happening? What is going on right now with my life?" I cried while sitting on the closet floor. That was my place of refuge whenever I needed to have a one on one with the Father.

"Brooklyn, Sam is your husband and you have to submit to him. Betty is your mother and you have to honor her."

"What does that mean? I can't just put my mother out on the streets. I am all she has right now and no one else is trying to help me."

Just then my cell phone vibrated in my pocket and interrupted my conversation with the Father.

"Hello," I said sounding drained.

"Brooklyn, I need you to meet me at Starbucks right by the house. We need to talk right now," Sam was very persistent and I didn't waste anytime getting myself together to meet him.

"Okay, I am on the way."

"Why couldn't he come to his house and talk to me? Was he going to try to do something to me away from the house because of Mama Betty being here?" I let the many thoughts run loose in my mind before I left the house.

"Should I take a knife or gun with me just in case this man tries to jump stupid?" I wondered.

I reached the Starbucks and saw Sam sitting at one of the small tables on the outside of the building. There were two cups at the table with him and once again my mind began to wander.

"Hey Sam, what's going on? Why did we have to meet here?"

"Brooklyn," Sam spoke softly, "that is your drink. It's a white chocolate mocha. Is that okay?"

"Okay Lord, is he trying to poison me? Should I drink this mess?"

"Yes, it's cool. Thank you. So what was the urgency about for me to get here?"

"Brook, I love you and I told you a long time ago that when I accepted you I accepted your family too, but today threw me for a loop. I was not expecting the drama today at all and I blew up. I didn't do anything to anyone but I was so pissed off that I had to leave the house."

"Sam I know . . . ," I started.

"Wait Brook, let me finish. I was so upset that I needed someone to talk too. I needed someone to be there for me before I lost my mind. You told me to figure things out because you were working but I couldn't figure it out so I . . ."

"You did what Sam? Who did you call?"

I was prepared to throw that cup of coffee in his face if he said the wrong thing and get my locks changed on my house.

"Brooklyn, like I said I love you and there is no one that can take your place. We have been through a lot together and I need you in my life . . ."

"What is it Sam?" I said beginning to get irate.

"I called Delicious and went by her house. We did sleep together and I immediately left because I felt so bad. But Brook, I needed you and you weren't there for me. She told me that she was going to call you, but I wanted you to know before she called you with something made up."

I sat there for a while with one hand on the hot cup of coffee waiting for the perfect moment to let him have it. I could not believe my ears and what I was hearing from the man I had just married a few months ago. My mind began to think of all the ways I could hurt him and who I could call in the family to knock him off.

"Brooklyn, say something. I am so sorry baby, I really am sorry that is why I am telling you."

Again, I sat there trying to hold back a flood of tears and keep from embarrassing myself in public.

I grabbed the cup of coffee and my purse off the chair next to me. I didn't say a word as I began to walk to my red BMW parked on the other side of the parking lot. Sam looked at me but didn't open with his mouth I guess for fear of the coffee meeting it before the words came out.

"Sam, go back to her house and find yourself. I don't want you to call me or come to our house ever again," I said in a solemn tone. As I turned back to walk towards my car a black BMW speeding through the parking lot slammed on the brakes to keep from hitting me.

"Sam, are you finished? Let's go," Delicious yelled out of her car window. I took one strong look at Sam and shook my head. If he was going to settle for an Internet hoe then he could have her.

"Brooklyn," Sam yelled as he got up from the table, "Brook, don't leave."

"Uh-uh Sam, forget that bitch. Let her go. She don't have what I have Boo. I got you, so let that go," Delicious said.

I walked around the back of Delicious' BMW and headed to my car. The silence coming from me was very unusual and Sam looked puzzled. I thought about running smack dead into her BMW from the side Sam sat on, but there was something that wouldn't let me do it.

"It's not worth it Brooklyn. You are worth so much more than any man could ever give you. I want to give you an abundant life."

As I drove back to the house I thought about what the Father told me but I couldn't understand why everything bad was all happening to me.

"Lord, what are you doing? Why is Sam with that other woman and why am I left here alone again? This is not right, what did I do to deserve this?"

"Brooklyn, he might have left you but you are not alone. I promised to always be here with you. Trust me I will take care of you."

Chapter twenty-seven

The days seemed longer and longer without Sam at the house. Mama Betty and Chrissy were still there but it wasn't the same without Sam, I really missed him.

"Brooklyn, are you getting out of the bed today and going to work honey?" Mama Betty walked in my room and asked one morning.

She had gotten a better job working for ExxonMobil Oil Company and had normal business hours. I had called in to work again and really didn't want to see anybody except for Sam.

"No, I don't feel good. I will probably go to the doctor today," I said as I rolled back over. I hadn't really eaten much since Sam left and I was losing weight by the day.

"Brooklyn, come here," Mama Betty pulled the covers off me and pulled me towards her. Tears immediately began to run out of my eyes as she held me and hugged me tight.

"Baby girl I know you love Sam and miss him but you have so much more in you than just him. I hate seeing you like this Brooklyn. I need you to get up and at least take a shower and eat something. Listen, I am calling in to work today and staying home with you. We will go shopping and get some lunch together, okay?"

Mama Betty meant well but I wanted to be by myself. No one had really seen me like this before and I didn't want to put my pain on anyone else either.

"No mama! You just got that job and you don't need to miss any days. I will be fine. I am going to get up in just a minute," I lied.

"Brooklyn, are you sure? I can stay here with you. Come on and get up now so you can take a shower. I am going to cook you some breakfast before I leave, okay?"

Mama Betty went to my dresser drawer and pulled out a red velour warm-up and white tank top. She went into the bathroom and turned the shower on and lit a few candles.

"Baby girl, come on now and get up. Go into the bathroom and wash up. When you are done your breakfast will be on the table. I love you Brook, I need you to feel better for me. You are my strength so you can't be down right now."

I got out of the bed and went and hugged Mama Betty and laid my head on her chest just like I use to do when I was a little girl.

"Thank you Mama. Please don't tell Pearl or Mike or Asha or anybody that you saw me like this okay?"

"I won't baby girl, I won't. Brooklyn, just know Sam does love you but he is obviously going through some things right now and you cannot save him. The Lord is going to have to deliver him from whatever it is he is dealing with so you take care of you and don't you stop living just because he has."

Mama Betty let me go and walked out of the room and into the kitchen. I guess Mama Betty was right about Sam going through something because it had been several days and he had not tried to contact me at all. I wondered if he was with that slut or if he was with someone else.

"Lord, why did you allow us to get married if you knew he was like this? Didn't you know this would destroy me, your child?"

"Yes, Brooklyn and you did too. Sometimes when you have in your mind what you want you ignore all the warning signs. There were plenty red flags before you said I do."

"But couldn't you stop me from making a mistake? Where is the Comforter you promised who would guide me? Why didn't he say something to me before the wedding and the house?" I asked.

"He tried."

I wasn't trying to hear that because if he is God, the Spirit, then he could've gotten my attention. I got into the shower and stood there crying while the water danced on my back. Our bathroom had a separate shower from the tub that was large enough for four people. Sam liked inviting over a few friends that didn't mind sharing the shower with us. I wasn't too gung-ho about the idea but since he wanted to do it I went along with it. This time for some reason even with only me in the shower it still felt like I wasn't there alone. I stayed in for a while and cried until my head began to hurt.

"Lord, what do I do now? He is gone and I am not sure if he is coming back. He is gone," I yelled, "he is gone!"

There was a complete silence and the Fathers' still small voice I could no longer hear.

"DING DONG, DING DONG," the doorbell rang over and over as I was putting on my clothes that Mama Betty had laid out.

"Who knows I am home? My car is in the garage and the blinds are still closed," I thought as I continued dressing.

"DING DONG, DING DONG," whoever was at the door didn't seem to want to leave.

"Who is it?" I said sternly.

"Brook, its me Sam. Open the door!"

Sam, what in the world is he doing here at 8 in the morning? How did he know I was here? I took several deep breaths and wiped my face with my hands hoping to have no signs of crying or depression anywhere.

"Hey Sam, what are you doing here?" I asked as I opened the door halfway seeming to be all put together.

"Brooklyn, I miss you baby girl and I want to come home. I can't stand being away from you. Can I come in?"

Those same puppy dog eyes that attracted me to Sam years ago in college tugged at my heart again. I wanted to pull him in and make mad love to him right there at the front door. I couldn't let him see my weakness for him; I couldn't let him know he had gotten to me that bad.

"Sam, what makes you think it's okay for you to come to this house and try to come back when I hadn't heard from you in days? I didn't know if that crazy slut had killed you or if y'all had run off and gotten married in another country. I called your job and they say you took a vacation and you were not expected to be back until mid-November. So what the hell is that about? Who do you think you are?"

Tears were on the verge of falling but I prayed for strength. Sam stood at the front door quiet and looking extremely pitiful.

"You called my job? Why did you do that? I don't need those white people in my business Brooklyn. I am the boss up there and as soon as one of them think they have a little bit of juice on me they will try to use it to destroy me. Please don't ever call that job again. Look, can I please come in?"

I thought real hard about letting Sam in that house with Mama Betty and Chrissy not being there. What if he tried something again? I had Greg buy me a small handgun since I was now living in that house with two other women and if anything jumped off at least we had protection.

"Yes, you can come in for a minute because I'm leaving shortly." I opened the door a little wider and Sam slid in.

"Brook, what's that smell? Have you taken out the trash lately?"

"Uhmm, no. I forgot. I will take it out with you as you leave. Now what is so important that you needed to come here early in the morning and in my house?"

"Listen," Sam started as he began walking into the kitchen and on to the living room, "I know we have had our problems but Brook at the end of the day there is no other woman for me. I thought there was because I was getting tired of your nagging and you trying to push God on me. I love God just as much as you do

Left, but Not Alone

but I am not going to worship him like you nor will I go to church every time the doors of the church open. Yes, I went looking for somebody to be everything you weren't but I got something way worse. I love you and I am sorry for bringing another woman into our house, our bedroom and our life."

The whole time Sam stood talking to me in the living room he looked around as if he was looking for something or somebody. I hope he didn't think I would bring another man in this house, especially with Mama Betty and Chrissy being there.

"Sam, I hear everything you are saying but I need to see something. All I have seen is you deny me for a hoe and put her before this family. I can't take that anymore. I have seen you beat me like I was your child, curse me out and then talk to me like I was the slut you were paying. So if you want to be back here you got to show me something different because your words at this point mean nothing."

We stood toe to toe looking each other in the eyes. A sudden fear came over me and I backed up and braced myself for a fight.

"Brooklyn, stop doing that. I am not going to hit you anymore. I said I don't want to hurt you and I mean that . . . in any kind of way. I want to show you that I love you and that I am serious about us making things right."

Sam pulled an envelope out of his blazer inner pocket and handed it to me. The last time Sam handed me some papers it was for an apartment in college. I was skeptical about taking the papers from him in fear of them being for a divorce or a higher life insurance policy or something.

"What is this Sam? Are you asking for a divorce because you could've just called and I would've met you somewhere to sign the papers? I mean you didn't have to come all the way over here to bring me these damn papers!"

"Brook, stop, shut up and just open the envelope. It's not divorce papers!"

I picked my face up off the ground and opened the envelope. The contents looked like airline tickets but I was unsure so I kept looking and reading. The second page said congratulations on booking a trip to Paris, France for June 23-28.

"Sam, what is this? Are you trying to tell me something? Are you leaving?"

I knew Sam wouldn't leave the country but I wanted to see what he was going to say if I played dumb!

"Brooklyn, this is an itinerary for you and me to go to Paris this summer. I put it out a few months from now because I wanted to show you that I am here to stay. I am serious Brook, so will you go to Paris with me?"

Paris? I could not believe that he felt like he could just come back into this house with a trip itinerary and expect me to fall over into his arms.

"Paris?! Are you serious?" I asked cheesing from ear to ear.

"Yes baby! But like I said I have to move back into this house. We have to be together in order for things to work out, right?"

That was a rhetorical question that he knew I was not about to answer. Sam grabbed my hand and led me into our bedroom. I was prepared to give Sam whatever he wanted especially since I knew he loved me again for real.

Things were going really good for Sam and me for the past few weeks. We started going to church together; Mama Betty had saved up enough and moved into her own place with Chrissy and our love life was off the charts. I figured that I was at a place in my life where I was ready to start a family with my husband and begin again. Since I didn't know much information about pregnancy and multiple sclerosis I decided to do some research.

"What about me? Every since Sam came back we haven't talked much at all. Know that I love you Brook and I want to talk to you again."

There had only been a few times when I heard His voice as clear as I did that day. I thought I was still nurturing our relationship even after Sam came back. I mean I was still going to church, paying my tithes and praying sometimes. It wasn't because of Sam being back, I think.

"When he was gone you sought to please me. Now that he is back you have put the most valuable asset in your life down and picked up someone that needs me like you. I am your Source!"

This time I felt His words. My heart began to fill with pain and it seemed as if I had let my best friend down. I wanted to ask Him for forgiveness but what did I do wrong?

"Remember Father you told me to be submissive to my husband and that is what I am doing. Am I doing too much by trying to please him? What am I doing wrong?" I sat down at the computer in our office and tried to think of all the things I could be doing that made God upset. I recalled my sins but I also remember asking for forgiveness for them.

"It's about relationship Brooklyn, not religious practices. Remember that I am a jealous God."

I was starting to get upset so I ignored the voice in my mind and began to think about something that made me happy; starting a family. I remembered seeing a book about pregnancy and multiple sclerosis but I didn't buy it when I should have, so I did a Google search. All sorts of information came back and all of it was positive. The rumor of me not being able to have kids because I had MS was dispelled; I didn't need to take the god-awful shots while I was pregnant because pregnancy seems to have a protective effect in people with MS. Mainly because the immune activity levels are reduced and the level of natural steroids are higher. The research suggested that I stop taking my shots about three months before Sam and I got ready to conceive. Now was the time for me to talk to Sam since things were good and this was our time. As I began to close out the research page, a pop-up came on the screen advertising pornography. There was a picture of two nasty-looking ladies rubbing each other in very inappropriate places and a man in the middle having sex with one and fondling the other. I couldn't believe how people would subject themselves to such ridicule by showing their faces on a computer.

"Asha, girl I am here on the computer looking up MS and pregnancy and all of a sudden a pop-up comes on my screen with two nasty ladies and a man. Does this stuff come on your computer too?" I asked when I called Asha.

"Hell naw, I got a pop-up blocker. What are you doing looking up pregnancy and MS? Are you thinking about getting pregnant?"

Asha didn't really sound like she was too happy about the thought of me being pregnant since she knew most of everything that had happened between Sam and me.

"Yeah, I'm thinking about it. Why you sound like that?"

"Brook, you my girl and I know you sometimes live in this bubble where you think everything is and should be perfect. But look at the stuff that Sam has done. If y'all have a baby and he starts acting up again who is going to help you?"

"Well, lately he has been fine unless he doing some real undercover stuff. Girl, wait this mess keeps popping up and now this one has a black man being nasty."

I took a closer look at the screen and the man in the picture looked familiar. I clicked on the pop up to see if I knew him from Prairie View or somewhere . . . then I dropped the phone. On the website there were several pictures and advertisements inviting people to join and receive free videos of men with women having sex. The man in the advertisement was Sam, and he was sitting on a park bench butt naked with one other women giving him oral sex. The advertisement read, "This could be you if you join today."

"Hello, Asha I am so sorry but I got to call you back. Bye!" I hung up the phone without giving any explanation and I immediately called Sam.

"Hey, where are you?"

"I am on my way home. What's wrong? Is everything okay?"

"No, I need you to get here quick, fast and in a hurry."

"Brooklyn, what has happened now? Is someone there?" Sam asked, laughing.

"Sam, hurry up and get your ass to this house." I hung up the phone.

Why does this mess keep happening to me? God, I am trying to do the right things and love my husband without losing myself but I am failing in both areas. And this man keeps trying me . . . please help me.

"Seek me first and do what is pleasing in my eyes."

Here we go again, kick me while I'm down. I was doing the best that I could but obviously I was missing the mark somewhere. Sam barged through the door and I was still sitting at the computer in the office.

"Brooklyn, where are you?"

I heard him running upstairs and I braced myself in fear of his initial reaction.

"Brook, didn't you hear me calling you?" He said huffing from being out of shape.

"Sam, what in the hell is this?" I asked as I turned the monitor around for him to see. The video of the lady performing oral sex on him was still playing and my face had turned cherry red.

"Brooklyn, how did you get that?" he said as he sat down in one of the chairs.

"Sam, God said that you are the head of this house and he is holding you accountable for everything that goes on with us. How could you do something like this since everything has been so good for us? I know it's not me, Sam, because everything that you have asked me to do sexually I have done even when it was against my morals. I can't take this mess or understand what the problem is, so you better go get some help or I'm out of here."

I didn't shed a tear or raise my voice because now I was just tired. Mama Betty always told me that I wouldn't move on until I was tired of being sick and tired. I didn't want to hear Sam's explanation or what he had to say so I walked out of the office. He stayed sitting in the chair like he was a student in the principal's office. I always told Sam that everything that he does in the dark will make its way to the light and it never failed.

Left again . . .

Chapter twenty-eight

"Okay, Mama Betty here is the key and if you need anything my cell phone is international so I will get your calls. Please make sure you take out the trash and set the alarm when you leave. Thank you so much for staying here while Sam and I are gone. I love you so much!"

It was almost as if I didn't want to leave knowing how Sam had acted in the past.

"Brook, go and have a good time. You both need this vacation and some time to enjoy each other."

Mama Betty didn't know about half of the things that Sam and I had experienced in the short amount of time we had been married. I was not about to let her know anything either, because we would see the Rideaux clan pop up out of nowhere. I grabbed the last of my bags and gave Mama Betty a kiss on the cheek. As I leaned in, Chrissy limped over and grabbed my waist.

"Brook, you gone bring me something back right?"

"Yeah, I'm going to bring you and Jaz something back. Take care of Mama Betty and make sure my house stays clean and no boys allowed in it, okay. I am leaving you in charge."

Chrissy gave me a wink and a smile as she walked into the house.

"HONK, HONK . . . Brooklyn come on before we miss our flight, damn. I told you to have all this stuff ready before today. Let's go!"

"What in the hell are you talking about? I am telling my family bye. Please don't start that mess, I'm coming."

"Brooklyn, watch your mouth. Listen, really have a good time and don't worry about the house. Okay? Bye baby girl," Mama Betty said as she grabbed my arm and turned me around.

I gave her a look and went and got in our black Cadillac Escalade that Sam had just put a new set of rims on and slammed the door.

"What the hell is wrong with you? Don't slam my doors like you lost your mind," Sam barked.

"Why are you honking like you crazy? We have at least two hours before the plane leaves. We will not be late, damn."

I pulled my seatbelt strap over my shoulder and pulled my golden red natural curls up into a bun. The summer heat was in full effect and it felt like I had just jumped out of the shower.

"Brooklyn, wipe my seat off from all that sweat. I do not want that mess to leave a smell in my truck while we are gone," Sam said.

"This dude has bumped his head again and is about to receive that long awaited tongue-lashing of his life," I mumbled to myself. I could not believe that Sam couldn't even wait until we got out of America before he started clowning.

"Sam, before we get too far away from home let me just say this, I did not take you back because I needed you. As you saw I was doing just fine without you but I wanted you home. You have hurt me in many ways with that other woman and the stuff on the porn site. I did not want to see that side of you; the mean and arrogant person that I cannot stand and I don't want to see it now. I was hoping that the counseling helped you but you are starting to trip out again. So if this is how things are going to be please turn this truck around and take me back to my house and you can get your stuff and go back to be with that slut."

Sam remained quiet as he continued to drive. I wanted to reach across the console and slap him into the middle of next week but something inside knew things would turn ugly if I did.

"Brooklyn, all you have to do is what I tell you on this trip and we will be fine."

"Why in the hell do you think you have to tell me what to do? You are not my father, his name is Tommy Boy!"

"The hustler, the thug, the pimp! You are right that is not who I am. But I will tell you this . . . you ain't gone disrespect me on this trip, you understand?"

I grabbed my headphones and turned on Smokie Norful. I agreed to go on this trip with Sam and agreed for him to move back in the house because I believed he had changed. I needed to rest and relax like Mama Betty said and I was not going to let Sam ruin this for me and before I knew it I was out.

"Excuse me Mrs., can you please take off your shoes and belt? Any jewelry you have on as well and place your passport in the bin with the rest of your things."

The airport in Paris was nothing like in America. It was dirty and almost dark. Armed men with scowling faces marched around the small airport as if a terrorist was on the prowl.

"Sam can you hold my purse while I untie my tennis shoes?"

Without looking and expecting Sam to take my purse I handed it to him and it hit the ground.

"What the hell is wrong with you? You can't even hold my purse?" I could not believe Sam was acting like this and especially in a foreign country. I knelt down to the floor and began to pick up everything that fell out. Sam had already walked through the screener and left me there with one shoe on and one shoe off.

"Lord, please tell me why this is happening again? If he is not for me please remove him," I prayed silently to myself as I tried to gain my composure. One of the guards turned his machine gun around and held his hand out to help me up. I gathered my things with one hand and grabbed his hand with my other.

"Madame, are you okay?"

"I guess, my childish ass . . . ," I stopped not knowing who this man was and how they viewed women speaking to men in this country.

"I dropped it by accident. Thank you so much for your help, merci," I said.

I gathered my things and looked around for Sam. My hands began to shake and my nose drew little beads of sweat. I felt my heart pounding and a sudden fear began to come over me.

"How could he leave me alone in a foreign country's airport?" I thought.

"Brooklyn, I am with you and you are okay. Go through the security gate and he will be waiting for you."

As I made it through the security gate I saw Sam standing at the counter trying to exchange our money for the new currency.

"Brook, over here," he called out. I managed a smile and walked over towards him as if nothing had happened. My hands had stopped shaking and before I made it to him I wiped the sweat off my nose.

"Brook, how much money did you bring? Give it to me now and I will go ahead and exchange it."

"I didn't bring cash. I need to go to the ATM here and withdraw some money. Do they have ATMs here in Paris?" I asked Sam.

"Are you serious? I told you to get some money out of the bank before we got here. What if they don't have ATMs Brooklyn? Then what? I hope you don't think you gone come down here and spend all my money. Damn, can you do just one thing I ask you to do?"

Here we go again. I will feel Sam's wrath because I didn't do something his way. The words of Mama Betty played back through my mind, "go and enjoy yourself Brook and leave everything else here." I grabbed my headphones out of my purse and stuck them on my ears. Fred Hammond rang out, "no weapon formed against me shall prosperrrrr . . . it won't work. God will do what he said He would doooo . . ."

A huge smile came across my face as we headed to baggage claim. I knew that song was for me from God. As a matter of fact I didn't recall putting that CD in my player. Oh well, it was for me and it was working.

"Hey Mama, we are here and made it to our room! It is very small and the whole hotel only has one iron!" I needed a voice of peace, so I called Mama Betty as soon as we got into the room. I wasn't sure of the time change but I decided to take a chance anyway.

"Are you serious Brook? That is too funny! So how is everything else? Where is Sam?"

"So far it's okay. Everything looks very dirty and almost like the ward. There were armed soldiers walking around the airport because someone threatened to blow it up but other than that, so far so good. Sam went to the desk to see if they could locate the iron. He wants to hit the streets and do some sightseeing."

"Wow, Brooklyn. I heard a while ago that Paris was the ghetto. They show us in America the beautified parts to get us over there to spend our money. You and Sam doing all right?"

Before I could answer, Mama Betty began running off her list of things she wanted me to bring back. From coffee mugs to t-shirts for everybody it seemed I would need at least an extra $500 just for the family. As Mama Betty continued I heard stomping down the hall towards our room. I was hoping Sam found what he needed so he wouldn't have any reason to be pissed off.

"Mama, I got to go. I think I hear Sam coming down the hall," I interrupted her.

"Okay, Brook. Did you write everything down?"

"Yes ma'am," I lied.

"Okay, and if you don't feel like going out right now tell Sam you need to rest a little. I hear it all in your voice, Brooklyn. You know how your body gets when you've done too much running and not to mention jet lag. Lay down before you get out, okay?"

"I will. I love you and I will talk to y'all later. Give Chrissy a kiss for me. Bye."

Just as I hung up the phone Sam walked in the room, looking like he was ready to lay into someone.

"Brook, get up so we can go see some things before it gets dark. I talked to the man at the front desk and he told me where to catch the subway that will take us to the shopping areas."

I could feel the excitement in Sam's voice, but I didn't really feel it. I was tired and I needed to rest or I wasn't going to be good for anything.

"Sam, I need to rest for a minute. You know I took my shot before we left home and now I am feeling it. Give me thirty minutes and then we can go."

"Are you serious? I did not come all the way down here to sleep. Listen, no one told you to take that medicine before we left. I am ready to go see Paris, and I am going with or without you."

The room was about the size of a matchbox with one small black and white television, an even smaller tub and a twin size bed. The brochure about the hotel mentioned it was a four star hotel; I would hate to see what a two star hotel in Paris looked like. Sam's voice echoed throughout the room and I am sure down the halls.

"What is the problem?" I asked. "You know when I am tired my body shuts down. You know better than anyone else. I just need a little time to rest. Dang."

I rolled over in the twin size bed onto my side with my back to Sam while he stood near the front door.

"Get up now Brooklyn!" Sam roared.

I looked at him over my shoulder and rolled my eyes. I turned back over and began to see myself asleep within minutes. Before I could close my eyes tight, Sam grabbed my foot and pulled out of the bed and on to the floor. Shocked and scared I jumped up and lunged toward him with tight fists. I began pounding against his face as hard as I could hoping to knock him out. I wasn't sure what happened or why it happened but I was not going let him have a repeat episode of our honeymoon. Sam grabbed my face and punched me in my ear. I knew blood was everywhere but I kept fighting back.

"Leave me alone Sam! Let me go!"

I cried out, hoping someone would hear us and come to the door. Sam gripped both my hands together and tried to push them away from him.

"Brooklyn, who in the hell do you think you are hitting? Sit down somewhere before I hurt you little girl. I should've kept your ass in America. If it wasn't for me you wouldn't have left Texas. Now don't think you're going to come overseas and get all bad."

Sam threw my aching body on the bed and I bounced off and hit the floor. Immediately, an adrenaline rush took over me and I grabbed the lamp off the nightstand.

"LEAVE ME ALONE," I said as I swung the lamp and hit Sam across his chest. I was aiming for his head but my arms were too short and his body was too tall.

"What in the hell . . . ," Sam hollered as he fell back into the bathroom door. My mind began to rush and I grabbed my purse and ran out the door. I flew down six flights of stairs hoping he wasn't coming behind me. My hair had come undone and the little eyeliner I was wearing began to sting my eyes.

"Excuse me, sir," I managed to bellow out between breaths as I reached the front desk. "Can you please tell me how to get a cab to the airport and the police? My husband is beating me." I stood there hoping he understood English and that they didn't think women were beneath them.

"Madame please calm down. I will get you out of here. Come, let me get your things from your room."

"No," I loudly whispered, "I am not sure if he's coming after me. I need to leave now. Please, please help me!"

I wasn't sure where I was going to go or even if I had my passport and credit card in my purse. I was going into survival mode and needed to get out quick.

"Okay okay. Then come with me and I will get Jesse to take you to the airport. What about your things?"

"I don't care! I just need to get out of here before I get killed."

I didn't really think Sam would bring me all the way to a foreign country and kill me but I had seen it happen on television before and I was not about to be another statistic. The gentleman whistled for a heavy-set bald man to come from a side table in the waiting area. They began to talk in French and even shared a smile that made me all the more nervous. I began to pray for God's angels to protect me and hope this man he was calling wasn't a murderer or rapist.

"Madame, Jesse will take you to the airport but you have to pay."

"That's fine," I said angrily. "Can we go now please?"

I walked swiftly behind the fat bald guy while looking back hoping Sam was nowhere near. What seemed like an eternity standing waiting to get a ride actually was just five minutes and within the next ten minutes I was at the airport. The dark had taken over the city of Paris and it looked like the postcard we received in the mail. I sat in the back of the cab stiff and praying that Jesse was really taking me to the airport. He didn't speak English so I couldn't ask him any questions.

"Lord, please let me make it back to America safely."

"Brooklyn, I promised I would never leave you nor forsake you. Your life is in my hands and there is nothing that can snatch you out."

At that moment time seemed to stop and a blanket of peace came on me. Even though I was scared and unsure of my safety I maintained control. Not because of Jesse and his two-mile an hour driving but because the Father had spoken.

"Jesse is this it? They look closed." Jesse smiled and nodded. I handed him three Euros hoping that would cover the bill and he smiled. I grabbed my purse and jumped out of the cab. Before I could close the door all the way Jesse sped off faster than I knew his car could go.

"Okay, Lord, I am in a foreign country and I don't know anyone here. I don't speak their language and I know I look different. Please direct me."

The doors to the small airport were propped open with chairs and I couldn't see any workers in sight. I looked for international flights in hopes that someone would be there to get me out of France. The airport looked a lot different than when we first came. There were no armed guards standing around ready to blow someone's head off and there were no currency exchange lines with workers who spoke no English.

"God, please don't let them be closed," I said, "What kind of airport closes?"

I walked around looking for anyone I could ask about a flight until I stumbled upon international departures. The desk was vacant and I stood there as if someone would soon show up. I held my purse close to my chest and dropped my head.

"God are you serious? You know what Sam was going to do to me and now this place is closed? What is going on?" I cried. Just as I turned around a tall slim black women came hurriedly to the desk looking for something of importance.

"Excuse me ma'am! I need to get a flight out to America tonight," I said with urgency. She looked at me as if I was speaking a foreign language. I stood waiting for a response until finally I broke the silence.

"Palais vous English," I said trying to speak her language.

"Yes," she giggled, "I speak English. But I am sorry the airport is closed and we do not have any flights out to America again until the morning."

I dropped my head again and began to cry. I couldn't believe God would do this to me!

"Ma'am are you okay?" she asked.

"Look, I just got into a huge fight with my husband and I couldn't take him beating me anymore. I left the hotel with nothing but my purse and cell phone. I need to get back to America. Back to my home."

She looked at me with a very long face as if she understood what I was going through. I wiped the tears from my eyes and began to walk away before she could respond to my request.

"Ma'am! Excuse me? There are no flights out but you can get a room across the street for the night and I will make sure you're on the first flight to America tomorrow. Is that okay?"

"How much are the rooms? Because I don't have much money. I may have to just sleep here in the airport."

"Oh no! You will get killed if you stay here alone! Don't worry about the room, I will call over and let them know you are my special guest. I will walk you over there as well! This airport reeks with terrorists and if they see a single female by herself that will be the last we see of you. Just let me find my keys and we can go. It's so crazy that you caught me because I am usually gone way before now. Wait here sweetheart; I think I know where they are."

"Excuse me, what is your name?" I asked.

"It's Karen. Wait here, I'll be right back. Oh, wait what is your name honey?"

Karen? Where do I know that name from? Maybe one of the teachers at the school or somebody at the church?

"I am Brooklyn Rideaux Johnson and thank you so much for helping me out. This really means a lot to me."

Karen walked away quickly and I dismissed the thought of possibly knowing her from somewhere. I walked over to the propped open doors and looked out at the quiet almost serene streets. My mind wondered where Sam was and what he was doing. He hadn't tried to call my cell phone and he didn't follow the cab trying to come after me.

"What is wrong with me, Lord? Why can't I have the love I need and want?"

"The love you need and want is within you. Stop looking for a man to do and give you only what I can!"

"Okay, sweetie! You ready?"

I looked around and Karen had let down the tightly wrapped bun from her hair and took off her green vest. It seemed that I knew Karen and that we had some unspoken things in common but I didn't want her to think I was crazy so I again dropped the issue. As we walked across the street to the only hotel around I stayed close to Karen not knowing if a terrorist was watching us or if Sam had snuck in the airport and followed us over.

"Salut Charlie. Ceci est mon Brooklyn d'ami et elle a besoin d'une pièce pour ce soir. Sur moi bien?"

I stood behind Karen trying not to look pitiful or scared. I wasn't sure what she was telling him, but I prayed that she was legit and not one of the terrorists she spoke of.

"Aucun Karen de problème. Un ami du vôtre est ami du mien. Je m'occuperai d'elle et s'assure qu'elle obtient son vol à l'heure."

"Brooklyn, this is Charlie and he is going to take care of you," Karen said as she turned around and gently grabbed my arms. "And don't worry about money here. Anything you need Charlie will make sure you have it."

Karen turned back to the desk and grabbed a business card that was left and a pen.

"Here is my number honey if you need anything. When you get to the airport in the morning I won't be there but tell them you spoke to "I AM". It's our code name and that means to let this person go through. Take care of yourself honey and I wish you Godspeed. Charlie, je vous dois l'un. Vous remercier autant de pour occuper de mon ami. Vous voir demain!"

As Karen walked out of the hotel, Charlie handed me a key and held up three fingers on one hand and five fingers on the other hand.

"Merci," I said with a faint smile. I was hoping he didn't expect more than that because my little book that translated terms for me was left back at the other hotel room. I managed to find my way around the circular hotel to room 35 and I again became scared walking through the deserted looking halls.

"How come Sam didn't see this hotel online? It looks way better than that rat hole we were in," I thought as I drew a brief half smile. My head had begun to pound and I knew I needed to eat something. The side effects of the medicine had worn off but now my body was aching from the fight with Sam. I sat on the full size bed in the room and rubbed my temples.

"Father, I know you are here. I need help. I am afraid, lonely and hurting. I am your daughter and I need you now."

Tears poured out of my eyes and through my fingers that covered my face.

"I am here Brooklyn. You need to eat and rest. Weeping is only for a night, but your joy will come in the morning."

I wiped the tears from my eyes and grabbed my purse and keys on a mission to find something to eat. When I made it back to the front desk, Charlie was not there and I really began to get worried. He was the one Karen advised to take care of me and now he was nowhere to be found.

"Excuse me, is Charlie here?" I asked a lady standing behind the counter.

"Désolé mais je ne parle pas l'anglais."

The young lady turned away and walked behind the tall light blue wall that separated the lobby from the back offices.

My head had a little drummer boy going to town inside and I needed something to stop his madness quickly. I walked over to an out-of-date vending machine hoping that something would magically fall out.

"Salut madame. Je suis allé au dos pour obtenir quelque chose. Avez-vous faim pourtant?"

"I am sorry but I don't speak French," I said. I must have looked totally confused.

"Are you hungry yet?" Charlie spoke up. He came out of nowhere like a ghost and scared the living daylights out of me.

"Yes," I said. "And I thought you didn't speak English?"

"I do just not too much around here. People treat you differently when they know you know the American dialect. So I learned French and I stick with it. I am from California."

I burst out laughing, which made my head pound even harder. Charlie laughed too but quickly regained his composure.

"Bien, aller à côté du restaurant et les dit je vous a envoyé. Commander quoi que vous voulez et l'amenez de retour à votre pièce."

I gave Charlie another confused look especially since he knew I had no idea what he was saying. Two housekeepers passed by with their carts without looking in our direction.

"Okay, go next door to the restaurant and tell them I sent you. Order whatever you want and bring it back to your room," Charlie whispered.

I shook my head and raced out of the door. When I reached the dimly lit restaurant with the huge wooden frame door, an older lady with an apron came to meet me at the front. She was heavyset with wide rim glasses that reminded me of Harry Potter.

"Peux-je vous aider?" she said.

"Charlie sent me here," I hurried and said.

"Oh, you're the lady from America! What would you like to eat dear?"

No she didn't? Is everyone here an imposter? This place was getting weirder and weirder by the minute and I couldn't wait for morning and my flight back home.

"Yes that's me. Do you all have chicken?"

"Uhhm, yes but it is not the chicken you eat in America. How about a hamburger?"

I really didn't care what she brought out as hungry as I was.

"That will be fine, thank you. Oh, do you have French fries to go with it?"

"Look where you are honey, of course we have 'French fries 'and I will get you plenty of them!"

Even though my head was pounding and I was still a little scared I pulled out a smile.

Chapter twenty-nine

The food and shower did the trick of getting that little drummer boy out of my head. As I lay down I prayed that I wouldn't oversleep and miss my flight out of Paris. To be sure, I slept sitting up facing the front door. Not only did I not want to miss my flight but since I was in a foreign country I didn't want to be caught off guard if someone tried to come in my room. I sat in the bed staring through the dark trying to hold the tears in and forget about Sam. I managed to doze off and before I knew it the alarm on my cell phone was going off.

"Oh my God, what time is it?" I said as I jumped up off the bed and grabbed my phone. The sound of the alarm and the shock caused the little drummer boy to show his face again as I squinted to read the clock.

5:30, it was time for me to head across the street and back to America.

"Father, thank you for keeping your angels watching over me and protecting me all night long. I love you so much."

"Brooklyn, remember that no weapon that is formed against you will prosper."

I washed my face and brushed my teeth in a matter of minutes and headed out of the door. The lobby was crowded with tourists that all spoke several different languages. There was a lot of commotion coming from outside so I looked around for Charlie, but I didn't see him or any of the workers from last night. I walked over to the large glass window and peered out across the street at the airport. Smoke was coming out of the roof and armed soldiers were lined up in the front not allowing anyone to enter or exit.

"Dear God, please don't tell me the terrorist attacked over there today. Lord please, not today."

I looked around again for Charlie and he was nowhere to be found. I walked out of the hotel holding my purse tight and trying not to look at anyone in the face in hopes that they didn't think I was a terrorist. I approached the airport doors and was immediately stopped by an armed guard.

"NO, STOP, NO," he yelled as he began to push me back.

"No, sir my flight leaves this morning to America," I yelled back at him while trying to push past him.

"NO, No enter. You must leave NOW!"

His face began to turn red and his voice escalated but I knew I had to get out of there and quick fast and in a hurry. Police cars continued flooding the area and cops started roping off the main entrance where I was trying to enter.

"No, you don't understand I need to leave. I need to leave today, RIGHT NOW," I yelled as tears began to flow. Then I remembered what Karen had told me to say for them to let me through.

"I AM . . . I AM," I shouted over all the ciaos that seemed to get louder and louder.

The soldier stopped pushing me and quickly grabbed my arm. He pulled me over to the roped off main entrance and nodded to the guard that was standing there. The guard lifted the rope for me to walk under and the once furious soldier held my hand tight as he drug me through the crowded corridors without saying anything. We made our way through and several stretchers were laid out on the floor with bloody bodies on top and some covered completely with white sheets. The smell in the airport was gruesome and something I hadn't smelled since moving from the ward.

"Come, don't look," the soldier said as he pulled me close to him and covered my eyes.

"This is very sad for lady to see. Just go and get on plane and don't get off until you get to America. When I leave you at plane don't look back."

His words were choppy but I understood what he meant. There had been a terrorist attack in the airport and several people had been killed. He took his hands off my eyes and let my hand go.

"Go there, they will take you home," he said as he pointed me in the direction of a long and empty walkway.

"Thank you so much for your help," I started to say and began to get emotional.

"GO, Go NOW," the soldier demanded as he pushed me in the direction of the airplane.

I ran as fast as I could down the hallway until I saw a flight attendant waving at the end for me to hurry and get on. I had a strong desire to look back and see where the soldier had gone but I kept going until I reached the flight attendant.

"Hurry and get in a seat and put your seatbelt on. Don't get up until we tell you we're clear," she said while pulling the door closed and locking it tight.

"Were they waiting on me?" I began to question myself but at that point it didn't matter because I was going home. I looked around and saw that there was no one else on the plane but me and the flight attendant. I didn't want to question her, but I was beginning to get more and more scared thinking about the bodies I saw lying on the ground in the airport.

"Excuse me, where is this plane going? Where is everyone else?"

"Brooklyn, we are taking you back to Texas. This is a private plane that Karen asked us to have here for you this morning. Please sit back and relax," the flight attendant said as she began to loosen her necktie. "This is a thirteen-hour flight so please try to get some sleep. I will let you know when we arrive."

What in the world is going on? Did Karen own the dog gone airport? Why did she do all this for me? She doesn't even know me. But wait, my nurse in the hospital was Karen too.

"She doesn't know you Brooklyn but I do. I know the plans I have for you. Plans Brooklyn to prosper you and not to harm you. My plan is to give you hope and a future."

"Father did you send Karen to me? You saved me again and made sure I was not alone, again?"

"There was a terrorist attack Brooklyn," the flight attendant interrupted our conversation. "And we wanted to make sure you were safe and not alone."

Okay, now I am really freaked out. How did she know I was alone? I didn't want to give off a scent of fear so I smiled and looked out the window.

"Lord, thank you . . . thank you . . . thank you," I whispered as I let the tears gradually fall. My mind was running a mile a minute but my body still was sore and the little drummer boy was still beating his drums. I sat back in the chair hoping that I would fall asleep and the little drummer boy would too. Out of nowhere a loud noise came bursting out of the ceiling of the airplane.

"Lord, please don't let this be another attack," I mumbled as my heart began to skip beats, "if it is Lord please take me quickly and make sure my mama is taken care of."

"Sorry, Brooklyn. I see that startled you honey," the flight attendant said as she looked over at me from across the walkway. Her face was calm and angelic almost. The noise didn't seem to bother her at all since there was still a smile planted on her face. "This is classical music honey by the Kodaly Quartet . . . it will help you sleep. You still seem shaken up, so lie back and relax. You are safe now and we will have you home real soon."

A faint smile came over my face and even though I still didn't know the flight attendant from Adam it seemed as if we had a past relationship. Since the little drummer boy must have gone to sleep I decided to follow his lead.

"Brooklyn, wake up honey. We're here."

I jumped up not really sure of where I was or what was going on but I obviously startled the flight attendant since she moved about ten steps backwards.

"Where am I and where is Sam?"

Still half sleep and oblivious to what had taken place almost twenty-four hours ago I looked around the plane for Sam.

"Come on sweetie, it's time for you to go home now and for us to get back."

The flight attendants smile was even more comforting than before and I began to remember what happened when I recognized the bruises on my arms. My heart began to beat rapidly again at the mere thought of the fight so I grabbed my purse that I had tightly stuck between my legs. For some reason that seemed to be all that was important that I had left. I didn't know where to go from here and immediately my street mentality mind shot back into hustle mode. I knew I had to now get out of that house before Sam came back. I had to call Mama Betty and ask her to come and get me from the airport and explain to her why I was by myself. That was not going to be easy so I started getting my story together.

"Brooklyn, when you get into the airport there will be a tall slim man holding a sign with your name on it. He will take you home from here and anywhere else you need to go, okay? No more worries."

The flight attendant hugged me and took my hand and led me off the plane.

"I am sorry but I never got your name. I want to send this airline a thank you card for all your help. Do you all have business cards?"

The flight attendant looked at me and broke a wide smile.

"My name is Ruth and this Angel Airlines. You don't have to send us anything; we're always there when you need us. Be safe honey and know from here on out you will be fine."

"Uhmm, okay but may I at least tell the captain thank you for such a safe trip?"

"He heard you! Now hurry and look for the tall slim man that's holding a sign with your name on it."

"Thank you so much, thank you!"

"Good-bye Brooklyn," the flight attendant said as I walked out of the plane and as she pulled the door down and locked it.

I hurriedly walked out of the gate and looked hastily for the man she described and the sign with my name on it. I didn't know if he was black or white or even if he knew who I was. Everything had been so weird with people knowing who I was so I hoped this man worked for that same company and knew my information too. After about fifteen minutes of searching for someone I did not know, my cell began to ring. I had totally forgotten that I had the phone and that it was in my purse. I sat down in one of the dark blue chairs at gate C3 hoping to see the driver or at least the sign with my name on it.

"Hello?"

"Brooklyn Rideaux-Johnson, please."

"This is she, whose calling?"

"Mrs. Johnson I am Sam, your driver, here to take you home. Where are you located?"

Sam? Is this fool trying to be funny? I knew darn well my Sam was not calling my phone just trying to find out where I was; but how would he know I had a driver waiting? Is he responsible for getting me out of France?

"Brooklyn, I AM responsible for making sure you are safe. Remember no weapon that is FORMED against you will prosper. Let him know where you are so we can get you home."

"I am at Gate C3. Where do I need to go? Where are you located?" I said sarcastically.

"Stay there ma'am and I will be right over to get you in a second. Please Mrs. Johnson don't move."

The urgency in his voice made me a little nervous and the phone hung up before I could say anything else and gave me a busy signal. I clutched my purse close to my chest and sat in a seat near the door of the gate just in case I needed to make a fast getaway.

My heart continued to skip a beat and now it began to beat more rapidly than before. I prayed that this person that was looking for me was really legit and not sent by someone trying to take me out. I knew I should call Mama Betty and let her know what happened but I didn't want her to worry about me. I was the baby technically and she and Tommy Boy would be over in France trying to find Sam. I knew it would be better for me to just wait until I made it to the house. It was almost still early so I hoped she and Chrissy would be home.

"He hasn't called to see where I am," I said as I looked at my phone hoping for any missed calls.

"Mrs. Johnson," a deep masculine voice called out over my shoulder as I searched through my phone, "Excuse me, are you Mrs. Johnson?"

I turned around in a hurry and was stunned by what I saw. A tall, slim fair-skinned man with salt and pepper curly hair and green eyes. His wide smile stretched from ear to ear and his white teeth were aligned perfectly.

"Papa," I said excitedly and feeling relieved that someone I knew was there to take me home.

"Excuse me? I am Sam and I was sent to drive you where you needed to go."

I sat still in my chair turning a full 180 to make sure I wasn't losing my mind. This man looked exactly like my Papa except he passed away years ago. Now things were really starting to freak me out, but since I was back in Texas and knew I would be home soon those fears faded quickly.

"Mrs. Johnson, do you have any bags that I need to get for you?"

"No, I left everything back in Paris. Uhmm, are you from New Orleans?" I asked as we began walking away from the gate toward the outside where his Lincoln Town Car was parked.

"No, where I am from you probably have never heard of."

"Try me," I said dodging the men on the cart coming at us 50 miles an hour.

"Don't worry little lady. Here is the car, stand over there and I will open the door once these shuttles buses pass."

The last yellow shuttle with black dots passed and he opened the back door and signaled for me to get in. The car was clean and smelled like piña colada. But before I got in I turned around and stared at him one more time. Every one of his facial features resembled my Papa's and I had to know where he was from. Maybe this was Papa's long lost brother or something.

"Sir, do you know any Rideaux's? They are mainly from New Orleans in Louisiana but could be anywhere by now."

He smiled showing his pearly whites again, "I know a lot of people," he said, "now let's get you home."

Sam, the driver, slid on his dark black shades and closed my door.

"Lord, those are the same shades my papa use to wear and would let me play with when I was a kid!"

Water filled my eyes as I felt the same butterflies in my stomach like before when Papa smiled at me.

My mind quickly shifted back to reality and back to the Father for the answers I needed.

"Father what am I going to do when I get to the house? What if Sam is there already? Where am I going to live since I know I can't stay in the same house with him?"

Once again my mind was flooded with questions and back into survival mode I dove.

"Brooklyn, trust in me with all your heart. I promised to meet your every need according to my riches in glory. I will take care of you."

"But God, once again I am left to figure things out on my own. I am tired of running and moving and running and moving. Please give me stability so I can pursue what you want for me. I can't keep giving all my love and heart to a man that doesn't want to share his with me. I know you hate divorce but do you want me to stay in an abusive relationship? Father, I need answers! I need to know what to do when I get to this house. I need your help!"

I could never express my weaknesses or desperate state to anyone other than the Father; they wouldn't understand. I was the strong one, the tough one . . . so everyone thought and I couldn't show them any different.

We pulled up to my seemingly deserted house and boy was I nervous and didn't want to get out of the car.

"Mrs. Johnson, are you all right? Do you need me to help you with something?"

"No, I am fine. I am just a little nervous," I said trying to crack a half smile. "Can I have just a few more minutes?"

"Yes ma'am! Take all the time you need. I am going to step out of the car and take a look around. No hurry!"

Sam the driver jumped out of the car and closed the door quickly. I knew I gave off some scent of fear and anxiety that caused him to kindly peruse the perimeter of the house. I took my cell phone out of my purse to see if I had missed any calls from Mama Betty or Sam. The battery on my phone was dead so if he did try to call it wouldn't come through. I wondered if Sam had thought about me at all. Did he miss me? Was he still in Paris? I shook my head and dropped the issue. This time it was over . . . no more games. I wanted Brooklyn back!

My feet and legs felt like a ton of bricks as I got out and walked up to the house.

"Mrs. Johnson, I am going to go now. Are you okay? Do you want me to wait until you call someone to come over and be here with you?"

"No, I think I am okay. I am just going to lie down and rest for a minute. I will call my mother in a few. Thank you for all your help. I would give you a tip but I am sorry all my money is in the form of Euros, so I have no cash."

Sam, the driver, came over and touched me gently on my shoulder, "Brooklyn, your bill has already been paid in full. No worries!"

Overwhelmed with peace and gratitude, I dropped my head and began to sob.

"Please don't cry Ms. Brooklyn. You are safe now and I am going to tell you like my grandpa use to tell me . . . no weapon that is formed against you will prosper!"

I looked up and Sam, the driver's, warm smile and comforting words sounded like what my Papa would say.

"Thank you so much," I said.

Sam, the driver, winked and quickly got in his car and disappeared.

Chapter thirty

I walked in the house not knowing what to expect and hoping Sam hadn't come back. Our house was cold and dark even though the sun was out and in full effect. My body was still sore and the bruises on my arms were still very apparent. If I was going to call Mama Betty to come over I would need to cover up and take some Advil for the pain before she came. Walking through the house memories of Sam's mistress and the police all ran a marathon through my head. I needed peace and at this point I was going to get it by any means necessary. Even if it meant leaving everything I had worked so hard for and starting all over again. The material things didn't mean that much to me since I knew I could get them again but leaving the man I loved was the scary part.

"You may love him but does he love you? Brooklyn, you need to get to know two people."

"Now we're talking," I thought, "now I am about to get the answers I need to continue on with my life. Who Father? Anyone . . . just tell me who?"

"You and I."

"HUGHHH? What does He mean by that? I know who I am!"

"You need to know the YOU I created and not the YOU that you created."

"Father, all my life I have looked for someone to love me and you let me test the waters. I am tired now and I need to know your love for me, FOR REAL. I tried everything out there in the world and there is nothing that satisfies me like you. Take this pain and hurt I allowed away and give me your love . . . unconditionally."

I sat down on the couch baffled by the words I heard and spoke. I grabbed the spiral tablet and pen off the coffee table to satisfy the urge I felt to write. I began to write down everything I heard Him say and my hand couldn't move fast enough to keep up with the words in my mind flowing out onto the pages of a nearby notebook.

"You can't tell other people anything about pain unless you've experienced it firsthand. I didn't and I won't let the enemy take you out. I will bring you through everything you're faced with, trust me."

I wrote and wrote until the voice in my head stopped and the pen fell to the floor. The 300-page notebook was full from cover to cover and my fingers were bleeding. Sweat streamed down my forehead and stung my eyes. The house was dark as the night crept in; only a small lamp illuminated the room. The street lights shone through the dining room window and voices came from the other side of the front door that sounded familiar. I looked at the filled spiral notebook and then at the clock on the microwave in the kitchen. It read 10:26 and then I heard the voices again get even louder.

"I know she is here! I called her phone but it is going straight to voicemail. Mama knock on the door again," the female voice said.

I wanted to get up and open the door but my body was numb and weighted. All I could do was look at the pages in the spiral notebook and my bloody fingers in disbelief.

"Father, what is this?" I thought.

"The final chapter in this story is over and the first chapter of your new life begins. The love you have always looked for you've discovered. It's time to move on and experience me not only as your Lord who will provide but now as your Lover."

"I have a key to the house," a male voice interrupted and the locks began unlocking.

"Brooklyn, Brooklyn you here baby girl? Cut some lights on so we can see if she is here," Mama Betty said with a squeaky worried voice as she entered through the front door.

"Lord, please don't let that be Sam," I thought as I sat idle on the couch with the notebook in my lap.

"Brooklyn, baby girl you okay?" Pearl yelled as she walked into the living room. "Mama Betty, here she is and look at her fingers! Mama Betty look at her fingers! She is bleeding."

Pearl grabbed me off the couch and pulled me on the floor close to her chest. She cried loudly as she began to physically search my body. Mike and Mama Betty ran into the living room and assisted Pearl in checking me out.

"Girl, are you okay?" Mike asked. "Someone called Mama Betty from an unknown number and said you were home. Are you okay Brook?"

I wanted to spill my guts about what had happened to me but nothing would come out of my mouth. I stared at Pearl, Mike and Mama Betty knowing they would not understand even I began to tell them the story.

"Brooklyn," Mama Betty began to gently speak. "Who did this to you baby girl?"

She held both of my thin arms in her overworked hands turning them back and forth revealing their bruises.

"Where is Sam?" Pearl asked.

"How did you get here Brook?" Mike asked.

The storm is over now. And the baby you are carrying will know who she is because you now know who you are.

"Y'all, it doesn't even matter," Mama Betty said as she looked deep into my eyes with her mesmerizing look. "She's home and she's safe. Pearl, get her into the shower and Mike put on some soup.

Her storm is over now! She won't be left again!"

About the author

De'Monica is a native of Houston, Texas where she is currently an educator and former radio personality. She graduated from Prairie View A&M University with a Bachelor of Science degree in Interdisciplinary Studies and a minor in English. De'Monica soon returned and completed her Masters of Education degree in Educational Administration. She is an energetic leader, educator, author and motivational speaker. Her vision is to help youth and young adults discover and build their self-esteem, self-love and self-worth.

Her passion and dream for developing one's inner self prompted her to form De'Monica Cooper Enterprises which is comprised of a publishing company, life coaching services and speaking tours.